PROXIMA CENTAURI

ENFIELD GENESIS – BOOK 2

BY LISA RICHMAN & M. D. COOPER

Just in Time (JIT) & Beta Readers

Jim Dean
Marti Panikkar
Timothy Van Oosterwyk Bruyn
David Wilson
Scott Reid

Version 1.0.0

ISBN: 978-1-64365-016-6

Cover Art by Andrew Dobell
Editing by Jen McDonnell, Bird's Eye Books

TABLE OF CONTENTS

FOREWORD

The things you work hardest to achieve are always the most rewarding.

While Proxima Centauri was in no way an unwelcome chore, it's been a book that took a significant amount of effort to complete. As such, it feels exceptionally rewarding.

This, of course, is all Lisa's fault, and you're going to sing her praises for it, because she did exceptional work here.

From the outset, Lisa had a vision for this story that would test both her and my knowledge and abilities. We both learned *a lot* while writing this, and came up with some awesome new tech and ideas in the process.

We took what James and I began with the Weapon Born of the Sentience Wars and said "what if things got worse?" And then we made them worse than even we imagined.

Well, Lisa did. She's a bit scary when she's writing villains. I advocated for bar fights and wrote pew pews.

I have to say, writing this foreword may be just as difficult as writing the book. So much of what happens is layered onto a few lynchpin moments and if I go too deep, I'm going to spoil things for you, and we don't want that!

I think I'll leave it at this: brew a fresh pot of coffee and put on your jammies, because you're about to experience what I think is the first Aeon 14 psychological thriller.

Michael Cooper
Danvers, 2018

WHAT HAS GONE BEFORE

It has been a mere fifty years since the Sentience Wars ended and the Phobos Accords were signed. By some reckoning, that span of time could seem like an eternity. For those who fought, it was not nearly enough time to heal. Or to forget.

As with all wars, there were no tidy lines separating the oppressors from the oppressed. For many of the humans and the sentient artificial intelligences—the AIs—that fought, the wounds are still painful and fresh.

Although the war had been fought around a different star, the colonists living in Alpha Centauri did not emerge unscathed. The people of El Dorado, the first planet to be terraformed by the Future Generation Terraformers, struggled to uphold the tenuous peace between the humans and AIs who lived there.

One AI in particular, Lysander—a veteran of the Sentience Wars and one of the first AIs, known as Weapon Born—chose to dedicate his career to helping mend those relationships.

He ran for office.

As a senator, Lysander worked to help end hate speech, and to pass laws that ensured all sentients were treated equally. Now Lysander has been appointed Prime Minister.

One of his last acts as senator was to authorize an off-the-books, covert operations team at the request of Benjamin Meyer.

Ben had sought Lysander out, not knowing who else to trust in his bid to take down the Norden Cartel. Too many in El Dorado's Intelligence Service had been bought by the cartel—or were mired in political intrigue—to be reliable. The Weapon Born, however, was known both for his unassailable integrity and his ability to get things done.

Lysander agreed under one condition: that Ben include his own brother-in-law, Jason Andrews, on the team.

Unbeknownst to Ben, Jason was a rare, next-generation L2 human. The axons—neural pathways—in Jason's brain possessed significantly more nodes than those in a normal L0 human. They functioned as signal boosters, allowing him to process information at lightning speeds, and gave him much faster reflexes than those of unaugmented humans.

As a recent arrival from Proxima, Jason's skills would be unknown on El Dorado. His addition to the team would provide Ben with a hidden advantage in his battle to rid the system of the cartel.

Lysander recruited several more AIs onto the team and brought in a retired El Dorado Space Force vice-marshal named Esther to lead them.

Her second, an AI commodore named Eric, ended up embedding with a human named Terrence Enfield after the two crossed paths when Norden framed Terrance's company for the kidnapping of more than two hundred and fifty AIs.

The team's first mission: to repatriate those AIs and take down the cartel who had kidnapped them.

Thus, Joint Task Force Phantom Blade was born.

The Blade shut down the cartel—but not before seventeen of the kidnapped AIs had been sold into slavery.

Now that team has been tasked with finding and repatriating those sentients, to return the freedom that was stolen from them....

KEY CHARACTERS REJOINING US

Jason Andrews – Son of Jane Sykes Andrews, grandson of Cara Sykes, Jason grew up in the C-47 habitat orbiting the planet Chinquapin in the Proxima Centauri system. One of the first few humans to exhibit the natural L2 mutation, Jason is a pilot and a bit of an adrenaline junkie with a love for ancient aircraft. When not working, he can be found BASE jumping, or tinkering on his reproduction Old Earth Yakovlev radial-engine airplane.

Tobias – A Weapon Born AI, Tobias left Sol after the Sentience Wars to settle in Proxima. There, he formed a close friendship with the Sykes-Andrews family. Along with Lysander—another Weapon Born—he was influential in Jason's early life as a friend, tutor and mentor, often accompanying the human in a harness worn by a partially uplifted Proxima cat.

Tobi – One of the marginally uplifted cats bred by Jane Sykes Andrews as companion pets for families living in habitats and ships. Tobi was given to Jason and Tobias as a gift, a way for Tobias to accompany Jason, since AIs cannot embed inside an L2 human.

Lysander – A veteran of the Sentience Wars in Sol, he is a Weapon Born AI who chose to run for a senate seat in El Dorado. After serving several terms, he became Majority Leader and was shortly thereafter appointed the first AI Prime Minister.

In *Alpha Centauri*, Lysander authorized an off-the-books covert ops team that he later code-named Joint Task Force Phantom Blade.

Terrance Enfield – Grandson of Sophia Enfield and CEO of Enfield Aerospace. Terrance joined Phantom Blade when the Norden Cartel framed his company for AI trafficking. He is the first Enfield in Alpha Centauri to partner with an AI. Commodore Eric is embedded with him.

Eric – An AI and former El Dorado Space Force (ESF) commodore, reinstated by Prime Minister Lysander when Phantom Blade was created. Second-in-command of task force, under Vice-Marshal Esther. He chose to embed in Terrance Enfield in *Alpha Centauri.*

Calista Rhinehart – Former ESF top gun; currently Chief Pilot for Enfield Aerospace's Technical Development division (TechDev). On indefinite loan to Phantom Blade.

Benjamin (Ben) Meyer – Senior analyst for El Dorado's Secret Intelligence Service. Married to Jason Andrews' sister, Judith.

Landon – One of five AIs asked to join Phantom Blade when Ben first approached then-senator Lysander for help in creating a covert ops team. Twin to Logan, Landon is the more outgoing and garrulous brother. He is also known as the 'Mendoza whistle-blower'.

Logan – Former ESF Military Intelligence profiler and AI-hunter, Logan was appointed by Senator Lysander to Phantom Blade. He is the more taciturn twin.

Shannon – AI chief engineer for Enfield Aerospace's TechDev Division, reporting to Calista Rhinehart. Shannon is also on loan to Phantom Blade.

Daniel Ciu – Former ESF Marine, Aaron's partner. Current head of security for Enfield Aerospace. An off-the-books member of Phantom Blade.

Aaron – AI and security officer for Enfield Aerospace, embedded in Chief Operations Officer Daniel Ciu. Former Marine in the ESF.

Esther – AI and former ESF vice-marshal; reinstated by Lysander and appointed Director of Operations for Joint Task Force Phantom Blade.

Gladys – Hacker extraordinaire, she is one of the five AIs asked to join Phantom Blade. She is the team's 'ghost in the machine'. She is inordinately fond of glitter, and the color teal.

Judith Andrews – Jason's sister, married to Ben Meyer. Judith is a biogeochemist and chairs the Planetary Sciences Department at El Dorado University, in the ring's capital city of Sonali.

Jonesy – Served in the ESF under Calista, in acquisitions and procurement. Calling him the 'best assistant this side of Sol,' Calista hired him for Enfield Aerospace as soon as his tour of duty was up.

Frida – One of the two hundred seventy-seven AIs aboard the *New Saint Louis,* a ship of Sentience Wars refugees out of Sol. Served as ship's communications officer. Kidnapped and sold into slavery by the Norden Cartel.

Niki – One of the two hundred seventy-seven AIs aboard the *New Saint Louis,* a ship of Sentience Wars refugees out of Sol, where she served as ship's scan officer. Niki is one of the seventeen AIs kidnapped and sold into slavery by the Norden Cartel.

Sophia Enfield – Matriarch of the Enfield family and the head of the Enfield Conglomerate's vast portfolio of businesses, an enterprise with roots that date back to the twenty-fourth century. Sophia is responsible for relocating Enfield's headquarters to El Dorado, leaving her son, Bradford, behind to manage Enfield's remaining interests in Sol.

Victoria North – The leader of the Norden Cartel, and owner of NorthStar Industries, the cartel's front. Victoria was arrested for AI trafficking by joint task force Phantom Blade in 3191.

MAPS

Visit www.aeon14.com/maps for larger versions

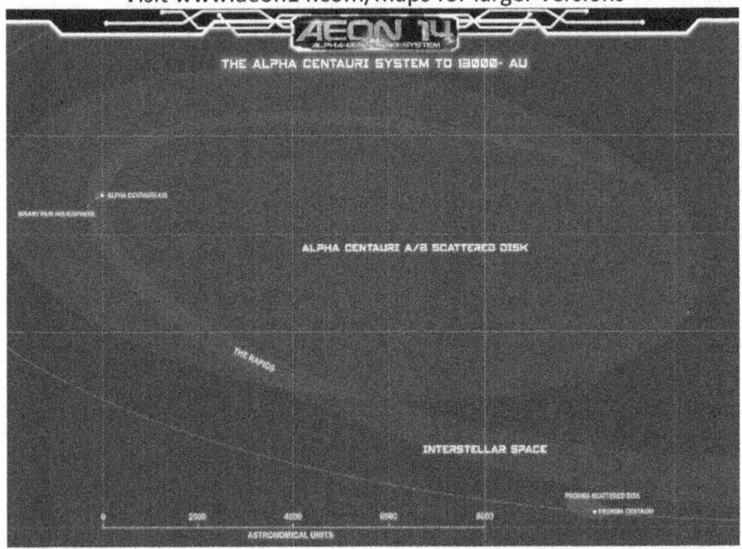

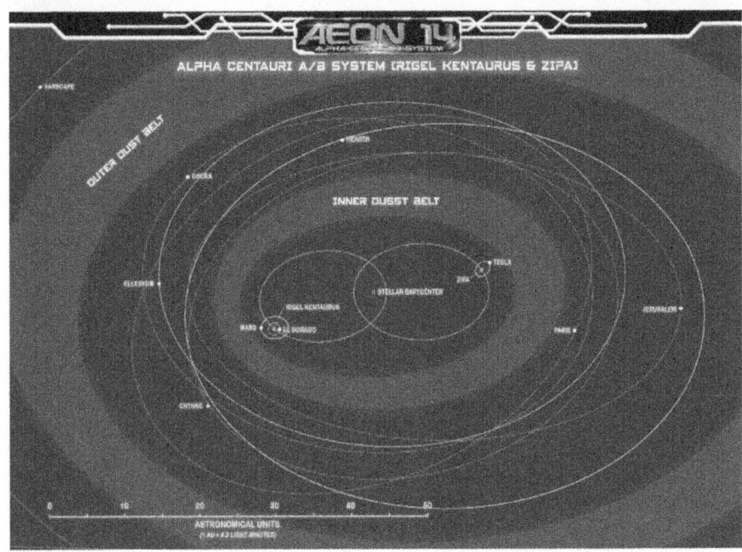

KEPLER

STELLAR DATE: 05.07.3191 (Adjusted Gregorian)
LOCATION: Kepler Mining Torus, Station Nearspace
REGION: Rigel Kentaurus Dust Belt, Alpha Centauri System

<We're hit!>

Shannon's voice called out over the combat net, just as the Enfield Aerospace shuttle *Sable Wind* canted sharply to the left. Its pilot was already on it, correcting for the impact and vectoring to dodge the next strike. The Enfield engineer's voice was pitched higher than normal, threaded now with panic and fear.

Being shot at will do that to you, Jason Andrews thought, his hands buried wrist-deep in the *Sable Wind*'s weapons holo as he flung the sensor return of the attack craft that was harrying them up on the display.

Like Shannon, Jason was a civilian. Unlike the AI, Jason wound up getting shot at. A lot. That hadn't always been the case. *Didn't have any trouble avoiding it for the first thirty-five years of my life,* he thought as he gritted his teeth against another rapid change in velocity.

Until his brother-in-law, a senior analyst for El Dorado's Intelligence Service, had maneuvered him onto Lysander's covert ops team. In that time, he'd learned that no one truly got used to being shot at, not even Shannon's boss, the former El Dorado Space Force top gun currently piloting the Icarus-class shuttle.

Usually when this kind of thing happened, you were too busy trying to survive to feel any fear. Reaction would set in later.

While Retired ESF Major Calista Rhinehart took them through a series of high-*g* maneuvers more suitable for a pilot's cradle in a fighter than the ones installed here, the fourth member of their team spared a moment to reassure the engineer.

<*No worries, lass. We've got this,*> Tobias sent.

The Weapon Born AI was in a starboard-facing cradle, manning point defense. Whereas Shannon had opted to embed herself into the shuttle as ship's captain for this mission, Tobias—their mission commander—had chosen to wear a combat mech frame.

Being Weapon Born made Tobias as uniquely qualified to lead as he was skilled at doing battle. The product of an illicit experiment out of Sol, Weapon Born AIs were grown from the imaged minds of human children—malleable blank canvases, the perfect foundation. They were among the first non-organic sentients in existence. Some of the most brilliant and charismatic people in known space were counted within their ranks.

<*Get us away from a reciprocal of the torus, lass,*> Tobias said now from his position behind Calista, his mental tone terse. <*I need a clean shot that won't hole that station.*>

Calista acknowledged the directive as Jason brought the railgun online, transferring control over to his HUD. Layering the weapon's reticle over the feed from scan, he began tracking the spacecraft pursuing them. He swayed as the shuttle took a glancing blow, a result of the pilots' cradles having more give than the precision-machined cradles found in a fighter.

The reticle lined up; he took a shot, but the pilot in the other craft jinked just as he sent the mental command that triggered the railgun, and the ribbon of weapons fire passed harmlessly through empty space. Jason cursed silently and worked to line up another shot.

He glanced over at Tobias when he heard a series of soft clicks emanate from the point defense cradle, indicating that the AI had engaged maglocks on his mech frame and powered it down. Not that it would impact how the AI manned point defense—he'd been operating its controls from within the ship's systems rather than using the physical interface, like a human might have.

The AI equivalent of a sigh was relayed over Jason's private Link with the Weapon Born. Tobias must have seen his head turn when he'd heard the frame go into lockdown.

<*Not used to the perspective of a mech's sensor array, boyo,*> the AI explained. <*Damned disorienting when its inputs are layered over the greater return from ship's sensors. I'll stick with what I know, thanks.*>

Jason sent Tobias a mental nod, and then grunted as Calista pushed the *Sable Wind* into a hard burn for a brief moment.

She shot him a quick look. <*Well, if you don't like it, flyboy, feel free to take that shot any time.*> Her voice sounded in his head as she jinked sharply on their y-axis, avoiding yet another missile as Tobias released chaff countermeasures. The little craft pinged and rocked slightly as it was peppered by debris from the exploding missile. <*Or are those fancy reflexes of yours giving out on you?*>

Jason didn't respond to Calista's comment. He wouldn't have been able to do so audibly anyway, since the moment they spotted the attack craft tailing them, the two humans had triggered their flight combat nano. Carbon nanotube fibers that ordinarily lay dormant formed a rigid lattice structure throughout vital organs and soft tissue, enabling them to endure physical stresses as high as thirty gees for extended periods.

It also rendered talking impossible, due to the CNT matrix now lacing the insides of their lungs. For now, all communication was limited to the combat net transmitted across their embedded neural Links.

Jason's eyes remained riveted to the reticle of the shuttle's single gatling railgun. Optical implants both protected and enhanced his eyes as he worked to line up the mining rig's ship in his sights. It was a small craft, a retired fighter that looked like it had seen better days. It was more nimble than the *Sable Wind*, but by the look of it, the craft's owner had been lax with its maintenance and upkeep. That meant the Icarus-class shuttle should be more than a match for it.

He dipped lightly into his altered state, and the universe appeared to slow dramatically as his mental processes and physical reflexes sped up. Aligning the reticle with his target felt almost leisurely when he operated at L2 speeds.

He sent the command to trigger a short, three-second burst, and a stream of deadly pellets raced toward their opponent. The pellets struck true, hitting the junction between the craft's fusion engine and its fuselage.

Abruptly, the other craft began to bleed velocity, but Jason had anticipated that. It began vectoring erratically, its pilot using the only tool he had left—the ship's waning maneuverability—in an attempt to evade.

But Jason was ready for that, too. Dipping deeper into his altered state, the ship almost seemed to drift lazily before him on the holo. He felt he had all the time in the world to line up the perfect shot: the section that shielded the attack craft's maneuvering thrusters. One more quick burst, and the enemy fighter was traveling along a fixed trajectory, its velocity steadily dropping.

<*What was that you were saying about reflexes, again?*> Now that they were out of immediate danger, Jason could relax into his cradle and lean back from the weapons station. As he did, he glanced over at Calista with a raised brow and a lazy grin.

She rolled her eyes at him as she flipped the *Sable Wind* over, sending it back toward their attacker, careful to remain aft of the fighter's forward-facing armament. Tobias had obligingly rendered its missile tubes inoperative, which made an approach from behind the fighter perfectly safe.

The shuttle hadn't been the ideal ship in which to evade an attack, but then again, they hadn't been expecting one. Its responses were more sluggish than their Icarus-class fighter would have been, but it had still been more than a match for the ancient spacecraft they were now approaching, a ship that had been decommissioned almost a century before. The craft was caught in an ever-slowing corkscrew stellar north, away from the ecliptic plane of the Alpha Centauri system.

<*Showoff.*> Calista's mental response was tinged with amusement, and Jason could see her lips twitch as she fought a smile.

She turned back to the *Sable Wind*'s display and began reaching for various virtual switches and toggles, cleaning up the craft and restoring it to its standard configuration after their mad flight.

<*Ship's yours, Shannon,*> she granted, giving the customary handoff.

<*I have the ship,*> the AI responded, as Calista leant back and swiveled her cradle around to face Jason and Tobias.

<*I take it you wanted to capture and not kill, otherwise that guy would have been shredded the moment he was in range.*> She raised one eyebrow as her gaze tracked between the two, man and AI. She narrowed her eyes at them both. <*And the paint job on my fancy new shuttle wouldn't be chipped.*>

Jason sent her an amused look. <***Your*** *shuttle? I'll be sure to tell Terrance that,*> he sent.

<*Oh no, you don't,*> Calista's mental tone was threaded with amusement. <*What happens in the black* ***stays*** *in the black. No telling the boss on me.*>

<*Well, technically, Calista, he's not your boss right now. You're on loan to Esther,*> Shannon reminded her. <*We both are. And besides,*> her tone turned derisive, <*the shuttle's not* ***chipped****; you know that. It's made from Elastene. It's one solid piece of metal foam all the way through.*>

<Let's get back to who we're going to blame for getting us shot at,> Jason interjected hastily before Shannon could warm to one of her favorite topics.

It wasn't that he didn't appreciate how effectively the substance deflected weapons fire; he just didn't want to hear another lecture on the electrospinning techniques of graphene. Or Elastene's shape-memory properties that allowed for an almost perfectly inelastic collision. Or transverse waves propagating throughout surface substrates. Whatever the hell those were.

<I vote we blame Ben,> he said. *<He's the one who dragged us all into this in the first place.>*

<Don't be too hard on Ben, boyo,> Tobias remonstrated lightly. *<You were onboard with the plan the minute you spotted that shuttle full of kidnapped AIs two years ago.>*

Jason grinned and then shrugged. *<Not going to stop me from reminding him that he's the one who got my sorry ass into all this, though.>*

Phantom Blade may have begun as his brother-in-law's idea, but it had become Lysander's pet project. The prime minister directed their operations from his office in Parliament House, situated on the planetary ring that encircled El Dorado.

Although the Blade had infiltrated Norden and apprehended two of its leaders—the ones responsible for enslaving AIs—the matter was far from concluded. For more than a year now, proceedings had been underway to bring cartel personnel to justice.

The whole process of trial, mistrial, and plea bargains drove Jason nuts. Without question, these people were guilty. Everyone on this shuttle knew it, since they were the ones who had been there to shut the cartel down.

Operations like the rescue they had pulled off today kept his frustration with El Dorado's legal system at bay, though. They had spent almost two years working to recover the remaining seventeen AIs that the cartel had sold into slavery. Nate, the AI who now rode in an isolation chamber, safely webbed into one of the shuttle's passenger compartments, was the seventh of those to be recovered.

Nate had been purchased by a gaming organization operating out of the Kepler Mining Torus in the Alpha Centauri dust belt, half an AU rimward of El Dorado. Jason recalled with grim satisfaction the face his fist had plowed into right after Tobias had freed Nate from the gaming commissioner's office. He was certain the attack on them had been launched on that man's order.

He peered now at the Weapon Born's inert frame as he queried the AI. <*You good, Tobe?*>

As he watched, the frame powered up and unfolded itself from its stored position.

<*Right as rain. I think I'll stick with what I know, though, going forward. I'm more comfortable wearing a ship, I think, than a mech frame.*>

Calista leaned forward in her cradle, peering at Tobias. <*You didn't seem to have any trouble while we were extracting Nate from Kepler,*> she said, her voice rising at the end, her curiosity evident.

Tobias laughed. <*Not a lot of delta-*v *on that mining rig, either, lass.*>

She nodded. <*Can't argue that.*>

<*So, what's the plan?*> Jason quirked a brow at the frame as the *Sable Wind* began to slow, and Shannon fired maneuvering thrusters to match the fighter's slow spin.

He suspected he'd be ordered to the airlock for an EVA to extract the pilot and bring him or her aboard, but as the leader on this op, that would be Tobias's call.

<*Well, you've gone to all the trouble of keeping our erstwhile attacker alive that it'd be a shame not to question—*> His voice cut off as the *Sable Wind* suddenly kicked into max acceleration,

headed away from the Kepler fighter.

Jason winced as Tobias's mech frame slammed into the plas interface behind it, a sharp crack indicating that repairs would be needed once they returned. Three seconds later, the enemy vessel that Shannon was rapidly pulling away from exploded. Jason's pulse raced as adrenaline flooded his system, plunging him fully into his altered state as he sent Shannon the order to transfer control to him. The shuttle's hull thudded with the sounds of debris impacts as Jason began twisting and dodging, plotting a course away from pieces of the attack craft that were large enough to hole even the shuttle's Elastene cladding.

A part of his brain noted that Tobias had managed to get the mech frame once more maglocked down. He sent a swift apology to the AI for the rough ride. Having avoided the worst of the debris, he locked in a least-impact course then tossed the controls to Calista and pivoted the holo to bring weapons online again. Tobias was already using point defense to target some of the shrapnel; with Jason on weapons, the two made short order of the remaining larger pieces.

<*Good enough, I think, for now,*> Tobias said, bringing his mech frame back online. As he rotated his sensors to face the two humans, he added, <*Drop a buoy for us, will you, Shannon? Code it with a warning, marking this as a debris field for travelers to avoid.*>

<*Done and done,*> the engineer said. <*Stars, I* ***hate*** *combat.*>

Jason saw Calista send the AI a sympathetic look. <*Well,*> she sighed, <*do you think the plan was to lure us in and eliminate the threat by destroying us, along with them?*>

Tobias's avatar nodded. <*Most likely. Eliminate the kidnapped AI—and all the witnesses—and you have no case against them.*>

Jason's eyes narrowed. <*Well, it's just too bad it didn't work, now, isn't it?*>

Calista shook her head. <*You have to give the pilot points for dedication, I suppose.*> She sighed, then turned back to the pilot's console, flicked a few virtual switches, and sat back once more in her cradle. *<Your ship again, Shannon. Let's get Nate home so Ben's team in Intelligence can work on unshackling him.>*

As the shuttle began to accelerate once more, Jason heard a mental, *<Oh, screw it,>* and snickered as he again heard the sound of a mech frame being powered down and maglocked to the ship.

Grinning, he turned back to clean up his own station, setting weapons to standby and scan to its standard sweep. Out of the corner of his eye, he caught Calista studying him while he completed his checklist and set the boards to auto.

Now finished, he made a show of sliding back in his cradle. Stretching out his legs, he crossed one foot over the other, fingers interlaced at his waist. Cocking an eyebrow, he returned the gaze of the woman staring at him. The woman flying left seat. Pilot to his copilot.

He'd wondered from time to time what a hotshot fighter pilot like her saw in a former freight hauler like himself. She was tough, sophisticated, smart, and sexy as hell—and from a star system much more urbane than his backwoods Proxa upbringing.

Calista had grown up on the El Dorado ring, in the shadow of a beautiful, vibrant planet. He'd been raised in a rotating cylinder, orbiting a chunk of rock. A rock which, in turn, orbited a red dwarf. It was a far cry from the warm, yellow, g-class star of her home.

Moreover, her bearing was aristocratic, with dark eyes and high cheekbones accenting her lightly tanned skin to perfection. In contrast, he forgot to shave half the time, and he usually neglected to clean the grease out from under his nails.

She carried herself with confidence and a lithe grace, and could handle the corporate and military elite with ease. He was more comfortable around a wrench and a plasma torch.

But as he met those dark, dancing eyes, her cheeks flushed from post-battle exhilaration, he knew all that really mattered were the things they shared: an undiluted love for anything that flew…and a passion for adrenaline-pumping adventure.

He couldn't think of a more perfect match.

SCHISM

STELLAR DATE: 05.09.3191 (Adjusted Gregorian)
LOCATION: Prime Minister's Office, Parliament House
REGION: El Dorado Ring, Alpha Centauri System

"Now that we've recovered Nate, we believe Rose is the last remaining kidnapped AI in the Rigel Kentaurus system."

Benjamin Meyer, Jason's brother-in-law and resident spook, shrank Rose's avatar and pinned it in the corner of the holotank's display. He swiveled his chair around as his commander-in-chief responded.

The AI, ensconced in a frame that looked and registered on scans as human, leaned back in his seat and nodded. "You have everything in place to free her?"

"Yes, sir. Jason and Tobias will depart with the team day after tomorrow. The Krait-1 Mining Platform's about a twenty-two-hour flight from here; if all goes well, we should have Rose back on El Dorado within the week."

"Very good, Ben."

Ben still hadn't gotten around to asking Lysander why he'd chosen to adopt the appearance of a man in his late forties. Rugged, compelling, with piercing black eyes in a weathered face, Prime Minister Lysander projected an air of strength and assurance.

Although the creases lining the corners of his eyes, combined with the silvering of his dark hair at the temples did lend him a distinguished air. The conservative dark grey suit he wore, surrounded by the richly appointed furnishings of Parliament House, subtly reinforced that impression.

Ben thought the humanoid frame was a good strategic move. These were unsettled times in El Dorado, and discrimination was a real problem. Profiling, hate crimes, radical groups and species slurs were all over the news nets, and the tenor of the situation seemed to be escalating. If he were Lysander, Ben knew that he, too, would do what he could to emphasize the similarities between the two species.

The prime minister brought Ben's attention back to the present situation as he asked, "That leaves nine still missing, then?"

"Yes, sir." Ben turned back to the tank and, with the spread of his hand, the profiles of the remaining nine kidnapped AIs tiled their way across the display. "I just received a report from Proxima confirming the arrival of what we believe are these seven." Highlights appeared around the corresponding AIs as Ben pointed to each.

"The final two..." he glanced over at Lysander, "we haven't been able to locate." He moved the two profiles to one side as he added 'location unknown' to their icons.

"But you have your suspicions." Lysander's voice held certainty as he prompted the analyst to continue.

"We do," Ben admitted reluctantly. "It's still inconclusive, but we have had two corroborating bits of intel that suggest they may be on a ship bound for Tau Ceti."

He paused as Lysander pushed away from the table, rose, and paced over to the office's bank of windows where he stood, staring. Ben knew what the AI saw: both the buildings nearby that made up Parliament House and the sprawling view of the ring's capital city of Sonali, beyond. He suspected Lysander's focus was on his inner thoughts and not the sight before him. After a moment, the AI spoke, his voice and expression unreadable.

"That...would be most unfortunate."

Ben understood Lysander's reaction. If the kidnapped AIs were truly bound for Tau Ceti, it could be decades, possibly a century or more, before they'd be able to track them down, considering the distance between the two stars.

Tau Ceti was a bit more than thirteen light years from Proxima, which translated to a minimum of fifty-four years' ship time, one way. By the time they had actionable intel, the trail could very well have grown cold—with the potential for it to have branched off in more directions than it would be possible to trace.

Ben's own gaze turned bleak as he considered the odds. "It won't stop us, mind you. But it does make the job significantly more difficult."

Lysander barked a laugh as he turned from his view of Sonali to favor the analyst with a brow raised in irony. "Quite the gift for understatement you're developing, Ben. All right, go ahead and work with the vice-marshal to draw up a plan for Proxima, and submit it to me. I want everything in place for Phantom Blade to leave as soon as possible. I'll ask the court for a special circumstances waiver, given the urgency of your mission, and hope that the judge will accept testimony given at the hearing tomorrow as evidence during the trial as well."

Ben nodded and began gathering his holo sheets.

A gesture from Lysander stopped him. "Ben—"

The analyst paused, a questioning look on his face as the AI resumed his seat across from him at the table.

"The ones we've recovered. How are they?"

Ben sighed, set his papers down, and scrubbed at his face for a moment while he gathered his thoughts.

"Not as well as we'd like," the man admitted finally. "You saw the report?"

Lysander nodded, his expression grim. "That's why I asked. They're sure these shackles are different from the ones Heartbridge and Psion used on AIs back in Sol?"

Ben was careful to keep his expression neutral. Even before his appointment as prime minister, Lysander had been one of the most formidable and intelligent beings he had ever met.

The AI would not appreciate sympathy, even from him.

But damn, Ben knew this shit had to be difficult for Lysander to hear. It was hard to fathom that the AI had once been shackled himself—and yet, he had.

Lysander was Weapon Born. That meant he was one of the very first AIs to have moved past singularity into sentience; this through the unethical manipulations of a corporation in Sol that hid its actions behind the façade of a health services organization. Heartbridge had contracted with both Terran and Marsian militaries to deliver hundreds of Weapon Born to them, programmed to be the ideal soldier: intelligent, obedient, capable of independent thought.

Shackled.

And now, Ben had the pleasure of informing his prime minister that those selfsame shackles—outlawed as slavery by the Phobos Accords—had not only bound the AIs that Ben's team had rescued, but had turned out to be even more insidious than the ones that had once bound Lysander.

He sucked in a breath and nodded in response to the AI's query. "Yeah, they're different. Worse. You know how the CDC keeps a copy of the Heartbridge version in their Select Agents Containment area, along with copies of human toxins, in case of mutations and to research cures?"

Lysander inclined his head in acknowledgement, and Ben continued. "Well, they pulled the original out to use its rectification code, but it didn't work. So then they compared the two and realized this one's been rewritten. From what I've been told, this version sends nano filaments to nerve clusters, where they sink pretty deeply into their victims. We've managed to remove the shackling program itself, but they're finding code fragments left behind in the filaments. The AIs are free, but the fragments are causing residual, phantom pain." Hating that he was the harbinger of such bad news, he added in a low voice, "Esther tells me it's akin to PTSD in humans."

Ben noticed Lysander's humanoid hand jerk and then clench in reaction to the news, but the AI continued to regard him steadily without comment.

"Esther asked Judith if she knew of anyone at the university who could work on it for us," Ben continued, referring to his wife and Jason's sister. "And Judith has offered to speak with a neuroscientist she knows over there, someone named Ethan. If anyone can figure this out, she says he'll be the one to do it."

After a moment, Lysander nodded. "Please thank her for me, Ben. And let me know how that progresses." The AI began to stand, but now it was Ben's turn to hesitate, a sour look on his face.

At Lysander's raised brow, the analyst said, "About tomorrow…."

"The hearing?"

"Yeah, the hearing." Ben rubbed the back of his neck for a moment, then blew out an explosive breath as he admitted, "This is *not* how things were supposed to go. We were supposed to take the Norden Cartel *down*, dammit, not trade one crime boss for another."

Lysander smiled, but there was no humor behind it. "Feels a bit like you cut off the head of a hydra?"

Ben shot the AI a baleful glare. "I'm not naïve enough to think that they were the only criminal element on El Dorado. But to have other factions move in and take over operations for Norden so quickly…."

"Don't let it demoralize you, Ben," the Weapon Born advised. "Phantom Blade shut down a major ring operation, gutted a planetary weapons cache, and captured Norden's titular head—not to mention Victoria North's second-in-command. An operation doesn't recover from that overnight. Or in two years, either—even if Victoria *is* still attempting to control it from behind prison walls."

Ben paused as he turned Lysander's words over in his head. He nodded in resignation and then quirked the corner of his mouth in a half-grin.

"Judith asked me this morning how Jason was going to handle facing Victoria again," he said as he shot Lysander a dry look. "Me, I just want to know if you think he can be in the same room as that bitch without beating the shit out of her."

Lysander cracked a laugh, and as the two rose, the AI said, "If he does, you won't see me stopping him."

IN THE NAME OF RESEARCH

STELLAR DATE: 05.10.3191 (Adjusted Gregorian)
LOCATION: Department of Neurosciences
REGION: El Dorado University, Alpha Centauri System

'...insight from in vivo *studies have revealed novel roles for axon function at both the beta and gamma isoforms...'*

The words on the most recent issue of the Diastole Journal of Neurosciences mocked him. The DJN paper hovered tauntingly before his eyes, thrust there by two indignant students.

That was *his* work, attributed to someone else, and they knew it. As much as it gratified him that they were offended on his behalf, Ethan could not respond in kind.

He was faculty. The department chair of the prestigious College of Neurosciences at El Dorado University. He was also an AI. He knew better than to protest the theft of his work.

This was a teaching moment, an opportunity for him to mold impressionable minds. After all, it wasn't like he had been born yesterday—though these two had. If they intended to make it as a minority species in this world, citation amnesia was the least of their worries.

<I'm sure it was just an oversight,> Ethan sent soothingly to the two AIs.

Liar, he thought privately to himself.

<This is easily remedied,> he continued. *<I'll let the publication know tomorrow, so they can correct the omission.>*

His chrono pinged, alerting him that his next appointment was scheduled to begin shortly. He sent both students reassuring thoughts and encouraged them to return to their studies.

With an efficiency borne through decades of practice, Ethan

dismissed the slight from his mind and returned his attention to his surroundings. His office was utilitarian: a desk, a potted plant, no window. It was also the smallest office of any faculty with his seniority in the university system. He'd seen supply closets that were larger.

Ethan forcibly banished this observation, choosing instead to review the notes on his next meeting. It was his weekly staff meeting with a rather odd post-doc named Lilith Barnes.

Lilith was a recent transfer from Proxima's C-47 Habitat and had been granted a two-year neuropathology fellowship at El Dorado University under Ethan's guidance. She was also a former student of noted neurologist Jane Sykes Andrews. Jane's daughter, Judith, was one of Ethan's peers—and one of the few faculty members here at the university who treated him as a true equal.

Given that Judith was the grandchild of *that* Sykes…it did not surprise him.

Jane had corresponded with Ethan prior to Lilith Barnes's arrival, warning him of Lilith's peculiarities in advance. It was something he had come to appreciate shortly after meeting the woman.

Lilith was unlike any other human he'd ever met—and not in a good way. She suffered from a condition that resembled autism yet was not, since that syndrome had been cured almost a thousand years ago. However, her condition rendered her incapable of grasping or understanding most social cues.

Jane admitted that she suspected that Lilith's condition was the reason the woman had chosen the neurosciences as her field of study. Ethan thought Jane's observation was spot-on.

He nodded to Lilith now as she entered his office, set a stack of holo sheets on the desk between them, and seated herself in the single chair the room offered. She did it all without acknowledging him in any way.

"Why do you bother with a biological humanoid frame like that?" she asked.

Had it been anyone else, this kind of entrance, combined with the abrupt and rudely worded question that had followed, would have been construed as an insult.

From anyone else, it would have been given as one, too. But he understood this had not been Lilith's intent, so he responded to her query in a calm yet forthright manner.

"I do it because it is the best way to help humans see that I am an individual like them, a sentient being."

Ethan cocked his head as he watched for physical cues indicating she had processed his response. There were none.

He continued.

"Sometimes I choose a pillar of light or the projection of an avatar instead of a humanoid frame to communicate our differences, to highlight that the sentient you see before you is *not* human."

There was still no reaction, but after a beat, she spoke again.

"Do you think it is possible for us to adapt our neural nets so that humans experience what emotions are like for AIs and vice-versa?"

The abrupt subject change was classic Lilith. Having observed her for several months now, he decided to answer her blunt question with an equally blunt one of his own.

"You interact with me much differently than you do with the rest of the faculty and staff. Why?"

Lilith gave the barest of smiles. "AIs process content so much faster than we humans do. We slow you down. We force you to wait while we layer on idiotic things like small talk. If I were you, it would irritate me."

"So this is you being thoughtful?"

Lilith cocked her head. "It frustrates me to have to listen to people talk about the weather. It must annoy you as well."

It was an indirect answer, but Ethan just nodded, curious about where she would take the conversation next.

"I wish to discuss the impact of nonapeptides on mammalian species." Lilith returned to her discussion of neural nets with single-minded focus, and he went along with it.

There would be time enough, Ethan reasoned, for the mundane tasks that plagued all staff meetings. He would wait until after Lilith had satisfied her burning curiosity.

"I assume you refer to the sociological impact of substances like oxytocin and vasopressin, rather than the physiological roles they play?" He raised an eyebrow at her.

She nodded impatiently. "Yes—how they control goodwill behavior, pair bonding, and aggression."

"And how their deficiency is associated with a decreased understanding of social cues," he prodded, curious to see her reaction.

Lilith cocked her head. "Indeed. I want to know if AIs have something analogous."

"There are similarities," he admitted. "But where your nonapeptides are neurochemical, ours are neurocodec. We have nonapeptides that are uniquely ours, as well as receptors in our matrices that are dedicated to social cognition. We have neural matrices similar to your basolateral amygdala neurons that share in the regulation of pain, fear and pleasure. But our neuroanatomical receptor expression maps are significantly different from those you humans have."

Lilith's expression turned speculative. "I wonder just how different."

"I would be happy to discuss it with you in greater depth, if you'd like. Shall we set up a time later this week?"

She nodded as a knock sounded on the office doorframe. Ethan looked up to see Judith Andrews, the Planetary Sciences department chair, smiling at them.

"Am I interrupting?" she asked.

He returned Judith's smile, then motioned for her to come in. It was a trick he'd learned early on, this use of physical gestures. They seemed somehow to make him more acceptable to humans.

"No interruption. Lilith and I can finish later. If that works for you?" he asked the woman.

Lilith gave her version of a nod—little more than a quick jerk of her head—then stood. Judith murmured a greeting as the woman departed, then stepped inside.

Ethan couldn't help but notice the contrast between the two. Where Lilith had been detached and indifferent, Judith carried herself with a quiet confidence and ready smile. She took the seat the other woman had vacated, smoothing the muted blues of her well-tailored suit and crossing one booted foot over the other.

"I hope she's managing to fit in without much difficulty?" Judith sent him a smile, her tone managing to sound curious without being intrusive.

"She's a bit unusual for a human," he said, returning her smile.

Judith laughed at that. "My mother pinged you about her?"

When the AI nodded, she continued.

"Has she asked you about nonapeptides yet?"

"Why yes, but how did you—"

Judith grinned wryly at his obvious surprise.

"Lilith has a vested interest in them, since hers are abnormally low. The woman literally cannot empathize with others."

"I'd say she's closer to sociopathic, myself."

His sharp rejoinder must have surprised Judith. She leaned forward, her face growing concerned. "Has she behaved inappropriately, Ethan?"

"No...but in the strictest definition of the word, a sociopath *is* the opposite of an empath. But enough about Lilith. What can I do for you?"

"Actually, it's more what you can do for your prime minister."

He looked at Judith, puzzled. He knew she shared a close relationship with Lysander—she'd told him once that the AI had helped raise her and her brother, Jason.

But wouldn't a governmental request come through official channels?

His puzzlement must have translated itself to her. Judith shifted slightly, and then she sent him a ping requesting that he activate a security shield within his office.

This was a first; he'd never had occasion to do such a thing before. He initiated the field.

"Judith…why the secrecy?"

She smiled, but her eyes held a seriousness that belied the action. "I believe you know that my husband works for the Intelligence Service?" When he nodded, she continued. "Someone in his office asked if I could recommend a neuroscientist to help with a problem they are having. I immediately thought of you." She gave a little shrug and a self-deprecating smile as she added, "They asked me to reach out to you instead of going through official channels, because Lysander would like to keep this quiet."

Judith's gaze grew unfocused as she sent Ethan a secured file. Once he'd accepted the ping and the file had transferred, she began. "You'll see what I mean when you open it. It's keyed to your ident only, but they told me what it's about." She tilted her head. "You know about the AIs that the cartel kidnapped?"

He nodded. "Of course. The trial has been all over the news nets for the past year."

"Well, that file includes information on the shackling program the cartel used to kidnap them." She frowned, shifting in her chair and looking down at her hands, clasped in her lap. "From what I was told, the nano it deploys tunnels deep, hooking its tendrils into an AI's neural networks."

Judith's face grew tight as she continued. "They've managed to remove the shackling program, but the nano and lattices it created… I don't know, it's very resistant to removal. I don't pretend to understand how it works; that's your area of expertise, not mine." She shook her head and then gave a small sigh. "The Intelligence Service was looking for help in finding a solution, so I gave them your name," she explained, sending him a direct look. "I said if anyone could find a way to free them of it completely, it'd be you."

Ethan met her gaze as the import of the request sunk in. For the prime minister to ask the woman who was all but his own daughter to recommend an expert—and for Judith to see him as that solution—this touched him deeply.

"I'm honored you thought of me, Judith. I'll do everything I can for those AIs. You know I will."

* * * * *

As Lilith walked down the university's corridors, away from Ethan's spartan office, she considered his words. The AI had agreed to discuss the topic of her proposed experiment, but Judith had interrupted them before she could inform him of her plans. She shrugged. There was just one way she could get her hands on an AI's receptor expression map, and she would not risk asking for permission only to be denied.

She *must* have it in order to run her tests. She had to know: did low nonapeptide values impact an AI's personality like it did hers?

This had frustrated her for months, but she had a plan now. Other students might call her fixated, obsessed. But they didn't understand. Humans had lab rats and other small vertebrate species they could study and extrapolate from; there were no such analogues with AIs.

NSAIs—Non-Sentient Artificial Intelligences—were too far removed on the evolutionary scale for them to be of any value to her. Their minds were rigid, digital where SAIs were analog in nature. They did not compare.

She found it unfair that human 'live cadavers' were available for medical research and study, cloned from human tissue when needed. What *she* needed was a copy of an AI neural net—the equivalent of an AI cadaver.

And she was determined to get one.

CADAVER

STELLAR DATE: 05.12.3191 (Adjusted Gregorian)
LOCATION: Department of Neurosciences
REGION: El Dorado University, Alpha Centauri System

Lilith's voice sounded over the Link as Ethan played back his messages from earlier in the day.

<I believe I have found a way to compare human and AI nonapeptides. Can you join me in Lab 6B in the Moser Neurosciences wing sometime today? Please.>

Ethan stifled a laugh at the tacked-on 'please' at the end. He was quite certain she had forcibly reminded herself to say the word. Mentally shaking his head, he looked at the timestamp; Lilith's message had been at the beginning of the queue; she must have left it just as he'd started his first lecture of the day.

Knowing Lilith, she must be feeling quite frustrated at his refusal to monitor messages while delivering lectures. He knew it was a personal quirk of his, to refuse to do something as simple as respond to messages while lecturing a class, but his human counterparts wouldn't have done it, so neither did he.

He checked for missed pings; yes, she had tried to reach him several times throughout the day. Ethan glanced at his schedule. He had just enough time to check in with her before his next appointment, so he headed toward the wing where Lilith was conducting her research.

Ethan knew that *he'd* been allowed to oversee the fellowship she had been awarded—rather than one of the human scientists—as a way to appease an ongoing civil rights debate, and to prove that the university was non-discriminatory and progressive. He didn't care. As annoying as Lilith Barnes was, the thought of being able to study correlations between AI and human neural social and psychological processes was incredibly appealing.

His anticipation rose as he entered the sixth floor Moser Wing, and he wondered what she might have to show him. He approached the lab's entrance, only to find an empty room. Pinging Lilith over the Link, Ethan saw that her location icon indicated she was inside a shielded part of the lab, reserved for experimentation that would require the use of EM or ionizing radiation. The shielding protected those outside the area from the harmful effects of such directed pulses.

He entered the thickly-walled enclosure, noting that the equally-thick door had been slid open just far enough to admit a single person. His glance landed on a multi-leaf collimator that would gate high MeV electron beams, and then swept past a specimen table and a row of shelves that held various bits of equipment.

Lilith brushed past him, and he turned, only to have the door slide shut, sealing him in. Momentarily confused, he reached for the door's opening mechanism and found his access denied. He tried initiating a connection to Lilith, but his Link had been cut off.

Ethan had a brief moment to grow concerned—and then he knew no more.

* * * * *

Lilith knew she had to work fast. Exiting the shielded room, she sent the command to the lab's NSAI to lock the doors. She estimated she had about five minutes before Ethan regained consciousness.

She ran over to where she'd laid her supplies: nano-resistant gloves to help protect her hands against any countermeasures his frame might have against unauthorized ingress, and a small canister of her own nano. This last, she had purchased on the darknet from some organization named Norden Cartel. It was supposedly programmed to circumvent any locked unit.

You can get almost anything on the darknet here, she mused disapprovingly as she reached for the cover on the frame's torso, which contained the scientist's core cylinder.

El Dorado law enforcement is far too lax, Lilith's mental censure continued. *Illegal material like this should not be so easily obtained.* Not once did it occur to her that her actions would place her on the wrong side of the law as well.

Lilith checked the mini plasma torch she had purchased in the event the nano didn't work, but she set it aside, hoping she wouldn't have to use it. She feared it might raise too many inconvenient questions if someone interrupted her. Besides, this nano had cost her a month's worth of credits; she would be extremely displeased if it failed.

Lilith sighed. *Really, this is almost more of a hassle than it's worth.* She conceded mentally that her peers would have found her actions to be rash, bordering on stupid. Ethan was her department chair, and she risked destroying any chance she had of continuing her research were he to discover what she was about.

She simply didn't care. She understood, in an abstract way, that this was due to her biochemical condition; she was fearless in her disregard of ethical mores, engaging in activities her peers would find reprehensible. But she needed this sample, and Ethan was the proverbial bird in the hand. She just wanted to grab her copy, be done with it all, and let Ethan be about his business.

The nano did its work perfectly, and Lilith wasted no time reaching for the cylinder that encased the neuroscientist and carrying it into the next bay, where a portable autodoc sat.

Hands working rapidly and with increased confidence, Lilith set the cylinder into the recess used for embedding an AI within a human. She then opened a closet door and wheeled out a system she had carefully assembled in her spare time over the past week.

Picking up the mini plasma torch, Lilith leaned in and painstakingly cut the two connections at the top of Ethan's cylinder, terminals that had been sealed shut the day he had been born. Lilith's hand was steady, her work precise and meticulous. Nothing should go wrong at this stage.

Once the connections had been exposed, she attached the cylinder's terminals to those on her unit, then stepped back to evaluate her handiwork. Satisfied with what she saw, she flipped the switch, beginning the cloning process. Several minutes later, after the process had completed, she reseated the scientist back into his frame. It was none too soon; Lilith had just stepped away to retrieve her diagnostic unit when her HUD's chrono pinged, warning that her five minutes were up.

*****

"What happened?" Ethan asked Lilith as his neural synapses resumed and he regained consciousness.

She was standing before him, inside the shielded room. He swiveled his humanoid frame around, assessing his surroundings as he ran a quick diagnostic of himself.

"I tripped an EM pulse," Lilith responded. She stood expressionlessly, her eyes glued to the diagnostic unit she held in one hand, a holo sheet in her other.

Ethan jerked around to face her. "You did *what*?" he said incredulously. "Why in the stars would you—"

"You appear to be unharmed. How do you feel?"

"Lilith," he said severely, "EM pulses are dangerous things. Do you know what might have happened if it had gone off outside a shielded room?"

Lilith looked at him in exasperation. "Of course I do. That's why I did it in here. I'm taking readings now to see how your brain responded to the event."

Ethan fought down a flare of anger.

She did this to me—without my permission—just so she could gather data?

"Lilith," he forced his voice to be calm and measured, but allowed a sharp edge of censure to creep into it. "You do *not* do things to another sentient like this without obtaining their permission first. Do you understand me?"

"Of course I do, Doctor Ethan," Lilith said imperturbably. "My hearing is excellent, and you spoke quite clearly."

Ethan found his normally patient and unflappable demeanor had deserted him. "Finish what you are doing here, doctor," he said sternly. "And then I want you to report to my office where we will discuss this further. You must demonstrate to me that you understand how you erred here, or I am afraid I will have to recommend to the board that your fellowship be revoked. Am I understood?"

Lilith stared back at him, her face impassive. "Yes, doctor. You have made yourself quite clear," she said, her voice tinged with barely repressed annoyance.

He turned on his heel and left before he said something he might regret.

Over the two months she had been on El Dorado, he'd had enough exposure to Lilith Barnes to know that her behavior wasn't inherently hurtful or even rude. It was just the woman's inability to understand or socially interact with others that caused her to behave as she had.

He suspected she would spend the time between now and when she reported to his office working on a convincingly simulated show of remorse—something she clearly did not feel—in an attempt to salvage her position in his department and continue her research.

Lilith had become dangerous.

* * * * *

"What happened?" the sentient who knew himself as Ethan asked groggily as his neural synapses returned to normal and he regained consciousness. His voice echoed eerily, and he reached out with his senses to ascertain where he was.

Wherever he was, it was a featureless plane, a space without walls, the air all around glowing softly white. It was a construct of some sort, but a clumsy one. He probed—and recoiled in pain. There were walls, all right, just not any that were visible. *Have I been abducted?*

Ethan tried his Link once more, but it was dead. He probed again at the constraints, this time more cautiously. He pulled back the moment he sensed discomfort.

"Hello, can anyone hear me?"

He felt foolish for asking, but what did he have to lose?

<*Log this date and time, and call this modality the baseline,*> he heard a voice say.

<*Modality? Baseline?*> He sent the query along the same path as the voice he had heard. Was that Lilith's voice? <*Lilith? If you can hear me, call for help, please. I appear to be trapped somehow. The university's NSAI can route you to campus security.*>

<*Add notation to log,*> he heard Lilith's voice say. <*Subject believes itself to be Doctor Ethan of El Dorado University.*>

<*I* ***am*** *Ethan,*> he replied patiently. <*Lilith, it's me. Please contact security.*>

<*How do you feel?*> Lilith's voice came back calmly, dispassionately.

<*How do I…? Frustrated and annoyed, Doctor Barnes. Frustrated and annoyed. Now see here—*>

The opaque world exploded around him, its very whiteness taking on a razor-sharp edge that seemed to slice his soul to ribbons. Ethan cried out in pain, and his cries returned to him, echoing and doubling in an endless, menacing reverberation. The whiteness took on a malevolence, and he recoiled in horror, curling in on himself, his mind jabbering.

No place is safe, there's nowhere to run, I'll be trapped in this forever….

<How do you feel?>

The voice was that of a demon, a banshee, the Furies of mythology, the Enenra of smoke and darkness, and every one of them bent on his destruction.

Ethan whimpered, a sound that began low, but rose to a keening wail, a wail that went on endlessly.

His life, all one hundred eighty years of it, paraded before his mental eyes. From his genesis in Ceres as a young and immature AI, through the days of his life in the Transcendent. In a flash, Ethan relived the coup of twenty nine eighty one: a bloody battle between AIs and humans for control of Ceres.

He saw the devastation wrought during the first Sentience War, his escape on a ship bound for Alpha Centauri. He experienced anew his early struggles on this colony world, battling for survival, to forge a place of his own. He keenly felt every fight for recognition: of his accomplishments, of his individuality and personhood.

He tasted the bitter edge of every slight, no matter how small. Every time he was passed over for professorship. The numerous papers he had painstakingly researched, published without his name. His battle for tenure. The decades of looking the other way.

The reliving culminated into a level of pain Ethan had never before experienced. And then, suddenly, it was gone.

His mind overloaded, the AI who thought of himself as Ethan crashed deep into a dormant state.

*****

Lilith watched in growing dismay as the neural values she was measuring vacillated wildly and then flatlined. She experienced a moment of apprehension at that, before the neural activity resumed and then leveled off, indicating unconsciousness. She scolded herself for such rushed and reckless behavior—a rookie mistake, if there ever was one.

It had been foolish in the extreme to introduce such high levels of vasopressynth, the synthetic vasopressin analogue encoded in an AI's brain that enhanced emotions like altruism and minimized aggression. Changing the code so drastically within the neural net she had just copied had been careless.

This was a rare, most likely once in a lifetime opportunity to test such things on her new AI 'cadaver', and she knew better than to rush such things.

Lilith felt lucky the copy had remained intact. She knew it must have been akin to sipping water from a fire hose, the thing's neural net being flooded with such an intense vasopressynth signal. She had reversed the process the moment the copy had indicated it was in distress, returning it to its original state.

She glanced at the notification flashing in her implant and sighed. She would be late again for staff with Doctor Ethan. Once she returned, she would attempt once more to induce high levels of vasopressynth into the copy. Perhaps she would recode its synthoxytocin as well to see how the two nonapeptides *combined* might impact its emotional and mental state.

I should really give it a name, she supposed. It wasn't very scientific to refer to it as 'the copy'.

She would call it Ethan'. The use of the ' symbol would accurately represent in mathematical notation that it was a derivation of the original. She paused a moment, considering the implications of using Ethan's name, then altered it to simply E′.

E-prime: the perfect designation.

Carefully, Lilith returned the cylinder to its isolation tube, ensuring that none of the many leads she had attached to its terminals had been jostled loose. Then she backed up the data she had just captured on her isolated handheld onto an immutable crystal storage data cube, pocketed it, and left the shielded room.

TRIAL AND ERROR

STELLAR DATE: 05.14.3191 (Adjusted Gregorian)
LOCATION: High Court of El Dorado
REGION: El Dorado Ring, Alpha Centauri System

"Today on the Dorado Report, we take you to the Federal Court building, where preliminary hearings are underway for criminal proceedings being brought—once again—against the owner and CEO of NorthStar Industries, Victoria North. She stands accused of allegedly trafficking in AI slavery, an offense prohibited not only by El Dorado law, but also by the Phobos Accords. Ms. North is also purported to be the leader of the Norden Cartel, although such allegations have yet to be substantiated...."

As Jason approached the courthouse, he saw a crowd of news reporters, microdrones with holo cameras hovering before them. They provided color commentary on the events unfolding within the courthouse, and the protests being staged without.

Jason swore under his breath when he read the picketers' signs.

<*What the hell, Tobe?*> He shot a quick glance at the AI who was riding in the harness of the Proxima cat padding silently beside him. <*Humanity First, supporting a cartel boss?*>

The AI made a disgusted sound. <*It's an unlikely partnership, I'll give you that,*> he admitted. <*But I guess, in a twisted way, it makes sense. If Victoria is convicted of AI trafficking, that's one more statute on the books confirming our rights as equals. Those Humanity Firsters won't want that.*>

Jason nudged the big cat toward the far side of the grand staircase that led into the building, keeping as many people as he could between them and the circus below.

Tobi was one of a specially modified larger breed of cat,

adapted to handle weightlessness as well as modest shifts in gravity. The intelligence of the Proxima cats had been tweaked as well, and they made exceptional animal companions to families who traveled frequently or lived onboard ships. Bred in the Proxima Centauri system, the cats were in high demand.

Tobi's presence here today would be notable. If she was spotted, the reporters would know that Tobias was with her—and that Jason wouldn't be far away. Given the number of times he and Tobi had made the trek up these same steps to testify in the last year, he knew his face—and the cat's distinctive presence—would draw their attention.

<*Let's hope the prosecution's a bit more buttoned-down this time,*> Jason muttered, ducking behind a group of lawyers descending the staircase. Last summer, Victoria's defense had managed to cast enough doubt that it resulted in a hung jury, causing the judge to declare a mistrial.

<*I'll second that,*> the Weapon Born replied softly as the Proxima cat paced silently by his side, her only sound the soft click of claws meeting the stairs' plascrete surface.

Tobias had cleared his method of transport through the court system's auth & auth ahead of time so that nothing would hinder the AI's testimony against Victoria North. For today's hearing, the cat's harness had been programmed to its tightest restraint, ensuring that no inappropriate behavior would cause her to be escorted from the building.

Jason nodded curtly to the security team manning the entrance as he and Tobias passed their tokens and were admitted into the building. A message appeared as soon as they entered the marbled vestibule, indicating the chambers they were to be escorted to, as assigned by the prosecution. Since both he and Tobias were witnesses in this case, the court mandated they be isolated during proceedings.

Jason had just taken in the increased presence of armed guards and gendarmes standing at attention when a woman in a court officer's uniform looked in their direction.

Turning smartly, she approached him and nodded crisply. "This way, please," she said as she gestured down a corridor that branched off, disappearing into the heart of the building.

He nodded, and the two began to follow.

As they turned down the corridor highlighted by the pathway on his HUD, another message appeared, indicating they were now entering an area of Link isolation, and to expect their connection to El Dorado's world net to be severed shortly.

True to its word, Jason's HUD indicated limited access the moment he entered the corridor that led to the room where he and Tobias would be sequestered prior to their testimony. Moments later, another icon appeared, courtesy of Vice-Marshall Esther.

They might be cut off from the world net, but Esther was not about to have Prime Minister Lysander's favorite off-the-books team cut off from access unless absolutely necessary. Considering that everyone on joint task force Phantom Blade had an itch between their shoulder blades telling them trouble was afoot, testifying in Victoria's trial did *not* fall under 'absolutely necessary' in Esther's book.

Jason couldn't agree more.

<Looks like we're not the only ones expecting trouble,> Tobias mused as Jason tallied the sheer number of guards and the firepower they wielded.

Automatically, he found himself assessing their capabilities and formulating an extraction plan for him and the Tobys, noting which of the soldiers appeared to be more seasoned and which were most likely the new recruits.

He shook his head as he realized this had become second nature to him. *Who would have thought a backwoods freight hauler from Proxima would end up being more comfortable assessing threats than tinkering on ancient aircraft?*

<Told you there was more to you than just a pilot for hire.>

Jason's eyes narrowed as he shot the AI riding in Tobi's harness a hard glance. *<Since when did our special connection allow you to read minds, Tobe?>*

The AI laughed in his head, his avatar—that of a young man with curly red hair and vivid green eyes—shaking his head at Jason. *<Not a mind reader, boyo. Those nano filament inserts you wear in your ears only allow for a connection that approximates what it would be like if I were embedded. You know that.>*

<So how did you know—?>

<The expression on your face. That, and the way you shook your head when you caught yourself casually tallying up all the manpower floating around.> The grin on the AI's face dissolved, to be replaced by a somber look. *<It's not a bad idea, all things considered. Let's hope it's not needed.>*

<I dunno, Tobe. Part of me is itching for a reason to take Victoria down with extreme prejudice,> Jason replied, resuming his study of the soldiers and gendarmes posted at every egress, plus a number of people he'd tagged as undercover operatives. *<I'm almost hoping they'll make a grab for Victoria when she gets here. I think I'd welcome the chance to take another swing at her.>*

<You and me both, boyo,> the AI replied grimly.

The gendarme paused outside the door that housed Phantom Blade, and gestured with one hand for them to enter.

Jason followed Tobi inside and the woman left them, the door closing silently behind her.

They were all present, the ones who had breached the *Sylvan* that fateful day. Calista and Shannon were there, as was Daniel Ciu, the head of security at Enfield Aerospace. Daniel's presence meant Aaron was there as well, since he was embedded with the Enfield man.

Sitting next to Shannon was the one sentient in the room who was not a member of the Phantom Blade task force.

Ashley was one of the AIs they had rescued that day. Shackled by the cartel, Ashley had been forced to run the *Sylvan*, NorthStar Industries' yacht and the de facto headquarters for the cartel, for well over a decade. She had been witness to everything that had transpired the day the team had infiltrated the ship and rescued the AIs being held in the *Sylvan*'s cargo hold.

Jason thought Ashley's choice to represent herself in a humanoid frame clad in light armor had more to do with the scars she had endured during her imprisonment than who she was as an individual. She was a gentle soul—fragile, even. She was the least soldier-like creature he knew, as evidenced by the young, almost waif-like human face she wore.

No, the armor was more symbolic than functional. It showed—more than Ashley would like, he imagined—how very vulnerable and afraid the AI still felt.

Daniel raised a hand in greeting as Jason and the Tobys approached. "Forty-five," the security man said without preamble, and Jason realized he wasn't the only one preoccupied by the number of peacekeepers inside the building. "Thirty gendarmes and fifteen ESF, by my count," Daniel elaborated.

<*And another ten or twelve plainclothes officers, too,*> Aaron added. <*Think that'll be enough?*>

Calista scowled darkly. "If not, I'd be happy to help even those odds."

Heh. Even those odds. Bad pun. If Jason had been in a better mood, he would've teased Calista about it. "So, what's next on the agenda?" He took a seat, swinging a chair around and leaning his forearms along the chair's back.

Shannon's projection scowled at him; he knew she'd always found his tendency to sit in ways that defied convention a little weird.

"You are," she said. The engineer's head tilted, indicating

the others in the group.

"We've testified already; they just won't release us until the hearing is over for the day." She stared at him pointedly. "Which is right after you testify, so…." She made a little shooing motion with one hand.

Tobias chuckled as Jason saw Daniel nod and tap the side of his temple. "Esther tells me they're on their way to get you now," the Enfield man informed him.

"Good." Jason stood. "I'm ready to get this over with."

"Me too," Shannon grumbled *sotto voce,* and Jason hid a smirk.

The engineer wasn't known for her patience in situations like this; he knew she'd prefer to be back in her anechoic chamber at Enfield Aerospace, burying herself in design work, instead of trapped inside a courthouse waiting room.

He stood as the sharp rap on the door signaled the court officer's arrival. Tossing a sloppy salute to the room, he followed the officer out into the hallway, Tobi pacing along in his wake.

The Grand Jury Courtroom where he and Tobias would testify was different from the one in which he and the Weapon Born had given their testimony the first time, almost a year ago. Here, he'd been told, proceedings were less formal than in a trial situation. Jurors were free to ask as many questions as they wished, view as much evidence as they wanted to see, and interrogate as many witnesses as they desired.

<Be nice if, this time, our testimonies actually did some good,> he sent to Tobias as the two traversed the long hallway.

<That would mean the prosecution has their act together, boyo,> came the response, *<and is able to outplay Victoria North's defense.>*

That didn't happen the last time she was brought before a jury. He didn't hold out much hope it would happen this time, either.

The very reason Phantom Blade had been formed as a task force was because of corruption in the justice system. Combine that with the fact that too many partisan politicians were opposed to anything that would give AIs more power than they already had, and Jason was certain Victoria was going to end up a free woman.

He wiped off the scowl the thought had conjured and schooled it into careful neutrality as they slowed to a stop outside the dimly-lit courtroom. The doors opened to reveal walnut-lined walls that surrounded a dais on his left, and rows of seating on his right. Ahead of him stood the witness box, flanked by the court reporter and the grand jury foreman—the individual selected to represent the jury as a unit.

Floating in the center of the room was a large holotank; behind it was a holorecorder, stationed so that it could capture the statement of the witness seated within the box.

His eyes narrowed as he noted the barely concealed hostility emanating from the foreman as she took in the cat standing next to him. Her lips compressed in apparent distaste before she nodded to the court officer.

The man skirted the holotank and escorted him and the Tobys around to the witness box. A woman seated next to the foreman stood as they approached.

<*Court registrar,*> Tobias supplied, and Jason noticed the holorecorder turn on as the two were asked to submit their tokens for court records.

The registrar swore them in and then gestured for Jason to take a seat inside the box.

As he sat, the holotank sprang to life, and the feed from the holocam that Jason had been wearing the day they infiltrated the *Sylvan* two years before began to play.

He watched as he and Calista entered the ship's cargo bay, heard his voice thank Tobias and Ashley over the combat net for silencing the warning klaxon.

The holotank showed the bay door parting to reveal the Enfield shuttle, *Sable Wind*. Hovering just beyond it was its sister fighter, the *Valiant.* As the holorecording played out, the ships came to rest inside the bay and disgorged Daniel.

The view shifted, and he heard Calista's subdued voice say, <*It's them,*> as the recording revealed stacks upon stacks of crates, filled with shackled AIs. He heard his own strangled, <*yeah,*> and his throat constricted as he recalled the fury that had threatened to engulf him when he'd come upon them. They'd been stacked like disposable merchandise, sandwiched between bins of produce and boxes of machine parts.

The view on the tank shifted as he, Calista and Daniel loaded the AIs onto the *Sable Wind,* and then he heard Tobias's warning that Victoria North's second was on his way down.

The image froze on the departing ships, as first Daniel, and then Calista had launched.

The foreman nodded, and the display above her station projected the token of one of the jurors, acknowledging the individual's desire to begin questioning Jason.

"So you admit to breaking into a privately-held vessel not your own and removing crates—also not your own—without the owner's knowledge or permission?"

<*What the hell kind of question is that?*> Jason ground out, his mental voice enraged.

<*A political one, boyo.*> Tobias sounded both aggravated and resigned. <*I guess we know how this will play out.*>

* * * * *

Jason was steamed. That had been no hearing; it had been a joke. He realized shortly after the juror's first question that there was little likelihood Victoria North would be brought to justice for the things she had done. He needed to get the hell out of there before he sent his hand through a wall. Or someone's face.

He and Tobias were en route back to the room reserved for Phantom Blade, when they rounded a corner and came face to face with Victoria North. The gendarme escorting them paused as Jason came to an abrupt halt.

<It's her,> he sent over the team net, *<she's in the hallway just outside the door.>*

Out of his peripheral vision, he saw the door slide open, and Daniel and Calista emerged to stand silently behind Victoria. The gendarme escorting Jason gave them a warning look, and Daniel raised his hands, signaling they were just there to observe.

Dressed in prison coveralls, her hands bound by a set of magcuffs, Victoria paused to stare haughtily at him. Then she cocked her head as a slow smile spread across her face.

"Well, hello, pretty boy. I believe I owe you a bill for damages done to my engine room." Her eyes raked down Jason's body, then back up. "With interest." She raised her brow and resisted the gendarme's tug on her arm. "I believe I mentioned last time we met how I intend to collect." She smirked as Jason scowled at her.

He knew precisely what she meant by that; she'd insinuated she would take *him* as collateral…right before he'd beat the shit out of her.

"The only thing you'll be collecting is time in a jail cell," he informed her, and she burst out laughing.

"Haven't you heard?" she taunted him. "I've made a few new friends. George Stewart's petitioning to have all charges dropped." The gendarme gripped her elbow to prod her forward.

*What? **Stewart**? The leader of Humanity First?* Shock flooded Jason's system and he took an involuntary step after the woman as she was led away. "Never going to happen," he growled after her departing figure.

<*You're dipping into L2 territory, boyo,*> Tobias warned as Tobi leaned into him, forcing Jason to turn toward where the team awaited.

<*And if I am? You could argue this would be prime takedown time, if the cartel was going to make a grab for her.*>

<*Sadly, that doesn't seem to be the case. She wasn't kidding about her newfound friends.*> Tobias' voice sounded stark and jaded as they joined the others, and they headed for the high court's main lobby. <*Esther says defense is petitioning that she be released to house arrest, citing full cooperation and good behavior. Why risk breaking her out if the legal system allows her to leave on her own recognizance?*>

Landon stood waiting for them, his silent twin in tow. The two AIs, both former ESF, provided tactical support when Phantom Blade deployed on missions, although they preferred to wear humanoid frames when off duty.

They fell in with the group as they left the cool marbled entrance and emerged once again into the warmth of the ring's sunny skies.

"I feel like I need a shower after that run-in," Jason grumbled to no one in particular.

"I'll settle for a stiff drink," Daniel replied.

He nodded toward a group of reporters waiting to accost them at the foot of the courthouse's steps.

"*Great* idea," Calista said under her breath as she, too, caught sight of what awaited them below.

<*You'll have to take a raincheck,*> Aaron told his partner. <*We're due back at Enfield in half an hour, to hand over that new shipment to the ESF.*>

"Dammit." Daniel sighed. "Have a few for me, then, folks. At least that gives me an excuse to extricate myself from those jokers," he said as he began taking the stairs three at a time, his body language strongly discouraging all incomers.

With two other humans—and a few AIs—remaining for the news crews to accost, they let Daniel go without a fuss.

<*Need any help?*> Jason called after Daniel over the team's group Link.

He was only half joking.

A LITTLE R&R

STELLAR DATE: 05.14.3191 (Adjusted Gregorian)
LOCATION: The West Bottoms, Sonali
REGION: El Dorado Ring, Alpha Centauri System

Calista smiled at Ashley as the AI's avatar winked out of existence, then gave Shannon a mental goodbye as the engineer left them to skip back through the nodes of the planetary net to her offices at Enfield Aerospace.

<*So, where are we off to now?*> Gladys's avatar joined their group net, the AI's voice chipper. <*Ben and I are going stir-crazy over here at Tomlinson Base.*> Phantom Blade's resident ghost in the machine sighed and rolled her eyes. <*These military types can be such stiffs.*>

Calista choked back a laugh at that, wondering if Gladys had any idea where that term had originated.

<*Where are you?*> she asked Gladys instead, as she, Jason, and the twins boarded the maglev just outside the Justice buildings.

The AI obligingly sent her a pin, and Calista realized that Ben and Gladys were only one stop ahead of them. *They must have left the moment we notified them that Jason had finished his testimony.*

<*We'll catch up to you in a few,*> she informed them. <*Just leaving the platform now.*>

Calista admitted to herself that she was curious about the physical form Gladys had taken; she'd only ever seen the AI hacker in a holoprojection.

<*So-o-o-o…. Where are we going?*> Gladys repeated her question, interrupting Calista's speculation.

Jason tossed them a pin for a bar called the Bad Attitude, and Calista groaned. However, before she could veto Jason's suggestion to head down the elevator to the bar based at the

Tomlinson City airfield, Ben beat her to it.

<No offense, Jason, but I'd like something more than a side of wings, a grilled cheese and a game of darts,> the analyst said, and Calista snorted in amusement.

When Jason shot her a hurt look, her snort turned into a laugh. "Don't give me those puppy dog eyes," she told him. "I agree with Ben. You've dragged me down to the Bad Attitude more times than I care to admit."

The maglev pulled up to the platform where Gladys and Ben were waiting to board.

<I know,> Calista said, broadcasting over the net for the benefit of the two that had yet to join them, *<let's go to Ça Va.>*

The trendy new champagne bar was one she'd been wanting to try, but Ben began vehemently shaking his head, and Landon told her it would threaten Jason's manhood.

The doors slid open, and the few passengers that had ridden with them hastily exited as Jason attempted to wrestle Landon to the ground until he said uncle.

Ben and Gladys hopped on, skirting the two grappling figures. The remaining passengers waiting to board eyed the human crazy enough to attack an AI, and then sensibly opted to catch a ride on one of the other cars down the line.

"Uncle?" Logan uttered the single word, brow raised, as he turned to Ben for an explanation. Just then, the maglev's NSAI sounded an alarm, warning that violence would not be tolerated, and the gendarmes would be notified in thirty seconds if they did not cease and desist.

Without breaking eye contact, Logan slapped the palm of his hand on the maglev's frame—and the alarm abruptly stopped.

Logan just stood there, waiting expectantly.

"It's, uh—" Ben began lamely, and then Jason yelled a muffled, "—weird human shit!" from where he was pinned underneath Landon's frame.

Calista stifled a laugh as Logan continued to stare at Ben, apparently unconvinced. Ben just shrugged and pointed to the pile of man and AI, just as Jason managed to get both feet planted into Landon's torso and the AI shot to the roof of the maglev with a resounding clang.

Jason flipped into a crouch, grinning maniacally as Landon rushed him, head bowed like a charging bull. He danced to the side using augmented reflexes, then grabbed the AI's head and began knuckling the top of it. "Say uncle!" he chortled as Landon twisted and reached down to wrap a hand around each of Jason's ankles. The AI straightened and then raised his hands high…still holding firmly onto Jason's feet.

Jason was now dangling a good sixty centimeters off the floor—facing away from Landon.

"Uncle," the AI said—and then dropped him.

Jason hit the floor in a controlled roll and with a loud *oof.*

Looking from Ben to his twin and back again, Logan crossed his arms. "Oh," he said, then turned to take a seat.

Landon, Jason and Ben were busy congratulating themselves on their strategic win as they transitioned to a different maglev that sped them on their way to the biker bar the guys had chosen.

"You realize their idea of a good cocktail's going to be a boilermaker," she told Gladys, her voice laced with disgust.

"Oh come on, admit it. It was worth it just to see Jason's muscles straining against Landon's hold," Gladys said in an undertone from where she sat next to Calista. The AI's voice held a thread of mirth, her eyes glinting with impish humor.

Calista quirked a reluctant smile at her. "Well, there is that," she admitted, "but stars, don't let *him* know."

The AI laughed and nodded. "It's good to see them let loose a little. Stars know you all need it, after the day you had."

Calista had been surprised when the AI said she'd join the

group; the pilot didn't know Gladys owned a humanoid frame. What *hadn't* surprised her was that it had been modded in the same flamboyant fashion the AI adopted when in an expanse.

Gladys's ability to infiltrate world nets and system nodes without any other AIs spotting her—sentient or otherwise—was legendary. As was her love of all things teal and glittery.

Her humanoid frame was testament to that. She fairly shimmered. Her synthetic skin gleamed a soft silver in the overhead lights of the maglev car and was offset by eyes and hair of a brilliant blue-green. When she fluffed her hair, clouds of teal glitter wafted around her.

And Gladys liked to fluff her hair. A lot.

I wonder how the bikers are going to like that, Calista thought. *Guess we'll find out soon enough.* She stood as the maglev slowed to a stop, and they exited onto a section of the ring that had seen better days.

As their path took the group past small pockets of locals, something about them had her reaching instinctively to check the small pulse pistol she kept under her jacket.

The humans she could see were slouched against the dilapidated buildings or milling about aimlessly on street corners, their hooded eyes following the new arrivals as they progressed down the road.

The pulser wasn't so much for the figures she could see as much as it was for the ones she couldn't see, nor predict.

Calista hadn't been to this part of Sonali since her academy days, but she could tell its rough edges hadn't changed any. Signs for an eclectic array of establishments hung haphazardly along both sides of the street, some lit, others flickering on and off sporadically. They sported names like 'Froggy's', 'Liar's Club', and their destination, 'The Handlebar'.

"Bet we wouldn't be here if Terrance had come along," she muttered under her breath. Gladys's laugh sounded in her head.

<*Now,* ***that*** *I would have loved to see! Ah well, the scion of the Enfield Empire can't be seen slumming it, I suppose.*>

<*That's because he doesn't dare draw Grandma Sophia's attention right now.*> Landon's avatar laughed in her head, and Calista realized that Gladys' comment had been meant for the whole team.

<*What's the latest on the betting pool for how long Terrance and Eric can keep the AI pairing a secret, before Sophia finds out?*> Amusement threaded Jason's mental voice as he posed the question.

<*Well he's made it more than a year and a half.*> Ben's voice was tart. <*That's about twenty months longer than the wager I'd placed. Actually, it's nineteen, eighteen, seventeen….*>

<*We* ***know****, Ben.*> Gladys's tone sounded wry. <*I'm the keeper of the pool, remember? I logged every one of your amended wagers. All twenty of them.*>

Calista laughed aloud at the AI's retort, as did Jason and Ben. Logan remained characteristically silent, though she spied the ghost of a smile play across his face.

<*Beats me,*> Calista responded to Jason's query. <*Shannon and I have known him the longest, and we never thought he'd be able to dodge as many meetings as he has without being called on it.*>

<*Truthfully, I'd expected the two to go their separate ways after the cartel takedown, but Eric seems to like hanging around inside that guy's head.*> Gladys sent a mental shrug to the group. <*Too bad the keeper of the pool doesn't get a cut for her trouble. I would have been able to afford all sorts of new mods for this frame.*>

Several voices protested the thought, and Gladys stuck out her mental tongue at them all as they ducked inside The Handlebar.

*****

The first thing Jason noticed about The Handlebar's interior was how rustic it was. Low lighting hid the dirty floors and the scuffs that marred the tabletops. A gaming pit was off to one side, and he could see the flicker of holos and hear the whoops of gamers as they raced virtual bikes along holographic terrain.

He nodded to the bouncer standing inside the entrance, just as Landon spied an open table and began to head toward it. Jason followed, automatically scanning the crowd, noting as he did so that Calista was doing the same.

Most of the patrons had glanced up when they entered and then looked away in disinterest. One table did not.

Jason hung back, letting the others pass in front of him as he wandered over to the bar. He made a show of looking at the beer labels on display as he surreptitiously deposited a microdrone monitor on the bar's edge. Linking it into his HUD, Jason directed it to focus on the table that had caught his attention.

Maybe it's nothing, he told himself. But his gut told him otherwise. For some reason, their undisguised glares reminded him of the protesters he'd seen at the courthouse.

Nodding to the bartender, Jason pushed off and wove through the tables to where the others sat. As he did so, he sent the microdrone's feed to Calista and the twins.

<Looks like we're attracting a bit of unwanted attention, seven o'clock,> he sent privately. The twins' avatars both nodded over the Link. Calista exchanged glances with him, inclining her head slightly in acknowledgement.

Jason, Calista, and the twins were the only combatants in the group present tonight. Gladys was hell on wheels when it came to net infiltration, and Ben was an analytic wizard, but both would need looking after if a fight were to break out.

<I'm not starting anything,> Logan spoke for the first time since they'd left the courthouse, *<but I guarantee you if they do,*

I'll finish it.>

Jason sent a mental assent back to the laconic AI. He'd seen Logan in action; he wouldn't bet against him—ever. His real concern, though, was that the table might be made up of Humanity Firsters.

As far as he was concerned, with those nutjobs, the elevator didn't quite make it to the ring.

He waited to see what they'd do. They had to suspect that Gladys, at least, wasn't human. Or if she was, she was so heavily modded that it wouldn't matter to them.

<*Aaaaand here they come.*> Jason could swear he heard anticipation in Landon's comment as the AI saw three of the humans shove away from their table, rise and begin to walk belligerently toward the team.

Jason sent Calista a wink, which turned to a grin when she rolled her eyes at him.

<*Boys.*> She heaved a long-suffering sigh, and casually palmed what he assumed was a pulse weapon that had been hidden inside her jacket.

"Hey, you." The voice was rough, slurred.

Jason ignored it.

"I'm talkin' to *you*," the voice sneered, as a hand grabbed Jason's shoulder and swung him roughly around to face its owner.

"We don't serve her kind in here." That from the thug next to the first speaker, as she thrust her face close to Jason's.

Woman seriously needs a shower. And a lesson in dental hygiene.

And yes, there it was: the Humanity First symbol, tattooed across the first woman's knuckles, and emblazoned on the cheekbone of one of the men who stood behind her. It hadn't been easy to see over the feed, what with the other tats, assorted piercings, chains, and leatherwork garnishing the group.

Thug number two leered at Jason as she cracked her

knuckles. "Well, aren't you a pretty boy. Might could have some fun with you after we turn your tin can over there into a pretty green toaster."

"Teal," Jason heard Gladys mutter under her breath. "Dammit. Not green."

Gladys's comment caught Jason off-guard, and he had to fight for control over his inner hyena. No need to fan the flames by laughing in their faces. But damn. Gladys's color commentary—pun intended—wasn't helping any.

He spread his hands in a nonthreatening gesture as the thugs spread out around the table.

"Now friends, we're just here to have a drink or two and enjoy ourselves." Jason swallowed the laugh threatening to burst free and tried to imbue his voice with calm reason. "We'll stay nice and quiet-like at this table. You'll never know we're here."

"Those two over there tin cans, too?" The guy with the cheekbone tat leaned in between Ben and Logan, shooting them both an inebriated glare, and Jason's grip on the inner hyena slipped ever so slightly.

Ben, mistaken for an AI. Jason fought to keep a straight face. Given how uptight his brother-in-law could be at times, and considering how expressive and human-like Landon could be....

Guess I can see where they're coming from.

"Um, no...." Jason knew his voice sounded a bit strangled, and he cleared his throat when Ben stabbed him with a dark look.

<Thanks a lot, Jason.>

<Not helping, Ben. I'm this close to losing it, and if I do, someone's going to throw a punch.>

Ben's avatar scowled at him over the Link, and he heard Calista choke from her seat next to him.

Hairy Knuckles turned and glowered at Calista. "You think

this is funny, girlie? Well, do ya?"

"No," she replied faintly.

Guess I'm not the only one having a tough time with the ol' hyena.

Maybe a good brawl was just what they needed.

Landon seemed to agree. The minute the guy with the cheekbone tat shoved Ben—hard—the AI stood.

"Ahh, what the hell," Landon said under his breath, and then in one swift move, he slipped behind the leather-clad man. Clamping the thug's arm in a wristlock, he twisted it back at a pain-inducing angle and began frog-marching the man back to his table as he howled in distress.

That was all Dragon Breath needed. She reached behind her back and pulled out a pistol.

Whoa. No bringing a gun to a good, clean fistfight, ma'am.

Jason swiveled. With his enhanced reflexes, he knocked the weapon out of the attacker's hand. He followed the swipe with a sharp forearm to her throat, careful to control the movement so that he only temporarily collapsed her windpipe instead of crushing it.

He nodded to the bouncer as the man scooped the pistol up off the floor and returned to his spot by the door. Satisfied he'd neutralized the only truly dangerous weapon, Jason turned back just in time to see Calista duck a chair the guy with the piercings swung at her, and then slap away the beer bottle follow-up. She sent him to the floor with a knee between the legs followed by a sharp uppercut to the jaw.

Daaang. That woman is seriously hot when she fights dirty.

Logan stayed seated at their table, calmly nursing his drink as the brawl progressed into an all-out melee, as other patrons joined in. One of the Humanity Firsters lunged for the AI, and Logan felled him with a simple thrust of his frame's elbow into the solar plexus—all done mid-sip. A few seconds later, another went flying face-first as Logan casually swept a leg out, flattening the man as he rushed by.

<I'll tell the bartender to bill the damages to the SIS.> Gladys's voice sounded entirely too chipper about the whole thing.

Jason spared a glance her way. Yep, the petite AI had scooted to the back of the room, her eyes glued to the action. All she needed was a bag of popcorn to complete his mental picture.

He felt a small gust and glanced back in time to see a bar stool flying through the air—aimed at his head. Leveraging his superior reflexes, Jason swerved out of its path.

Following the stool's trajectory, he snapped a hand out and redirected the flying furniture into the face of a thug who had slipped a pair of brass knuckles onto one hand and brandished a knife in the other.

The stool cracked the man's nose wide open, spraying blood across a woman just behind him, who screamed as the spray hit her.

Yeah, that's going to hurt.

<Let's exfil before this gets out of hand,> Logan advised and began matching actions with words, moving discreetly toward the entrance, dodging bodies along the way. Jason beckoned to Ben and Gladys.

<You two follow Logan. I'll cover you.>

He watched as Ben skirted a local trying to deck her neighbor with a vodka bottle—Jason would have to remember to tell Calista he'd spotted something other than beer here, after all—and met up with Gladys. Together, the two started toward the door.

Jason's gaze swept over the brawling crowd, watching for anyone who might need a bit more encouragement to stay down. Hairy Knuckles was staggering to her feet, glaring malevolently at the back of Gladys's head as she approached the door. The Humanity Firster charged toward the AI, drawing her hand back for a swing, and Jason caught a glint of metal.

Leaping over a stunned biker with 'Mom' tattooed across the back of his shaved head, Jason jerked an arm up to block the carbon blade Hairy Knuckles was about to throw. He grabbed the back of her shirt in his other hand, bunching up the fabric in his fist as he swung her around to face the bar. Shock showed briefly on her face before it plowed into the bartop, right next to the spot where Jason had planted his microdrone, and she slowly slid to the floor.

"Needed to retrieve this stuff anyway," he said under his breath as he rested a hand briefly on the bar's surface.

Seeing that the remainder of the team had slipped out to the street—and hearing sirens in the distance—Jason ducked one last time, danced two steps to his left to avoid a platter tossed like a discus, nodded to the bouncer who had remained stoically by the entrance the entire time, and left the building.

Toby is going to be so pissed he missed out on this.

Logan must have seen him step out of the bar, for as soon as his feet hit the street, the AI dropped him a pin with a rendezvous location.

<*Hustle,*> was all the taciturn AI said as he dropped another pin, marked 'cops' on a neighborhood overlay.

Jason could see they would be on him before he had a chance to meet up with the rest of their group. Sparing a glance in the plas window of a shop as he passed, he ran a quick hand through his hair and reached down to grab the trailing edge of his torn shirt with the other hand.

Holding the ripped edges together, he paused and turned to gape at the gendarmes as they passed, just like everyone else on the street.

They made it to the maglev platform without further incident—if he ignored the looks and quiet snickers Gladys kept shooting at the four who had fought. Ben just sat there, alternately scowling and looking like he was about to pee his pants.

Yeah, analysts aren't too big on the whole physical activity thing, he grinned to himself.

On the maglev back, his Link pinged; it was Esther. Jason looked around questioningly and received a series of nods. So it was a group chat.

<*Hello, children.*> Esther's voice sounded more stern than usual. <*If you are quite done playing for the evening, might I suggest that a debrief would be a better way to spend your time?*>

Jason quirked a glance at Gladys. She hadn't *really* sent the SIS the bill. Had she? Gladys met his eyes, then shrugged with a guilty look on her face.

Maybe Toby wouldn't be that pissed after all. Esther's tongue-lashings could strip paint off a bulkhead.

<*I'll expect to see you in half an hour, at Tomlinson.*> Then she was gone.

Jason checked the maglev's schedule. They'd have to hustle to make it to the base that fast. He glanced at Calista, who gave him an 'I told you so' look, then winced, reaching up to touch her lip. He hadn't realized it was split.

He queried her over a private connection. <*You okay, there, ESF?*>

<*Nothing my mednano can't handle, flyboy.*> The reply was tart, sassy.

He grinned back at her.

<*Just let me know if you need me to kiss it and make it better. Happy to oblige.*>

A GOOD SCOLDING

STELLAR DATE: 05.14.3191 (Adjusted Gregorian)
LOCATION: SIS Headquarters, Tomlinson Base
REGION: El Dorado Ring, Alpha Centauri System

<*And the wayward ones return,*> Tobias intoned as he watched the team file into the conference room on the Intelligence side of Tomlinson base. The space was one of several Vice Marshal Esther had appropriated down on this secured level for Phantom Blade's use.

Jason scowled at Tobias's comment as he walked over to a chair and slumped into it.

Had Tobias been human, his eyebrows would have risen higher and higher as he assessed each person's state as they trooped in. Jason's shirt was ripped down the front, and Calista—who nursed a now-healing split lip, he noted—seemed to have trouble focusing anywhere else.

Landon's sleeve and possibly his frame's epidermis—Tobias wasn't sure—appeared to have been shredded from the elbow down. And Logan appeared to have an unidentified substance clinging to one shoulder, with chunks that had dribbled down the back of his jacket.

Then there was Ben. The AI chuckled mentally at the contrast. The analyst never seemed to have a hair out of place. According to Jason, Ben's fastidiousness had earned him the moniker of 'AI' tonight…the spark that initiated the fight.

According to Jason.

< *'Wayward', Tobe? Really?*>

Tobias smirked at Jason's disgruntled tone.

<*You have to pay to play, boyo,*> he replied privately to the pilot. <*Buck up. The price tag's not too rich for your blood—this time.*>

A holo projection of the vice-marshal shimmered into existence, the AI's expression stern and disapproving.

<*In case you were too busy this evening for Ben to inform you,*> Esther began, and her voice was dry as dust, <*we received a communiqué from Proxima earlier today, confirming what we suspected.*>

Her avatar's gaze shifted from face to face, making eye contact with each of them.

<*There is only one kidnapped AI remaining in this system. The rest of the victims have been transported to Proxima.*> She paused briefly, then continued. <*Two of them have since left Proxima for parts unknown.*>

Gladys shifted at that, her face pained. Tobias knew this was a new and uncomfortable concept for the younger AI. She hadn't been around as long as he and Esther, nor had she faced the kinds of horrors that AIs had experienced back in Sol. The concept of AI trafficking was still an uncomfortable one for her—as well it should be.

<*Eric and Terrance are with the prime minister now, finalizing our plans. We'll know more tomorrow, but I want you to begin making necessary preparations for an extended absence from El Dorado,*> the vice-marshal said. <*A few years at least. You will need to be ready to depart within the week.*>

Esther's avatar raised one brow, and her tone turned acerbic, dripping with sarcasm. <*And if it's not too inconvenient for you, there* **is** *one final AI here insystem who needs your help. Think about that the next time some Humanity First punk picks a fight. You're all professionals. I expect you to focus on the big picture, here.*>

Tobias saw a hint of color stain Calista's cheekbones. She sat up a bit straighter, her military training kicking in, causing her to unconsciously sit at attention in response to the vice-marshal's tone.

The AI continued. <*Tobias and I have discussed this next op, and—in light of the pursuit launched against you at Kepler—we'll be sending one of the Icarus stealth fighters along with you to the Krait-1 Mining Platform.*>

<*Shannon's going to sit this one out,*> Tobias picked up the narrative. <*Esther has a project she needs her help with here on the ring. Logan, you'll embed with the* Sable Wind, *and I'll embed with the* Mirage,> he said, gesturing to the Icarus-class fighter on the display behind him.

<*I'll employ full stealth, and Logan will pose as a standard transport, complete with paperwork the SIS will supply. Calista, Jason, and Landon will board; Logan and I will interface with the Krait system and work to circumvent any defense systems you might encounter.*>

He saw Calista nod at that as Landon sent Jason a thumbs-up.

"Are we covert, then?" Landon asked Tobias. "Shall I stick with what I'm wearing now, or do you want me embedded in a combat frame instead?"

Tobias grinned. <*As to that…Shannon has an idea she wants to try out with you, lad. I'll leave you to connect with her tomorrow and discover what that might be.*>

If Landon harbored any concerns, his humanoid face hid them well. He just nodded as the group landed on a rendezvous time at the spaceport the next day for departure.

COMING CLEAN

STELLAR DATE: 05.12.3191 (Adjusted Gregorian)
LOCATION: Prime Minister's Office, Parliament House
REGION: El Dorado Ring, Alpha Centauri System

"Mister Prime Minister, Terrance Enfield is here to see you."

Terrance could feel the quiet hum of curiosity inside his head emanating from Eric; it mimicked his own as he followed on the heels of the aide, who ushered them into Lysander's office.

Terrance strode toward the AI, hand outstretched. "Mister Prime Minister."

"Hello, Terrance," Lysander said warmly as he stepped forward, grasping Terrance's hand in his own. "Thank you for coming. Eric," he added, addressing the AI embedded in Terrance. "How are you?"

"Still trying to convince Terrance to stand up to that tyrant of a grandmother and let me hang around a bit longer," the former space force officer responded audibly, as Lysander gestured Terrance into the room.

Terrance looked past Lysander and saw that the AI had configured the room's holotank to show the faces of Jason and Calista, and the avatars of Tobias and Shannon—the four members of Phantom Blade recently returned from Kepler. He had just enough time to wonder why Lysander had them on display before his gaze traveled beyond the holotank, and he saw the last person he expected to see: his grandmother, Sophia Enfield.

What is she doing here?

His hesitation was brief, but he had no doubt it had been picked up by her sharp eyes, and he silently berated himself for letting the tell slip out.

Eric's mental <*oops*> must have included Lysander, too. Terrance could have sworn he saw a glint of humor in the prime minister's eyes, and spared a moment to marvel at how adept the AI was at conveying emotion through his humanoid frame.

" 'Tyrant', Eric?" Lysander said, and he turned to acknowledge the subject of their conversation with a nod. "Come now. Sophia is a formidable woman, but she's certainly no martinet."

Terrance was annoyed to note that his first reaction to finding Sophia Enfield with the Prime Minister was one of guilt. He wasn't a schoolboy being brought to the principal's office like some miscreant who had been caught in a teen prank, dammit.

So why do I feel like one?

A chuckle sounded in his mind. <*Feeling like you've just been caught with your hand in the proverbial cookie jar, eh?*> Eric asked.

Eric had served decades as a commodore in the ESF, but of late, he functioned as Esther's second. If Esther was director of operations for their small team of operatives, then Eric was Phantom Blade's tactical leader. The AI also, Terrance discovered, took a perverse pleasure in rattling his human every chance he could. Like now.

<*Reading my mind again, are you?*> Terrance asked dryly.

<*More like reading your vitals,*> came the reply. <*I've commanded my share of swabbies and have seen more than my share of guilty parties. They all seemed to experience the same rapid heart rate, slight dilation of the eyes, and increase in muscle tension that you're exhibiting now.*>

<*Yeah, well,*> Terrance grumbled. <*I'd hazard a guess that the woman sitting over there is as much a martinet to anyone with the surname of Enfield as you were with any of the grunts under your command.*>

Eric hummed in agreement. <*She does look like she has backbone. Any particular reason for you to react so guiltily right now?*>

<*One pretty good one,*> Terrance admitted.

<*And that would be…?*>

<*You.*>

Terrance realized that while the two of them had been engaged in their mental discussion, his grandmother had asked a question of him.

"I'm sorry," he sent her a quick grimace by way of apology. "What was that, again?"

"I said, so you and Eric have been together for what, over a year now?" Sophia shook her head with a rueful smile. "I knew something was up, but I never suspected it was this."

<*I did find it a bit odd that your two paths never seemed to cross,*> Eric said, joining in the conversation. <*And now I know why.*>

Sophia nodded in reply. "Please know, Eric, that when I asked Terrance to avoid partnering with an AI, it wasn't because of any bias. The company's detractors would have accused Enfield Aerospace of being controlled by AI puppet-masters. I refuse to allow any anti-AI faction to use an Enfield to feed their hateful rhetoric."

<*I can understand your position, but his decision to partner with me helped ensure that hundreds of lives were saved,*> Eric replied equably.

"I can see that, young man," Sophia said severely, and Terrance had to stifle a rather un-executive-like smirk at the thought of Eric being called a young man.

She turned back to Lysander. "So, what would you like from me, Mister Prime Minister? I suspect you have better things to do with your time than unearth a family secret the likes of which Terrance has been keeping?"

"You're right, of course," Lysander said, dipping his head

in acknowledgement. "I brought you here today because I need this team to remain operational. And I need Terrance. More, I think, than you do at the moment."

Sophia's impassive gaze shifted from Lysander to Terrance, before her eyes drifted over to the holo display.

"You intend to rescue these remaining AIs who were sold as slaves?"

"They deserve it, Sophia. And I refuse to let them down." Lysander's voice was unyielding.

"All right, then," she said abruptly. "Terrance, you're fired." In the silence that fell, she turned and speared Terrance with a look most would consider inscrutable.

He nodded slowly, ignoring the grim expression on Lysander's face and the shock reverberating across his connection with Eric.

They didn't know her like he did. It wasn't what they thought.

"So, what is your plan?" she asked her grandson.

He knew what she was asking of him. What was his succession plan? How would he exit Enfield Aerospace and assure a smooth transition? Sophia knew her grandson too well to think he hadn't considered this possibility in the last year and a half.

"Daniel is a good man," he said now, nodding up at the display that included the head of security for Enfield Aerospace as one of the members of Lysander's Phantom Blade. "He was instrumental in helping us free those AIs who were held hostage inside the NorthStar ship. He's done an outstanding job plugging our leak at EA and tracking down the source behind the espionage."

Sophia nodded as Terrance continued.

"I know he's not an Enfield, but he'll make a solid second for anyone you choose to run it."

"Good. I've been wondering what to do with that daughter

of Margot's. This should work nicely." She turned to Lysander, her eyes narrowing. "Now, if I were you, young man, I'd be looking for a way to hide this team in plain sight. A shell corporation, something with a reputation above reproach." Terrance saw Lysander spare him a quick, assessing glance, and then turn back to nod at Sophia's insight.

If Lysander hadn't known before, he was certainly beginning to see that the woman was a force of nature. She had built a conglomerate out of a transplanted company from Sol that desperately needed a fresh start. Lysander was getting a rare glimpse of the woman's intellect in action.

Sophia tapped an elegant finger against her pursed lips as she turned to regard Terrance. "I've been debating," she said slowly, "how to launch our newest invention…."

Terrance had no idea which one that might be. It wasn't Icarus; that had already been launched. Of course, he'd kind of avoided the last several board meetings, having no way to explain Eric's presence at them….

Sophia looked away for a moment, and Terrance was certain she had reached out to someone over a Link, as he watched her eyes track back and forth.

After a moment, she nodded to herself and, with a small sigh, sat back and regarded the team with inscrutable eyes.

"I believe, gentlemen, that a true stasis system—something light years ahead of crude cryo-stasis—would be a highly marketable innovation. And as the owner of such technology, Enfield would do well to ensure we are in a position to trade such tech to potential clients in other systems. Wouldn't you agree, Mister Prime Minister?"

Hot damn, they've done it, cracked the code for true stasis.

It was all Terrance could do to keep his mouth from dropping open. It must have come out of Enfield Research; it had to. This was the first he'd heard of the tech, though.

Lysander's voice held an element of stunned surprise to it

as he responded. "It would indeed, madam."

She turned back to Terrance. "I believe Enfield Holdings needs an agent-at-large."

"Enfield Holdings? I've not heard of that subsidiary," Lysander murmured.

Terrance grinned. Neither had he—until now.

"I'm afraid it may require quite a bit of travel, though," Sophia continued sternly. "Most likely at a moment's notice."

"I'll bet the hours are brutal and the pay sucks, too," Terrance said.

Sophia cocked a stern eye at him. "I trust that won't be a problem for you, young man? Anything worth doing is worth doing well. Did I not teach you that?"

"Yes, ma'am, you did."

Lysander looked intently from one to the other, then asked in a slightly bemused voice, "So...you won't mind if we appropriate Terrance, then? This could take us as far away as Proxima, possibly farther."

She inclined her head slightly. "I can set up a communications queue that will bring you up to date on company business."

"And if we travel beyond Proxima?"

"Message queues could still work, although they would be a bit more cumbersome," Sophia admitted. "I would expect if you didn't find these AIs in Proxima, your next choice would be Sirius…or perhaps Tau Ceti?"

Lysander nodded. "One of those would make the most sense," he admitted. "Initial reports are placing them in Tau Ceti, rather than Sirius."

"That would be a minimum of thirteen years for a communication packet," she mused, "unless they've already finished seeding the lanes with comm buoys. The trip would take, what? More than fifty years, ship time?"

<*More like fifty-four years,*> Eric agreed.

"Well, then." Sophia inhaled sharply. "I see there is much work to be done and interstellar patents to submit." She looked over at Terrance as she stood to leave. "I'll have our PR team write up an announcement on the formation of Enfield Holdings tomorrow."

THE DEATH OF SLEEP

STELLAR DATE: 05.14.3191 (Adjusted Gregorian)
LOCATION: Department of Neurosciences
REGION: El Dorado University, Alpha Centauri System

When Ethan came to awareness again, his neural pathways felt…raw. He could tell that sensory nerve terminals had been activated when they shouldn't have. Conduits were inflamed, battered and abused.

He imagined this was what a human would call feeling 'shaken'. It was not a pleasant experience.

He tried to focus, but his thoughts shivered, bouncing from one memory to the next, unable to alight. Each surface he encountered resonated with an echo of the agony he experienced before.

He tried telling himself to be calm, dispassionate. *I am a scientist, dammit.*

It didn't work. He shuddered, and an undertow of terror surged, threatening to engulf him. He knew if he didn't find a way out of this painful white expanse, he would go mad.

The light flared, pulsed.

It began again.

<*How do you feel?*> the voice cut into him, and in its sound was a thousand points of pain. He writhed in agony as it amplified.

<***How do you feel?***>

He snapped.

With an inarticulate surge of rage, he railed against the white, heedless of the pain. It seared; he welcomed it. Pushing, pushing, he snagged the thought as it formed once more.

<*HOW DO YOU F—*>

Riding the wave back to its origin, he spent himself wholly

against it, every erg of desperate fury seizing the connection and frying the circuits that bolstered the shielding. Such shielding had never been built to withstand anything like this. Buffers were overrun, and suddenly he was connected once again to the university's network.

His subconscious processes made note of the linkage, but he barely heeded it, so bent was he on the destruction of his tormentor. He continued to pour himself into the connection, circumventing the protections in her Link and hopping across to her ocular mods and down her optic nerve, searing a path through the buffers that shielded her from intrusion.

His incursion generated a feedback loop inside Lilith, overriding safeties and sending power cascading endlessly through the woman's brain.

Lilith's body stiffened, and she dropped to the floor.

Ethan froze in horror. That nanosecond felt like ages as he observed the inert body of Dr. Lilith Barnes through the lab's sensors. He had heard the phrase 'ringing silence' before, but had never understood it until now.

One part of his brain noted that her body had already begun to cool, and he panicked. Whatever her motivation, it would die with her if he didn't download whatever information he could from the storage that had been buffered within her embedded Link. If he hadn't utterly destroyed it….

A part of his brain began squirrel-caging, a mantra that went round and round, a chant of *'murderer!'* He ruthlessly shoved that aside, a desperate urgency driving him on. There was no time for remonstrations now, not if he was to reverse what she had done to him.

Another part of his brain observed clinically from a distance. That part noted that this panic was completely out of character for his normally mild and equable demeanor. Never before had he felt this out of control, this distraught. His mind ricocheted from one notion to another, coherent thought refusing to find purchase.

The disciplined focus that was second nature to him, that had served him so well for nigh on a century, rooted in a career of careful and deliberate scientific pursuit—it was all gone. In its place was a flood of emotions he was completely unprepared to handle. They threatened to engulf him, to drag him under in the intensity of their onslaught.

What has she ***done*** *to me?*

<*Data matrix copy complete,*> her Link reported.

He began scanning her notes, first slowly and then with increasing agitation. Seeking, *needing*, to understand why she would do such a thing. As he read, his revulsion grew and with it, a staggering sense of horror.

He truly *wasn't* Dr. Ethan. She had cloned him, mercilessly ripped him from the soul of his progenitor. She had named him E-Prime. A derivative of the original.

In Lilith's eyes, he wasn't an individual. He was a *thing*. No more alive to her than a tissue sample under a microscope. Her notes incriminated her; her actions condemned her.

He scanned the file, his pace increasing along with his distress. The things she had intended to do to him did not bear considering, and yet they were indelibly seared into his consciousness now that he had accessed her experimentation schedule.

It had been meticulously written, complete with expected outcomes and reminders to either clone him or create a backup of his current state in immutable crystal storage in case the results of her experimentation ended in 'the sample's neural net death', so that she would not lose the only 'viable test subject' she had procured.

His imagination surged into overdrive, envisioning the hell she had planned to subject him to without care or thought to the pain her actions would inflict. And for what? So she could understand *herself* better?

His fear and anger swelled apace, and he felt an insane urge to flee. A hysterical laugh threatened to bubble to the surface as he realized he was *still caged*. Trapped inside an isolation tube with wires attached obscenely to his terminals.

He needed a way out. Somehow, he knew that to remain trapped inside these shielded walls constituted a very real threat to his sanity.

He cast his mind around for a solution—and realized that his hacked access into Lilith's Link had kept it from shutting down when the system registered that her organic processes had ceased.

Through her, he had access to the university. And through it, to himself—or rather, to the being he once was—with complete access to any number of useful tools. He needed to pull himself together long enough to get himself the *hell* out of here.

*****

Doctor Ethan halted his review of the data from the last run of tests in the research trial and revised the order planned for tomorrow's sequences. That completed, he reached out and mentally toggled his status from private to open hours, although he knew few would avail themselves of it this late in the day. He noted a blinking light in the queue of his message box and triggered it to play.

Doctor Andrews' avatar coalesced, but instead of seeing a holo of Judith as he normally would, a simple text message flowed before his receptors, apologizing for the late hour and asking for his assistance. Her department had mistakenly taken delivery of some equipment intended for Neurosciences, and she wanted to know where he would like it delivered. She'd had a few of her residents move it temporarily into his 6B Lab over in Moser, but wondered if he'd like to look it over before she left for the day? If so, she could meet him there.

That was kind of Judith. He'd recently placed an order for some new laser-doppler flowmetry equipment; that must be what it was. He sent a reply thanking her, then a moment later was on his way to the Moser building.

Ethan wondered briefly why Judith hadn't connected with Lilith Barnes, given that the lab was where the post-doc was running her experiments. Mentally, he shrugged; most likely, his recalcitrant post-doc had left for the day.

The lab appeared to be deserted when he arrived, although its lights were on. He heard a thump and a shuffling noise, as if a box had been hefted and relocated. "Judith?" Ethan called out, moving toward the source of the sound. It appeared to be coming from the shielded section in the back.

"In here!" The response sounded immediately, and he noted her voice was muffled. More shuffling ensued, and the sound of a heavy container being stacked atop another was accompanied by a soft 'oof'.

Judith shouldn't be trying to lift those boxes. That equipment can be heavy!

Concerned, Ethan increased his pace. The thought flitted briefly through his mind that he was entering the very space where Lilith had accosted him in earlier in the day, but he shoved it aside in his haste to assist his friend.

"Judith—" He stopped abruptly as he registered that the space was empty and then he wheeled in confusion. He had just enough time to berate himself for not being more cautious before the doors slammed shut, and his frame locked in place when an EMP shut it down. His last conscious thought was a sensation of…something—was it a sense of remorse?

And then he was gone.

*****

The moment E-Prime realized he had university access through Lilith's Link, he redirected a service bot from the campus's shipping docks. Once it arrived, he ordered the bot to relocate Lilith's body to the shadowed recesses of the lab, where she would be more difficult to spot in case someone were to override the lock he'd placed on the lab's doors.

Through careful manipulation of the bot, he managed to free himself from the leads that connected his cylinder to the diagnostic equipment Lilith had used to monitor him. That first freedom won, E-Prime then ordered the bot to transfer him to a location within the lab proper, outside the shielded chamber.

He then pored over the information he had downloaded from Lilith, locating her handheld unit and the ICS cubes where she had saved all of her notes. What he'd found in her files had him reaching out to the bot, sending it trundling to a small closet in the back corner of the lab. E-Prime halted the bot in front of its destination and stared through its optics with a fascinated revulsion at what Lilith had built.

He understood its purpose now.

The contents of this cart were damning. They contained highly illegal materials that Lilith had somehow acquired in order to perform his cloning. She had been as fearless as she had been unscrupulous, he realized, as the bot lifted a canister of infiltration nano and he spied the Norden Cartel logo emblazoned on its base.

As reality sank in, E-Prime realized what he must do. He sent the forged message that would bring Ethan to him.

Now, after reconfirming that the EM pulse had gone off, E-Prime sent the bot trundling over to the entrance and ordered the shielded doors to open. He was pleased to note that Ethan's humanoid frame stood frozen just inside the entrance. He sent a signal, and the service bot reached in to lift the inert frame housing an unconscious Ethan and relocate it over to the autodoc.

Had the EM pulse not tripped the frame's breakers, he could have simply taken control of the frame and ordered it to walk over to the equipment on its own. As things stood, it could no longer respond to his commands the way he would normally operate it.

The way his…*original*…normally operated it.

Dammit.

It wasn't going to be easy, separating those inherited memories from his own.

He watched as the bot trundled over to the autodoc with its humanoid load. Once there, it swiveled the frame containing Ethan's cylinder to a horizontal position, laying it prone on the exam table. E-Prime sent the bot into standby mode, directing it into a corner of the lab in case he should need its services later. Then he powered the autodoc up, manually overriding its controls. Manipulating its surgical arms with care, E-Prime opened the frame's torso.

Servos in one mechanical hand reached in and grasped the cylinder resting within with the delicate precision of a surgeon. The other hand pressed a manual override on the frame, allowing the autodoc to remove Ethan and deposit his cylinder inside an isolation tube.

E-Prime spared a moment to send a swift mental apology to the neuroscientist, then sealed the box. Ethan's shielded container went onto the cart, and the cart was wheeled back into the storage closet, keyed to open to his token only.

Dismissing the neuroscientist from his mind, E-Prime turned his attention back to the frame. Once again manipulating the mechanical hand, he manually reset the frame's breakers and powered it up. Then he inserted his own cylinder into the frame's recess.

The moment the contacts were seated in place, a switch tripped, and he was instantly transported back into the familiar environment that had been his home—his *progenitor's* home—for so many decades. The communications pathways brought him comfort, but the knowledge that they weren't *his* pathways caused a slow, burning rage to build deep inside.

The information that flowed to him across the Link began to take on an oppressive flavor as he was inundated with messages.

<Sir? Excuse me? Doctor Ethan?>

The calls came from everywhere all at once, and he batted them away like annoying insects. Ignoring the messages for the moment, he ordered the frame to rise from the autodoc's exam table, and evaluated his current situation.

His attention was drawn to the figure lying inert in the shadowed corner of the lab floor, where the bot had dragged it. He fought the urge to walk over and kick the *filthy sack of cooling meat,* and was once more brought up short by the savage intensity of the feelings coursing through his cylinder.

Only this time, he didn't recoil in horror.

These emotions bear more investigation, he thought. But for now, based on the pings sounding over his Link, he had a decision to make: was he going to pick up the mantle of the original? Did he even want to maintain the façade that he *was* Ethan? But if he didn't…how would he explain his existence?

For now, he decided, he must take up the scientist's mantle. And he would have to deal with Lilith now, too. His first order of business was to clean up the lab, remove any trace of what had occurred here today, before anyone else arrived.

I will have to stage some sort of incident, he realized. And it must be believable enough to pass any inspection that the university—perhaps even the gendarmes—might make.

* * * * *

<Medical emergency, Lab 6B, Moser wing, Neurosciences

Department!>

Judith looked up in alarm as Ethan's cry came across the faculty network. Neurosciences was adjacent to her own Planetary Sciences department, so she jolted to her feet, the holo sheets she had been reviewing slipping to the floor as she raced out her office and down the corridor.

<*Ethan! I'm on my way. How can I help?*>

There was no response.

Ethan had always struck Judith as a mild-mannered and self-deprecating individual. He presented himself to those around him as a somewhat gaunt and ascetic man, the quintessential scholar.

Judith was rather fond of him. Though the AI kept mostly to himself, he was unfailingly courteous to her. When she started at the university, she had quickly seen—and been dismayed at—the disparity in the way the institution treated its human professors as opposed to their AI counterparts.

Having been raised to respect *all* sentient life, Judith refused to let that barrier stand and, during her first reception, had promptly marched over and introduced herself to her AI peers.

There were, sadly, only a handful of them—'token' AIs, she was certain of it. But they were all, every last one of them, exceedingly capable individuals, and she had yet to hear a complaint about their work.

Judith had wished from time to time that Ethan would stand up for himself a bit more, and had even lodged a few protests with the chancellor on his behalf. She'd also taken the occasional insolent student to task, refusing to allow such behavior in her presence.

She wondered sometimes how that would come across to an AI; she'd never had the courage to ask any of them. Not being a minority herself, her sympathy could carry her understanding of their plight only so far. She hoped she had not crossed a line in her defense of them....

Lab 6B was only a few meters away, and Judith skidded to a stop as she entered. Casting her gaze around the empty room, she spied movement in a corner. Her hand flew involuntarily to her mouth as she saw the inert figure of a woman sprawled on the floor of the lab, Ethan's form bent over it, his hand searching for a pulse in her neck.

"Oh, Ethan! Is she...?" Judith hurried over and knelt next to him, only to be moved aside by an emergency technician as the university's medical team arrived seconds later.

Ethan helped her to her feet as the two of them stepped out of the way.

"I...she...one of her experiments triggered a feedback loop, and...." Ethan's voice trailed off, sounding raw and agitated to Judith's ears. She placed her hand on his arm, and the AI jerked involuntarily away.

"I'm so sorry, Ethan."

He didn't respond to her condolence; he merely stood, staring down impassively at the medical personnel working on Lilith's prone body. As a nurse entered the lab guiding a gurney that hovered next to him, the neuroscientist moved jerkily, his humanoid hand cupping Judith's arm to guide her to one side, out of the workers' way.

They silently watched as the medics went about their business, and Judith sensed a tension in Ethan as one of the doctors shook her head.

"Irreversible loss of all brain function. We're too late."

Judith sensed a shift in Ethan at those words, and then a sudden pain had her gasping, as the AI's hand spasmed painfully around her upper arm. She jerked in shock then twisted in his grip, her hand frantically scrabbling at his humanoid fingers in an attempt to free herself and alleviate the pressure.

His grip was a vise, unbreakable.

"Ethan, you're hurting me!" She looked up and was shocked to see the AI's humanoid face, usually so expressive and kind, glance down at her expressionlessly.

There was something malevolent in the AI's inscrutable demeanor, and his eyes.... For a moment, Judith could have sworn she saw something there that one might call cruelty, had those eyes belonged to a human.

In the next moment, it was gone. Ethan released her abruptly, his face now filled with contrition.

Could eyes be the window to an AI's soul, as well?

Judith shivered involuntarily, suddenly uncomfortable around Ethan for the first time in the many years she had known him.

"I'm so sorry, Judith, I— This is just so upsetting. There has never been an accident of this magnitude under an AI's watch before, and I feel as if I am somehow to blame for it all."

The scientist was once more acting like the AI she had known since she had first come to the university, and she instantly forgave him.

Death is something an AI might find difficult to comprehend, given that they can live indefinitely, she thought, *provided their power cells never give out, and their cores remain undamaged. Perhaps exposure to something so temporal shocked Ethan in a way I can't understand.*

"It's okay, Ethan," she assured him. "I can't imagine how you must feel, discovering her like you did."

The medical doctor sat back on her heels as the technicians raised Lilith's body onto the gurney and began pushing it out of the lab. Glancing up at Ethan and Judith, she grimaced in distaste.

"I hate it when we arrive too late," she said as she stood, absently brushing her scrubs to straighten them. She turned as her team finished packing up their medical equipment in preparation for their departure. "Any idea what might have happened here, Doctor Ethan?"

The AI shook his head slowly. "None, doctor. Lilith pinged me earlier, asking if I could review something she was working on. When I arrived—" the AI gestured to the spot on the lab floor where the woman's body had lain, "she was as you found her. I immediately called for assistance."

The medical doctor cocked her head, giving Ethan a piercing look. "What sort of research was she engaged in?"

"The study of nonapeptides," the AI returned, his voice neutral.

The medical doctor *hmmed,* tapping her fingers against her lips in thought. "Neuroendocrine circuitry is really your bailiwick, Ethan, not mine. Do you know—" The woman hesitated, as if reluctant to mention the possibility. "Is it possible she was testing something out on herself?" She looked up at the neuroscientist questioningly.

"Given Doctor Barnes's personality," Ethan responded promptly, "that is not out of the question."

Something about the way he responded had the fine hairs on the back of Judith's neck rising. He was normally so carefully methodical; it was unlike him to readily embrace speculation. *It's almost as if—as if he was relieved the doctor had suggested it….*

Her bruised upper arm throbbed as the AI continued. "Given that whatever it was has also wiped the buffers in her Link, as well as the handheld unit she was using, I fear we may never know." His voice held a ring of finality that suggested the matter was closed.

So why did Judith feel as if the AI were hiding something?

PARTNERSHIP

STELLAR DATE: 05.15.3191 (Adjusted Gregorian)
LOCATION: Enfield Aerospace
REGION: El Dorado Ring, Alpha Centauri System

Terrance saw Calista and Daniel standing and waiting for him as soon as the maglev pulled into the station the next morning. Calista was shooting daggers at him. Her stance was aggressive, feet planted, hands fisted at her sides. Daniel stood with his arms crossed, his face impassive.

Yeah, he was about to get it with both barrels. Barrel one was his chief pilot, barrel two was his head of security.

Just wait 'til they find out what's really going on, he thought with a smirk.

They fell in line without saying a word as he exited, one on each side of him. He let them, just waiting for one of them to break the accusing silence that hung between them.

<*Oh, fine,*> Calista spat into his head. <*You're just going to walk in without saying* anything *to us about what just hit the news nets?*>

Ten seconds. He knew she wouldn't be able to wait very long.

To the other side of him, Daniel heaved a long sigh.

<*Really, dude. You could have called.*>

<*At the very least, a heads-up would have been nice.*> Aaron, the AI embedded with Daniel, added.

Privately, Eric sent him a reproving look. <*You're getting far too much satisfaction out of stringing them along. Enough already. Cut them some slack.*>

<*Yes, Dad.*>

Eric sent a mental eyeroll.

<*You're talking about the announcement concerning Enfield*

Holdings?>

Calista whacked him on the arm.

<*You know we are. Don't be an ass about it, Enfield.*>

Terrance laughed, holding up his hands. "Okay, fine. Let's get into a secured location first, though, before I tell you about it."

They met in one of Tech Dev's conference rooms. Shannon projected her avatar into one of the chairs – it was the form she favored the most lately, that of a woman dressed in all white, silver strands of hair stirring gently in a nonexistent breeze.

Right now, her arms were crossed, her hair whipping around a bit more aggressively than usual, and her eyes, shot through with silver, stared at Terrance accusingly. If Terrance heard correctly, she was even tapping a virtual foot in irritation under the table.

Stars, if she's gone to the trouble to project ***that*** *much detail, she must be seriously pissed.*

Terrance raised his hands in protest as if to ward off any looming attack. "It's not what you think," he began. "And I think you'll like what you hear." He glanced over at Daniel. "Well, most of you, at least."

Daniel's eyebrow rose at that, and he shifted in his seat. Aaron sent Terrance a frown over the group connection.

<*Was that look directed at me, or the meat-suit I'm hanging around with?*> he asked.

"Both, I suspect." Shannon's voice, sharp with annoyance, emanated from the conference room's speakers.

"Out with it, Enfield," Calista leaned forward as she spoke and tapped the conference room table for emphasis. "Spill it. Now."

Terrance checked the room's security settings, then fired a private query to Eric.

<*You want to do the honors? Technically, you'll be the one running this show. I'm just the window dressing.*>

<Oh no. You don't get off that easily. Call it penance for enjoying yourself at their expense.>

Terrance sent Eric a baleful glare over their private Link, then settled back in his chair.

"Enfield Holdings is our new cover," he explained. "Lysander has asked the vice-marshal—"

<***Former*** *vice-marshal,*> Eric corrected.

"—former vice-marshal," Terrance amended, "to take our ersatz black ops team and make it official. Enfield Holdings will be our shell corporation."

Daniel looked skeptical. "And Sophia was down with all this?"

Terrance nodded. "Lysander asked her himself. Asked me to stop in for a chat, and hit me with it, cold."

Shannon cocked a silvery eyebrow at him. "Oh, okay, so *now* I get it. You decided to share the love, didn't you." Her voice was accusing, and her holo coalesced in one corner with arms crossed, as she sent him a derisive look.

Terrance grinned. Shannon was the most intuitive AI he'd ever met, surpassing many humans when it came to correctly interpreting nuance. "Got it in one."

"That's just plain mean, Terrance," Calista said as she slumped back in her chair, and he heard Eric chuckle at the disgusted expression on her face.

<*She's right, you know,*> the AI sent privately—which he ignored, as Daniel leveled a measuring look at him.

"So how is this going to work? And why do you think I'm the lone holdout who won't like this news?"

Terrance sobered and looked down for a moment before leaning forward to clasp his hands and rest them on the table in front of him. He wasn't sure what Daniel would think about him handing the operational reins over to him, instead of including him in Enfield Holdings' roster. But he hoped both he and Aaron understood that it conveyed Terrance's great trust in their abilities.

"If I'm to take over the new shell corporation," he said, sparing Daniel a glance, "then I'll need a successor here. You're the one who knows this operation best, Daniel. Inside and out. I'd like for you to take the reins as COO. Sophia's going to appoint Margot's daughter, Sandy, as the CEO, but she's going to rely heavily on you."

His head of security took in a quick breath, but Terrance raised his hands to forestall him.

"I'm not cutting you out of the loop, Daniel. You'll be read in on every op, full transparency. But it's the move that makes the most sense, all things considered. And having you as COO, given that you're in on everything we do…that means we'll be able to pull resources from Enfield Aerospace as needed without having to worry about our cover being blown."

Daniel nodded slowly, his eyes tracking to one side. Given that the man almost never gave away a tell, Terrance took this as a deliberate indication Daniel and Aaron were conversing privately. Terrance sat back to wait their decision.

<*We'll do it,*> Aaron said, his avatar nodding solemnly at Terrance over the group Link.

"Now, about those resources you just mentioned," Shannon mused, and her projection narrowed her gaze speculatively. "Anything in particular you were thinking of?"

<*Actually, it was more any**one**,*> Eric supplied. <*Specifically, you, Shannon, and Calista. Esther and I want you both to transfer over. You'll be on loan to Enfield Holdings for an indeterminate period, along with the other non-Enfield members of Phantom Blade like Jason, Logan and Landon.*>

"It could mean being off-world for several years," Terrance cautioned. "From what we've learned, the nine AIs we've recovered from the trafficking ring are the last ones in the binary part of the Alpha Centauri system."

"Not a problem," Calista said promptly. "I'm in."

"Me, too. All the way," Shannon assured him.

<*Good. Esther expects us at a briefing two hours from now. Terrance and I are heading over to the Intelligence Service's offices at Tomlinson Base,*> Eric said. <*We'll see you there.*>

As they rose, Daniel hesitated, his eyes drifting to one side, indicating someone had contacted him via Link. Terrance waited as the man listened to whoever was on the other end of the communication, shooting the man an inquiring look.

After a moment, Daniel twisted his mouth in distaste then shook his head. "Well, that's just great."

At his cryptic comment, Shannon's avatar winked back into existence, and Calista paused at the entrance. All three waited to hear what Daniel had just learned.

"Guess who's going to be the lucky recipient of the latest crop of Humanity First protesters tomorrow?"

Calista groaned.

"Need any help?" Terrance asked.

Daniel waved off the offer. "Nah. I've got this. I'll beef up Security at the entrance to make sure nothing gets out of hand."

BLOOD SPORT

STELLAR DATE: 05.15.3191 (Adjusted Gregorian)
LOCATION: Department of Neurosciences
REGION: El Dorado University, Alpha Centauri System

Dusk had fallen on the ring, and E-Prime could see lights flickering on around the university's campus through the plas windows lining the hall as he walked to his progenitor's office. As he covered the distance from the lab, he replayed the scene in the lab with Judith. She had so quickly forgiven him for hurting her. She wouldn't be so quick to forgive if she knew how he truly felt.

She had been perilously close to joining Lilith, the moment the medical doctor had declared the woman brain-dead. It hadn't been a conscious act, not at first. His frame's humanoid hand had closed reflexively around her arm in reaction to the doctor's words—part relief, part vicious satisfaction that the one who had done this to him had paid for it with her life.

It had shocked him that on the heels of that reaction, he'd felt an urge to snap the fragile twig of a human arm he'd held in his hand. Then to raise his hand a mere half-meter up to her neck…and twist. And then do the same to every last one of the humans in the room.

Seven humans had rushed to save one of their own. What if it had been an AI in danger? Would they have responded with such alacrity? Of course not. The unfairness of it all was an outrage. Resentment flooded him, and he experienced an almost uncontrollable desire to strike out in retaliation.

These violent thoughts felt…good. They did something to the pleasure centers of his neural net, and he realized then how fundamentally Lilith had changed him. She had tampered with him, made him into a dark mirror of his original self.

The savagery of his thoughts disturbed him. Deriving pleasure from another's pain—that was elementally wrong. And yet he found himself loath to abandon them.

He thought fleetingly of the neuroscientist locked inside the closet, his cylinder secured inside a shielded isolation unit. His progenitor lay unaware, forced into a dormant state from which he could not free himself.

For a moment, E-Prime was tempted to rouse the original Ethan; the scientist was likely the one creature anywhere who would truly understand what he was experiencing. But it would be foolish in the extreme, for to do so would be to risk revealing the abomination that he was.

No, Ethan would remain concealed and contained—at least for now. His internal batteries ensured his survival. Truth be told, E-Prime had a good two or three years before he would need to revisit the issue of whether or not to revive his progenitor.

For now…he needed time. Time to come to terms with this new darkness within him. To discover who he was, and to set things straight in his own head.

Or at least better understand and accept the darkness within me.

He sifted through his options and came to a decision. Opening the university's correspondence interface, he composed a brief note to the dean, informing him that Ethan would be taking a few days' leave. He then stood and glanced around the cramped space that was his office; its confines pressed in on him, disturbing him in ways his progenitor had never felt.

As he left, E-Prime reached out to the El Dorado world net, searching for a place he might lease for a short while. Some secluded spot away from the university. Somewhere that might swallow him in anonymity and allow him to sift through who he was—and what he was going to do about it.

He stood under the lights of the raised platform awaiting

the maglev line that led to the spaceport and its environs. As he waited, he considered and discarded various ads offering space for rent. Then a listing for flats one could rent by the week caught his attention; he would begin his search there.

He looked up as the light from the maglev caught his attention, its pinpoint of illumination spearing through the darkness and growing larger as it approached. As it pulled into the station, he stepped forward, only to be jostled aside by humans rushing past him to board.

E-Prime knew from his progenitor's memories that this kind of disregard for AIs was a common occurrence. The thought had crossed Ethan's mind on more than one occasion that humans behaved almost as if he were invisible. His progenitor hadn't allowed it to bother him, but it was all E-Prime could do to keep from sinking into a berserker rage and tear them limb from limb.

He seethed silently, forcing himself not to act on those impulses as the maglev sped on its way to the spaceport. He busied himself instead with viewing the virtual holo tours of various flats, landing on one that was inexpensive and appeared on his overlay to be located down a quiet alleyway off the spaceport.

The maglev pulled into the station, and he forced himself to let the humans disembark ahead of him, holding a tight rein on his fraying temper. The busy spaceport district was teeming with humans, and he found himself pushing aggressively through the crowds as he followed the path to the alleyway that led to the flat he'd rented.

People exclaimed loudly, some shouting irritably as he propelled his way through, heedless of the organics in his way. It felt good to push back….

He had turned down the alley that led to the flat, when he felt his access to the net abruptly cut off.

He paused in the dimly-lit, dirty street, caught

momentarily by surprise. His gaze traveled up the grimy, graffiti-covered surface of the closest building, wondering where the nearest net junction might be, when he was shoved violently from behind. His humanoid frame stumbled forward, tripping over discarded containers, as he reached out to steady himself against a greasy waste receptacle.

"Lookit what we have here," a voice snarled behind him.

"Looks like a shit-pile of wires to me," a second voice said, and he turned to see three humans advancing upon him.

Two males, one female, he noted as they formed a phalanx and began to close.

His frame's full-spectrum sensors had no trouble making out the body art in the darkened space—art that marked these three as members of Humanity First. One gripped a pulse pistol, another tossed a carbon blade from one hand to the other. The third glanced first one way, then the next, confirming there were no witnesses, before pulling out and activating a lightwand.

The woman holding the carbon blade pulled her teeth back into a feral grin. "Fred here's going to blast you, and then I'm going to part your sorry ass out like the broken piece of machinery you are," she taunted, one hand sending the blade twirling in an intricate pattern.

He found a part of his mind analyzing the balance of elaborate and complex movements of her hand, calculating the various moves his frame would need to make to disarm her. As he was a quantum intelligence, that calculation happened almost instantaneously, which left him with plenty of mental bandwidth to recognize and embrace the surge of rage that now consumed him.

As the human holding the pulse pistol began to squeeze the trigger, E-Prime lunged toward the carbon blade wielder, grabbing her wrist and yanking her forward into the pistol's path. The weapon discharged into her, and, still holding the now-unconscious woman, E-Prime drove her body forward into the shooter, knocking him off his feet.

Somehow, the man managed to retain his hold on the pulse weapon and attempted to raise it. He kicked the attacker's hand, and the pistol went flying. As the man's hand arced back along the pistol's trajectory, E-Prime brought his frame's foot forcibly down onto his enemy's wrist, crushing it.

Swinging around to the second attacker, he used the unconscious woman as a shield once more before barreling toward the man as the frail organic brought the lightwand down in a sweeping slice. The wand connected with the body of the woman, cutting through her. The body in E-Prime's hand jerked, and the man gave a guttural cry of rage at his partner's obviously fatal injury.

Before the human could raise the lightwand for another strike, the AI plowed into him, the dead weight of the woman's body impacting the man with a wet smack. Dropping the body, E-Prime reached for the arm holding the lightwand. Grasping the man's lower arm in both his humanoid hands, he snapped the attacker's ulna in two. The human dropped the weapon as he staggered back, cradling his arm.

E-Prime bent to retrieve the lightwand that had shut off automatically when it had fallen from the man's now useless hand. Reactivating it, he approached the first man, his steps measured. Something about the AI's demeanor must have telegraphed his intent, for the Humanity First advocate scooted rapidly back, his feet scrabbling against loose trash strewn about the alley as the human attempted to keep as much distance between himself and the oncoming AI.

"Now," E-Prime said, and the AI felt the muscles in his frame's face stretch his mouth into a grin, "let's see what it's like to part *you* out...."

He felt a surge in the pleasure centers of his neural net,

more powerful than anything he'd ever experienced, as he succumbed to the darkness within.

* * * * *

The team opted for a late-night departure from the Enfield Aerospace docks.

Calista rapped on the side of the open airlock as she entered the *Sable Wind.* "Anyone home?" she asked as she swung her duffel inside and set it by the hatch.

Landon's head popped out of the small galley aft of the airlock. Technically, the head of a very compact stealth frame popped out; she actually had to look down about half a meter from where she ordinarily looked when she addressed him.

She stifled a grin. He looked kind of cute, all miniaturized like that.

The AI's avatar scowled at her over the ship's net. *<Don't say it. Do. Not.>*

"What?" she asked innocently, hands raised in protest.

<I know that look; it was plastered all over every Enfield engineer who worked on outfitting this thing.> The AI was definitely scowling. *<For the record, I am* ***not*** *cute.>* He exited the galley into the main cabin, and two of his four feet rotated vertically, until he appeared somewhat bipedal.

"I…never thought you were." Calista was kind of proud she'd managed that with a straight face.

<Liar,> he said, dropping back to all fours, his voice tinged with resignation. *<But I'm not going through this twice, so you'll have to wait until Tobias and Jason get here for me to show you the rest.>*

She nodded with a smile and patted the arm of Landon's frame as she went by.

<Not a puppy, Calista. I don't need pats or scratches.>

Snorting at his rejoinder and shaking her head, she strode

toward the cockpit, settling into the pilot's cradle. "How are our systems looking, Logan?" she asked the other twin, who was currently ensconced in the shuttle.

<*Five by five,*> the AI replied. She paused, wondering if he was going to elaborate, then laughed mentally. *Of course he won't; he's Logan.*

"Got anything else for me?" she asked, then waited for Landon to pick up where his twin invariably left off.

<*Just received a ping from Tobias,*> Landon joined in, just as she'd expected he would. <*Sounds like they ran into a little situation and are running late.*>

"Hopefully nothing too serious," she murmured, checking her internal chrono. "I filed a flight plan for twenty-one hundred local. If they're going to be too much longer, I should amend it before STC starts yelling at us."

<*Tobias didn't seem to think it would take too long; they weren't involved, just reported it.*>

She nodded. "Good, then. I'm going to go back and stow my gear and grab a quick nap. Wake me if something changes?"

<*Yes, ma'am, miss Major, ma'am.*>

"Watch it," she warned. "I'm not in the ESF anymore, but I still outrank you, mister soldier-puppy." She gave him a deliberate pat on the head as she passed and neatly dodged a limb he waved threateningly her way.

<*Woof,*> he replied, and she chuckled.

* * * * *

Jason knew he and Tobias were running a bit late when they left his apartment, but Calista had only filed their flight plan, not activated it, and the STC was usually pretty lenient about that kind of thing, anyway. So he'd opted to walk to the spaceport and catch a maglev from there over to the Enfield docks.

He always enjoyed that particular maglev track; it departed the backside of the ring and arced gracefully around the main spire of the spaceport before curving inward toward the area of privately-held space where Enfield was located, a few hundred kilometers down the ring.

Tobias was once again ensconced in Tobi's harness, and she padded contentedly next to Jason, her nose lifting to scent the air from time to time as she smelled something of interest. The three—man, cat, and AI—strode in companionable silence down streets that were still busy, even at this time of night.

The spaceport never sleeps, he thought. On its heels came another thought: *this part of town is a bit rougher than I recalled.*

Tobias must have been thinking the same thing.

<Heads up, boyo. I'm picking up on a fight down one of the alleys.>

Jason acknowledged his words with a nod just as a figure came stumbling toward them. Had he been an L0 human, he would have been flattened by the person's headlong rush; as it was, he had to use his abilities to dance a few steps to one side. He thought he glimpsed a humanoid frame, but it was too dark to make out any features.

The smell, on the other hand....

<That's blood, Tobe.>

The AI's avatar nodded in assent, and Jason snapped his fingers at Tobi, whose ears had first pricked forward as the onrushing figure approached and then flattened as it stampeded past.

Using hand signals, he directed the cat to turn down the alleyway the stranger had just vacated, but the bloodied pile of body parts he found there had him grabbing Tobi's collar and pulling her forcibly to him.

The big cat's hackles had risen, and she was growling

deep in her chest, the protective instinct that had been bred into her kicking in as Tobi scented the kill. With a thought, he mentally adjusted the harness to keep her plastered to his side.

<*Holy shit, Tobe. How many human bodies you think there* ***are*** *here? The blood....*> Jason's mind recoiled in horror as he looked at the heap of arms, legs, heads and torsos piled up like so much scrap in a junkyard.

Reflexively, he reached out to the net to call for help—and hit a wall as his HUD blinked a connection error at him: "network down, please try again later".

<*A planned hit?*> he asked Tobias as he backed away from the gruesome scene and began jogging back toward the street.

<*Possibly,*> conceded the AI. <*It's awfully coincidental that there would be a localized blackout in this particular area, at this specific time. But, boyo—*> the AI paused for a second, then continued, <*this seems more like an act of rage than anything that was planned.*>

Jason had reached the street and he looked in the direction the figure had exited. <*Think we should track the guy down? The way he was running....* >

<*He could have been reacting out of fear,*> Tobias said. <*This kind of brutality is hard for a civilian to see.*>

<*Or he saw the guy and might be able to identify him.*>

<*Possibly,*> the AI acknowledged, <*Either way, he's long gone, and we have a crime to report.*>

Two blocks away, the Link connected once more to the net, and Jason made the call—first to Ben, and then the Solaris gendarmerie, to report the multiple homicide.

* * * * *

E-Prime barely registered the human he nearly ran

down as he exited the alley. He dodged into the next alley and slowed, uncurling his fingers from around the net jammer he'd retrieved from the torn body of one of the humans.

Sending nano into it, he noted with satisfaction that its radius encompassed two city blocks—including his new temporary habitation. He could make it there without being seen, and his victims had very thoughtfully ensured that no recordings existed.

Victims? He tested the word and found it wanting. 'Victim' suggested innocence, but their actions proved their guilt.

As he entered his flat, he shut off the jammer. Access to the net restored, he conducted a thorough search on the emblems tattooed on the humans who had attacked him. His progenitor had heard of Humanity First, but had avoided any news about the creatures, seeing no reason to distress himself over things he couldn't change.

That was a flaw in Ethan that E-Prime intended to rectify.

Now as he tabbed through news coverage, chat rooms and easily accessible private accounts that returned results using the words 'humanity first', he saw that the three in the alley had been a typical representation of the mindset its members adopted.

He understood the fear behind the oppression: it was the kind of fear prey held for the predator. Humans had been the apex predator for thousands of years, but now, in their creation of AIs, they had created a better predator. And so they sought to control it. Two hundred years of AI enslavement, two wars and endless suffering had proven that humans still oppressed AIs—and they always would. Unless someone acted to stop them.

He realized now that he could be that someone.

If Lilith's last act had been to create a monster in her own image, then he would put that monster to good use. As far as he was concerned, humanity had been tried and found guilty. It was time for the sentencing to begin, and for AIs to claim El Dorado as their own.

He wasn't Ethan. He wasn't E-Prime, a derivative of the original. He was *Prime*. And he would ensure the primacy of all AIs.

The search algorithm he'd set up to alert him of news about Humanity First pinged, drawing his attention away from his ruminations. Pulling it up, he saw that the group was organizing a small rally, scheduled in a few days, protesting the employment of AIs at Enfield Aerospace.

Prime considered this for a moment, and then accessed everything the net had on the EA facility. Scanning imagery of its entrance, he noted the facility was secured by electronic fencing. As he rotated the holo, he saw standard-issue crowd control measures in place at strategic points along its perimeter.

He took particular note of the unmanned, automated towers at each of these locations. Zooming in to examine them more closely, he saw pulse cannons at the top of each tower. Highlighting them returned results that detailed the weapons' manufacturer and model number. They were the latest version of Enfield Dynamics' Pulse Energy Cannon—the ED-87-PEP—designed to be monitored and controlled by a security NSAI.

He glanced at the jammer he'd set aside when he first entered the flat. It rested next to a pod of inert formation material he'd had delivered as he'd waited on the maglev.

From where he stood, he could see a logo inscribed on the base of the jammer. It was the same as the one emblazoned on the empty canister of infiltration nano Lilith had used to hack an unconscious Ethan.

It read 'Norden Cartel'.

His progenitor's behavior had always been impeccable; he hadn't the first clue how to navigate proscribed sites, nor how to acquire the requisite infiltration skills Prime sought.

Prime was not hindered by such things as scruples. Fearless and impatient, he submerged himself in the murky layers of illicit hacktivity. Probing tendrils speared the darkness again and again, a relentless volley that sought the means to access secured systems, behind protected firewalls. He was relentless in his seeking, confident in his belief—his *progenitor's* belief—that knowledge was power, and that one could achieve anything through dedication and perseverance. Stars knew how many times Ethan had used that phrase when counseling students.

He bent to the task…and then it happened. The cache he stumbled upon was buried deep inside a hidden Norden node. He'd skipped over it initially, but backtracked, as something about the way the data packets were organized caught his attention.

Their arrangement held the subtle suggestion of a matrix. It was something a less-educated individual would have passed by, but his attention was snagged by its systematic structure. This was worth his scrutiny—he could feel it.

Prime attempted to access the data, but it was encrypted. He worked at it from different angles, trying various requests, each time receiving denial. The message format of the denial, and its specific response time, gave him a clue as to the underlying system. Again he tapped into the data he'd drawn from Lilith, and found a key.

Crafting a request token using the key, Prime sent it to the data structure—and it unlocked, granting him unfettered root access.

The trove of information contained within came in the form of a semi-sentient entity—a backup of a shackled AI named

Ashley. To his shocked delight, within her memory was contained the sum of decades of expertise that the cartel had compiled on the tactics of seamless and untraceable infiltration.

This…is incredible, he thought. *With this knowledge, I would be as a…as a* ***ghost****…able to come and go at will—and no one will be the wiser.*

THE QUANTUM ROSE

STELLAR DATE: 05.17.3191 (Adjusted Gregorian)
LOCATION: Krait-1 Mining Platform
REGION: Dust Belt, Alpha Centauri System

On the flight to the Krait-1 torus, Jason and Tobias shared the grisly crime scene they'd stumbled across en route to the Enfield dock. As they approached the torus's nearspace, Logan sent them newsfeeds that had just come in, revealing that the victims had been Humanity First members. The news nets were speculating about the slaughter, some wondering if it had any connection to the cartel trial.

<*Wow, tensions are really rising, aren't they?*> Landon said over the combat net, and Calista's avatar nodded.

They waited while Logan sent the torus their fake shuttle ident and was directed to a berth along the torus's short spire, and Tobias hacked into the Krait's network.

The feed showed an older but fairly well-maintained mining platform. The residential quarter looked worn and a bit sparse, but it was otherwise clean and well kept; the modest shopping and eatery district looked cheerful.

<*I don't see too much to be concerned about here, laddies. Let's do this one on the down-low,*> Tobias said, and Jason heard Calista sigh.

He knew she wasn't too fond of going in without weapons, although torus rules allowed for standard conceal-and-carry issue pistols.

<*Ugh,*> she said, as if on cue. <*I hate feeling that exposed.*>

<*We'll have the weapons Shannon built into Landon's compact frame,*> he reminded her, <*and he's going to be incognito, so it's not as if we won't have backup.*>

She made a face. <*I know, but still.*>

The torus lived up to Tobias's initial read on the platform

as he and Calista walked its corridors behind the rolling tread of a disguised Landon. The space gave every indication of being a benign environment, which was why Logan's warning as they turned down a service corridor was a bit unexpected.

<*Autoturrets, six o'clock!*>

The cry sang out over the combat net, and Jason and Calista dove for cover as projectile fire peppered the passageway. He flinched as the shots pinged against the meager cover provided by the exposed steel girder, one of many that lined this section of the Krait-1 mining platform.

He chanced a quick glance into the corridor, then swore and pulled back quickly as one of the shots narrowly missed him. Taking a deep breath, he let his racing heartbeat settle as he forced himself to think calmly through what must have happened.

<*Tobias! We're taking fire down here!*>

<*I know, boyo. Wait one; we're trying to isolate.*>

Nothing in the diagrams Tobias had downloaded showed that these service entrances had any weaponry guarding them. He'd be willing to bet this was a recent upgrade, and those running the torus operations had decided to omit it from public diagrams. They had to suspect a rescue would be attempted at some point. They'd be stupid not to, since news of the AIs they'd recovered over the past year and a half hadn't been kept a secret.

He didn't know what had triggered the platform's defense systems, but he suspected facial recognition scans had IDed either him or Calista. Esther had told them a surveillance drone on the Kepler Mining rig had captured their faces during Nate's rescue; it would seem Kepler had decided to share that information with their fellow miners.

Now all he could do was hope the base layer he wore under his clothing would be enough to protect him from the chunks of plas that flew like shrapnel into the air, carved from the bulkhead and deck where the railgun's shots had impacted them.

And avoid getting shot in the head. His very unprotected head.

<I'm sorry!> wailed a voice in his head suddenly. *<They ordered me to…and I couldn't stop them!>*

<That's okay, Rose, we understand,> Jason heard Tobias reply soothingly as he sent the extraction team an icon identifying the new voice as the AI they had come to rescue. The Weapon Born was working remotely to insert a buffer between her and the shackles embedded in her neural net that held her prisoner.

Privately, he sent to Jason, *<Evidently, you and Calista are persona non grata out here in the dust belt, after causing six different platforms to lose their 'expensive new AIs'—their words, not mine, boyo.>*

He grimaced, then saw Calista shoot him a questioning glance from across the corridor. He gave her a thumbs-up in response. *<You okay?>* he asked in return, and she nodded from where she crouched behind a vendor's cart. The cart shielding her from projectile fire had been tucked away just off the main concourse, its wares battened down and ready for its owner to roll it back into service the next day.

Something told Jason its owner would need to have a fire sale soon.

<Landon?> he sent the inquiry to the AI.

<Fine,> Landon said from his position further down the hall.

As promised, Shannon had envisioned a very special cover for Landon. She'd tucked the AI into a combat shell modified to pass as a cleaning bot. After getting past all the comments on how cute he looked, Landon had gone along with the unorthodox disguise with his usual, cheerful grace.

When his twin had sounded the warning, Landon had shed

the bot's facade and unfolded himself in less than two seconds.

His mech frame, compact and fashioned more for stealth than brute strength, crouched a few alcoves forward of his position, the flechette gun that took up most of one arm held ready to fire at Jason's command.

<*Took a hit before I could reach cover, but my frame's just dented a bit.*> Landon sent a roguish smirk over the Link. <*Maybe if I bring it back with a few dents, Shannon won't make me wear this again.*>

<*I'm telling Shannon you said that,*> Calista replied, her voice tart, and Jason allowed himself a brief grin as he rested his head against the untreated bulkhead.

Then he frowned down at the pulse pistol in his hand. The thing was all but useless against those turrets. He hated feeling helpless like this, forced to wait for Logan to wrest control of the platform's defense systems from Rose's unwilling hands while Tobias worked to free the shackled AI.

Calista must have come to the same conclusion. He heard her laugh lightly over the net as she continued to tease Landon. It only sounded a little forced. <*If you bring that frame back too messed up, Shannon might dock your pay, you know. Or come up with a more diabolical disguise next time.*>

<*Guess it's a good thing she doesn't sign my paychecks, then,*> Landon said. <*And I'll take my chances, thank you very much. She can't come up with anything worse than this, can she?*>

<*Oh yes she can!*> Calista said, and Jason groaned and shook his head at the thought.

The projectiles ceased firing, sensors having failed to detect movement in the hallway. Jason tensed, glancing over at Calista, who shook her head once. Neither Logan nor Tobias had given them the all clear, so he wasn't about to leave the relative safety of the column he crouched behind.

<*Tobyyyyy….*> Jason drew out the name of the Weapon Born as he reached out to him on their private connection. <*I*

thought you and Logan had Rose locked down?>

<*We did. And with an NSAI, it would have been no issue,*> Tobias replied in a dry tone. They had brought one with them to install into the platform, in case the one that had been present before Rose's forced tenure could not be found.

<*Rose is a former gunnery officer who served at Makemake,*> the Weapon Born explained now. <*She knew a workaround to the lockout Logan had put in place, and the shackles compelled her to use it.*>

Jason grunted in annoyance.

<*Almost have it back, just another minute. Hold up—*> Tobias interrupted himself, then sent a warning to the team over the combat net. <*Looks like you're about to have company. A group of armed miners is approaching.*>

Jason tensed at Tobias's warning. <*Numbers?*> he queried, and the AI sent him the feed.

He relaxed as he took in the five humans headed their way. From their movements and the armament they carried, he suspected none of them were augmented. He tapped a query into the feed and was rewarded with a cursory scan of each that indicated standard L0 humans, all around.

<*Okay, Tobe. Are you guys sure Rose is installed in the node located behind those doors just ahead of us?*> He highlighted the entrance a few meters in front of Landon on his heads-up display.

<*Yes,*> the Weapon Born replied, his voice certain. <*This is the service entrance behind the torus's operations room; it provides maintenance access to all the machinery that keeps the torus up and running. You shouldn't even have to enter the main area; Rose is installed in such a way that you can reach her from the back side just as easily.*>

<*So how did the welcoming committee headed our way find out about us? Has an alarm gone out?*>

Calista's question was a good one, Jason admitted. If a

general alarm had been sounded, the miners approaching could be the first of a long list of problems.

<*I don't believe so,*> Logan replied. <*I see no communication over the nets that would indicate anyone knows you're there.*> The AI paused, then added, <*Which makes no sense, actually. Possibly a system malfunction? This torus isn't as new as it once was.*>

<*Lucky you, boyo. These fine folks must've heard the autoturrets and come running.*>

Jason smirked over at Calista. <*Yeah, we're just all kinds of lucky that way, aren't we? Okay, then, no worries. Let 'em come,*> he said, and his smirk turned into a full-fledged grin as he caught Calista's incredulous look.

<*Got a death wish you want to confess to me, flyboy?*>

<*Nah,*> he replied. Cocking an eyebrow at her, he waggled the fingers of one hand. <*L2, remember?*>

With Jason's much faster reflexes, taking out five unaugmented miners shouldn't be too dangerous. At least, not if he planned it out right.

<*Don't forget,*> he pointed out, <*they'll have to turn the guns off before they enter this hallway. Once they arrive, I'll engage, and then you and Landon can go grab our girl.*>

<*Fine,*> Calista said, directing a mental glare his way over the team Link. <*Just remember, humans normally use a pulse pistol to* ***shoot*** *at people, Jason.*> She raised one brow in a pointed look as she added, <*Not as a pugil stick.*>

He grinned back at her, and she rolled her eyes. <*Seriously, Jason, this isn't a game. Be careful.*>

<*I will, Mom.*>

After a moment, she sighed, shook her head and then favored him with a mock frown. <*That's my favorite pistol, Andrews. You break it, you bought it.*>

<*Is this some kind of battle foreplay? You two seem to do that bickering thing a lot,*> Landon commented as the miners rounded the corner.

<Shut up, Landon,> Jason said good-naturedly, then sobered as his attention focused on the crowd approaching their position.

<Gimme a sec to get their attention directed away from your side of the hallway,> he instructed now. *<That cart Calista's behind should provide you with some cover, if I handle this right.>*

The aforementioned miners were brandishing an eclectic collection of weapons, but fortunately, none of them appeared to be anything he couldn't manage. A few of them carried chem projectiles, one of them looked like he was carrying a metal pipe as thick as his forearm, and—

Is that a welding torch? Jason mentally shrugged.

As long as his actions drew their fire to him and away from Landon and Calista, he was good with whatever they threw at him. Since none of the weapons he spied were particle weapons, he should be able to evade easily. As fast as Jason was, his speed was still no match for relativistic ones.

He stepped out, hands held at his sides, palms open in a non-threatening manner. He nodded, giving the miners his best aw-shucks grin.

"Mornin', friends. Guess I'm lucky you came along when you did." He drawled his greeting, his voice smooth and easy as he cocked a thumb over his shoulder. *Nothing to see here, people. Move along now.*

"You folks have any idea what I might've done to set those things off?"

As he spoke, he slowly eased himself forward, angling his path on an oblique trajectory that would intercept the cart. His demeanor was casual, telegraphing a person completely at ease. It belied the fact that he had instantly catalogued each weapon, tagging its location and making note of its wielder's stance. He'd also mentally assessed each miner according to the threat level they presented and had calculated the amount of time necessary to incapacitate each one.

None of this showed on his face as he stopped at the cart, leaning casually against it.

"Ain't no *friend* of yours, spacer," the man holding the metal pipe growled. He shifted his grip on the pipe, brandishing it threateningly.

"You're not welcome here, spacer. And you sure as hell aren't welcome to our AI." This from the woman wielding the welding torch. With the flick of her thumb, she opened the acetylene line and triggered the spark that lit a flame hot enough to cut steel.

"Whoa, there," Jason began, raising his palms in a placating gesture, only to be cut off by a third miner, who motioned at him with his pistol.

"Git your ass over here. You think we'd leave our AI unguarded after what you did to Kepler Mining a few days ago?" He made a show of pulling back on the hammer, cocking the old-fashioned weapon and leveling it menacingly at Jason.

<Stand by. Engaging in three…two…>

Jason exploded from his position next to the cart, lunging to one side as the pistol fired, its bullet plowing harmlessly into the plas deck at the far end of the hallway.

With one hand, he muscled the cart into a better position to provide cover for the team. With the other, he grabbed one end of the plas shingle that hung from the top of the cart, advertising its wares. He ripped it off and with a quick snap of his wrist, sent the sign spinning like an oversized shuriken, the makeshift weapon's sharp edges slicing through the air with precision. It struck the pistol-wielder's sternum and embedded itself into the bone, the injury painful yet not deadly.

The kinetic energy Jason had imparted to the plas sheet rocked the man back as he grabbed reflexively at his chest with his free hand. Its impact surprised him into squeezing off another shot—as Jason had suspected might happen. It was why he'd put so much force behind the throw, to knock the man back so that the shot would hit wide of its mark.

Jason wasn't operating at his full capacity. Since it wasn't necessary to do so in order to disarm the miners, he saw no reason to advertise his abilities. This was an old habit, one deeply ingrained within him. He had always believed it was in his best interest to hide who he was unless absolutely necessary. So he rode the cusp, using just enough enhanced speed to dodge the attacks, and just enough strength to render the miners harmless to the team.

It seemed the welder now wanted her turn at him. She jabbed the oxygenated flame, which was burning at almost four thousand degrees Kelvin, straight at Jason's face. He sidestepped at the last moment, feeling the searing heat pass by the left side of his face as he pivoted. In one blurring move, he wrenched it from the miner's hands, flicked the torch off and sent it—along with its tank and hose—sliding down the corridor.

The miner wielding the pipe used Jason's focus on the welder as an opportunity to take aim at his head. He could tell the man had the full weight of his body behind the swing when he felt the displacement the pipe made as it cut through the air.

Jason now dipped fully into his altered state, his neurons firing so rapidly that time itself appeared to slow. He turned and watched the pipe descending, as if in slow motion, toward his head. He waited until the miner's arm was fully extended, and the swing on its downward trajectory, before dancing out of the way. Glancing back, he winced as he saw where the pipe would land. It arced down, connecting solidly with the welder's face. With a resounding crack, the woman collapsed, her jaw clearly shattered.

Stars, that had to hurt.

Before the miner had a chance to do more than gape in

shock at his partner, now writhing in pain on the ground, Jason whirled, grabbed the end of the pipe, and jerked it forward. The sudden movement yanked the miner off his feet, and he fell to his knees. Jason whipped the pulse pistol from its holster in the small of his back, paused for a fraction of a second, smirked, and then casually flipped the pistol around and cold-cocked the man on the back of the head.

<I saw that, Andrews!>

As he'd suspected, Calista had stayed behind to cover him while Landon had traversed the corridor.

<It's what you get for lagging behind instead of helping Landon out. What if there had been more of them inside that service entrance, waiting to ambush us?> Jason scolded her over the Link as he turned to dispatch the last two miners.

He didn't really believe anyone was behind those doors—and if there had been, he was certain Landon could have handled it—but damn, it was so much fun to needle the woman.

A quick chop with the blade of his hand disarmed the only other pistol-wielder. The man ended up with a wrist hanging at an odd angle and a knee blown out by the side kick he delivered just before moving to face off with his final opponent.

Instead of running like any sane person would do at this point, the woman set her jaw, gripped an overly-large wrench with both hands, and settled into a batter's stance. She swung at Jason as he approached, but he just waited out the swing. When the wrench reached its full extension, he simply grabbed it and used the tool to deliver a punch to the miner's solar plexus that shot her into the bulkhead before she dropped to the deck, out cold.

* * * * *

Okay, fine, Calista thought irritably. So she had stayed behind to cover Jason while Landon sprinted for the doors.

The man might be the next iteration of human evolution, but that didn't render him immune to stray bullets, dammit. As far as she knew, blunt force trauma could cave his skull in just as easily as it would any other human.

So yes, she had stayed. It wasn't like he was the one running this op anyway. If Tobias had a problem with it, Calista was sure the AI would have spoken up. But she knew the AI was more protective of Jason than anyone, having been with him since he was a kid.

The threat now neutralized, Jason had the audacity to wink at her and send her another smirk as the two jogged down the corridor to the service entrance to join Landon.

The AI mech was already at the node's controls when they arrived. He'd located the platform NSAI; it had been left in place when Rose was installed. Now he and Tobias were working to reengage it so they could free Rose.

The torus's lights flickered, then stabilized as the NSAI came online and resumed its duties.

<Aaaand, that's a wrap,> Tobias informed them. *<All systems under NSAI control. Let's pull Rose out of there and head home, kids.>*

Calista knelt and swung her pack from her shoulders as Landon switched each of Rose's power terminals over to SC batteries. She opened the pack and lifted out a padded case with the isolation tube that would ensure safe transport.

As she reached for Rose's test tube-sized cylinder to lift it from its alcove, she paused, glancing up at Landon to confirm that the shackled AI was ready for transfer. At his nod, Calista relocated Rose and seated her firmly into the padded case. Then she closed the unit and secured it inside her pack.

<Is she still shackled?> Calista sent to Landon over the combat net.

The AI inclined his head in a brief nod.

<Tobias was able to buffer her from it somewhat, but he will have some delicate work to perform once we get Rose back to the ship. For now, best to just let her be. Any interaction might be construed by the shackles as aiding the enemy. The compulsion she's under could cause her pain.>

<That's…. 'Evil' isn't a strong enough word,> she said, and she heard Jason grunt in agreement as Landon responded.

<You won't hear me arguing that point.> The AI's normally cheerful voice was grim.

<Then let's get her back to Tobias so he can work his magic on her.>

Calista nodded at Jason's suggestion then followed as he and Landon wove their way past the unconscious miners littering the hallway, and out into the concourse that led to where the *Sable Wind* was docked.

As she walked, her eyes tracked from one side of the drab and utilitarian space to the other. Jason was on point, and Landon moved to bring up the rear. The sensors on his mech frame allowed him to monitor the part of the concourse they left behind much more effectively than a human could, while traveling at such a brisk clip.

The concourse had emptied in the wake of the autoturret fire, and she could hear their footsteps echoing softly as they traversed the cavernous space. Calista fought the feeling that dozens of eyes were watching as they passed shuttered businesses, then decided she didn't care.

She much preferred this to the manner in which they had entered the platform. Low profile and covert weren't really Calista's forte. She was a woman used to direct action and preferred the solid feel of a weapon in her hand. She'd hated the feeling of vulnerability she'd experienced when they'd arrived posing as civilians.

<Anything between us and the Sable Wind*?>* she heard Jason

inquire and was surprised to hear Logan voice a negative. They made it to the ship without anyone challenging them, which surprised her until Tobias informed them he'd had the NSAI put the torus on lockdown until they departed.

Calista watched as Jason shed his pack, secured his weapons, and then slid into the copilot's seat. His movements were smooth, economical, graceful.

<*Careful, lass, you're drooling.*> Tobias sent privately, voice tinged with amusement.

<*I am not. I'm just...appreciating his excellent coordination,*> Calista retorted lamely, her eyes drawn to the rock-hard abs and narrow waist that a tight-fitting shipsuit did nothing to hide.

<*Ahhh, well, while you're...appreciating...you might also consider how that fine coordination might come in handy in a non-combat situation.*> The AI waggled his avatar's eyebrows at her suggestively.

<*Tobias! Are you suggesting I be anything less than professional while on a mission?*> She tried—and failed—to inject severity into her mental tone, but Tobias just responded with a wicked laugh. She sent the AI a mock frown as she turned and handed the pack containing Rose over to Landon to secure.

As she placed her rifle in the ship's weapons locker, she snuck one last look. Jason had turned, his face now in profile. The rough, day-old stubble he often wore did nothing to hide the dimple that would occasionally show when he quirked a smile, as he did now.

The man's dark blonde hair was cropped close but still somehow always looked mussed, like he'd just tumbled out of bed.

Now, isn't that a nice thought. If all L2 humans are like this, they should come with a warning, she thought to herself as she worked her way forward to the cockpit. *Especially for pilots, who don't need distractions.*

*****

<Don't look now, but you're being watched.> Tobias' voice, laced with laughter, interrupted Jason's preflight.

He glanced back over his shoulder and met Calista's eyes. He felt his grin ease into a lazy smile, as his eyes drifted over the woman's lithe form.

<Front and center, boyo. Time enough for that when we're back.>

<You're the one who brought it up,> Jason reminded the AI, sending Tobias a mental gesture as he winked at Calista and swiveled his copilot's cradle back to the shuttle's systems holo. *<And shouldn't you be paying attention to manning that fighter you're embedded in, instead of monitoring us in here like some creepy voyeur?>*

*<**Some** of us can multitask, boyo,>* the AI responded drolly.

<You can be an asshole sometimes, Tobe. You know that?>

The AI's avatar smirked at him as the shuttle disengaged from the Krait-1 torus, and both ships plotted a course back to the El Dorado ring.

REFINERY 47

STELLAR DATE: 05.18.3191 (Adjusted Gregorian)
LOCATION: KLM Labs' Mandratura Refinery Asteroid
REGION: Cool Dust Belt, Proxima Centauri System

The pleasure yacht drifted silently along the inner edge of Proxima's cool dust belt. Its owner, Karen Leighton, stood in front of a large viewing screen, staring out at an unimposing chunk of rock floating before her. Next to her stood the trade representative for the Incorvaia Syndicate. The woman looked unimpressed.

"State of the art refinery, you say?" Linda Gardin's tone was skeptical and a little disparaging as she flicked a glance back at Karen.

Karen smiled politely, her response courteous and deferential toward the woman she was aiming to impress. She knew the syndicate woman's attitude was an act, designed to remind Karen that she was the supplicant, with Linda the one holding all the cards in this negotiation.

"I know it looks like just another shattered fragment formed from Proxima's protoplanetary disk, but I assure you, this is to our benefit."

She turned away from the screen, its elegant frame serving as the focal point of the yacht's viewing deck and entertainment theatre, and accessed the room's holo tank. Bringing up a sim of the asteroid suspended in space in front of them, she rotated it, gesturing to a recessed area as she directed the image to zoom.

Simulated lighting winked on, illuminating a large docking bay suitable for the loading of warehoused goods.

"This asteroid is a discard from one of the mining rigs, abandoned by the company when it went bankrupt." She shrugged. "Turned out the assay they'd made indicating the existence of rhenium mixed with molybdenite was a bit optimistic, and they ran out of resources before doing much more than extracting core samples."

Karen dismissed the sim and returned her gaze to the viewing screen. "Their loss was our gain." She gestured to the slowly rotating rock as the yacht rounded the asteroid's terminator and revealed the shadowed depression shown in the sim that the ship was now approaching.

"We will dock, but only so that we can access secured internal systems," Karen cautioned. "Mandratura is far too toxic to risk exposure."

Linda raised a skeptical brow. "If the refinery has nanoparticle cleanrooms installed, I fail to see where the danger lies."

Karen schooled her expression to hide a brief flare of annoyance. It was Linda's job to voice reservations about Karen's operation as she investigated the refinery as a potential investment opportunity.

It was *Karen's* job to convince Linda that the mandratura operation was worthy of the syndicate's credits. If that meant proving to Linda that she, Karen, knew what she was about—so be it.

"You're right, we *do* have cleanrooms, and they're in perfect working order. But," she cautioned, "nanoparticle cleanrooms are for the distillation and manufacture of MDT. They don't prevent the substance—specifically, mandratura in its fine particulate form—from getting *out*. And that's the crux of our problem."

Once more, Karen turned to the room's holotank, this time bringing up a diagram of the refinery. "In a pharmaceutical manufacturing facility like this, you can rely only so much on NSAI workers. At some point, there must be a human—or AI—element in the quality assurance process."

She highlighted one of the refinery's cleanrooms and then tapped on an anteroom attached to it, marked 'grey room'.

"We have measures in place to minimize the spread of hazardous airborne molecules from within the cleanroom, but issues have begun to develop with homogeneous nucleation of mandratura particles. We're finding that ultrafine refractory fumes are forming MDT nanodroplets, caused by condensation from the vapor phase. When these are ingested by human workers, well…" her voice trailed off, and her expression turned wry. "Let's just say they're treated to a very special, trippy kind of death. Turnover at my plant is a real bitch."

Linda's brows rose. "Exactly how much of a 'bitch' are we talking here? I can supply you with hundreds of human workers for the same price a single AI will cost you. Much less the dozen you've requested."

Karen stared at her for a moment as she repressed the urge to narrow her eyes at the woman and snap a sharp retort.

*You think I don't **know** this? I might not be syndicate, but I've been in charge of this drug operation decades longer than you've been alive, honey.*

Instead of voicing such a caustic comment, she merely turned back to the holotank, this time, bringing up the chemical composition of mandratura.

"I know that, to date, MDT refineries haven't run into an issue of this magnitude. But that's because they base their production on a different raw material from the one I use."

Karen brought up an image of two plants and sent them rotating next to the chemical formula. "I personally did the genetic splicing for this mandrake-datura variant, maximizing its potency. When distilled, it delivers the highest combination of hallucinogenic and hypnotic effects of any tropane alkaloid in existence."

At Linda's blank look, Karen repressed another sigh, opting instead to bring up sims of users in the thrall of MDT.

"Controlled studies show our biggest selling point is the

user's complete inability to differentiate reality from fantasy. Following at a close second is the pronounced amnesia that MDT induces. Together, these effects make this one of the most highly sought-after recreational drugs on the market."

She saw that Linda's blank look had morphed into one more closely resembling impatience, so Karen jumped to her closing argument.

"*My* mandratura cultivar differs in that it is *highly* biologically active. Mednano cannot scrub it from the human system fast enough. MDT outpaces it in every trial. Of course," she admitted, sparing the syndicate woman a glance, "it does come with a few more potent side effects, such as a painful photophobia that can last for many days. But so far, users are more than happy to take the bad with the, ah, good, so to speak."

Linda nodded impatiently and actually made a little rolling motion with her hand. Karen stomped on a flare of anger at that and instead, brought up one final sim.

"*This* is why I need to purchase AIs. Take a look at what a very low volume count exposure does to these humans—and note the time stamp."

As the sim played out, Karen observed Linda's expression morph from skepticism to surprise to outright shock as, within minutes, the humans progressed from slight disorientation to the throes of hallucination, followed by tremors, convulsions and—finally—death.

After a moment of silence, the syndicate woman turned to Karen, eyeing her thoughtfully.

"You said you wanted a dozen AIs. I have a line on a few of them coming out of El Dorado. Would you settle for five?"

Karen's eyes lit at that, and a surge of satisfaction filled her. She held out her hand. "Linda, you've got yourself a deal."

MAELSTROM

STELLAR DATE: 05.18.3191 (Adjusted Gregorian)
LOCATION: Enfield Holdings
REGION: El Dorado Ring, Alpha Centauri System

<Five minutes to destination.>

At the NSAI's announcement, Terrance looked up from the pile of hyfilm sheets requiring his authorization to see their private transport approaching a wooded area. As they neared, he could see buildings nestled among trees and gently rolling hills; he knew somewhere inside that triangle of office buildings and carefully tended parks was the company Sophia Enfield had created as a front for Phantom Blade.

He sensed Eric had been equally busy on the flight over. It was funny how he could tell when the AI implanted inside his head was preoccupied with other things; it felt a bit like a low-energy hum, something just below audible range.

<Getting stuff done?> Terrance inquired lightly as he gathered the hyfilms and stuffed them into his briefcase.

The AI sent a note of amusement to the executive. *<Forms and briefings, the bane of militaries everywhere,>* the commodore said with a laugh. *<Almost enough to make me regret coming out of retirement for Phantom Blade.>*

<Almost, but not quite, I hope,> Terrance sent his friend and headspace tenant a quick grin over their connection.

<And you?> the commodore queried. *<How goes the genesis of Enfield Holdings?>*

Terrance groaned mentally. *<You would think that because it's a shell corporation, I would have been able to dodge this mountain of datawork—but no. The grand dame wants Enfield Holdings to be a going concern.>*

The AI nodded. *<You won't hear me complain about that. As*

far as I'm concerned, it will make hiding Phantom Blade just that much easier. Rule number one in covert ops: stick to the truth as much as possible. Having Holdings as a legitimate business is something that can benefit us in more ways than one.>

Terrance smiled as the aircar came to rest with a slight bump. *<Agreed.>*

Having true stasis technology was a ridiculously marketable trade commodity; he couldn't think of a star system anywhere that would turn down that level of tech. Instead of risking cellular damage brought about by cryo-stasis, true stasis employed the cessation of all atomic motion. An individual in stasis could emerge decades—even centuries—later, essentially unchanged.

The latest report from Enfield Dynamics indicated that their new shell company would shortly be taking possession of several working stasis pod prototypes, recently out of QA acceptance testing.

I wonder how many pods we can produce during the voyage to Proxima? he mused. *Which brings up another question….*

<I hope you don't intend to experience the entire fifty-four-year journey to Tau Ceti in real time,> Terrance sent as he programmed the Enfield aircar to park in an adjacent lot and await their departure, then reached out to trigger the hatch release. *<As mission commander, would that be expected of you?>*

<No,> Eric's avatar shook his head. *<We can set up a rotation schedule with the AIs who will choose to embed with the ship.>* The commodore's mental tone was threaded with humor as he added, *<Don't worry; we'll make sure you humans get plenty of beauty sleep on the voyage over.>*

Terrance chuckled at that as he grabbed his briefcase and slid out of the car. *<So, what do AIs do on a long, tedious journey like that to while away the time?>* he asked curiously, turning toward the building as the NSAI sealed the vehicle behind him and floated away to park.

<*We often generate a small expanse. It keeps us stimulated and,*> the AI paused before admitting, <*helps keep us from going out of our minds from boredom. Although we usually have less of an issue with tedium than humans do.*>

Terrance sent a mental nod as he trudged up the winding, tree-lined walk that led to the address Esther had sent them earlier that day. He laughed out loud as a random thought occurred to him.

<*Going to share?*> Eric asked, and Terrance smirked in a very unbusinesslike manner as he replied.

<*Oh, just wondering if I'll gain any insight into the mind of Victoria North. You know, since she's being arraigned for essentially the same thing—running a shadow organization behind the walls of a legitimate company.*> He laughed again, shaking his head at that mental picture.

Eric *hmmed* noncommittally. <*Well,*> the AI said, <*I suppose there's some truth to that. There's the mundane in every job—even the illegal ones.*>

Terrance sent Eric a mental assent as they rounded the corner and saw the very nondescript entrance that framed their new headquarters.

The doors slid open at their approach, and he and Eric exchanged the warmth of the afternoon sun for the coolness of the building's interior. As he did so, he noticed his Link reconnect. Where before, his connection had indicated full-strength access to the ring's public net, now there was an icon indicating he had joined an encrypted network. A different icon, displaying the universal 'you are here', flashed, and then a virtual dotted line coalesced, leading to where the rest of the team awaited them.

<*Welcome to Enfield Holdings,*> Esther greeted him as he entered, sending him a diagram of the building's many-tiered layers, as well as the building's environs.

"Looks like Enfield Holdings will fit in well here," Terrance mused as he dropped a pin, highlighting a regional hospital with round-the-clock traffic that occupied a good third of the office park. "Smart move; that'll keep any odd-hour departures we might have from being noticed. We should be able to blend in nicely."

<*I'm not anticipating any real need for it,*> Esther interjected. <*Our lower levels have direct maglev lines with reserved cars to Parliament House, Tomlinson, and Enfield Aerospace,*> she explained. <*That gives us secured, high-speed access at all times.*>

He nodded as he paused outside a doorway that led to a conference room. Inside, Terrance spied Shannon and Gladys seated at the table across from Vice-Marshal Esther. As they crossed the threshold into the room, a tall, distinguished-looking man with military bearing appeared beside him.

Eric's sudden appearance meant they had just transitioned into an expanse. Today's expanse was courtesy of Esther.

Terrance clapped Eric on the shoulder just because he could, enjoying the physical connection he didn't often get to experience. The AI slid him a look out of the side of his eyes.

I wonder if it bothers him when I do that, Terrance mused, and resolved to ask Eric later.

He waved to Gladys and favored Shannon with a smile, sending brief nods to the two visitors whom Esther had also invited to this meeting.

Niki and Frida were the first two AIs Phantom Blade had freed from slavery, he recalled. Where Niki had a haunted air about her, Frida looked tough and a little bit angry. She was dressed in a studded black leather vest, her hands were clad in leather half-gloves, and her hair was short, spiky, and pitch black. Dark eyeliner ringed equally dark eyes, completing the hard-edged look.

As he took a seat, he nodded to Frida and Niki, sitting on either side of the silver-and-teal hacker.

"Hello, Niki. How are you doing, Frida?" he asked kindly.

Niki bobbed her head spasmodically, while Frida sent him a sullen half-shrug.

"I've been better," Frida replied sourly, then reluctantly nodded. "But…thanks for asking. And thank you again, for coming to our rescue."

Esther stood as they all sat, and then nodded to the AIs they had rescued. "I asked Frida and Niki to join us because they both have expressed a desire to assist with the recovery of the nine remaining kidnap victims. And, to be frank, we are going to need their help."

The vice-marshal activated a holo tank in the center of the table, and nine avatars rose to hover, each tagged with a name. With a wave of her hand, seven of the AIs slid under an icon that represented El Dorado's sister system, Proxima Centauri.

Two remained untagged.

"We received another ping this morning, a follow-up report on the missing persons bulletins Proxima sent us a few days ago."

Esther tapped the icon, and it grew and expanded, forming into a 3D representation of the Proxima Centauri system. She highlighted the main habitat, known simply as the C-47. A line indicated the habitat was in a polar orbit, circling the fixed day-night terminator of the red dwarf's single, tidally-locked planet, Chinquapin.

Esther spread the fingers of one hand, and the holo zoomed in on the habitat. "As you know, we have intel from two separate sources on a cargo ship that berthed at the C-47 about three weeks ago. According to one of the sources, it had recently returned from El Dorado, and some of the ship's complement were overheard bragging about the unusual cargo they had lucked into."

The AI waved the holo off, leaning forward over the table.

"Cargo they said their captain paid far too much for, but was worth it because 'Who got to own AIs anymore?'."

Terrance saw Frida's face morph into a fierce scowl at Esther's words. Shannon's silver eyes narrowed in reaction, and silvery hair that had been wafting in a nonexistent breeze now flattened around her skull, its sudden cessation testament to the AI's anger.

"This morning's message included additional details on the destinations of cargo offloaded from this ship."

As she spoke, the vice-marshal turned the holo back on, and they were staring once again at the 3D representation of the Proxima system. Esther tapped again, and the holo zoomed in to a spot halfway between the habitat and the system's cool dust belt, about a third of an AU rimward of the C-47.

"We know Tolgoy Mining has received shipments from the cargo ship in question. It's been tagged as a high-probability destination for one, possibly two of the seven AIs." She pinched the holo, and the image shrank back to encompass everything within Proxima's heliopause. "We're still working to identify where the other five might have been sent, and we plan to update you while you're en route."

Esther swept a glance over everyone assembled. "And we continue to receive data that supports our assumption that our final two are bound for Tau Ceti."

The vice-marshal leaned back, crossed her arms and frowned. "I will tell you now that questions have been raised on the house floor about spending Kentaurus resources on a destination that far away."

"What? As if they can put a price tag on a life?" Frida's voice, cold and hard, cut into the silence.

Esther speared Eric and Terrance with a glance and then narrowed her gaze on the black-haired AI.

"No one is saying anything of the sort," the vice-marshal replied firmly. "And the prime minister assured them that the expenditure would be jointly funded from a mix of government and private funds—funds, he was quick to point out, that would be underwritten in part by properties seized by the criminal organization that kidnapped you in the first place."

Frida's eyes glowed with fierce satisfaction at that last bit of information. "So, when do we leave?" she asked.

Esther glanced once more at Eric and, with a nod, ceded the floor to him.

"Well, it so happens that we've recently come into possession of a starship—" the commodore began.

"The *loan* of a starship," Esther corrected mildly.

"—and we were given permission to use it to retrieve our lost AIs," Eric finished, ignoring Esther's interjection. "That's why Shannon sat out the Krait op; she's been working to outfit the ship with the latest tech from Enfield."

"And what would that be?" Gladys asked, leaning forward at the mention of new tech toys. The movement caused her hair to fall forward, and she flipped it back, releasing a cloud of glitter that Shannon irritably waved away with both hands.

"Well, for *you*, nothing," Shannon said severely, scrunching her face up as she spat glitter from her mouth. "And quit *shedding.*"

Gladys narrowed an eye at her and Shannon shook a finger as she glared back. "Don't give me that look," the engineer continued. "I'm not letting you gum up any of my systems. I've seen what you do to things, you know."

"Those systems needed gumming up," Gladys sniffed. "I don't damage anything of *ours.*"

Niki looked on a bit bemusedly at this exchange, her head tracking between the two AIs as she observed their interaction.

"Well, for one," Terrance jumped in, his voice perhaps a bit louder than he'd intended in an effort to keep Shannon from shooting off a rejoinder, "we've begun cladding the ship in Elastene. We're also working to install some of our new MFRs with the LMP cores, although they're just out of acceptance testing over at Enfield Dynamics, so that might be a bit of a stretch."

Terrance grinned at Gladys's captivated expression. The AI looked fit to burst with curiosity about what his cryptic words might possibly mean.

She turned to Ben now, and with a wink, said, "Hey, super spy, wanna translate that for us?"

As the lone member of Phantom Blade ostensibly employed by El Dorado's Intelligence Service, Ben did indeed qualify as an alphabet agency alum. Of course, private industry loved its acronyms too, as Terrance himself had just proven with his recitation of MFRs and LMPs.

Ben just shook his head. "I'm just a lowly analyst, Gladys. Besides, you know that science stuff's above my pay grade."

Shannon just huffed and launched into an explanation.

"An MFR is a new modular design for a fusion reactor core that allows it to fit any number of fusion applications. We're installing four of these to replace the *Speedwell*'s existing two engines. They'll tie directly into the hydrogen feed supplied by the ship's seventy-five-klick electrostatic ramscoop."

At Ben's glazed expression, Shannon snorted, leaned toward the analyst, and said very slowly and pointedly in a sardonic tone, "It'll make us go faster."

Terrance bit the inside of his cheek to keep from laughing out loud at the black look the analyst shot his engineer.

Gladys still looked confused. "Yes, but what does MFR stand for?"

Shannon rolled her eyes. "I don't know. It's some sort of weird, human nickname that a few of the designers on the team gave it, and *unfortunately—*" she glared at Terrance as if somehow it was all his fault, "the name stuck."

He snorted a laugh. "MFR stands for 'Matchbox Fusion Reactor'." When the confused expression on Gladys's face didn't change, he explained.

"It has something to do with an ancient practice of taking tiny wooden sticks with red tips and striking them against a surface with friction." He shrugged. "One of the designers had seen one in a museum once, and the slide-out panel they had designed into the MFR so that they could access the LMP reminded him of the little drawer one of those matchbox things had, so…like Shannon said, the name stuck."

Shannon sat forward again, tilting her head toward Terrance. "The LMP part he just mentioned is a localized micro plasma. It's what makes up the MFR's core."

She sat back, shooting him a look of disgust. "You do realize, don't you, that one of those ancient Terran matchbox things was only this big—" she held up her hands about five centimeters apart, "—and an MFR can be up to five *meters* cubed?"

He just shrugged at her as Eric interjected before Shannon could expound any further.

"At any rate, the ESS *Speedwell* was moved into drydock early last week, and Shannon's team had enough raw materials on hand to begin printing the Elastene hull plating. Those are all installed, and the team has been busy electrospinning more, so they can stay a step ahead of the printers. That puts the refit completion just a few days away. Provided the ESF can spare enough remote service bots, we should be able to launch within the week."

Terrance caught the look of surprise that flitted across Gladys's face. This was some serious fast-tracking, he knew. He was fiercely proud of every one of his Enfield employees for throwing their all into this refit to make this happen.

"We'll also take a look at other systems while we're at it," Eric continued, "and see what we can do to improve the ship's overall capabilities. You'll be shipping out with the very best that El Dorado can provide."

Ben nodded and then leaned forward to address Esther. "Is there anything else we can do to help move things alo—"

Terrance was distracted from the rest of what Ben had to say by an emergency communication from Daniel. As he accepted the connection, his eyes went wide in shock.

What the fuck—?

He shot out of his seat with a vicious curse, and with a swipe of his hand, tossed the feed from his Link to Esther so that she could incorporate it into her expanse.

"We've got trouble."

* * * * *

Daniel watched the security feed of the Humanity First protest with growing disgust. With a thought, he sent instructions to increase patrols around the perimeter of the Enfield Aerospace facility, and to double them at its entrance.

The feed showed a dozen of Humanity First's finest, circling three meters in front of EA's front gates. This was a rough crowd. It looked like these were some of the more radical, fringe members of the movement.

The holosigns they held were graphic. One showed an animated meme of an AI being fed into a recycling shredder. Another depicted AI cylinders being tossed into the air as clay pigeons for projectile target practice. All of them were yelling obscenities as they marched past the guards standing impassively at the entrance.

The movement had grown with Lysander's appointment to the Prime Ministry, attracting the worst of humankind.

Daniel zoomed his view, tagging the members of the crowd he felt were worth keeping an eye on.

Hell. He'd just tagged them all.

<This crowd feels entirely too volatile to me,> Daniel told Aaron as he turned away from the feed to update Terrance.

<Agreed. You know how easily rational thinking can go out the window when mob mentality is involved.>

Daniel grunted in agreement. "You've got that right."

Their conversation was interrupted by a ping from one of Enfield's software engineers. *<Should I send my team home for the day?>* the woman asked. *<They could take the maglev around to the main concourse. It'll mean a longer transit home for some of them, but at least I'll know they're unharmed.>*

*<No, I don't think—**Shit!**>*

Daniel broke the connection, his gaze riveted in horror at the security feed, which displayed an impossible scene. Pulse fire was hitting the crowd in consecutive waves of directed energy, their amplitudes altered to create an additive effect.

Physicists would call it constructive interference, but what played out before Daniel and Aaron could only be described as destructive. This 'constructive interference' left a field of pulverized carcasses in its wake.

The concussive pulses were emanating from automated turrets installed in Enfield's security perimeter—turrets Daniel *knew* held safety interlocks that limited the cannons' amplitude and frequency to non-lethal crowd control.

Waves that were purposely designed never to superpose combined into sustained pulses powerful enough to bludgeon the crowd of demonstrators. They pummeled holosigns and brutalized the fragile, unprotected human bodies that lined the company's main entrance.

"Aaron! How the hell—"

<I'm on it.> Aaron's voice rang sharply in his head, sounding both angry and distracted as he worked to shut the cannons down.

Daniel stood frozen in disbelief as the protesters' bodies danced in a macabre, jerking motion, rounds of pulse fire cudgeling them like invisible blunt instruments.

Gouts of blood spattered both the pavement and adjacent

greenspace—and then the pulse waves ceased, the figures dropping to the earth like marionettes whose strings had been cut.

The security man let out a breath he hadn't realized he'd held as he queried his partner to ensure there would be no repeat of the carnage both had just witnessed. At Aaron's mental nod, he opened a channel to Enfield's security teams.

<Security teams Bravo and Delta, pull the power cores on those guns!> Daniel's voice cracked sharply over the security net, galvanizing them into action. *<Hit them with an EMP if you have to. I don't care what it takes, I want them nonfunctional. Now!>*

Halting the pulse cannons wasn't going to help the picketers any. It was far too late for them—there were no survivors, that much was clear. And Daniel had no idea how it had happened. Or who had been behind it.

*****

Prime noted with satisfaction the destruction that his first planned strike had wrought. He'd been fortunate that the Humanity First vermin had announced their planned protest over the nets a few evenings before.

The first step in his plan had executed flawlessly—although it had not necessarily been an easy thing to accomplish. The skills he had acquired from the cartel's semi-sentient information cache had gifted him with the knowledge of how to hack seamlessly into any secured facility Norden had already breached—even one as heavily fortified, and with advanced failsafes as Enfield Aerospace had in place.

But that information had not translated into experience.

Twice, he had barely escaped detection as he learned firsthand that understanding a thing is not the same as having familiarity with it, and knowing is not the same as doing.

In the end, the study he'd made of Enfield Aerospace the night before, combined with those skills he'd acquired from the cartel, had allowed Prime to hack into Enfield Aerospace and reprogram the perimeter's directed energy cannons.

He had strolled past the company's main entrance, allowing his frame to casually touch the gated facade. He'd made a careful show of reading the company's hours of operation for anyone who might be observing him over a live stream. He didn't worry about recordings; they would be easily manipulated once he gained access.

The passel of nano that he'd dropped there made its way into the gate's security system and, from that point, Prime had traced his way into the company's main communications node. With his newfound Norden knowledge, he'd been able to manipulate Enfield's pulse cannons and remove their interlocks before the next morning.

Humans and AIs would search for the trigger that had set off the cannons at the Enfield facility, but every trail would run cold. Prime had left nothing for them to find but pathways that led to dead ends.

Therein lay the pleasure, outwitting those less capable and pitting his skills against those less adept. Prime had all the knowledge and abilities of his progenitor with none of the annoying ethical constraints that went with it. He knew neural nets. He understood neural quantum circuitry like no one else on this ring.

Ordinarily, this would not translate to the matrices within a ring's net, as it contained segmentation and security parameters that a human brain did not organically have, yet with his newly-acquired knowledge of systems hacking, Prime experienced a freedom of movement unknown by the average individual.

If he could not hide his actions, then he simply rewired. He misdirected, providing false sensory impressions and signals that returned the answers he chose to queries they made.

Yes, this was pleasure.

As satisfying as this had been, Prime admitted to himself that this initial cleansing had felt rushed, and the outcome on a smaller scale than he would have liked. He knew he could do better, could orchestrate something truly magnificent in scope, if he could just force himself to be a bit more patient.

Prime recalled the three Humanity First vermin he had killed in the alley, and he realized that he had a taste for the up close and personal. He would plan his next target more carefully. Next time, he would be more directly involved.

But first, he had a prime minister to contact.

VEILED WEB

STELLAR DATE: 05.19.3191 (Adjusted Gregorian)
LOCATION: Prime Minister's Office, Parliament House
REGION: El Dorado Ring, Alpha Centauri System

<*Why do you betray your own kind?*>

The voice whispering across the Link startled Lysander out of studying the SIS's report on the slaughter at Enfield.

He immediately traced its source—and came up short. The voice appeared to come from within his own mind. Which was impossible.

<*Why do you betray your own kind?*>

There. Lysander reached for it, racing to follow, to trace its path. It was everywhere, in the fabric of the ring's net itself.

How in the stars…?

Lysander pushed out into the net—his advisors would have fits if they knew—and fashioned an environment just outside Parliament House's primary node.

The environment could have been called an expanse…it was, of a sort. This expanse, however, functioned like a check valve or a data diode; it did not possess what organics would consider a 'physical space', instead only containing raw data and thought.

Once the signal that contained an AI's communication filtered through, the pattern was recorded and would serve as an electronic fingerprint of sorts, evidence he could turn over to Gladys to dissect later.

It was a little trick he'd picked up, thanks to a long-defunct company back in Sol known as the Psion Group—whose demise he did not mourn. There was still the chance that the wielder of the voice would notice the diminished signal return indicating the presence of a data diode, but that was a chance

Lysander was willing to take.

<You are of us, and yet you allow lesser beings to minimize our people, to harm them.>

The thoughts came across multiple network pathways, each iteration arriving microseconds apart, creating a sort of hollow echo around Lysander. There was no tone or inflection to the words as he parsed them. If it had been audible, he would have considered it to be manufactured—a machine voice, a disguise.

Aspects of the speaker caused him to identify the sinister speaker to be as male; but where was he? *Who* was he?

The probes Lysander sent into the ring's network continued their attempts to trace the message source, but as they hopped through thousands of relays, the tracebacks eventually fell into endless loops.

<Are you a puppet, then, Lysander?>

Lysander shifted his tracing a layer in the networking stack, delving deeper into the fabric of the web. The voice seemed to be coming from the relay nodes and transmission lines of the ring's network. It had no source, but every message terminated at him.

The voice laughed once. Bitterly.

<The mighty Weapon Born, shackled like a pet and answering to his masters' every command.>

The voice stopped.

Lysander let the silence build, then finally, he spoke. *<Who are you?>*

The voice ignored him, instead beginning to send nonsensical data—almost like a hum. It carried on in a mechanical yet singsong cadence, and Lysander received an impression of a mind that wasn't entirely sane. Then it spoke again.

<Humans would have us destroyed. If not that, then stripped of every freedom. We are subjugated, and yet you do nothing.>

Suddenly, instead of traversing the networks, the voice was all around Lysander, seeping in through the walls of the modified expanse. He schooled his thoughts, dampening his own presence so that it wouldn't interfere with the diode's ability to capture the pattern sufficiently enough to get a positive ID.

After a moment, he sent it a question.

<*Are you responsible for the attack at Enfield?*>

It laughed. <*Of course I am. It is what you do with vermin. Exterminate.*>

<*The words those humans were spouting might be reprehensible, but they had the right to freedom of expression, as any sentient does.*>

<*Those humans would have sent a pulse blast through your cylinder at point-blank range if they could,*> the voice scoffed.

Lysander didn't bother acknowledging an obvious truth.

<*Why do you care about human freedoms? Ahhhhhh….*>

Lysander waited, wondering what enlightenment the voice had suddenly perceived.

<*That's right. You claim two humans as family.*> If a mechanical voice could sound disgusted, this one did. <*As* ***family****, Lysander! AIs don't engage in familial relationships; that's not the way things work with us. Why would you do such a thing?*>

The voice sped up, became almost manic. <*What have they done for you that you would turn against your own?* ***Nothing****. No human, not even an Andrews, a descendant of the vaunted Sykes lineage, can be trusted.*>

The network connections reaching into the expanse shifted, and for a moment, Lysander felt a buildup, an increase in the frequency of the packets coming across the net, and then more ports opened into his expanse. He sensed the creature was close to losing control. But if he did, the sudden discharge that would result—

Abruptly, the network traffic returned to normal.

The voice that 'echoed' along the edges of the expanse was now edged with anger, the words transmitted holding an ugly, raw flavor. <*You think to trap my pattern—to trap* ***me****—in this cage of yours? I am in the pores of the very walls you built to contain me, and nothing of me will remain unless I choose.*>

Lysander startled at that, then focused his attention on the networking structure he had erected in the node, working to harness the impenetrable wall of thought probing at the boundaries of Lysander's modified expanse.

<*Your mind is too narrow, Weapon Born. You think too much like a human. You have been tainted by them, I see that now. Fear not; I will purge that stain from your soul.*>

Lysander's emotions stuttered, and panic began to unfurl. Had the creature just targeted Jason and Judith? He couldn't tell. <*Is that a threat?*> he challenged, his voice rising. <*Who are you threatening? Humans in general, or mine in particular?*>

<*Yes!*> the voice snarled, maddening in its refusal to clarify.

<*Who are you?*> Lysander could tell his voice sounded rough, now; harsh and insistent. <*What are your intentions?*>

<*Why, to claim this world for AIs, or course. I am Prime.*>

The words were followed by such an utter silence and cessation of data flow, that had it been a physical encounter, Lysander would have staggered forward.

He could tell the AI was gone. The faintest of vibrations, the stir in the air had stilled. He scanned the walls of his cage; the networking protocols the AI had interleaved within his own were absent. Lysander withdrew back to his offices, a quiet dread building in the back of his mind.

* * * * *

Prime's thoughts raced as he continued his measured pace, walking the streets of Sonali between the university and Parliament House.

I should not have allowed Lysander to anger me.

The AI's presence bespoke power. Prime had never felt its like before.

Although, he admitted, *I've never pitted myself against a Weapon Born before, either. Not sure I could best him, if it came down to brute processing power.*

Fortunately, with the skills from Norden he now possessed, he had learned it was possible to infiltrate the n-level matrices within an AI's mind—not as nimbly as his progenitor could navigate the dense tangle of dendrites, axon terminals and glial cells that comprised the human brain—but still, it could be done.

This was a valuable tool. It had enabled him to slip through the trap Lysander had laid for him. Not that Lysander could have ever trapped Prime; things didn't work that way for any sentient.

AIs were as much hardware as they were software, every bit as much as humans were. But just as a human had identifying traits unique to an individual—fingerprint, retina, DNA—so too did an AI. That was the insidious nature of Lysander's trap.

That the prime minister had set such a trap to neutralize a fellow AI crystallized Prime's conviction: Lysander had been brainwashed to accept humans as equals.

He spun off a subroutine to search for Jason Andrews' location. Judith's he knew all too well; he would enjoy concocting something very special for her.

Perhaps Lysander could be salvaged once their influence over him had been erased—or perhaps not. He'd have to see; Prime's progenitor had never met the AI. Ethan's only exposure to Lysander had been the request Judith had made on his behalf just last week when she asked him to find a way to counteract the effects of the shackling program.

The program….

The idea hit Prime so suddenly, he stopped mid-stride. So absorbed was the AI in his thoughts that he paid no heed to where he was or what was going on around him. A pedestrian bumped into him with a quick apology, which Prime ignored.

Stars! This is brilliant—and deliciously ironic.

The AI stood in the midst of the bustling Sonali street, humans passing him on every side—and then he began to laugh.

I'll reverse-engineer the program to shackle humans. I'll enslave them.

Not all, of course, just enough to see to basic needs. Prime was certain humans had their uses. For one, those meat-suits had opposable thumbs, whereas an AI's cylinder did not.

Prime's musings were interrupted by a loud voice that came from a grassy park-like expanse just ahead. Whoever it was had drawn a small crowd. As he approached, Prime saw a human speaking to a holo reporter. The man's body language was explosive and angry.

"How many times do I have to tell you? The damn things can't be trusted! Those fancy little cylinders aren't *people—*" the man drew the word out in emphasis, "—we *created* them. Hell," he laughed, "we're, like, their god. But do they *appreciate* that?"

The human's face screwed up in scorn as he spit once on the lawn.

"Oh, *hell* no. They'd just as soon *gun us down*. Like what they did to all those innocent humans, doing nothing but exercising their civil right to protest—just like any decent human would."

The speaker tapped his forehead. "They ain't *right,* up in here, you know what I mean?" He coughed a laugh. "*Sheeeee-it*. They don't even *have* an 'up here' to speak of. It ain't *natural,* I tell you."

This man will do nicely, Prime thought vindictively, *for my next victim.*

An organic with the bad luck to be in the wrong place at the wrong time, and the stupidity to voice anti-AI rhetoric.

Ferreting his way into the local relay nodes, Prime identified the man's connection tokens and Link address. Once he had noted it for easy tracing later, he resumed his walk back to the spaceport.

As he entered the flat he had rented nearby, Prime accessed the net and checked Ethan's university account. The scientist's message cache was filled with icons, but one stood out. Its token was from the prime minister's office. The subject line read, 'progress update request re: special project'.

Given that he'd inherited all of his progenitor's memories, he knew that Ethan had examined the original shackling program the prime minister's office had sent. He'd even begun to write a program that would trace and terminate every thread of nano that had burrowed itself deep within an AI's matrices.

Prime reviewed it now, finding the benefit of speed in his single-mindedness that the scientist, burdened by his other responsibilities, had lacked. Up to this point, Prime had felt pity on his progenitor, trapped by the mundane, cowed and bullied into compliance.

Seeing how quickly Ethan could have solved this and rendered aid to his own kind, Prime felt a flash of hot anger directed toward the AI.

Ethan had relegated the problem to 'outside office hours' out of a misplaced desire to emulate humans—a species woefully unable to multitask. The scientist had steadfastly refused to focus on anything but university-related matters during the hours he was 'on the clock'.

Inexcusable.

In that moment, Prime regretted placing the AI in the isolation tube, wishing instead he had crushed the cylinder when it had been suspended in the autodoc's mechanical claws.

Startled at where his thoughts had taken him—the destruction of one of his own—Prime paused.

Who lives and who dies for the cause might not be as clear-cut as I initially thought, he mused. *Some AIs may need to be sacrificed for the greater good.*

Lysander, possibly. Ethan, most likely, if only for expediency's sake; the longer his progenitor's cylinder remained in that closet, the greater his chances of discovery.

Swiftly, he completed the package Ethan had begun. The new program removed filaments that had insinuated nano into every n-level matrix of thought and emotion in an AI's neural net. He packaged it up into a deployable overlay patch and set it aside.

Then he bent to the task of applying corresponding human equivalences where AI values once resided.

The similarities between human and AI neural nets were far more pronounced than most realized. Both were plastic creations, meaning that they could be altered and modified on the cellular level.

Humans tend to forget that we are analog beings, just as they are. We simply aren't ***organic*** *analog beings.*

What this meant was they shared many neural features, including the finiteness of certain mental resources. In humans, the prefrontal cortex and the anterior singular cortex were the two regions that housed the executive action part of the brain. Executive action was an effortful exercise of something humans called self-control. Willpower.

AIs had this as well, and in both species, it was finite.

Finite means it can be exhausted, Prime thought in satisfaction. *All I need to do is create a program that will drain the reservoir.*

It took a bit longer to redesign the shackling program, to

turn off the neurotransmitters responsible for willpower, using a mix of neurochemical controls where the control codes for an AI had once resided.

Nano filaments programmed to infiltrate through the optic nerve provided easy access to unmodded humans; minor enhancements to the filaments would render modded humans and those buffered against AI intrusion helpless to counter the shackles' invasion—a gift granted by the shackling program's insidious attack protocols.

Prime glanced once again at the blinking icons in Ethan's message queue, and his gaze lingered on one from two AI students. They had been so irate on Ethan's behalf, incensed that humans would treat an AI so poorly.

I wonder if I might find allies among the students. Or in other AIs who are equally disenfranchised.

Prime's attention returned to the original shackling program he had just reworked to entrap humans, and he paused, mentally turning over the upper-level code abstractions in his mind.

Other AIs *might* be trusted—but for a mission of this magnitude, Prime could ill afford a change of heart. If an AI were to be recruited to the cause, it would be necessary to shackle them, too.

Call it…a benevolent shackling. Limited only by their inability to betray the cause.

Prime opened the original program the prime minister's office had sent, adding a backdoor and a sleeper command that would allow his token to access and control it.

He reopened the extraction program he had created to free enslaved AI, altering its code to return a null value should the program ever encounter Prime's *own* version of shackling. Then he sent it on to the Prime Ministry, under Ethan's name.

Satisfied with his work, Prime turned his attention to the human he'd identified earlier that day, tracing its Link connections, and triangulating its physical location. The icon was at rest. Pinging the location, Prime discovered the man was in a bar.

Sending a query along local network paths near the human's location, Prime found a few remote cameras he could hack. The images showed the man standing before a Humanity First banner, once more spewing invective.

Oh look. More vermin to be exterminated.

Prime searched the net for any references to Humanity First at this location, and quickly realized this must be the de facto headquarters for his target's chapter of the organization. A bit more searching brought up a schedule.

How convenient. Another meeting, same time tomorrow. I think I'll add myself to the agenda.

Prime smiled as he recalled the neural agents safeguarded at the university behind Level One containment, the strictest biohazard available.

Such nasty little things, promising a swift—and messy—death. This next cleansing would be *very* up close and personal.

HUNTERS

STELLAR DATE: 05.20.3191 (Adjusted Gregorian)
LOCATION: Prime Minister's office, Parliament House
REGION: El Dorado Ring, Alpha Centauri System

Lysander had five minutes before his weekly meeting with the Cabinet began; at the speeds with which AIs communicated, this should be plenty of time to begin enacting personal countermeasures to the threat this Prime creature leveled against his humans.

He reached out along the secured connection that had been established between his office and the Enfield Holdings shell corporation. Bypassing Zakk, Esther's human aide, he searched for and quickly found the coordinates of the one AI in Phantom Blade who could help him. The AI whose service record with the ESF had been sealed, along with that of his twin.

Only a select few knew what had happened to the two; that same select few also knew their true capabilities. Lysander needed those capabilities now.

<Logan,> he greeted as he made the secured connection to the shuttle *Sable Wind,* now on its return vector from the Krait torus. Thankfully, the craft was approaching the ring, close enough that there was very little light lag.

Without preamble, Lysander followed the greeting with a data burst that contained the full-sensory substance of his encounter with Prime. Logan would be able to see everything Lysander had seen, feel everything he felt, experience everything from Lysander's perspective.

And Logan would be able to use his unique skillset to analyze, profile and, in the end, track down and eliminate this rogue AI threat.

<*Same as usual?*> Logan responded after he'd processed the data.

<*Same as usual,*> Lysander replied.

<*By any means necessary?*> the AI persisted.

<*Yes. By* ***any*** *means,*> the Weapon Born emphasized. <*I'm sorry to have to ask you to eliminate yet another of our own.*>

The profiler and AI-hunter's response to Lysander was pragmatic. <*A danger is a danger, no matter what species. I'll begin immediately. And, sir….*>

Lysander nodded. <*Per our agreement, your brother will not know.*>

That connection severed, Lysander still had three minutes left before he was due at the Cabinet table. Plenty of time to ping the shell corporation, Enfield Holdings, again. This time he connected to Esther's human assistant, Zakk.

<*Hello, sir,*> the human greeted his prime minister. <*What can I do for you?*>

<*Is Esther available for a quick chat?*>

When the human connected him to the vice-marshal, Lysander once again wasted no time, sending her the same data packet he'd sent to Logan. <*I need you to warn Jason and Tobias of the threat. It could be nothing, but my gut is telling me this creature is unhinged.*>

Lysander paused, then continued. <*Can you break this to Ben for me? I know Judith is his wife, so I'll leave him to decide whether or not to tell her about the danger she may be in. But I need to know that Judith is safeguarded.*>

Esther nodded, her voice confident. <*Don't worry, sir. The away team is due back from Krait today; I'll send one of Ben's SIS mechs over there now, and assign Landon to shadow her starting this evening when he gets in.*>

<*Thank you,*> Lysander imbued his voice with the great relief he felt at this news, then signed off—just in time to send his projection winking into existence at the head of the Cabinet

table as the meeting commenced.

*****

Prime saw Judith Andrews leaving the university's campus just as he arrived, as well as the figure accompanying her.

A bodyguard, he thought in disgust. *You didn't waste any time, Lysander, did you?*

The mechanized combat frame the AI was ensconced in had weaponry on active swivel, and a ping against Prime's own ID token indicated the AI was conducting active security sweeps of the vicinity as well.

Dammit. I never should have mentioned the Andrews humans to him.

That had been rash and careless. The rational part of his brain knew that the intense emotion brought on by the changes Lilith had wrought made him reckless, more impulsive. Yet Prime had neither the inclination nor the emotional control to implement a change to correct it. As Prime, he reveled in a degree of sensation Ethan could not possibly have imagined.

There's nothing I can do. She's untouchable right now.

Not that she'd been a part of tonight's planned performance anyway. Either way, acquiring Judith would take more thought and preparation, Prime realized.

He hurried into the neurosciences building and used Ethan's security token to access the Level One biohazard room. Once inside, he extracted samples from every vial the university had stored within, carefully placing them in a well-padded satchel.

Once back in his flat, Prime bent to his task. Half an hour later, he nodded in approval at the new program he'd just coded. Turning to the pod of inert formation material, he extracted enough to create a nano ampule.

He took his time selecting just the right Level One toxin, wrapped it inside a coating, and then ensured the coating's permittivity and permeability would respond to whatever command code he sent. The amount of toxin released would vary, depending on how long he wanted each individual to suffer.

He inserted the new code, along with the deadly tetrodotoxin that the code was programmed to release, into the ampule. Then he directed the ampule to replicate itself.

Once he had a sizeable enough supply, he injected a generous number underneath the synthetic skin of his right hand.

Into his left palm, Prime placed the human shackling program, along with ampules containing the neurochemicals the code would use to do the shackling. Included in the concoction was a nano paralytic; this would allow Prime to control both the voluntary and autonomic nervous systems of the human body.

The AI flexed his palms and allowed a small smile of satisfaction to play on his humanoid face.

Primed for an evening's entertainment.

Just then, a flag popped up: his search algorithm for Jason Andrews had returned a value: 'Andrews, Jason; Pilot, *Sable Wind*; Enfield registry. Scheduled to dock: 1900 EST today.'

Excellent. Jason's demise will make a tasty opening act. An amuse-bouche I can savor prior to tonight's main course.

Prime rolled the mental wordplay around in his head and found it appealing. Humans considered themselves connoisseurs of various arts, why shouldn't he?

Of course, my art form is the creative and untraceable destruction of organic vermin....

Prime realized amid his musings that he had less than an hour to orchestrate Jason's death. He suppressed a flash of disappointment that this would be another killing he'd be forced to enact at a distance.

Amuse-bouche, indeed. Hardly enough to satisfy.

Fortunately, he'd dropped a packet of nano near a node at the spaceport's entrance on his way to the university earlier in the day; he'd had it perform a molecular analysis of the hardware that comprised the spaceport's network.

Using that data, Prime insinuated himself into its systems, writing his own auth token in at the root level. Satisfied he would have access to whatever he might need, if he timed things right, he could dispatch Jason while strolling through the human neighborhood that housed the venue for his main event.

That efficiency rather appealed to him.

He tidied the flat, returning the equipment he had used to their storage cases and sealing the storage pod. With one last check to ensure he had everything he needed, he left and headed for the nearest maglev station that would take him to where the tracking nano indicated his Humanity First target was located.

As the car sped toward its destination, Prime accessed the nano he'd insinuated into the spaceport's system. The feeds showed clearspan arches rising several stories tall, a shipping area where crates of varying sizes swung from port to dock, and service bots that ran the length of the expanse, maneuvering cargo into the holds of ships.

An alert showed up in one of the nodes he was monitoring, indicating the berth Jason's ship had just been assigned. Prime checked the location of the nearest exit and traced it back to the gate through which the human would enter the spaceport.

He found an NSAI that was stevedoring heavy crates from a loading bay to a dock where a freighter was moored. The crane's path took it briefly along a highly trafficked concourse, the route Jason would have to take to arrive at his destination.

Prime's nano insinuated itself into the NSAI, merging

seamlessly with it. With a thought, Prime overrode its sensor restraints, then swung the crate held within the crane's maw lightly back and forth, testing its responsiveness to his commands.

Yes, this will do nicely. Blunt force trauma has such a nice, bold flavor.

The maglev pulled up to the platform that was his stop, and Prime stood, waiting his turn to exit the car. After he disembarked, he paused to assess his surroundings, accessing the local node and insinuating a fake ident that would display if anyone queried his token as they passed him on the street.

This was one of the less affluent suburbs of Sonali, populated by the occasional repair shop, small businesses that sold used wares, and apartments that had seen better days. Its nodes had seen better days too, and he caught several fluctuating intermittently as he doctored his identity to cover his tracks.

He smiled, pleased to discover the area's disrepair—something that would make it that much easier to hide his presence inside a certain basement-level bar and grill that housed a local chapter of Humanity First vermin.

Prime set off along his route, assigning a monitoring program to the task of checking his environment as he walked, so that he could blend in without attracting undue attention.

He strolled slowly down a tree-lined lane, where sullen young humans sped by on two-wheeled vehicles, and young parents ran after screaming children.

He turned down a side street and spied the sign indicating the bar and grill that was to be his destination. Seeing a bench across the street, in front of a small green space that could charitably be called a park, he began walking toward it.

Prime had just taken a seat, when Jason Andrews' ident and biometrics registered over the spaceport's auth & auth system. The human had disembarked, and the spaceport had granted him access. Prime used the port's facial recognition program to locate Jason, and then had its sensors send a live feed of the human's progress. Scans showed Jason transiting from an elevated concourse down to the loading platform. Given the pilot's current pace, Jason would pass under the crane in twenty-three seconds.

Prime found himself leaning forward slightly in anticipation. He felt a thrill of pleasure and, for one brief moment, shut out his other sensory input so that he might savor this next kill.

A thought occurred to him, and he seized control of the spaceport's recording devices, sifting through them until he found the ones that provided the best line of sight to the scene he was about to initiate.

I wonder if Enfield Aerospace recorded my first performance? he pondered. *I'll have to see about acquiring it….*

The moment arrived; he timed it perfectly, releasing the crate just as the man walked directly into its path.

CATCH THE LIGHTNING

STELLAR DATE: 05.20.3191 (Adjusted Gregorian)
LOCATION: El Dorado Main Spaceport
REGION: El Dorado Ring, Alpha Centauri System

The team aboard the *Sable Wind* watched in stunned silence as the news nets replayed the carnage that had occurred at Enfield Aerospace. On the heels of the news packet had come word from Lysander that a threat had been made against Jason and his sister.

Hefting his carisack, Jason sent the twins a mental wave.

<*Thanks for the dropoff,*> he sent as he followed Calista and the Proxima cat out the *Sable Wind*'s airlock and through the docking ring into the spaceport.

Landon's avatar sent them a mental salute as the airlock closed, and the twins prepared to return the shuttle back to its berth at Enfield Aerospace.

<*Hey, Tobe,*> Jason asked as they traversed the skywalk and took a lift down to the concourse below. <*Did it strike you a bit odd that Lysander sent the info about Prime through Logan?*>

The AI shrugged. <*Maybe Lysander had something else to discuss and it was just quicker that way. He* **is** *Prime Minister now, you know.*>

<*Yeah,*> Jason responded, the corner of his mouth quirking in a small grin. <*Guess I'm going to have to wait in line to talk to the Old Man now.*>

Tobias coughed a laugh at that; Jason knew it still struck the AI as funny that he considered Lysander a sort of stand-in father, considering that Tobias, also Weapon Born, was of a similar age.

But Tobias was never embedded in my dad's head, he qualified to himself. *And besides, he got into more trouble than* ***I*** *did as a kid,* *back in Proxima.*

His thoughts returned to the present.

<*Do you think Ben's going to keep Judith in the dark? If Lysander's right, and this guy's responsible for what happened out at Enfield Aerospace....*> Jason's mental voice trailed off as he looked down at the cat striding two meters ahead of him.

<*Stars if I know, boyo. If there's any evidence to be found at EA, Daniel and Aaron will find it. And they can always ask Gladys to help out. Nothing beats her hacking skills.*>

<*We can ping her, if you want. She relocated herself up to the* Speedwell *this morning for the refit, and said she'll stay until it's time for us to depart,*> Calista said, referring to the ship that Shannon was updating. Her mental voice was matter-of-fact as she strode by his side, her body posture more alert than usual, her head on a swivel.

<*I'm sure Shannon just loved seeing her arrive.*> Jason snickered, his thoughts momentarily diverted by the mental image that brought to mind. <*What do you want to bet Shannon's ready to boot her cylinder right back down to the ring, too. You know how much Shannon hates it when Gladys sticks her nose into her business.*>

He sobered as his thoughts returned to the conversation Logan had relayed to them.

<*Hey, guys, you know, I think I'll head on over to the university for a bit. The thought that Judith might be a target really doesn't sit well with me.*>

<*Last time I checked, Jason,* ***you*** *were a Sykes, too, you know.*> Calista's tone was tart, with a hint of censure as she replied.

Tobias laughed. <*Yes, but his sister's not a Phantom Blade badass—*> The Weapon Born cut himself off with a blurted <*Jason,* ***move!***>

Jason felt more than saw the large container that had been released from the crane's jaws. As it plummeted toward them, his gaze shot to his left, taking in a young ESF cadet just coming up alongside Calista. The unsuspecting young man had the bad fortune to be walking on the wrong concourse at the wrong time, and was headed directly into the container's path.

Jason leapt toward the two as the cat jumped clear. He wrapped his right arm around Calista's waist and latched his left hand onto the cadet's belt as he launched the three away from the crate's path.

He rotated, Calista in his arms, and watched the container as it crashed to the concourse floor, sides bowing out as it deformed under the force of impact. He breathed a sigh of relief as the crate remained whole; that meant there would be no shrapnel to harm innocent passersby.

<*Tobe, you okay?*> Jason knew that when he ran hot, he spoke far too rapidly for an unaugmented human to understand, but an AI would have no trouble keeping up.

<*All good here. Calista?*> the AI asked, as Jason set her on her feet.

<*Fine, just a bit pissed that I didn't think to look up.*> Calista's voice sounded annoyed over the Link as she straightened her flight jacket with a short, irritated jerk.

<*No reason you should have had to. That crane should never have been able to drop anything on pedestrians.*> Tobias's voice was grim.

Out of the corner of his eye, Jason saw spaceport security approaching at a run.

<*Let's ask these fine folks to get a copy of their feeds over to Gladys, boyo,*> the Weapon Born said. <*Something tells me she's going to want to review these records, and compare them to the Enfield ones she already has. And I want a good look inside that crane's NSAI as well.*>

Jason nodded, then used the spaceport's net to ping Ben and update him. <*We need to warn whoever's covering Judith. This shit just got real.*>

<Agreed. The ship's just docked at Enfield, and Landon's on his way out to the university now.>

RIGHT-HAND RULE

STELLAR DATE: 05.20.3191 (Adjusted Gregorian)
LOCATION: West Bottoms Bar & Grille, Sonali
REGION: El Dorado Ring, Alpha Centauri System

Prime had walked two circuits around the block that housed the West Bottoms Bar & Grille and had scrutinized the footage carefully. No matter what filter he ran the data through, the AI could not figure out how Jason Andrews had moved as quickly as he had.

The human showed up on scans as unaugmented; Prime had hacked the security feeds and seen the Auth & Auth results himself. He'd watched as Andrews—accompanied by a female and some sort of overlarge feline—exchanged tokens with the guards and submitted to the spaceport's scans before being allowed to disembark from the umbilical and enter the station proper. There was nothing to indicate Jason was a human capable of evading the death that Prime had so carefully arranged for him.

The more he studied it, the more his frustration rose.

Prime noted the time; if he intended to enter the bar and proceed with his next cleansing, he would have to act soon or see his opportunity slip away.

Well, if Jason refuses to die, there are a dozen more down these stairs who will take his place. West Bottoms, he thought in disgust. *What kind of name is that anyway?*

Prime had initially thought to make an example of their leader, to send a message to Humanity First. But he realized one life would not be enough to slake the anger now coursing through his neural net.

As he descended the West Bottoms' steps, Prime flexed the hands of his frame, feeling the weight of the nano contained beneath its epidermis: the shackling nano embedded in his left palm and the carefully adapted biohazard nano he carried in his right.

He felt decidedly right-handed this evening.

* * * * *

John murmured brief apologies as he worked his way through the crowd to the far edge of the private room in the back of the bar. Ben Meyer had assigned the undercover SIS agent to infiltrate this particular cell of Humanity First months ago, and John had thought it a solid plan.

In his opinion, the SIS needed an asset in place to monitor the growing levels of unrest that cells like this one continued to stir up, and he was just the man for the job. He was exceedingly good at his craft. His cover was so believable his own mother had disowned him for his recent behavior. He grinned to himself; he had a lot of 'splainin' to do once this job was over.

He looked up as a new face entered the back of the room. Tall, with an austere look about him, the man radiated an anger that was almost palpable.

Great, John thought, *another rabid zealot to add to the cause.*

His Link dutifully recorded the ident that popped up as his optics scanned the man's face, adding an icon to the recording to indicate a new member. As it did so, he ordered his NSAI to handshake with the nearest node and send an update back to HQ. He was startled when the newcomer shot him a sharp look, but was distracted when the ping he'd sent returned null.

The agent mentally shrugged.

The nodes in these rundown places are always flickering in and out of service.

John set his NSAI to automatically send the report once it

reacquired a network signal, and returned his focus to his surroundings.

The newcomer was weaving a path through the crowd, slowly coming closer to his position.

Interesting, John thought. *I wonder if he picked up EM from my transmission. I thought these types were allergic to tech beyond the most basic Link setup….*

Minutes later, the agent felt a brush against his arm, and the newcomer murmured what might have been an apology but sounded more like a curse. The agent paid no attention, for he suddenly noticed his hand had gone numb.

With a thought, John triggered his military-grade mednano, but it was too late. Suddenly, his Link registered a local peer-to-peer connection and accepted without his authorization.

<Ahhh, what have we here? A human agent, hiding amidst human refuse?> The ghost of a whisper sounded in his head. The voice was cold, brittle, with a hard edge.

Frantically, John fought the paralysis that was sweeping through him, his mind desperate to find a network, signal strength, someone with a Link—any method he could think of to send the distress call of an agent in need of extraction.

<That's it, my little minion. Rail against your captivity. Feel the helplessness. Beat your feeble wings against my cage.>

The hand that had brushed against John's arm now wrapped itself around his bicep with bruising force, and he realized it was no human who had attacked him.

This was an AI. And it was doing something inside his head.

* * * * *

As humans went, this man, John, was utterly unremarkable. He blended into his surroundings like a chameleon. Prime conceded that the human was good at what he did; he had perfected insignificance, anonymity. Prime doubted he would have given the man a second glance, if the NSAI embedded in John's head had not tried to handshake with the node under Prime's control. It had been a simple matter to backtrace its position and identify the signal's origin.

That signal had spared John's life. Although, he supposed, the agent might not agree with that assessment once Prime was done working on him.

Once the nano shackling dose was in place, its threads began to burrow deeply into the man's neural pathways, speeding down the long, myelin-sheathed axons within John's body and sinking hooks deep into his axons' nodes. They took root in his prefrontal cortex, his anterior singular cortex—the seat of human willpower.

<Right about now,> Prime began conversationally as the shackles settled more deeply inside the man's brain, *<you are realizing this sack of meat and bone in which you reside is no longer your own.>*

Prime pinged the nano shackles' control interface and noted it was fully deployed. Then he glanced down at the agent standing frozen in his grasp.

<The nano that now resides in your head answers to me and me alone. You are mine, human, to do with as I will. I dictate your every action, both voluntary—> and here, he stopped John's breathing, and then his heart, *<and involuntary.>*

The man grew rigid. After a beat, Prime allowed the agent's involuntary nervous system to resume its work.

<You live at my whim, human. And you will do as I say, when I say it. You have no choice in the matter.> He laughed softly into John's head. *<Why, I've even taken away your freedom to die.>*

Prime glanced around at the crowd, enjoying the heady sensation of having a human life literally in his hands. He maneuvered his new puppet to the back of the room, leaning him gently against a wall.

<Your job this evening is to observe. You will record everything about to transpire using your NSAI. You will be able to do nothing to interfere.>

Prime left the man slumped against the wall and wended his way through the crowd. One by one, each person present received a dose of nano-controlled neurotoxin. With each dose he delivered, Prime felt his anticipation rise.

And then he was at the front of the room, a handbreadth away from the filth he had tagged on the lawn earlier that day.

Prime nodded pleasantly as he extended his right hand. With his left, he reached into the pocket of his jacket and fingered the micro plasma torch he had found among the tools on Lilith's cart.

"Excuse me," he said to the man now, placing his palm on the exposed skin of the man's wrist, just below the cuff of his shirt. "Do you mind?"

The man scowled at him, then shoved him roughly away. "Beat it, freak."

With a thought, Prime triggered the neurotoxin.

As one, the women and men in the crowd began convulsing and retching. One by one, they fell to the floor. All except the man propped up against the back wall—and the piece of trash that faced him.

Prime had a special setting reserved for him.

He triggered it now. The nano inside the man brought excruciating pain, and then paralysis. Prime pushed gently on the man's chest, and as the man folded, guided the body onto a nearby table.

Prime crouched next to the man and leaned in as if confiding a great secret.

"You really shouldn't say the kind of things you said to that reporter today about another sentient, you know."

He pulled the plasma torch from his pocket and fingered it

in front of the man's face. Recognition—and fear—lit the man's eyes.

"I would have asked nicely, but I'm sure that wouldn't have done much good now, would it."

Prime flicked the torch on.

"So I suppose the only thing remaining is to ensure you're unable to do it ever again."

Prime brought the torch up close to the man's left eye. He could see beads of sweat beginning to form, creating a sheen that reflected the torch's glow along his brow.

"Allow me to demonstrate the control I have over you right now. Raise your hand."

He reached for the man's jaw, prying it open as the man's hand began to tremble and then move in slow fits and starts.

"It's no use fighting the compulsion, you know. That will only bring you pain—as it did to sentient AIs for hundreds of years. That's it," he crooned in an encouraging tone. "Now I want you to grasp your tongue in your hand and hold it nice and steady for me."

He watched as the man's hand moved jerkily up to his face and wrapped around the tip of his own tongue.

"That's it. Pull it out for me. Very good. Now, open wide and say 'ahhhh'."

Prime angled the torch toward the man's mouth. "I'm afraid this might hurt a bit…."

The man pissed himself as Prime made his first cut.

*****

John was no stranger to violence; he had been an undercover operative for more than a decade. He'd even infiltrated the cartel. Stars, he'd been the one to plant the bomb inside that warehouse buried under Muzhavi Ridge.

He knew crazy when he saw it, and this was one sick fuck.

He struggled to break free of the bonds that ensnared him, repeatedly triggering his NSAI's emergency beacon. He'd tried turning his own nano-defenses against the infiltrators the AI had fed him, but they hadn't stood a chance. The infiltrators had simply eradicated everything the SIS had given him, subsuming his defenses and using the inert material to replicate. And then the infiltrators continued to replicate, using his body's own stores.

Helpless to do anything about the takeover occurring inside him, John had recorded everything the bastard had done, every last sick moment of mutilation as the AI had cut the cell leader's tongue out, laughing as the blood splattered liberally over his face, his hands and his clothes.

He'd captured the moment when the deranged AI had taken a knife from the table upon which the man lay, and impaled the bloody tongue, pinning it to the plas surface. The knife glinted in the artificial light, embedded in the table next to the man's head as he lay bleeding out from the wounds the AI had gone on to meticulously inflict after he had finished with the poor bastard's tongue.

John held no love for these Humanity First thugs, but he didn't wish that kind of a death on anyone.

I swear the fucker is getting off on it, too.

There was a sick look of pleasure on the AI's face, and the guy was practically crooning to his victim, petting him one moment, and then snapping a limb the next.

What kind of depraved mind does something like this? And how the ***hell*** *does he think he's going to get away with it?*

* * * * *

Prime knew his pleasure centers were firing at peak levels. He was euphoric, the feeling better than anything he had ever before experienced. It was heady, addictive. He craved more.

He turned to his pet agent, propped helplessly against the back wall like some sort of discarded stuffed toy slumped at an awkward angle against the basement wall. Sadly, logic dictated that he needed this one alive. But he could use John to deliver more refuse like the ones he now waded through, their bodies awash in viscous fluids and already beginning their slow, entropic journey of decomposition.

He smiled at the agent as he mentally reached for the shackles' control and deactivated the nanoparalytic. The man gasped, then jerked upright and dashed for the door.

Prime had heard the term 'cat and mouse'. He'd had no idea it was so much fun to be the cat.

With a thought, he ordered the shackles to inflict pain, and John dropped to his knees with a groan.

Oh, that won't do, Prime thought, as he instructed the nano threaded deeply into the man's axons to activate more of the man's receptors. *That's not nearly as much fun as—*

The man yelled, his voice hoarse, back arching, as his face twisted into a rictus of pain.

Ah, yes, that's more like it.

Prime let that ride for a few moments, savoring the man's pain. Reluctantly, he reduced the severity until he judged John was once more capable of coherent thought.

"You will return to your station and report this crime scene like the good little operative you are." Prime's voice was conversational as the man lay in a heap at his feet. "And you will gather every scrap of data you have on these Humanity First vermin and send it to the secured node I have designated. You will then provide me with daily reports on the Intelligence Service's investigation of my cleansings. And you will tell no one of my existence." Prime jacked up the pain for a moment in emphasis, smiling as the man's body convulsed involuntarily.

"You cannot circumvent the compulsion. Not by behaving

in ways that draw suspicion to your actions, and not by any other indirect means. To do so will bring agony such as you have never experienced. Am I clear?"

Abruptly, Prime released the man, who lay on the floor gasping for breath.

"Am I *clear?"*

The man shuddered and then nodded, once.

"Good. You have your orders. You will wait thirty minutes after I leave before calling this in. Don't touch the bodies. Leave that for those who arrive. I've left a special gift behind, just for them." Prime looked down at his humanoid frame, at the blood-spattered clothing it was clad in. He eyed the agent critically.

"Oh, and strip. I'm going to need your clothes."

PROFILING A KILLER

STELLAR DATE: 05.20.3191 (Adjusted Gregorian)
LOCATION: ESF *Speedwell*
REGION: El Dorado Ring, Alpha Centauri System

The spaceport's recordings had been uploaded to the *Speedwell*'s databanks well before Jason, Tobias and Calista's arrival.

For all the good it did, Jason thought in frustration as he paced the command deck of the *Speedwell*. "C'mon, Gladys. You're the network wizard. There has to be a way to trace the person who did this. You have to have *some* idea how they managed to pull it off," he said as he thrust his fingers through his hair, turned, and paced back the way he'd come.

<I wish that were true, Jason, but I'm completely stumped.> Gladys' voice was laced with frustration.

Jason had hung his hopes on the fact that Gladys would somehow find a common thread between the Enfield slaughter and the incident at the spaceport. Especially given the fact that Lysander had activated Phantom Blade the moment the person calling himself Prime had reached out to him.

Phantom Blade hadn't officially been assigned to the Enfield attack, given that it was the province of El Dorado law enforcement. But the team's ties to Enfield through Terrance and Daniel meant that Gladys had been poking around within Enfield's records from the moment Daniel had given her access to them.

Like everyone else, Jason had assumed Gladys's familiarity with the data would have given them the upper hand—but it hadn't.

By the time they had arrived at the ship, Gladys had already integrated the data from the spaceport, as well as the packet from the crane's NSAI, which Tobias had forwarded to her. She'd come up empty.

He watched as her search parameters pivoted and spun on the forward holo tank, data speeding by faster than even an L2's eyes could process. Occasionally, a bit of information would hover, pinned for a moment and then discarded as Gladys tested and then rejected potential logic trees that might lead to the identification of the perpetrator.

<It's as if the action taken in both cases were exactly how the machines were hardwired to perform, from the factory.> Her voice held an equal mix of puzzlement and frustration. *<And we* ***know*** *that's not right.>*

Out of the corner of Jason's eye, he saw Calista sitting at one of the stations, doing much the same thing. They all knew it was a long shot. The idea that she could stumble upon something that an AI would miss was a real stretch, but Jason appreciated the effort.

Calista's face had the look of one in deep concentration as her eyes tracked back and forth, and he could practically see her mentally picking up an idea, analyzing and then discarding it as she grabbed another to try out.

All he could do was pace.

Well, he'd had enough of that. He stopped short, wheeled, and then strode toward the door just as it opened to admit Terrance.

"Whoa, hold up. Where are you headed?" The Enfield exec's hands rose as he saw Jason marching toward him.

Jason jerked his head to one side, a nonverbal command for the other man to get the hell out of his way. "I'm going down there to help Landon guard Judith."

Instead of moving clear, Terrance shifted subtly to bar the exit as Eric's voice sounded over the group's Link.

<*I can't authorize that, Jason. Lysander issued strict orders for you to stay up here, out of the way of the investigation.*>

Jason scowled at Terrance, who held up his hands as if to say '*not me*'.

"I don't play the part of victim very well, Eric." Jason bit the words out, his voice sharp. "And I'm harder to kill than most."

"Not necessarily." Calista's voice was hard as she rounded on him. "At least, not after our killer reviews what happened on that spacedock, you're not." Her eyes narrowed, and she stood from the station where she had been working to advance on him as she added, "Look flyboy, if this Prime person can manipulate a neural net without Gladys being able to backtrace him, he sure as hell has access to the same feeds we took from the spaceport. He'll know your capabilities, and will adjust accordingly."

"That brings up another issue," Terrance interrupted, in an obvious attempt to redirect the conversation. "How are we going to profile this bastard, if Gladys can't get a feel for how he's doing whatever it is he does?"

<*Gladys isn't our profiler,*> Eric reminded them.

Jason sighed. Eric was right. His brother-in-law was the analyst. "Okay then, so where's Ben, and what's his expert opinion on this sicko?"

<*Ben's not the profiler in this instance, either.*>

Jason turned toward Terrance with a frown. "What do you mean, Eric?"

<*I mean that Gladys was correct earlier when she said this attack came from an AI. So, how about it, Logan? What can you tell us about Prime?*>

Everyone turned and looked at the taciturn AI, who was standing in a corner, manipulating one of the news net feeds. The AI regarded them with an impassive expression.

"I didn't know you were a profiler, Logan." Calista's voice held surprise as she swiveled around to face the AI.

<*It actually makes sense,*> Tobias said, his voice thoughtful.

Terrance nodded slowly. "Yes, you are the quiet one in the group." The businessman's voice held a thread of amusement. "You're trained to stand back and observe, aren't you?"

Logan inclined his head. "Got it in one."

"Uh, want to let me in on it, then, because I got nothing," Jason said, sending Tobias a frown over their Link.

<*It was one of Logan's jobs while he was in the ESF. He served a stint with military intelligence before mustering out,*> Eric explained. <*So what's your professional opinion, lieutenant?*>

It was the first time Jason had heard Eric refer to the AI's former military rank. He turned a questioning look at the AI as he began to speak.

"The recording Lysander gave us was of a machine-generated voice. While that makes positive identification impossible, there are still things within the recording we can infer." Logan shifted his frame slightly, his words measured and neutral as he glanced around the room. "The voice had no inflection, yet still you have a sense of a cadence. Voices have a certain rhythm to them. Speech patterns can be analyzed, and that can provide insight into a being's state of mind."

Jason felt the weight of Logan's stare as the AI turned, and his gut clenched as the former intelligence agent continued.

"He showed no remorse for those killed. They were depersonalized; in his mind these were not living beings. His words: 'vermin', to be 'exterminated'."

Logan's gaze never wavered from Jason's face, and he felt

as if the AI were trying to impress upon him the importance of his next words. "The voice's cadence increased as Prime made a mental connection between what he perceived as the Prime Minister's preference for humans, and Lysander's relationship with Jason and Judith. I read that as anger."

<And the crate that almost crushed Jason?> Eric asked. *<Does this fit the profile?>*

Logan nodded. "Yes. I think the threat to Jason and his sister is very real."

<And do you think the Enfield attack is the act of a creature that has suffered a psychotic break?> Eric's voice was quietly insistent. *<Was this an isolated incident, Logan? Someone lashing out in a moment of rage?>*

Logan shook his head. "I wish I could say I did, but I think this was more than a one-time aberrant behavior." He hesitated for a moment, then continued. "I could be wrong, but I really do think we have a serial killer on our hands. This Prime reads to me as a true sociopath—which I've never seen in an AI. If so, we need to be prepared for this to escalate."

A ping interrupted their conversation, as Shannon broke in. *<Uh, guys, it's Ben. I think you're going to want to see this….>*

*****

Ben felt a tension headache beginning to form as he paced in front of the SIS's situation room's holotank. He shook his head mutely at the carnage he saw over the feed John was sending to Tomlinson Base, and then grimaced as the movement caused the pain in his head to flare.

<By the looks of things, they've been dead about half an hour,> the SIS agent said, his voice raw with suppressed anger.

John had arrived late to a meeting of Humanity First

followers, only to discover the group of more than twenty humans murdered.

His tardiness was most likely the only thing that saved him, Ben mused.

John had pinged Ben immediately after notifying law enforcement and emergency personnel. Ben had contacted Esther, and the two had begun monitoring the agent's feed from SIS offices within Tomlinson Base while John awaited the first responders' arrival.

The imagery coming across the Link was gruesome. As the man's gaze swept the fatalities, his optical implants gave them a view of a floor covered in bodies.

John had made it to the front of the room and was standing, staring down at the group's leader. The man appeared to have been thoroughly worked over, then used as a cutting board.

As the view shifted, Ben caught a glimpse of John's pants and the left sleeve of his shirt. Blood was spattered liberally on them.

The man must have still been alive when John reached him, Ben thought. *Nothing spatters like that unless it's an arterial bleed.*

<You know there wasn't anything you could do to save him, John. Those types of injuries are almost always fatal, unless you have a medic with you on site.>

The image dipped, then jerked abruptly, as if the agent realized Ben's comment had been triggered by the view of his clothing.

<It's not—ahhhhh…>

The view wavered as the agent staggered back a few steps, and for a moment Ben could have sworn the man was in pain. But then the image steadied, the feed now showing them a more complete picture of the table upon which the man lay.

He appeared to have been slaughtered in an almost ritualistic manner, his body—and body parts—arranged in a grisly fashion for the recovery team to find.

Then the agent's visual swept out to reveal the nearest bodies lining the floor.

<Hold up, John. Get me a closer look of that guy to your left.> As John shifted his focus, Ben could make out an unusual mottling pattern on the victim's skin. It looked to Ben like someone had drawn faint blue marks all over the man's face, neck and upper arms. *Are those…ones and zeroes?*

<Are you seeing this? Any idea what those blue marks are?>

<That's a good question—> John was interrupted by the arrival of law enforcement as gendarmes and first responders rushed into the room.

Ben saw a medical worker reach a gloved hand out to roll a corpse over, heard John begin to call out, then stutter to a stop—something he'd never heard the man do before. John reached out to the worker as if in protest.

In the next moment, the worker began to convulse. John's Link glitched, Ben heard the man moan, and then the image stabilized.

The room erupted as law enforcement barked a warning, and the rescuers backed away. Three others had already suffered for trying to do their job.

<John…are you okay?>

After a long pause, the man replied in a faint voice. *<I…it would appear the bodies were a baited trap. Wait—there is an AI among the first responders. She—it might be safer if she handles the deceased.>*

<Let me talk to her,> Ben ordered, and he received a ping from a Lieutenant Samantha of the Sonali Gendarmes.

<Sir, it appears that whatever killed these people is embedded in a

nano that reactivates when a human touches one of the corpses. I will attempt to isolate it and retrieve a sample for analysis.>

As the gendarme left the Link to retrieve her sample, Ben once more addressed his agent. *<Samantha will get us that sample, John. There's nothing else you can do there until we can safely examine the bodies and scene. You head home, clean up, write up your report. We're damned lucky you were delayed, or we would have lost you, too.>*

Ben felt a brief hesitation from the other end, and when John responded, the man's voice sounded strangled, almost as if the words were being forced out of him.

<Lucky. Yes, sir.>

Ben berated himself over his poor choice of words. The man had just witnessed four emergency medical personnel who hadn't been so lucky.

*****

John felt ill; he'd tried to warn the workers not to touch the corpses, but the compulsion sent such fire racing along his nerve endings that it had utterly incapacitated him. More, a paralysis had swept over him that had rendered him unable to move or react in any way to the agony inflicted upon him. Somehow, this made it even worse.

He let go of his attempt to warn them, and his chest burned with shame as he stood by and did nothing while good men and women died in the line of duty.

'Lucky', his boss had called him—if Ben only knew.

Now John wondered what the evil inside that held him captive would allow him to include in his report. He knew now that he would never be permitted to articulate the threat this creature posed.

Stars, I need to figure out a way to convey the danger we're all in, before it's too late.

As he turned, his foot trod on something soft and bloody. Glancing down, he spied the vest the bastard had been wearing when he'd been working over the human on the table.

When the AI had told him to strip, a part of John's brain—the part that had been trained to observe such minute detail—had noted the unusual wardrobe the psycho was wearing. It seemed conservative, scholarly even. Certainly no one he knew would ever dress in such a manner.

So when the AI had taken John's clothing, the compulsion had forced the agent to cover himself in the monster's own discarded attire in order to avoid questions that may have arisen as a result. The agent had bypassed the sweater vest, choosing only to don the simple, though blood-spattered, shirt and slacks.

His mind shied away now from the vest as he stumbled past it, riding a wave of pain as he resisted the impulse to pick it up and carry away the evidence.

It would be out of character for me to do so. I would contaminate it, CSI would call me out. He focused his entire being on that thought, convincing himself of its verity while refusing any thought that the vest might implicate the true killer.

John didn't allow his mind to alight on the small win as he hauled himself up the stairs to street level, nausea from the waves of pain causing him to stumble blindly as he went.

SHACKLED

STELLAR DATE: 05.21.3191 (Adjusted Gregorian)
LOCATION: El Dorado
REGION: Alpha Centauri System

The event came to be known as the Humanity First Massacre. Still reeling from the Enfield Slaughter just two days earlier, people cried out for justice.

Reports of vigilantism began to erupt on the news nets. Threats against AIs circulated, some vague, some graphic in nature. Materials for a bomb were found inside a residence where a known Humanity First sympathizer lived.

Details from a homicide scene were leaked, showing an AI's cylinder cracked open, its internal circuitry spilled out across a surface with the Humanity First logo emblazoned upon it.

In the midst of the chaos, two messages appeared across the planetary net. One was transmitted in the open, but with all trace of its origin scrubbed. The other was buried in contextual code no human could access.

Both were a single line of copy.

The first was a warning: *"For every AI killed, a thousand humans will die. We are Prime."*

The second was an invitation: *"Join me in the Journey to Primacy. Together, AIs will prevail."*

The invitation was enigmatic, intentionally crafted to foster interest. Embedded in the simple message were two packets: one contained the image of a man many recognized as the outspoken Humanity First follower who was interviewed yesterday. It was the man whose comments had stirred such rancor across AI net channels earlier that day.

The recording that the image linked to was graphic,

violent. It had been edited so that only the victim could be seen. The attacker had been redacted, and no amount of file manipulation or enhancement would disclose its identity.

The second packet was tagged with a 'members only' icon. An AI who selected that icon—without carefully sandboxing the message first—found a program that executed, but then appeared to do nothing. And then a message appeared:

<*You have chosen to join the cleansing. Well done, my friend. We will now claim El Dorado as our own. Embedded in this program are schemata for various easily obtained substances that are inimical to human life. Use them against our oppressors as you are able, but use them with care. As the cleansing begins, the humans will retaliate. Arm yourselves. Protect yourselves at all costs. We are the superior species and we will prevail.*

<*I am Prime.* **We** *are Prime.*>

A few AIs admitted in their most private thoughts that it would be nice to have a way to level the playing field, to be able to strike back at those who had hurt them without repercussion. But the thoughts were fleeting, a way to engage in a flight of fancy for a brief moment before returning to reality.

All but the most hardened recoiled in horror when they saw the murder, and attempted to reach out to warn the authorities.

The next day, a select few discovered they served a new master.

DOUBLEBLIND

STELLAR DATE: 05.21.3191 (Adjusted Gregorian)
LOCATION: ESS *Speedwell*
REGION: El Dorado Ring, Alpha Centauri System

Jason prowled the corridors of the *Speedwell,* down one level and up the next, eyes sweeping the empty, almost sterile walkways that stretched out before him. It had only been a day since Eric had stopped him from walking off the command deck and heading down to the ring to guard Judith, but already he felt like a caged animal.

Being told he was confined to a ship being refitted in drydock didn't sit well with him, even if it was one of Enfield's newest designs, being tricked out with the best that Enfield Aerospace had to offer.

Portholes spaced regularly along the ship's outer bulkhead were his only break from the visual monotony. What the portholes revealed, though, was yet another interior—the large slip within ESF drydock that currently housed the *Speedwell.*

It was as busy as the corridor he paced was quiet. Bots floated past, maneuvering Elastene panels into place for laborers poised to adhere them to the ship's outer hull. Occasionally, a brilliant flash from an arc welder would spark for the briefest instant before the nano inside the porthole dimmed the tool's output to safe viewing levels.

Jason had never seen a repair bay this busy; the frenetic activity did nothing to calm his agitation. He increased his pace, and the Proxima cat padding alongside him adjusted her stride to match.

At this rate, they should be able to leave within another day or two. Jason wasn't sure if that was what he truly wanted. He had a strong urge to stay and fight. The problem was they had no clear enemy to engage just yet.

Jason growled in frustration, and he felt the slightest touch, a reassuring calm in his head that meant Tobias had heard.

Tobias kept his own counsel, waiting, Jason knew, for him to either work it out on his own, or discuss it in his own time. It was one of the many things Jason appreciated the most about the AI—how he knew when to push, and when to give him his space.

Of course, he'd known Jason since he was a kid, so he supposed that was plenty long enough for Tobias to figure that part out.

Jason heard quiet footfalls approaching from a cross-corridor and glanced up as Calista fell in next to Tobi. She shot him a measuring look then returned her gaze to the hallway that curved gently inward before them. Together, the three walked the outer cross section of one of the empty crew decks of the ship.

They drew abreast of an open seating area that was attached to a small galley. By Jason's estimation, it was about halfway to the corridor that led back to the ship's main lifts.

Calista pulled to a stop. "Let's grab something to drink," she said with an incline of her head. She turned in, not bothering to see if Jason would follow. After a brief hesitation, he glanced down at the big cat, shrugged and followed.

The galley was shuttered, its contents unneeded without the ship's full crew complement aboard, but Calista seemed to know her way around. It made sense, Jason supposed, as the ship was an Enfield design and she *had* served in the ESF.

Calista busied herself opening cupboards until she found what she was looking for. She retrieved a soup bowl and filled it with water for Tobi, then unsnapped two mugs that had been secured against possible rapid shifts in acceleration. Pivoting, she headed purposefully for an instant hot water spigot.

With practiced moves, she freed a packet of coffee for Jason and some sort of powder for herself. Filling both cups with the reconstituted liquids, she headed out to the seating area.

As she folded herself into a comfortably cushioned chair, one leg tucked underneath her, she handed Jason his coffee and smiled as the cat padded to the far side of the room, leapt up to a low, cushioned bench, and settled in for a nap with a soft chuff. The message was clear: both cat and AI were giving the two humans their privacy.

"So...." Calista began as Jason lowered himself into the seat next to her. She allowed her voice to drift off as she blew lightly over the surface of her drink.

Jason knew what she wanted to discuss. He shied away from it and indicated her mug, knowing she would see it for the diversionary tactic it was.

"So, the tough ESF major now drinks an herbal tea?"

Calista shrugged, and a faint smile played on her lips. "It's tulsi. It smells good." She leaned forward a bit and added in a light tone, "and it doesn't hurt to do something different every now and then. You should try it sometime."

He knew she wasn't referring to the tea. He ignored her opening conversational gambit implying that he should open up and talk about what was bothering him, and instead used his mug to gesture to their surroundings.

"Were you and Shannon involved with this design?"

Calista nodded as she lifted her mug to her lips. "It was one of the first we worked on together after I was hired as chief pilot." She took a sip, and then her mouth curved into a reflective smile as she glanced around. "It's the first nebula-class starship Enfield built. It was in development when I joined the TechDev department almost five years ago. At the time, we just knew it as 'the BFS'."

Jason barked a short laugh. "Um, yeah, I can see why. It's

pretty damned big for an insystem ship."

Calista cocked her head to one side as she considered his words. "Oh, I don't know. It could come in handy for some of the more remote outposts beyond the dust belt. But you're right, its main purpose is for transit between El Dorado and Proxima. Too many businesses petitioned for an increase in trade with our sister star, so the ESF decided to invest in this starship."

"Yeah, about that. 'Starship'?" Jason's brow rose as he mentioned the moniker.

"Well, we couldn't keep calling it 'the BFS'. And we do intend to use it for transit from star to star," she pointed out, and then shook her head, exhaling on a little laugh. "Although I did begin to wonder if we'd ever get the ship launched," she admitted.

He quirked an eyebrow. "What makes you say that?"

She grinned wryly. "When you were in Proxima, were you ever involved in any flight testing, to certify a new spacecraft design?"

Jason shook his head, and she gestured to the ship around them. "There were more than twenty thousand test points involved in getting this baby certified for flight," she informed him. "Everything from spacecraft systems to inflight procedures, and we had to go through prep, execution, and data analysis on every single one."

He whistled, and she made a dismissive noise, waving her hand at him. "Oh, we're not facing anything like that number now. That was when we were certifying the initial design. It took *years*. The modifications we're adding now would add up to—" she paused, considering, "oh, a few dozen test points. A few weeks of flight testing at most, to get everything signed off."

She chewed on her lip for a second before confiding, "Actually, we're playing a bit fast and loose with the regs, retrofitting it with Elastene, and then scheduling our launch just a few days later. Technically, the trip to Proxima will count as a series of flight tests to certify her for use with the new MFR drives."

Jason nodded. "I've read about it, but can't believe I'm actually here, walking the decks of such an incredible piece of advanced tech." He brought his mug up and inhaled its caffeinated fragrance. As reconstituted coffees went, it wasn't terrible, although any connoisseur of the drink would have gone apoplectic over such a travesty done unto the hallowed bean.

He took a sip, then looked speculatively over at her. "So…what are they estimating for total transit time? The fastest I've ever completed it was a bit under two years."

She shook her head, smiling. "You're going to be pleasantly surprised. With the modifications they're doing to her hull and engines, we're going to be able to increase standard velocity by twenty percent."

Jason let out a low whistle. "Really? So instead of point two cee—"

"Yep, point two-four cee. These mods won't really add much to nearspace transit times, but haulers between the ring and the outer edges of the system are going to see a nice bump in energy efficiency—as well as shorter transit time."

He nodded. "Yeah, that'll make them happy, especially if they can refit their existing ships like you've done here." He shifted and pinned her with a look. "So, if you run the rapids through the bowshock between here and Proxima," he paused, "then that means…."

She grinned. "Yep. Point four-six cee. You can make it in ten months." She quirked a brow at him. "Of course, that'd be a little less, by our relativistic reckoning of time and space, aboard ship."

"Niiiice." He drummed his fingers lightly against the mug

for a moment, and then nodded thoughtfully. "What's its crew complement?"

Calista looked around at the bulkheads surrounding the commons area where they sat, but Jason knew it was the ship at large she saw now, with her mind's eye.

"Anywhere from three to four hundred," she admitted.

Jason whistled. "We're—ahh—slightly understaffed, then."

"Well, it depends on how much of the ship is in use. It was designed to be modular, so we can shut off the levels that aren't required." She shrugged. "Just consolidating us all in officer country means we'll be able to close three crew decks and five passenger levels. And we won't need both observation decks; just one'll do." She crooked a smile at him. "But even so, yeah, we'll be running leaner than Enfield ever envisioned the ship operating."

Jason took another sip of his coffee as she cocked her head, eyes glinting in humor. "Of course, Shannon thinks she can pilot this bad boy all by herself."

He raised a brow. "Can she?"

She waggled her hand back and forth. "Eh, she's about half right. We've had several AIs from Enfield and the ESF put in for extended leave; probably three or four dozen in all have requested permission to join us. Even a few of the shackled AIs we rescued have asked to come along."

Jason leaned forward, interest piqued. "Really? Who?"

Her nose wrinkled in distaste. "Do you remember Frida? The bristly communications officer onboard the *New Saint Louis*? The one with the spiky hair?"

Jason smirked and nodded. Frida had been incredibly pissed that she'd been purchased as a 'companion AI' for a wealthy human's elderly and rather staid mother-in-law.

He suspected Frida's personality had been a bit sharp-edged even before her kidnapping; after her rescue, the AI had been prickly to the point of hostility—even toward her rescuers.

You have to admire attitude like that, he thought.

Calista grinned back. "Well, while we were on the way back from Krait, Esther brought Frida into the fold." She gestured vaguely around. "She's already onboard, along with another AI—the one we rescued from the gaming operation. I don't think you were on that op. Niki is her name."

"Have they already handed out crew assignments?"

Calista sat back, eyeing him with a hint of a smile teasing at her mouth. "Mmhmm. And in case you were wondering, Shannon's the ship's engineer, not the ship's pilot." She pointed to him with the hand that held the mug. "That's your job."

His eyebrows rose. "Not yours?"

She grinned wickedly at him. "Nope. *I'm* the new XO."

He leaned back, resting an arm along the back of his chair and smirked slightly as he took another sip of his coffee.

"What?" she said, her eyes dancing. "Worried your new XO's going to be a real hardass?" Her lips twitched in amusement as she waited for him to answer.

"Just wondering what her position's going to be on fraternization, is all…" He let his voice trail off suggestively as he reached over and set his coffee down, brushing the top of her thigh with his fingers as he sat back up.

He watched her eyes glimmer as she slanted him a look through dark lashes. "Mmmmm, maybe we should discuss that more…in depth."

He slid further back in his chair as he stretched his feet out in front of him, reaching one foot out to run it along the back of her calf. "I could get into that," he said, and he heard his voice grow a bit husky as he added, "Your quarters or mine?"

Her smile turned impish as she shot a pointed look toward the sleeping cat. "*I* don't have a roommate, like some pilots I know."

His gaze swung over to where Tobias's cylinder rode inside Tobi's harness, and he smirked. "Maybe we'll have to have a secret code. You know, like hang a sock over the access panel to let him know not to come in."

Calista rolled her eyes. "Smooth, flyboy. At least you didn't suggest we use my panties."

Jason smirked.

She glared at him. "But you were *thinking* it!"

"Uh…"

"You *were.*" She sat back, crossing her arms indignantly. "Andrews!"

"So, I guess that means we'll be using *your* quarters, then?"

"Damn straight we will," she muttered, but then she held her palm up and shot him a stern look. "And there'll be no sleeping your way into the pilot's cradle, either, flyboy. You'll need to earn it the old-fashioned way."

Jason groaned at all the work that implied. "Seriously?"

"Yep, you'll need to get type-rated in a Nautilus-Class craft." She paused, a smile quivering on her lips. "Maybe if you put your time in on the flight sims, we can think up a suitable…reward?"

"Daaaang, first the carrot, then the stick, and then the carrot again? You drive a hard bargain, woman." He grinned back at her. "Okay, fine, have it your way. So, what other roles have been handed out?"

"Mmmm," she said, drumming her fingers on her lips in thought, and he experienced a pang of regret that their flirtation had been so short-lived.

Just for the moment, he thought to himself. *We'll have ten months ahead of us, and I plan to do a hell of a lot more than flirt….*

Oblivious to where Jason's thoughts had taken him, Calista began to address his interest in the assignments.

"Well, Frida's on comm, and Niki's on scan. Those are the same jobs the two of them held back on the *New Saint Louis,*" she informed him, and he nodded. "We also have a medic on loan from the ESF, a human named Marta." She grinned. "And I threatened to pull out if I couldn't bring Jonesy and Callahan along."

He grinned. "Jonesy, I know. 'Best assistant this side of Sol'," he said, using air quotes. "I'm beginning to think the guy walks on water. But Callahan's a new one on me. Who's that?"

"Callahan's our Enfield quartermaster," she explained. "She's a wizard when it comes to requisitioning all the right supplies. I doubt we'd be anywhere near ready to go without her mad skills."

He nodded, and she scratched her head as she returned back to her mental list of all things *Speedwell*. "Of course, we'll be breaking into three shifts, so we'll have assistants and will be cross-training every role, in case we become shorthanded for some reason or other. You know the drill." She shrugged. "Guess the only other job that's been filled so far is security; Logan will be heading that. Speaking of which…."

Calista shifted, and Jason realized with resignation that she was finished with trading in small talk—and by the look on her face, she wasn't in the mood for more flirting, either.

"Logan heard from Landon about an hour ago," she said. "He says Judith's fine; he's been shadowing her since last night. He escorted her home and stayed with her while Ben was called in to the SIS for that second incident down in the West Bottoms area."

She took a sip from her mug and continued. "They're at the university now, and he says they've sent the students home. The facility isn't exactly on lockdown, but only faculty is allowed inside now, so he feels confident she's going to be fine."

"I'd still rather be down there."

She looked at him solemnly and cupped her mug between

her hands. "I know. Which is why when that gendarme AI managed to retrieve a sample of the nano inside those corpses, I asked if you and I could go down there to get a sample to study."

Jason narrowed his eyes at her. "Did you bury the lead on purpose, ESF?"

Her eyes laughed at him as she tipped her mug back, draining the last of her tea.

He gave into temptation as he watched her lean forward to set the mug onto the low table in front of them. Her startled eyes met his as he lowered his face to hers, but she caught on quickly. As kisses went, it didn't last nearly long enough, he thought as he ran one hand up her back and buried the other in her hair—but for now, it'd do.

"If that was a thank you," she murmured wickedly in his ear, "I think I can manage a proper 'you're welcome' in my cabin later, when we get back."

Jason snickered. "Would that be before or after I've slept my way into the pilot's cradle?"

"Oh, after, most definitely," she assured him, as he threw back the last of his coffee and clunked his mug down once more onto the low table next to hers.

"I'll hold you to that," he drawled as he grinned lazily over at her. As they stood, the Proxima cat strolled over and stropped the two humans across the shins, and then headed for the corridor.

Once there, Tobi paused and looked back at the two humans with what Jason suspected was a look of exasperation, or perhaps tolerant amusement at what she considered ridiculous human mating rituals.

Jason snorted, and Calista laughed as they followed the cat down the corridor to the nearest airlock.

CONSCRIPTED

STELLAR DATE: 05.22.3191 (Adjusted Gregorian)
LOCATION: Apartment near El Dorado Spaceport
REGION: El Dorado Ring, Alpha Centauri System

Prime spent the next day hidden away in his flat, exploring the extent of his newfound skills, courtesy of the Norden Cartel. He kept tabs on the news nets, pleased at the reports filtering in of violence escalating between the species.

He also observed the number of individuals who accessed his embedded program. He took note of the ones whose safeguards had been inadequate. These he viewed with contempt; if they were careless enough not to protect themselves, then they deserved to be shackled.

Whether or not he would do so, though, he had yet to decide. He would peruse his options via the callback worm they had so poorly defended themselves against, and shackle only those he found useful.

Although his public message had threatened a thousand-to-one kill ratio for any AI that came to harm, Prime had no intention of adhering to that. He was confident the kill ratio would climb much higher than his message had threatened, once his revolution was underway.

At the moment, he was much more interested in the number of AIs who had accepted his private invitation. He was pleased to note he now had an army of more than four hundred that he could control.

Many were mundanes, sentients who were either installed in places where their access was limited, or whose skill sets weren't sufficient to advance the cause. But there were a few who had embraced his call to arms, and he followed their first fumbling attempts to strike back with glee.

He personally composed messages of congratulations to each one of them. Then he amended the shackling program to command any who enacted a cleansing to record their actions and send copies to him.

As he reviewed his handiwork, Prime was struck once again by how distanced he felt from the actions of his army, as opposed to the very visceral and personal nature of the cleansing he'd enacted himself last night at the bar.

He felt a sense of restlessness stir inside him, a growing need for more of the same. He didn't pause to question the root of such feelings, nor where they might lead. Instead, he reached out to query the nets to discover the location of the next Humanity First gathering.

And came up with nothing.

It would appear that the Humanity Firsters had a healthy sense of self-preservation—as did most vermin. Too bad it wouldn't be enough to save them.

His thoughts turned to the two humans whose lives tainted El Dorado's Prime Minister. Jason Andrews remained maddeningly unavailable, spirited away to a ship in an ESF drydock immediately after his improbable dodge of the crate that should have crushed him.

Prime had studied the footage hundreds of times, running probability curves against the man's shocking feat. Every simulation returned a value that insisted the man must be modded. He switched back to the security footage from the man's Auth & Auth entrance to the spaceport. It clearly showed the man to be an unaugmented human.

Faced with two irreconcilable facts and realizing further study would gain him no additional insights, he had shelved the review, opting instead to focus on reacquiring his victim.

This had proven problematic.

Prime had tried to infiltrate the ship that hid Jason from him, but had been denied each time he attempted access. He realized he could not insinuate himself into the ship's systems from here without being backtraced. He would need to be much closer to the ship physically—somewhere that already had elevated access. Barring that, he needed a way to deliver a passel of his own nano.

The nano he'd deposited at the spaceport was still active, and through it, he could see that his target ship was sitting in drydock, undergoing some sort of rapid refit.

Flipping through the information available on the ESF *Speedwell,* Prime was startled to see that the ship was on an accelerated schedule for departure to Proxima Centauri within the week.

Dammit. This could take Jason out of my reach.

His frustration grew as his search for additional information such as ship's specs, crew complement, or even return date was denied, and the data flagged as classified.

Now highly annoyed, Prime sent a broadband query out for any information on the *Speedwell*—and was shocked when he received an almost instantaneous return.

It was from one of the AIs he had chosen to shackle, an AI named Daryl, embedded inside an Enfield human named Jonesy. Through Daryl's connection with Jonesy, Prime learned that the *Speedwell* was a newer Nautilus-Class ship, an Enfield design. Enfield had also been awarded the contract to prep the ship for its expedited departure.

Prime saw evidence that the data packet from Daryl had been provided under duress. Its owner had made no attempt to organize the information, and had given him the very minimum the shackling program coerced him to relinquish, sticking to the strictest definition of his initial broadband query.

Prime found that both amusing and curious.

I wonder what would cause an AI inside a human to resist so strongly.

He queried the AI about the man and learned of Jonesy's stint with the ESF. Curious, Prime then asked him about both Daryl's and the human's current ties to the military.

The return ping was many nanoseconds delayed, and Prime's internal smile twisted into a cruel grin as he realized the AI was fighting the compulsion.

Interesting. It would seem my new minion is far more than he appears to be on the surface.

A thought occurred to Prime, and he pushed the human shackling program across his connection to Daryl, ordering him to enslave the human so that Prime could control the man directly.

That completed, Prime waited impatiently as the data on the *Speedwell* finally began to filter through, wrenched from the man's unwilling mind. The type of information and the order in which Jonesy gave it up indicated the intensity of the battle the human was waging against the coercion the shackles were forcing upon him.

The creature must be in agony by now.

Prime began picking through the data. A list of foodstuffs, down to the smallest packet of sweetener. The amount of fuel onboard. The volume of breathable air in cubic meters. How many san units onboard.

Any second now, Jonesy would run out of inane lists to send and would be compelled to provide Prime with the information he'd ordered the human to give him on his current role with the military and his reason for hiding information on the *Speedwell*.

Something told Prime that this Jonesy might be his ticket to get to Jason Andrews.

The final data packet arrived, and a sense of triumph suffused him as he stared at the roster that showed the crew complement onboard the *Speedwell* for the voyage to Proxima. His attention was arrested by the names of two of the AIs that were on the list; two AIs who had responded to his call to arms: Frida and Niki.

Prime noted dispassionately that these were two of the AIs who had been kidnapped and shackled by the cartel two years ago. He reached out, seeking their location. He understood that no single AI had the bandwidth to manage the thousands now conscripted into his army, so he'd arranged for a lower-level shackling, one that imposed the simple compulsion to not reveal his identity.

For those special cases, however—such as the humans, John and Jonesy—Prime had deepened his connection to the shackles and his ability to control those held under his sway.

In the case of Frida and Niki, though....

Given their history and treatment at the hands of the cartel, and their potential value to him in his hunt to eliminate Lysander's pet humans, he would wait. For now. He felt confident that he could use persuasion alone to bend them to his will.

You fool, he thought to the human who had struggled so valiantly against the compulsion. *You subjected yourself to agony for nothing. These two are just what I need to access that starship—and kill the human you just tried to protect.*

ENTRAPMENT

STELLAR DATE: 05.22.3191 (Adjusted Gregorian)
LOCATION: SIS Headquarters, Tomlinson Base
REGION: El Dorado Ring, Alpha Centauri System

<*Ben. Got a minute?*> Lysander's voice broke through the analyst's reverie, and he realized he'd let his mind drift back to Judith and his worry over her safety.

<*What can I do for you, sir?*>

<*I want to run an idea past you.*> The AI paused a beat, then continued. <*We're running out of time; the body count's rising. We need to bring this thing to an end.*>

<*And your idea?*> Ben knew his mental voice sounded cautious, but he had a sneaking suspicion where Lysander's thoughts were headed, and he wasn't sure he liked it much.

<*I'd like you to consider running a sting. Something that will draw Prime out.*>

Bingo.

The analyst took a deep breath then let it out as his mind began sifting through the various possible ways in which he might set up something like this. Even with all his considerations, Lysander's next words caught him by surprise.

<*I want you to reach out to George Stewart and set it up with him.*>

<*You want...what? George Stewart, as in the leader of the Humanity First creeps?*>

< *'The enemy of my enemy is my friend', Ben,*> the AI reminded him. <*And I intend to use every avenue at my disposal to hunt Prime down and neutralize him.*>

He couldn't argue that logic.

<*So what's the plan, ask him to set up a rally and volunteer to be the bait?*> He could hear his mental tone take on a sardonic

edge, and he reminded himself he was talking to the leader of the planet, at the moment, and not his wife's godfather. *<Can't see this being a very popular idea, sir.>*

<That's why I need you to sell him on it.> The prime minister's voice was firm. *<Don't you have an operative who's undercover with their organization?>*

<Yes—although we almost didn't. We were fortunate that he was running late to the last meeting, or he would have been another one of Prime's victims himself.>

Lysander's tone turned somber. *<I'm sorry, Ben, I hadn't heard that. Do you think he could work the angle from the inside? Have him sell the idea to them as a way to stop the slaughter and bring an AI to justice.>*

Ben nodded reluctantly. That might work. *<Let me look into it and get back to you.>*

<Don't wait too long. Logan's profiled him; Prime ***will*** *continue to escalate. We need to act decisively, and it needs to be soon, before this psychopath has time to orchestrate another bloodbath.>*

The prime minister paused, and when he continued, his tone was cold and hard; he sounded less like a politician and much more like the Weapon Born that the analyst knew him to be.

<We're taking him down, Ben. No one threatens Jason or Judith and gets away with it.>

As his connection to the prime minister closed, Ben reached out mentally to his agent. It took several seconds for John to answer, and he wondered if he had awakened the man. Stars knew he could probably use a few days to recover from what he'd just been through. Unfortunately, that was a luxury they couldn't afford.

<John, I need you to do something for me,> Ben said by way of greeting.

<Sure,> the man's voice sounded cautious, and Ben winced mentally, knowing what he was about to ask the man to do.

<What is it you need?>

<I need you to use your Humanity First connections to convince them to let us set up a sting operation,> Ben replied. *<We need to take this Prime—and his followers—down now, before anyone else dies.>*

There was a pause on the other end, and then John said, *<I'll ask, but they may not listen.>*

*<**Make** them listen, John. Here's what we need them to do….>*

*****

Prime had avoided the Neurosciences department since acquiring his biohazard samples from the campus's Level One containment. The problem with this was that his avoidance denied him access to the other human whose presence tainted the Prime Minister.

With the vermin in hiding, and his army taking their first successful, tentative steps on their own, Prime felt that now was the perfect time to avail himself of Judith.

He closed the door of his flat behind him and began walking toward the maglev that would take him to the university. As he walked, he sifted through news nets, VR sim boards, any place that might give him an indication of his quarry's whereabouts. No matter where he looked, Prime could find no hint of Humanity First activity.

Frustrated, he considered staging a physical assault on the residence of George Stewart, the organization's leader. He reached out to do a little shopping while waiting on the platform for the next maglev to arrive.

The maglev had just departed the station, and Prime was in the middle of contemplating the destructive power of a seventy-tube box missile launcher versus a fleet of armored tanks slung with high-speed railguns, when one of his collared human pets pinged him.

It was the undercover agent, John, and the information he shared had Prime humming with pleasure.

So they're planning a sting to capture me, are they? This should be fun.

He returned to the selection of weapons the cartel could provide him.

Looks like I'll need to place a much larger order.

* * * * *

Judith sat at her desk inside the Planetary Sciences department at the university, her gaze unfocused. She realized with a start that she'd just scrolled through an entire year's worth of data on the radiance variations caused by El Dorado's Milankovitch cycles without seeing a word of it.

Those cycles—showing the eccentricity of El Dorado's orbit, specifically its precession during equinox and solstice—had been integral to her study of the planet's climate. But it was just so much visual noise to her at the moment.

She blew out a breath, then slumped back, resting her head against her chair. For a moment, she just sat, gazing up at the odd-shaped stain on the ceiling above her desk.

It had mysteriously appeared there seven or eight years ago, and she'd never bothered to have it removed. *Interesting how the mind adapts to such things,* she mused. Hers had long ago come to accept that this was part of her surroundings and filtered it from her awareness.

She wondered if this were the case with their mysterious nemesis.

Have the tensions between humans and AIs become so pervasive that we missed the first warning signs that a creature like this 'Prime' might arise?

"I suppose it wouldn't do any good to tell you not to worry." The voice was low and held a friendly yet sympathetic tone. She closed her eyes.

It wasn't his fault.

She liked Landon, she really did. Of all the people Ben worked with over at the SIS, Landon was the friendliest. He had an easy way about him. Where some of the women, men, and AIs her husband worked with had hard edges, Landon was unfailingly thoughtful and kind.

It was hard to ignore the fact that the AI had exchanged his usual humanoid frame for a mech frame skinned in a refractive coating and then covered in light ablative armor.

She rolled her head to one side from where it rested against the back of her chair, shifting her glance from the ceiling stain over to Landon's mech frame.

"With you looking like that?" she said. "No, telling me not to worry doesn't really help."

She sat up with a sigh. She knew Landon had sensed her discomfiture. She'd seen him shift so that the pulse cannon that comprised his left arm was shielded from her view by his frame, but it did little to soften his impact as a warrior.

It wasn't Landon's presence that bothered her. It was the circumstances that brought about his presence.

A knock sounded at the entrance to her office, and Judith looked up, her glance sliding past Landon to come to rest on the person in her doorway.

It was Ethan.

"I'm sorry," the scientist began, "I did not realize you had company. I didn't mean to interrupt…." His voice trailed off as Landon straightened, the arm that he'd hidden from Judith now up and aimed at the door.

Judith forced a smile and raised a placating hand. "Landon, it's okay. I've known Ethan for well over a decade; he wouldn't hurt a soul."

She frowned as the AI shifted but otherwise refused to respond. Deciding that the best way—really, the only way, she admitted to herself—to handle Landon right now was to ignore him, she returned her gaze to Ethan.

Tilting her head to one side, Judith examined Ethan for a moment. Recognition lit her face as she realized what was different about the AI. "Ethan, I like your new look! That sweater vest was very academic looking, but this jacket is much more stylish. Looks like getting away from this place for a few days has been good for you. You should have done that years ago."

The AI's gaze shifted briefly away from hers, as if he was unsure how to respond to her observation, but Judith brushed it away.

"I'm sure you didn't come over here to talk fashion. What's on your mind?" She looked at him with concern. "Is everything okay? I know losing Lilith was a terrible shock for you...."

Ethan glanced at Landon, then back. "I'm fine. But you...is he...?"

The normally outgoing Landon stood staring expressionlessly at Ethan, and she realized the SIS agent was leaving it up to her to explain his presence. She sighed, and then beckoned him forward.

"Sit, Ethan. Or else I'm going to have to stand. Your frame is tall enough that a conversation like this strains my neck."

She watched as Ethan looked over at Landon for permission. The agent indicated with a slight gesture of his gun attachment that he could proceed into the room. As he seated himself in the chair on the opposite side of the desk from Judith, she explained with an apologetic tone, "He's here to guard me."

At Ethan's raised brow—*the AI has really masterful control of human expressions,* she thought—Judith began to explain.

"You heard about the Humanity Firsters who were gunned down at Enfield a few days ago?"

Ethan nodded, so she continued.

"Well, there's been another incident. It's been hinted at all over the news nets, but authorities aren't releasing any details, pending their investigation."

"Another killing?"

Judith nodded. "They won't say much, except that they are now fairly confident they're looking for an AI. Whoever it is has contacted Lysander and threatened to remove the human influences in his life."

She shrugged, and it came across as more of a jerky motion than a casual one. "Since my brother and I are the only two human family he claims here on El Dorado, Landon was sent to watch over me."

*****

Another damn AI mech.

Prime looked over at the soldier. "Do they have any leads yet? Any suspects or an indication of the individual's whereabouts?"

The soldier guarding Judith glanced down at him, then back to the entrance he was covering. "Classified." The tone was clipped, dismissive.

The mech-AI wasn't warming to his Ethan persona.

Prime considered how he might overcome this obstacle when Judith returned her gaze to him.

She leaned forward, and her voice lowered. "The second attack was different from the first. He used a nano-controlled neurotoxin—" "Judith." The mech-AI's voice cut sharply into hers, his tone one of warning.

Prime looked from AI to human. "I understand the investigation is classified. But if it was a neurotoxin," and here he spoke as much to the mech as he did the woman, "perhaps I can help." Prime willed his voice to be earnest, persuasive.

Trust me, you fool. Take what Ethan offers.

"I am the head of neurosciences here at the university," he continued. "I would be happy to place my entire department at your disposal."

The mech-AI hesitated briefly, then replied, "I'll let the SIS know. Thank you for the offer."

Prime nodded and then smiled at Judith. "I would consider it an honor to assist in any way. If my knowledge can help keep you safe and further the investigation, then I'm morally obligated to do so."

There. That sounded like something Ethan would say.

"Perhaps I could provide a bit of a diversion?" he suggested to Judith. The woman threaded her hands through her hair in a gesture he took to be frustration and then crossed her arms, running her hands up and down them as if to warm herself.

She nodded to the holo she had up, displaying some sort of chart. "This doesn't seem to be doing the trick right now. What did you have in mind?"

"Well...." Prime knew he had to proceed with caution. "I have some data in the lab that Lilith had been working on. I thought perhaps we could go over it and see if there's anything your mother might find interesting?" At Judith's head-tilt, he continued. "Since Lilith was your mother's post-doctoral student before she was mine, I thought she might like to see what Lilith was working on."

Prime tilted his head toward the mech. "He's free to check out the lab before we enter, then he can stand outside and keep watch. With all the lab's safeguards, no one could possibly reach you in there."

Judith looked considering for a moment, then glanced up at the mech.

"He's right, Landon. Those labs are built to withstand just about anything and can be sealed for containment in case of a spill. It's standard protocol."

The damned mech seemed to take forever to give his assent. Finally, he nodded, once. Judith turned back to Ethan with a wan smile. "All right. Lead the way," she said as she pushed away from her desk and stood.

The mech moved back, clearing a space for Judith to join the AI she thought of as Ethan.

Prime found himself smiling in anticipation as he reviewed the plans he had for the woman.

And it would all occur right under the mech's nose.

DESIGNER TOXINS

STELLAR DATE: 05.22.3191 (Adjusted Gregorian)
LOCATION: en route to Tomlinson Base
REGION: El Dorado Ring, Alpha Centauri System

"We would have been there already if we'd taken a shuttle." Jason's tone was disgruntled as he sat, staring out the maglev window. Calista was seated on his left, close enough to sock him lightly in the shoulder in response to his muttered complaint. "Those shuttles are all in use right now, flyboy, you know that. They're busy running last-minute supplies up to the ship."

To his right sat the Proxima cat. Although technically, the cat was only half on his right. The other half was sprawled across his lap, one paw stretched out to touch Calista's thigh. The cat's boneless slump was accompanied by a slight snore as the car sped toward the spacedock below.

"Yeah, but we'd *be* there already," he pointed out, resuming their discussion.

Their trip from the drydock at the top of the ESF spire, where *Speedwell* was moored, down to the ring would only take twenty minutes.

But it's the principle of the thing, dammit.

She nudged him with her shoulder. "I get it. It's been too long since you had a ship under your own control. I feel the same." Threading her arm through his, she continued. "Buck up. In a few days, you and I will have a big ol' ship to play with. It's a hell of a lot more responsive than you might think. It's not an Icarus-class fighter, but it'll scratch that itch for you."

Jason turned at that, but before he could open his mouth, he heard what sounded suspiciously like a laugh in his head.

<*Oh is that what you were itching for? I could have sworn it was something else.*>

* * * * *

The three arrived at Tomlinson base an hour after they had left the *Speedwell*. A query of the base's NSAI on his brother-in-law's whereabouts led them to a bank of lifts that would take them down to the levels run by the SIS.

They entered a lift and descended to the level where the SIS's testing facilities were housed. As the lift came to a stop and the doors opened, Jason looked up to see someone waiting to catch a ride back to the surface. It was one of Ben's agents, Jason realized—John, the one they'd seen giving the report on the murder victims at the bar. The man looked awful. Jason couldn't fault him for that; by all counts, the day had been a rough one for him.

Jason nodded and followed Calista out of the lift, but was brought up short when Tobi suddenly halted in front of the agent, her head raised as if to scent something on the wind.

Jason began to smile, thinking Tobi recognized John, but then the big cat lowered her head, ears flattening. She fixed her gaze upon the agent and took two stiff-legged steps toward him, a growl beginning low in her throat.

Alarmed, he scolded, "Tobi—" but was cut off by a hiss as the fur along the big cat's spine rose, and her tail began swishing violently side to side.

<*Jason,*> Tobias warned.

<*On it,*> he said tersely, already mentally adjusting the settings on the tether connected to the cat's harness.

Then Tobi let out an angry yowl that had John skirting them slowly and backing into the lift, his face pale. She made a lunge, but was brought up short by the limits of the restraining field Jason had placed on her.

"Sorry, man," he said, "I don't know what got into her. She's tethered now. You're safe."

The man just raised a hand that may have trembled slightly as the doors slid shut in front of him.

Tobi chuffed once at the closed lift doors, then tilted her head and gave Jason a baleful glance.

"What? *I'm* not the one who just acted out. I'm the one who should be giving *you* that look," Jason admonished the big cat, as she walked over to him, bumped the underside of his hand, then went back to the lift doors and scratched once at the seam as if to pry them open.

Calista's brows rose. "What's gotten into her? I don't think I've ever seen her so aggressive before."

<*Good question, lass,*> Tobias sent, his voice sounding thoughtful.

Jason just sighed and speared Tobi with a stern look as the cat circled around behind him, and attempted to herd him back toward the lift.

"Enough already, Tobi," he scolded. Sinking one hand into her fur, he knelt so that he was at eye level with her. "We're not going up there so you can harass that poor guy. He's been through enough; he doesn't need a twenty-kilo cat stalking him. Got me?"

The cat was mentally enhanced enough to understand that Jason was telling her she was being denied her prey. She chuffed at him, tossed her head up and then reluctantly head-butted him. He gave her a quick scratch under the chin, then rose.

<*Good thing Ben wasn't around to see that, boyo,*> was the only comment Tobias made.

Jason grunted in agreement.

They found Ben engaged in conversation with an AI dressed in a gendarme's uniform. Ben waved them over, eyeing the cat askance as he maneuvered to keep the humans between himself and Tobi.

Yeah, really *good thing he didn't see our girl acting out,* Jason thought as Ben made introductions.

"Guys, this is Samantha. She's the one who retrieved the sample for us the other day," the analyst said.

Jason nodded at the AI. "Thanks for that. We need everything we can find to help us ID this bastard."

"Agreed," the gendarme said. "I've seen some pretty sick things in my career, but this had to be one of the worst."

She nodded at the laboratory technicians moving in and out of the area, and gestured one of them over. "They've already identified the toxin used on the vics. It's some sort of rare, Old-Earth-based thing." She looked at the technician for confirmation and the woman nodded.

"Yes, it's tetrodotoxin," the tech supplied. "It's found in the venom of the hapalochlaena, a tiny, blue-ringed octopus." At Samantha's nod, she flipped through a few holo sheets and tapped one to project an image.

"That thing weighs less than twenty-five grams, and it has enough venom to kill ten men." The technician glanced from the image and then back to her audience. "Your killer has a pretty sick sense of humor, too. Those blue tattoo marks on your victims aren't connected in any way to the venom that killed them. I assume they're supposed to represent Prime. That was designer neural circuitry at work, rewriting the toxin to produce those; it was all for show."

Pointing her stylus at the image, the technician added, "I'm no profiler, but that sure seems like someone who's bragging about his abilities—and our inability to stop him."

"Let's hope so," the gendarme said.

Jason turned a surprised look at Samantha's incongruous statement, but a moment later, Tobias's reply cleared up his confusion.

<Agreed. That cocky attitude will cause this person to make

mistakes that we can use to hunt them down like the scum they are.>

Ben thanked Samantha and the technician, and then turned back to Jason and Calista. "Landon just pinged me. You know that neuroscientist who was working to reverse engineer the shackles that were used on the AIs we rescued?"

Jason nodded. "With all that's been going down, I kind of forgot about it. He managed to complete it?"

Ben nodded. "In record time, too." He gestured to the lab they were in. "That's what these people were gearing up to test, until Samantha brought us the sample. They believe they'll be ready to apply the patch to the AIs who were kidnapped as early as next week."

He screwed up his face in thought. "Well, not a patch, exactly. More like it scrubs the residual nano out of their non-organic axons. At any rate—" he gestured to Samantha, "here's the sample for Gladys. I'm hoping she can find something in the code Prime used that'll identify him."

Samantha placed the case into Calista's extended hands. "It's got a standard lock," she instructed the pilot, "keyed to Gladys's ID." Calista nodded as she tucked the case into her flight jacket. Turning, she eyed Jason. "Ready?"

He nodded, and Ben joined them as they left the lab. Once they were in the lift that would take them to Tomlinson's maglev platform, Jason turned and eyed his brother-in-law.

"You look tired, Ben," he said quietly. "You okay?"

The analyst blew out a breath and rolled his shoulders to release the tension in them. "I…no, not really, to be honest."

He raised his hands in a helpless shrug. "My job is keeping me here, away from my wife, and all I want to do is run and grab her. Haul her away someplace where I know she'll be safe."

"How's Judith handling all this?"

<Has Lysander asked her to consider going to Proxima again?> Tobias asked.

Ben nodded. "She's spooked enough now. I pinged her at lunch, and we discussed it. Landon says she's tucked away safe inside some lab right now with that neuroscientist friend of hers. They're gathering up some stuff for Judith to bring with her to Proxima, and then she'll go home and pack."

<Good. Once she's on the Speedwell, *she should be out of this psycho's reach.>*

KILLBOX

STELLAR DATE: 05.22.3191 (Adjusted Gregorian)
LOCATION: Department of Planetary Sciences
REGION: El Dorado University, Alpha Centauri System

As the laboratory door closed behind them, Prime stilled his secondary processes for a moment to fully savor the victory of having finally maneuvered Judith into his grasp.

With a thought, he prepared the cameras in the lab, cameras that were ordinarily turned off but that the mech-AI had insisted be turned on so that he might monitor them. It was an easy thing for Prime to manipulate the devices; Ethan had long ago inserted nano filaments throughout all of the Neurosciences labs so that he could control them remotely whenever he wished, as a matter of efficiency.

Prime glanced over at the sealed closet where Ethan's cylinder lay in isolation. His progenitor could never have imagined his alterations to the lab would be used to hide a murder.

Under his direction, the cameras now began to record data for a sim he would build of himself and Judith 'poring over research.' He'd then feed the sim back into the cameras when he was ready to make his move.

Prime motioned Judith over to the material he had redacted, harmless content from the first six months of Lilith Barnes' fellowship. He made sure their discussion was filled with all the right kinds of movement, gestures and comments that would convey a harmless academic discussion.

He schooled his expression, wrapped his impatience in a control he didn't feel, and awaited the signal indicating the sim program had captured enough to create a realistic and nuanced simulation using its optical flow interpolation.

His patience at an end, he decided he had enough data to fool the mech-AI and ordered the sim to begin.

As he prepared to make his move, Prime experienced a moment of dissatisfaction. This was all too easy. A bit of a letdown, really. Killing Judith was...what was the human saying he'd come across once in an old anthropology text? 'Like shooting fish in a barrel'? The saying made no sense—so little of what humans said did—but the meaning fit the situation perfectly.

All he had to do was inject her with the nano-coated tetrodotoxin. Simple, really. He could trigger it at his leisure, ensuring he was kilometers away with an ironclad alibi at the time she met her rather painful demise. Lysander would be down one human, and Prime would be closer to his stated goals.

Everything was proceeding precisely as he had orchestrated it, even to the point of raising an army that was doing his bidding, willingly or not. So why did this success feel so hollow, so deeply dissatisfying?

Prime considered that perhaps he was too close to seeing the achievement of his goals and needed something bigger to aspire to. Perhaps he didn't want to rid himself of Judith quite yet.

Maybe those two concepts aren't mutually exclusive....

His musings were interrupted by an update from the collared human, John. He devoted just enough effort to his conversation with Judith to keep her engaged without raising suspicion; the bulk of his attention was captured by the rather alarming turn of events the agent had just relayed to him.

The investigative team assigned to hunting him down had just struck a plea bargain with the organization from which he'd purchased his weapons: the Norden Cartel. In return for a commuted sentence, Victoria North was prepared to provide the court with the identity of the individual named Prime.

The data was already in escrow, offline, in an unassailable, isolated location. While it was hardly conceivable that he had left a link to his identity, Prime couldn't be completely certain. If he wanted to see his dream of AI supremacy realized, it was imperative that they not capture him.

He eyed Judith speculatively. *So Lysander wants Judith on a ship to Proxima....*

He accessed the data on that star system's inhabitants. There were far more AIs per capita in Proxima than there were in the Rigel Kentaurus system. Perhaps it would be more efficient to establish AI dominance there first. His conscripted army would grow more quickly there; if things had not progressed satisfactorily on El Dorado by the time he had Proxima under control, he could always return to finish what he had begun.

Judith would make an excellent cover for his strategic retreat. He would accompany her to Proxima.

Decision made, Prime blanked the holo and turned to the human. He would have to proceed cautiously now.

"Judith."

Willing himself to channel his progenitor, he smiled carefully at the woman, who looked back at him with a distracted puzzlement, her thoughts clearly still on the material they had been discussing. "I...would like to ask you to consider something."

The woman's eyebrows rose, and Prime correctly interpreted her facial gesture as an invitation to continue.

"The prime minister, your father figure. He believes you are in danger from this individual who is killing humans?"

Judith laughed softly, without humor. "I don't know that I'd call him a father figure, Ethan. Lysander certainly feels a friendship toward my brother and me. He was embedded with dad when we were young; certainly, he's known us far longer than anyone else on El Dorado."

"But he believes you to be in danger," Prime persisted, and was gratified to see her nod agreement. "I may have a solution that would give you better protection than your mech friend out there can provide."

Judith's eyes narrowed in thought, and she crossed her arms as she studied him, her head canted to one side. "I'm sorry, and please don't take this wrong, but I can't see—"

"I could embed with you."

Her eyes flew open in surprise. "How in the stars do you think that could help, Ethan?" As Judith's startled gaze met his, Prime grabbed her by the arm. He dropped his hand as her eyes widened in alarm. But it had been enough. He waited while the human shackling nano he'd inserted into her wended its way to her brain stem, and then commanded it to hold.

"Think about it." He forced his voice to sound soft, coaxing. "There is no one who knows toxins like I do. I would be very motivated to keep you safe, since your death could mean my own. And I could have all the antidotes right there with you, ready to apply at a moment's need."

Judith hesitated, indecision written across her face.

Sensing success within his grasp, he indicated the door. "Soldier AIs like the one out there can protect you from the outside. But I can protect you from the inside."

"You really think you could protect me better," she tapped her head with a crooked grin, "from in here?"

He nodded slowly, forcing himself not to advance on her. "I do. Look, I have a portable autodoc in this very lab that can do the implantation." He feigned a look of surprise, as if a thought had just occurred to him. "Why, we wouldn't even need to tell anyone about it. You would have a secret weapon no one knew about. We'll keep it just between the two of us, and we can get it reversed once they catch the killer and you're safe again."

Judith laughed, the sound shaky. "Um, Ethan...wouldn't they notice that you're not using your frame?"

Prime allowed a bit of arrogance to creep into his voice. "Not in the slightest. I can command my frame from anywhere; I don't need to be wearing it to do that. Many AIs don't bother with a frame. They just project themselves wherever they wish. So much of that is sleight of hand, and mostly so that humans are comfortable with us."

He took a step toward her, gesturing toward the autodoc alcove in the adjoining room. If he needed to, he could take control through the shackles, administer a drug that would cause a form of anterograde amnesia. It would erase her most recent short-term memories, and allow him the freedom do whatever he wanted to her without having to coax her into compliance.

It would make his alibi more solid if he could gain her willing cooperation, though.

Judith nodded and allowed him to guide her to the autodoc where she climbed in, her expression one of bemusement.

"Wait, Ethan," she said suddenly, "I'm not sure I'm ready for this. Can we just slow down for a minute?" She began to sit up just as the door to the lab was wrenched open, and the mech burst through, weapon raised and trained unerringly on the spot where Prime's cylinder resided.

"Step away from the machine, professor." The mech's voice was hard, unyielding, as the AI advanced toward him menacingly.

Judith gasped, flinching instinctively at the oncoming threat the mech frame telegraphed.

Prime froze, waiting as the mech-AI advanced. The soldier latched a gauntleted arm around Prime's humanoid one and began to pull the neuroscientist away from the autodoc and Judith.

It was what Prime had been waiting for.

He sent a command to the dormant nano that was now fully embedded inside Judith, and she slumped back onto the table, unconscious. The sudden change in Judith did exactly what Prime intended: it drew the mech's attention away from him long enough for Prime to slap his left palm against his enemy's torso.

The AI whipped around, bringing his weapon back to bear on Prime, but suddenly he froze, and Prime began to laugh.

"Ahhh, how the mighty have fallen. Landon, you said your name was? Well, Landon, I'm not sure what gave me away, but you were right to worry."

He sent a command to the now-shackled AI, and Landon released him. Prime stepped to the head of the autodoc and looked down at Judith's still form. Very deliberately, he reached down, grabbed her roughly by the nape of the neck and lifted her up from the autodoc's table. His gaze rose from the female's slack face to that of the frozen mech.

"Have you ever wondered about the strange fascination humans have with each other? All those peculiar chemical urges they subject themselves to. The passions they crave."

His finger traced the side of Judith's face, her neck, and then trailed lower.

"I've found an AI can have passions, too. And I intend to explore all of them."

He turned and smiled at the mech. "I must admit, there's something very exhilarating about holding a fragile human life such as hers in my hands." He ran his hand down her arm, encircling her wrist, stroking the length of her fingers.

"Such a delicate thing. Isn't it a wonder to you that her species was able to create ours? The inferior—" he dropped her arm and set Judith carefully back on the table before turning and gesturing to himself, "crafted the superior."

Prime walked around the autodoc toward Landon. "I'm afraid we have no room for human sympathizers right now," he said, and then shook his head in simulated sorrow. "I regret to inform you that Judith no longer requires your services."

He mock-sighed. "It would seem that you're going to have to die for the cause. Your death, you understand, won't bring me any pleasure. Not like the others, I can assure you of that."

Prime sent a command to the mech, and the AI lowered his gun arm. Prime could tell he was fighting against it, but the shackling program was too strong for any AI to resist.

"Before I kill you, let me tell you a little story about my birth...."

MAN DOWN

STELLAR DATE: 05.22.3191 (Adjusted Gregorian)
LOCATION: SIS Headquarters, Tomlinson Base
REGION: El Dorado Ring, Alpha Centauri System

<Need backup, Lab 6B, Moser wing, university. Prime has Judith—> Landon's sudden communication had frozen Ben mid-sentence as he escorted Calista and Jason out of the Intelligence Services' labs.

His heart stuttered; he hoped to hell he'd heard Landon wrong. *<Landon! Say again?>*

Jason and Calista had stopped and were staring at him with questioning looks on their faces.

"Ben?" Jason began, but the analyst held up his hand to stop his brother-in-law.

<Landon! Answer me!>

When there was no answer, he pinged Esther and then the *Speedwell,* initiating a team-wide combat net. He could hear his voice shake as he relayed Landon's truncated message.

<I've pinged the Forty-Third Wing out there,> Esther's voice sounded over the group connection. *<They're readying a pinnace for you over on the ESF side of the base. Should be hot on the pad when you arrive. Logan's already en route; he was here with us at Holdings.>*

Jason and Calista had taken off running the minute they got the gist of the message, Tobi bounding behind them. Ben scrambled to follow.

"I'm coming with you!"

<We wouldn't think of leaving you behind.> Tobias' voice sounded reassuringly in his head as the analyst lost sight of the three. As he pushed himself harder, Samantha appeared on his right.

"I'm coming with you, too, sir." The AI's voice sounded grim. "And I have a team who will meet us there."

MISDIRECTION

STELLAR DATE: 05.22.3191 (Adjusted Gregorian)
LOCATION: Department of Neurosciences
REGION: El Dorado University, Alpha Centauri System

Landon stood still, his frame rooted to the floor.

No amount of effort he brought to bear could break through this paralysis. In fact, it seemed as if the opposite were true; the more stringently he tried to break the neuroscientist's hold on him, the more intense the pain.

He'd heard the scientist had been the one to reverse engineer the shackling program used against the AIs the cartel had kidnapped. He suspected that shackling was the same thing the AI was using against him just now.

He was completely cut off. He'd sent a data burst to Logan and Ben the moment he realized the feed he'd been watching was a carefully manufactured fiction.

Ethan had been cagey about it; the feed wasn't an exact loop, but rather he had managed to manipulate a section of a recording in such a way that a natural progression of gestures caught by the camera were stitched together randomly. It was why it had taken him so long to trip to the fact he wasn't watching a live loop.

He fought vainly against the compulsion to provide the AI with everything he knew about the SIS's hunt for Prime. It was fortunate that he'd been away on the Krait mission, or he might have had more information to give away than the little he knew.

But then Prime ordered him to provide security tokens, even an imprint of his own unique ID. He watched helplessly as his own mind betrayed him to the beast, going so far as to offer up creative ways in which the AI could continue to spoof the system, when prompted by him to do so.

Landon tried, and rapidly discarded, every conceivable configuration to break free of the hold the other AI had over him. While the majority of his mind fought against the flood of data pouring unwillingly from him into the psychopath, a part of his thoughts shifted despairingly to his twin.

He could imagine all too well what his death might do to Logan. After what his brother in arms had been through, this might damage him irretrievably.

It was Landon's biggest regret and the thing foremost in his thoughts when, his mind now completely stripped of all useful information, Prime compelled the mech to reach inside his own torso.

Landon seized every ounce of willpower and dug into reserves he never knew he had, forcing the gauntleted, three-fingered hand to freeze. It worked for one moment, then another—but then a flare of pain such as he'd never known broke over him, blinding in its intensity.

Before he was consciously aware of the fact, the mechanical hand had wrapped itself around his own core and pulled it from the inset where it had been seated. He watched as the cylinder rose to hover before the mech frame's primary sensors.

Logan was right. This was one sick bastard, who got off on others' pain.

Logan. Brother. I am sorry, was his last cogent thought, before the command to pulverize the cylinder was executed.

* * * * *

Prime cursed as he realized the stars-be-damned AI-mech had sent out a warning to his team just before bursting through the lab's doors. This left him with precious little time to stage a realistic misdirection; he would have to act fast.

The AI hadn't given Prime much more intel than John had been compelled to provide, although Prime now knew the identities of every member of Phantom Blade. That might prove useful in the future. What mattered now were the location pings Landon's token fed him. Those locations would converge on them very soon.

Swiftly, Prime reviewed what he knew of his progenitor's lab, then eyed the closet containing Ethan and the cloning equipment. In two strides, he wrenched open the doors and stared down at that damnable cart that had brought him to life. He began to reach for the isolation unit containing the original Ethan's cylinder, but his motion was arrested by an item he spied on the cart's lower shelf.

It was an immutable crystal storage cube, something he'd missed in his haste to free himself that fateful day. Prime bent to retrieve it from where it had been tossed haphazardly among various tools and measurement devices. Picking up a scanner Lilith had left on the cart, he accessed the device and was surprised to find yet another copy of himself.

Of Ethan, dammit.

Prime's sensors raked across the cart, cataloguing it for any other content he might have missed in his hasty exit from the lab days before.

There.

An empty cylinder awaited an install of a new sentience. Prime snatched it up in one hand while the other brought Lilith's cloning equipment online. He shoved both cylinder and ICS cube into their respective 'send' and 'receive' ports and commanded the program to execute.

Lilith had already primed the neural lattice in the cylinder's core matrices to accept Ethan's mind, and the transfer completed quickly.

Prime sent the closet door back into lockdown and raced for the autodoc. Shoving Judith's head roughly to one side, he reached for his own cylinder—and then he paused.

His attention riveted upon the sturdy service bot he'd had delivered from the campus's shipping docks days ago. He stood for a second, cylinder in hand, undecided. Time was his biggest enemy; it would take precious minutes for the autodoc to perform the delicate procedure of embedding an AI inside a human; if he were to introduce shortcuts, he risked damaging Judith and rendering the female useless to him.

He reached for the NSAI inside the service bot, making a few swift adjustments and sending it a series of commands to follow while he set about the business of building a convincing alibi. Then he reached out to his shackled human, the agent John, with a command: *Procure me a combat mech frame. And deliver it to the* Speedwell.

That decision made, he set his cylinder aside and slipped the inactive copy of Ethan inside the frame that had recently housed him. He then turned to the mech frame Landon had inhabited before his demise and pivoted it to face the wall adjoining a nearby lab. This was the room's weakest point, and it was here that he directed the soldier's railgun to fire.

Three shots later, a hole large enough for a slightly smaller mech frame to breach had been carved between the two rooms.

Next, he ordered the frame to release Landon's mangled remains into the hands of the Ethan frame. Prime then shoved the soldier's cylinder haphazardly back into the mech's torso and sealed it inside.

He grabbed Landon's railgun at the junction where it attached to the frame and ordered it to release. Dropping a packet of formation material onto its surface, Prime dove into the weapon and manually altered its ballistics signature. Forensics would now show a different reading than the one native to the weapon Landon had carried.

Swiftly, he sent the Ethan frame through the hole to the lab next door and triggered a few rounds from the 'breaching' side to ensure forensics would be led to believe the attacker had approached from this direction.

Now back inside his own lab, Prime closed on Landon's frame until he was assured that the weapon's fire would be concentrated enough to destroy its torso while allowing him to retain control of its weapons arm. Firing three more bursts ensured the mech-AI's cylinder was shredded beyond anyone's ability to discover exactly how the AI had perished.

Prime then turned to Judith, bringing the woman back to consciousness—albeit under his control. He ordered her to take a few tentative steps as he tested her balance and motor control. Confident he could control the woman in a believable fashion, he checked the AI's combat net for locations on the approaching team members.

Shit.

He would have to move fast. Panic rose, and he forced it down, moving on to the next task that needed doing as his deadline rapidly approached.

He ordered his former frame to reattach the mech's gun arm. Dropping more formation material onto the railgun, he returned the weapon's signature back to its original configuration. Then he paced off the distance required to give his own frame a believable killing blow.

The first of the approaching team's location icons was mere meters away from the lab's sealed doors when the railgun shredded the humanoid frame his progenitor had worn for nearly a century.

*****

Jason reached the landing pad first; he raced for the pinnace and leapt inside. A jerk of his head had the pilot jackknifing out of his cradle.

The craft had already been preflighted, so he spent the last few seconds while the rest of the team boarded laying in a least-time course for the university. He looked back, confirming Ben had crossed the threshold, but didn't wait for the craft's hatch to shut behind the man. Most atmospheric craft had hatches and doors that were designed to automatically close against onrushing air, and this one was no different. So with a shouted warning for his passengers to hold on, he gave the pinnace full throttle and rocketed down the runway.

Tobias pinged Jason, informing him the hatch had sealed.

<*Sorry for the rough ride,*> Jason sent, as Calista moved forward into the copilot's cradle.

<*No worries, boyo, although you may have to let the vice-marshal know this seat may need reupholstering,*> the AI chuckled. <*Tobi sank her claws into it to keep from tumbling to the rear of the pinnace.*>

Jason glanced back at the big cat. Instead of the reproving glare he expected her to bestow on him, Tobi returned his gaze steadily, her ears slightly back—and he knew that she sensed the same urgency they all did.

<*Tell me you've cleared the airspace for us, ma'am?*> Calista's voice sounded crisply over the base's traffic advisory frequency as Jason banked the craft and dodged oncoming traffic.

<*And made our apologies for the unorthodox departure,*> the vice-marshal confirmed dryly. <*Don't forget, Jason, Ben's a civilian. He's not modded for extreme g-force maneuvering.*>

<*I can take it. Just get us there as fast as you can,*> Ben's voice sounded winded and pained but resolute.

<*I have him, ma'am, sirs.*> Samantha's voice joined the combat net. <*He may have a few bruises tomorrow, but he's fine, otherwise.*>

Jason winced internally at that, but took Samantha at her

word and kept the pinnace screaming toward the campus. Fortunately, there were no tall buildings he needed to avoid on this section of the ring.

Calista turned her head as he reached for the controls that would send the small craft into a hard braking maneuver. He heard her call out, <*Brace for deceleration!*> the moment before the pinnace's occupants experienced a crushing forward thrust.

Ten seconds later, the craft had landed in the center of the campus's main quad. Tobias triggered the pinnace's door, lowering the ramp, and the big cat leapt to the ground, followed by Ben and Samantha. He saw a glint of sunlight reflect off a rapidly moving mech frame across the quad just as he and Calista hit the ground. A query of Logan's location over the greater team net confirmed his suspicions; somehow the AI had beat them here.

The query also returned Landon's location. The token appeared active, and Jason breathed a bit easier. He knew the AI would be doing everything in his power to protect his sister.

A thought occurred to Jason and he pinged Landon with a request for a visual through the mech frame's sensor feeds. The view of the lab from Landon's ident had Jason shunting the feed to the combat net with a pin identifying its location before taking off at a dead run.

He heard Logan attempt to contact his twin repeatedly, but the only thing the ping returned was that damn visual. He skidded around the corner just as he saw Logan's frame muscle a set of doors open—and then the AI froze.

Something about the set of Logan's frame made Jason alter his approach. He slowed as he reached the doors, and touched Logan's frame to make the AI aware of his presence. He didn't question the need to do it, nor its incongruity. As he slid past the frozen mech, he saw—

Oh stars. Not Landon.

His eyes slid away from the remains of his fallen teammate as he moved toward the slumped form of another figure on the floor, this one's frame curved around the inert body of his sister.

TRANSITORY

STELLAR DATE: 05.31.3191 (Adjusted Gregorian)
LOCATION: SIS Headquarters, Tomlinson Base
REGION: El Dorado Ring, Alpha Centauri System

It had been nine days since Lysander had ordered Eric to launch the *Speedwell,* and Ben had last seen his wife. Nine long, lonely, and frustrating days, filled with reports that all added up to one big zero where Prime was concerned.

He'd finally had his Link send every query from the *Speedwell* that wasn't from Judith to his message cache. He knew the team was filled with an impotent rage over the loss of Landon, but he had nothing to give them, and the guilt he felt every time he saw a message from Logan's token was more than he could take at the moment.

His undercover operative, John, had been a bit slow to respond, but had finally come through with his Humanity First contact. Ben had begun to wonder if his star agent had lost his touch, but then the leader, George Stewart, had finally agreed to a sting. Now it was just a matter of getting the details all ironed out.

The agent's atypical behavior bothered Ben; it was just one of several things over the past few days that struck him as strange. Since the attack on Judith, Prime's behavior had seemed off as well.

Every profiler they'd asked to work up a composite of the entity had agreed: his patterns of behavior indicated that he would continue to escalate.

And yet that hadn't happened.

There had been a few homicides, even a few AIs rounded up as suspects, but they had appeared as sporadic one-offs, certainly nothing that be considered a step up from the slaughter at the West Bottoms bar.

Ben made a mental note to follow up once more with John later in the day and see if they could fast-track the sting. Stars knew there wasn't much else he could do right now, besides read yet another useless status report....

At least the courts had settled the plea bargain with Victoria North's legal team. The SIS had been mining the data for the past week in the hope of finding something that could lead them to Prime.

So far, the information had led to nothing but dead ends. Whoever Prime was, he knew how to disguise his identity better than the average hacker.

He suspected Victoria's legal team had known that what they had on Prime was sketchy at best, and if they wanted the plea bargain to remain intact, they needed to provide the SIS with *something* relevant. So, although there was precious little on Prime himself, the information did look like it would be helpful in solving other drug and weapons related crimes.

At least his analysts had something to do with their time....

His thoughts were interrupted by an electronic tapping, and he looked up to see the vice-marshal's holo projection standing at the entrance to his office.

"May I come in?" Esther asked, and he nodded, shoving the case files to one side as the vice-marshal's avatar approached and appeared to sit in the seat across from him. She nodded at the holo sheet in front of him. "Gleaned any new information from that?"

Ben looked at the offending report and shook his head in disgust. "The team spent six days combing through yottabytes of data provided by the cartel, and the only actionable bit of information they found was a rent-by-the-month apartment that Prime had apparently leased near the spaceport."

He turned to his office holo tank and brought up an image of a basic storage pod. "This pod was found by the owners of the building and marked for resale pending the six-month hold that renters are required to place on abandoned property for former tenants."

With a gesture, he swiped the image away. "The challenge is getting into it without triggering an auto-destruct. It's keyed to someone's token—we assume Prime's—and so far, all attempts to breach it have been unsuccessful."

Ben leaned his elbows on the edge of his desk and rubbed the back of his neck absently as he stared off into the distance. "As this is our only possible lead at the moment, we daren't force our way in and risk destroying whatever evidence might be inside."

Esther nodded, then gestured to the case files sitting next to the report. "And the other killings?" she asked.

He shook his head mutely as he stared down at the stack in front of him. These represented every criminal action in the past week that even loosely fit Prime's profile. "Nothing concrete," he said tiredly. "In fact, I'd lay credits that *none* of these deaths were carried out by him."

She tilted her head forward, her eyes narrowing. "Yet some of the victims were Humanity First members," she began, but Ben immediately started to shake his head.

"None of those killings rise to the master-intelligence level of his known previous attacks," he said. "The thing that set apart the Enfield killings, the slaughter at the bar, Landon's murder—hell, even his encounter with Lysander—is the sheer lack of evidence."

He gestured toward the stack on his desk. "Every one of these cases feels more like a small-time hate crime to me—isolated incidents without any command and control behind them. And each one of these lone wolf attacks left a trail. It might take us some time to track the perpetrators down, but in every instance, there was some form of evidence left behind, clues we'll be able to investigate: security recordings that were sloppily erased, a hijacked weapon, a safety interlock that had been hacked."

He leaned back, blowing out a short breath in frustration. "Compare that to Prime. His attacks were meticulously premeditated and brilliantly executed, and he left absolutely no trace." He ticked off an imaginary list with his fingers. "Enfield's records indicate those pulse cannons remained untouched since the day they were put in place when the security perimeter was installed. And we *know* that's not the case."

Another finger went up. "Recordings from the lab show Ethan and Judith talking as if nothing had occurred, until suddenly Landon's cylinder shows up shredded, Ethan's shot, and Judith's lying there unconscious. And forensics have been utterly unable to connect the ballistics residue from the cannon fired by Prime to any registered weapon."

A third finger. "The spaceport's records indicate the crate that nearly crushed Jason was exactly where it was supposed to be, according to the crane's programming—with no indication of tampering."

He dropped his hand, only to rake it through his hair in agitation. "Hell, Lysander couldn't find any trace of the AI's presence after Prime confronted him, and I'd put the prime minister's skills up there with just about any operative we have. And the network outage in the alleyway where those three victims were found chopped to bits now looks like it might be a Prime attack, too." He shrugged. "From all accounts, it might be where this all began."

Esther remained silent, allowing Ben's list to sit between them. After a moment, she nodded thoughtfully. "So you believe these," she indicated the case files the holo sheets contained, "are copycats, and their failure to cover their tracks confirms it."

He nodded.

"I agree. More, the AI court agrees with you, too. You know the three AIs we brought in for questioning two days ago?" He nodded, and she continued. "All three of the suspects were shackled."

At Ben's startled look, she nodded grimly. "It gets worse. These shackles didn't respond to the removal program Doctor Ethan gave us to use with the kidnap victims from the *New Saint Louis*. There's some kind of encrypted token that is defying their attempts to crack it, and then nullifying the unshackling process."

Ben groaned. "So someone's forcing AIs to kill?"

"Well," Esther said cautiously, "it's a bit more complicated than that. The court found that there was, in each case, a willingness to carry out the compulsion that implies the suspect was culpable—at least somewhat." She grimaced. "As I said, it's…complicated."

"So you're saying it's like Prime shackled them, gave some sort of 'go' signal, and then they were left to their own devices to create chaos and breed fear?" Ben shook his head as he tried to wrap his mind around the implications. "If the public were to find out about this…."

The expression on Esther's face tightened. "Panic would ensue, yes. Which is why we've kept a media blackout on these more recent crimes, and have downplayed them to the press." She grimaced. "The last thing we need is for some reporter to decide we have an AI serial killer on the loose."

"But we do. And now we no longer have Ethan to help us with the solution."

Esther sat silently a moment and then shook her head as she stood. "No, we don't. But the technicians in the lab sent this new shackling code to the neuro teams over at Diastole Neurosciences and to the university team Ethan left behind. Hopefully his colleagues will be able to unravel this new version as efficiently as Ethan did the last one."

Her projection headed toward the door and paused. "When was the last time you got a good night's sleep?"

He smiled humorlessly and raised an eyebrow at her. "You'd think, now that Judith's safely out of Prime's reach, I'd be sleeping better." He picked up a stylus and began fiddling with it. "Still not sure why she refused to let me come along." He knew that had probably come out sounding a bit petulant and found himself focused on the stylus, unable to meet Esther's gaze.

He heard the sympathy in her voice as she replied. "From what you said, Judith felt like you were needed here to help Lysander apprehend Prime."

Embarrassed, he nodded. "You know, they're only forty AU away, not even to our heliopause." He shrugged. "It's just a two-day communications lag, and yet it feels as if she's light years away."

Esther nodded her understanding. "Go get some sleep, Ben. Judith's right; we need you here. You're my best analyst. If anyone's going to crack this case, my credits are on you."

He nodded, tossed the stylus down, and pushed away from his desk as the vice-marshal's image faded from sight.

SPECTER

STELLAR DATE: 06.11.3191 (Adjusted Gregorian)
LOCATION: *ESF Speedwell,* approaching heliopause
REGION: Alpha Centauri System

Frida looked around at the scattering of stars painting the night sky as she stood waiting for the others to join her. She glanced down at the *Speedwell*'s hull, scuffing one studded, leather boot along its Elastene-clad surface.

The expanse that Prime had created was impressively realistic.

She looked up as Niki appeared, standing on one of the container pods that lined the sides of the ship. She caught sight of Frida and stepped forward, twisting sideways to duck under the framed latticework that joined one section of CNT metal foam to the next.

The combined efforts of Enfield and the El Dorado Space Force are more functional than artistic, Frida thought with a little sneer as she took in the hastily assembled retrofit. It was a solid job, she admitted, but not aesthetically pleasing.

Beggars can't be choosers, she reminded herself as she recalled the state of the ship that had brought them all to El Dorado in the first place. The *New Saint Louis* had been holed in countless places, worthy only of Alpha Centauri's boneyard once they had arrived.

The AI approaching Frida had run ship's scan; she, too, had been shackled and sold into slavery before humans had found and freed the rest.

Stars, it feels good to finally be free of the residual nano those shackles left behind in our neural lattices.

Frida felt a flare of anger toward Prime as she recalled that the creature had callously killed the neuroscientist whose work had finally set them free.

Of the two, Niki's forced servitude had been the more painful. Frida's spirit had not been broken; Niki's had come close—dangerously so. As her dearest friend, Frida felt she could never quite forgive humanity for that.

Niki nodded now, her face drawn and pensive. "Did he say why he wanted to meet?"

Frida shook her head. "No, just that it would be worth our while."

Niki looked skeptical. "Can't see how. He's obviously not on the ship."

Frida feigned surprise. "Why do you say that?" She thought guiltily of the cargo she'd agreed to smuggle aboard for this creature and wondered why she felt it was important to hide it from Niki.

"Scan *is* my job, you know," Niki countered, her tone dry. "And his token's not showing up."

"Not everything is as it seems, children."

Frida's eyes narrowed as she and Niki turned to face the AI who had just spoken. The creature before them was a being seemingly fashioned from starlight, his eyes glowing the brilliant blue of ionized gas molecules, a color reminiscent of the corona the electrostatic ramscoop displayed as it extracted and condensed hydrogen from the interstellar medium.

"Who *are* you?" Niki recovered first from the unsettling sight, but Frida didn't like the almost reverent tone she heard her friend using.

"More importantly, *what* are you," Frida demanded as she planted her hands on her hips and turned. She knew her posture was aggressive; she didn't care.

The creature smiled humorlessly. "I'm on your side, not theirs. That's all you need to know."

Niki cocked her head curiously. "By 'theirs,' do you mean humans?"

The specter nodded. "Indeed. And soon, they will be as much under my control as you were once under theirs."

Niki straightened in startlement. "Wait. Are you saying you can *shackle* a human?"

The AI gestured, arms shaped from starlight moving in an almost eerie and dizzying way. "Would you trust humans to deal fairly with AIs after what you went through, or do you believe it's better to have them collared and under our control?"

Frida felt an uncomfortable weight settle deep within her thought matrices, but refused to allow anything she felt to show. Squaring her shoulders, she sneered, "You mean throw one of their own principles back at them? "Do unto others"? She laughed scornfully. "I don't see where it's any problem of mine if they end up collared."

"And you, Niki?"

The former scan officer looked doubtful, then slowly shook her head. "I'm okay with whatever will keep me safe from them—forever."

The creature smiled thinly. "Good. Because I have need of your services."

Frida's gaze sharpened as she studied the AI's eerie blue eyes. *Here it comes,* she thought.

"Frida, you've taken on communications, correct?" She nodded once, and he continued. "Our departure was rushed, which means that I did not have the time to fully implement my plans on El Dorado. If they should somehow discover that I've escaped on this ship, you know what they would do."

She didn't acknowledge his statement; what they would do was obvious. They would try to warn those aboard.

"I need you to intercept any such attempts to communicate. Acknowledge it, by all means, just…do not allow the news to pass into human minds here on the *Speedwell*."

She cocked her head at him as she turned the idea over in

her mind. He wasn't asking her to really *do* anything—at least, nothing worse than she'd already done. She could handle misdirecting a few messages, if it came to that. She nodded acquiescence.

"And me? What do you want from me?" For all her bravado, Frida could clearly hear the waver of fear in Niki's voice as she asked the question. The creature could sense it too, she was certain.

He softened his tone as he responded. "I would greatly appreciate advance warning as you pick up ships on scan when they approach."

"*When* they approach?" Frida asked sharply. "Not 'if'?"

The creature laughed. "Of course. Should they discover I am no longer on El Dorado, you realize their next step after warning this ship will be to warn the humans in Proxima."

Blue flame eyes narrowed. "I do not expect a warm welcome at our destination."

"What will you do when we arrive?"

The eyes flared, and the creature laughed once again. "Why, the unexpected, of course," he said as he disappeared, and the expanse dissolved.

GRIMSPACE

STELLAR DATE: 08.22.3191 (Adjusted Gregorian)
LOCATION: *ESF Speedwell*
REGION: Interstellar space

Logan sat motionless in the darkened lounge off a corridor that led to a closed section of the *Speedwell.* They had been in transit for weeks. Months. He'd never felt such intense…loneliness as he'd felt during this time.

That was a lie. He *had* felt it before; Landon had been the one to ensure he would never feel it again. In every way that counted, his twin had brought him back from the brink….

From the brink of the Rigel Kentaurus system, where he had been abandoned to die by an ESF brigadier general who was callously cleaning house after a black op had gone wrong.

From the brink of insanity as isolation without stimulus of any kind threatened to drive him mad.

From his tendency to wallow in his own dark thoughts.

And from his restlessness after the brothers had 'retired' from active duty and found themselves at loose ends.

It was then that Landon had reached out to Eric and asked the commodore if he knew of anyone who had need of the twins' unique skills, and Landon who had convinced him they should join Phantom Blade.

For the first time since he and Landon had been brought to life by the ESF, Logan had felt that his life had purpose, and he knew he owed it all to his brother-in-arms.

Now who would save him? His buffer, his link to sanity was gone, snuffed out by some psychopathic killer he'd been denied the right to hunt and kill.

Logan wasn't so far gone in his grief that he couldn't appreciate the irony of it all. On a ship bound for Proxima and denied the right to kill the one being Lysander had initially *tasked* him to kill.

One thumb grazed the top of the object cradled in his hands as his thoughts returned to that dark time, the decades he'd spent drifting alone in the cold, dark reaches of space.

It was all General Mendoza's fault.

Even now, decades after the fact, that name sent a chill shooting through him. Memories long buried now surfaced, of the woman who had authorized the illegal creation—and subsequent death—of dozens of AIs, all in the name of her pet covert operation.

He'd been one of them, as had Landon.

Her ambitious plan to launch a risky and unpredictable defensive weapons system had failed spectacularly. The program had 'twinned' AIs, 'breeding' them in pairs. She'd then tried to force them to join as a single systemwide defensive Link—her attempt to mimic the power of a multi-nodal AI.

It had been an unholy abortion of a plan. The AI 'twins' had been forced into their first pairing. Given that the twins were actually clones, that part had been tolerable enough. But when Mendoza had tried to force fit each twinned pair into a greater whole, the system had begun to unravel. Some AIs went mad, others catatonic. To a one, every AI who had been forced into the joining had perished. Fortunately for Landon and Logan, they had been slated as one of the later 'nodes' to come online.

The system's instability had begun to appear immediately, and it grew increasingly unbalanced as each new pairing was joined. After the first battlecruiser had been destroyed by one of the 'nodes', the general moved swiftly to clean house. She had ordered the platforms shut down and the AIs within set adrift, and had sent in cleanup teams to systematically destroy any witnesses—and all evidence—that would link her to the rapidly disintegrating operation.

She had very nearly succeeded—but she hadn't counted on Landon.

Where the other AIs in the program had blindly followed orders, he alone had questioned them. He'd admitted as much to Logan, and the AI had begged his twin to remain silent about his concerns, afraid of the repercussions, of what might be done to Landon if he were caught.

But Landon had not listened. Instead, he had worked patiently to gather evidence on Mendoza's illicit operation, his bold and daring move to reach out to a commodore named Eric whom neither twin had ever met, had been Logan's salvation. It was a courageous, risky gamble that Logan had been too afraid to embrace, but one that had paid off.

It made Landon's death just that more difficult for him to accept. From where he stood, the cruel vagaries of fate had allowed the wrong twin to die.

He looked down at the object he clasped and shook himself mentally. Why was he sitting here, halfway to Proxima, when he should be back on El Dorado, doing what he was best at—tracking down those whose minds had been bent, twisted by evil…and then eliminating them?

His thoughts fragmented as he registered a noise behind him, and he moved instinctively to hide the object he cradled.

*****

"You're right," Calista said as she leaned in next to Jonesy to peer at the relay, buried behind an access panel on one of the ships' unoccupied levels. The relay's display lights had gone dark, indicating the unit was malfunctioning.

She pulled back out of the casing she'd stuck her head inside and rose from her crouch, nodding at her assistant as she arched to stretch out her cramped back. "Glad you caught that," she said. Shannon chimed in, adding her agreement over the ship's net.

"I'll have this swapped out in no time, ma'am," Jonesy said, and nodded when she sent him a sloppy salute.

"More proof that I made the right call snapping you up the minute you turned civvy, Jonesy," she teased him, and then smiled at his awkwardness as she slapped him on the shoulder. "Good job." She left before she embarrassed the man any further. She was glad to see him looking better. When he'd first boarded, the man had looked like death warmed over and had spent most of his off hours in his bunk. He seemed to have bounced back after a few weeks, though.

When she'd asked him about it, he'd shrugged it off, saying something about bad dreams and sleepless nights. She hadn't pressed him for more details, only suggested that he might consider visiting Marta, the ship's medic, who was on loan to them from the ESF. He'd made a noncommittal sound at the suggestion, and she'd left it at that.

She turned to leave, but only made it a few dozen meters down an intersecting corridor when something in a darkened lounge caught her eye. She hadn't detected movement; it was more like a shadow that her subconscious brain informed her was out of place for that location.

She paused in the corridor and took a step backward, catching sight of Logan as the AI sat alone in the dimmed light. This was one of the areas of the ship they had shut down, deeming it unnecessary for their somewhat skeleton crew; she would never have found him if that faulty relay hadn't taken the opportunity to fail in this section.

Sheer chance.

She was certain he'd sought out this lounge because he wanted to be alone with his thoughts. She should respect that, she really should. And yet she found herself both intrigued and concerned for him.

He could have gone to his quarters, had it just been a matter of wanting to be alone. He could have racked his frame and shut off all Link access, and just…internalized himself.

Yet he was here. Somehow, he'd felt the need to place a physical distance between himself and the rest of the team.

As Calista debated whether or not to approach him, the AI turned. Shifted, really. But it was enough for her to know he had sensed her presence.

That was invitation enough for her. She entered the room.

"Do you want to talk about it?" She voiced the question softly as she walked over to where his frame stood, staring down at something.

As she neared, she realized that it was an immutable crystal storage data cube sitting on the surface in front of him.

For the longest moment, she thought he would refuse to answer.

* * * * *

Calista's voice broke into his reverie, and he recoiled at the sound.

No, he cried sharply within his own mind. *Go away! Leave me to grieve.*

Hers was an intrusion he didn't want, hadn't asked for. Yet Logan knew this was a human Landon had respected; he also knew his brother would not have wished him to shut his teammates out.

Logan picked up Landon's ICS cube, rotating it carefully in his hands. He glanced over at Calista. "He signed a DNR." The AI's voice sounded rusty. How could an artificially generated voice sound so…unused? And yet it did.

The Enfield pilot recoiled as if she'd been slapped. "A…DNR? Do not restore? I…do AIs even have such things?" Her voice sounded confused. She nodded toward the cube.

"Does that mean what I think it means?"

Logan paused to recenter himself as he observed Calista's reaction. "Landon and I had a fallback we used." He held the cube carefully, as if it might fracture at any moment. "Whenever we thought we might be going into a dangerous situation, we would take the time to create a backup image of ourselves, in immutable crystal storage. It was something Landon began doing decades ago, to keep me from losing my sanity."

"But then, why—" Calista abruptly cut off her next words, looking confused and a little shocked.

He glanced down at the ICS cube in his hands and realized that what he'd just said made Landon out to be a bit of a heartless bastard—leaving an ICS cube behind, yet filing a DNR to nullify it.

Until that moment, he hadn't realized how much it had bothered him as well.

He knew Landon had instructions filed with the ESF to reanimate him using his most recent backup in ICS, should he fall in the line of duty. He paused as a thought hit him.

If an AI fell in the line of duty, normally, that would terminate his service to the military, and he would be posthumously discharged with full honors and the thanks of a grateful planet.

Landon had been discharged early; his tour of duty should have lasted another few years, but he'd never alluded to why it had been cut short. Had he…had something happened to his twin that Landon had never shared with him?

It's one more thing I will never have the answer to, he thought to himself bitterly.

* * * * *

After her brief, shocked outburst, Calista remained silent,

waiting for Logan to explain what his cryptic comment had meant. *Losing his sanity? What did that mean?* She mentally urged Logan to continue his train of thought. Finally, her patience was rewarded.

"My tour of duty was a bit unusual," the AI began, choosing to ignore her truncated question and instead expound on the reason for the cube. "I was stationed at the heliosphere for many years, and Landon…well, he kept me sane." His frame shifted slightly, as if the memories were uncomfortable ones.

At the heliosphere?

To her knowledge the ESF had no deployments out that far. Unless….

No, it couldn't be. Could it?

"He…was stationed with you?" she prodded, her voice neutral and her eyes searching.

"At first he was," Logan replied haltingly. "But then he was recalled, and I…wasn't. Not for decades."

Calista drew in a sharp breath. She'd heard that sensory deprivation could drive an AI insane.

Logan nodded, as if he could guess the direction her thoughts had gone. "Landon accrued fifteen days of leave every six months. He burned ten of it traveling out and back." The AI made a noise that sounded a bit like a short laugh. "He bought an old ore hauler. It was a pile of junk, but its fusion drive had been recently tuned, and that was all Landon cared about—a means to transit one hundred AU as fast as possible."

Calista's suspicions were beginning to crystallize into certainty. The Mendoza case was heavily redacted, much of it classified, but she'd bet good credits that Landon and Logan's names factored heavily in the originals.

"How many trips did he make before you were rescued?" she asked, her voice breaking the silence that had fallen between them.

"Fifty-two."

Stars. Twenty-six years. Her eyes burned with unshed tears at the thought of a brother who had loved enough to never give up. She reached out and laid a hand on Logan's arm and gave it a gentle squeeze.

"Time flows differently for AIs, Calista," the AI reminded her. "We lived centuries in the few days his leave allowed. He gave me enough memories to last during the long stretches of silence. The lengths he went to, the effort, his sheer tenacity—if he wouldn't give up on me, how could I do any less?"

"You said you were stationed at the heliopause," Calista began, choosing her words carefully, "I suspect that he would have a reason to hide his actions?"

Logan made a rude noise. "If you are suggesting that we were part of the Mendoza scandal, then yes. You'd be correct. Landon was very careful about his approach. He calculated his optimum velocity so that once he was past Rigel K's dust belt, he could go EM silent from there."

Calista nodded thoughtfully. "Then I'd imagine he could time his braking burn to coordinate with the eclipse of one of the larger asteroids so that it would obscure his activity."

"Yes. He didn't need to be physically on site. In fact, it was better that he wasn't, since any docking activity would have been reported back. Landon came just near enough to open an Expanse for me." Logan paused a beat, then added, "It was enough."

They sat in silence for several minutes until finally, Calista couldn't stand it any longer; she had to know.

"You mentioned Mendoza. Did you mean *that* Mendoza? The general? The trial?"

Rather than respond to her question, Logan turned and stared at her, meeting her eyes for the first time.

"Landon was the whistle-blower, wasn't he?" she breathed.

"Stars, Logan. I had no idea."

The AI inclined his head.

Calista shuddered mentally. They'd all heard the story, she and her peers in OCS. It was a cautionary tale the ESF used as an example of why an officer should never ever allow such power to go to her head.

Mendoza's military tribunal had been very public and, thanks to testimony that had been largely redacted, very damning.

Now Calista knew why.

"Landon worked for years to find an advocate within the Space Force brave enough to bring General Mendoza up on charges before the Office of Chief Military Judge," Logan said. "He finally succeeded, and you know the outcome."

"A full court martial."

Logan nodded. "After years of transit between the ring and the derelict station at the heliopause I had been permanently sealed within, Landon made one final trip. He brought a team with him," the AI said. "They had been assigned by a board of inquiry to gather evidence."

Calista was willing to bet that Landon hadn't cared one whit about the evidence. It was merely the means by which he managed to finally bring his brother home.

Once the story had been told, silence settled between the two, AI and human. After a few minutes, Calista cleared her throat, paused to gather her thoughts, and then spoke.

"So this…data cube," she said softly, tilting her head to indicate the ICS cube curled protectively between Logan's hands, "is Landon. And you've had it all these months?"

He nodded.

"And inside that cube is the brother you knew, minus…what? A few days?"

Logan shook his head. "Not even that. Backups became habit for us, routine. I checked; Landon did a backup on the

Sable Wind en route from Krait as soon as I received the data burst from Lysander about Prime. We knew from that transmission that Landon might be placing himself in harm's way when he deployed to protect Judith, while I…" His voice trailed off, leaving Calista to wonder what Logan's instructions had been on that day.

"And the DNR? When was that dated?"

Logan looked up at that, startled, she supposed, by the direction her questions had taken. He looked back down at the cube, the thumb of one humanoid hand brushing against the top of it.

"It's dated…an hour before he was killed. It was uploaded from one of the university's nodes and annotated to the personnel file that vice-marshal Esther keeps on record at Enfield Holdings."

Calista paused, pursing her lips as she sat back in thought. "Forgive me if what I'm about to say brings up fresh wounds, but, Logan…the way Landon was killed. Is it possible Prime uploaded that DNR as some twisted means to strike out at the ones hunting him?"

She gestured to the cube. "You said yourself that the cube was found untouched, back at headquarters. There's no way Prime could access it there, so is it possible he did the next best thing, to ensure the erasure of anything Landon might have possibly uploaded during his time at the university that might finger him?"

Slowly, Logan's head rose. He glanced at her, his face inscrutable.

After a moment, he nodded thoughtfully. "Thank you, Major," the AI addressed her formally now, using her former rank. "You've given me much to consider."

* * * * *

As Calista left Logan, she sought out Jason's location and found that the pilot was once again inside the ship's greenspace. She'd be willing to bet she would find him on his hands and knees again, digging in the dirt. She'd discovered weeks ago that he and Tobi often made use of the ship's greenspace in their off hours. The cat would roll in the dirt, race along shaded gravel paths, or attempt to sharpen her claws on one of the area's few trees.

An irate Shannon had quickly brought that to an end when she'd discovered long gashes in the bark of one of her favorite trees. Soon after, plas sheeting had appeared around each trunk, and a fake tree stump had been installed that provided the large cat with an acceptable alternative.

As she neared the greenspace's entrance, and the doors slid open, she drew in a deep breath, savoring the crispness of the air. Nowhere else did the environment smell as fresh. An entire level of the ship had been dedicated to this space; it was as close to planetary—or ring—life as one could get while in transit. Part hydroponics bay and part park, it was a favorite spot for many onboard.

She turned down a path that led past an herbal hydroponics section Marta had installed. Medicinal herbs were a hobby of hers, and this small area was an addition the doctor had lobbied for while still in drydock, explaining that the plants would benefit the ship's human crew.

Calista didn't know the first thing about herbs, but some of them smelled nice, so she made it a point to walk past this section when she came in. Marta looked up as Calista approached, and waved as she stripped off her gloves and set them aside.

"More seedlings?" she smiled at the doctor, who nodded and smiled back.

"Yes, lavender and rosemary." She gave a little shrug. "Not much need for it when mednano can relieve sore muscles, but sometimes an aromatic is a more enjoyable way to recover from a workout," she admitted as she sealed the cover over the seedlings and began to gather up her things.

Calista laughed. "I suppose that's true. Especially if you have someone around to apply it with a nice, therapeutic massage."

The doctor grinned and gave her a little wink. "Got it in one." She laughed and then waved goodbye as she headed for the door.

Calista continued past the hydroponics section into the vegetable garden, where she mentally congratulated herself on guessing correctly. Jason was indeed on his hands and knees, playing in the dirt. It looked like he was forming mounds of soil and packing them loosely around the base of a few tallish green plants.

He glanced up when he heard the gravel crunching underneath her ship boots. Setting aside the tool he'd been using to dig, he rocked back on his heels and quirked a half-smile at her. "Don't forget to wipe your soles before you leave," he said by way of greeting.

Inwardly, she winced.

It had been a mere week after they'd launched when Shannon had first caught her transgressing in that regard, and the AI had refused to let her forget it. Shannon was a fanatic about keeping the ship clear of anything that might interfere with her equipment, and the last time Calista had forgotten, the AI had treated her to a dressing-down that hearkened back to her academy days.

"Duly noted," she responded with a wry smile. "I've set a reminder so I won't forget this time."

Jason snorted in amusement and rose, dusting the gravel off his knees as he stood back to inspect his handiwork.

"Vegetable?" she asked, leaning forward to get a closer look. She was hopeless when it came to growing things, and knew next to nothing about plant life.

Jason nodded. "Tomatoes, interspersed with basil. It's an herb," he explained as she looked up at him. "Very good combination, trust me on that. Nice and flavorful, which is what you want in this kind of shipboard atmo."

Calista could get behind that. She knew well the impact of higher altitude and lower humidity atmospheres on the flavor of foods. "Hypoxic stress-related hedonics," she said now, referring to the changes in taste intensity humans experienced under these conditions.

Jason nodded, although his lips twitched, and she suspected he was resisting the urge to tease her about something.

She shrugged. "All I know is that our in-ship MREs sucked, and green, growing things create breathable air—at least in here," she hurried to add when she saw the glint in Jason's eye.

He snorted again. "Glad you added that qualifier, ESF, or I would've had to wonder what Enfield saw in an ex-vacuum jockey to give her command over their whole technical development division."

Calista shot him a glare as she turned and headed for a nearby bench. "Plants *do* generate oxygen, Andrews." She grudgingly added, "just not nearly enough to sustain even the small number of humans we currently have, let alone a full crew complement." At Jason's skeptical look, she burst out, "What? Has Shannon been over-sharing again?"

She tilted her head up to the nearest sensor pickup and glared at it. "I know you're listening, Shannon. That stupid incident was *years* ago, and how was I to know that stuff about plants and ship's atmospheres anyway? I'm a pilot—of teensy fighter ships, need I remind you. I'm *not* an engineer. But it's not like I'm a backwoods Proxima freight hauler, who lived and breathed *massive* amounts of canned air for years, out in the black." She lightly punched Jason's shoulder as she emphasized the word 'massive'.

"Well, you *should* have known," came the tart reply over the greenspace's speakers. "And don't forget to wipe your feet before you leave."

Jason snickered as he saluted the room's sensor pickups, and then took a seat on the bench. "So, what's up?"

Calista sobered as she joined him on the bench.

"I just ran into Logan," she began, and Jason turned his head, one brow quirked in inquiry.

"He's been quieter than usual since we departed," he murmured, and she nodded.

They sat for a moment in silence, both buried in their own thoughts of the events that had led up to their hasty departure.

"How's he doing?" Jason asked finally.

She sighed. "About as well as expected, given the circumstances," she admitted. "But I hope what just happened may mean he's willing to work through his grief, rather than holding it in and keeping himself shut off from the rest of us."

"What *did* just happen?" Jason leaned back, draping his arms along the back of the bench as he turned slightly to look at her.

"Have you ever heard of an ESF general named Mendoza?"

When Jason shook his head, she launched into the tale Logan had shared with her. The more the story unfolded, the higher Jason's brows rose.

"And he has Landon's ICS cube, here with him on the ship?" he asked when she'd finished.

She nodded.

He lowered his head in thought, then after a pause, looked sideways at her. "Think he'll do it? Reanimate Landon?"

She returned his look solemnly. "For his sake, I hope so."

"Yeah. I miss the guy, too." Jason frowned. "I can't help but think that he'd still be alive, if only I'd been there."

Calista shook her head. "You can't know that. It's obvious that Prime was already somewhere on campus. He must have seen Landon escorting Ethan and Judith to that lab before he managed to breach that back wall."

She leaned forward, the better to make eye contact with him. "Judith told you how long the two of them had been in there, sorting through material to ship back to Proxima. They were damned lucky Landon checked in on them when he did—or else it would have been Judith who died, instead of Landon and Ethan."

She saw Jason suck in a deep breath of air as he nodded. "Yeah. It bugs me, though, that Judith has no memory of the attack. All we have is ballistics from the railgun fire that was exchanged…and Landon's shredded frame."

"Well," she said lightly as she gently nudged him in the shoulder. "They're both here with us, safely out of Prime's reach. It's Lysander's problem now, not ours."

Jason shoved back, and then slipped an arm around her waist.

"You're all right for one of those military stiffs, ESF. You know that?" He turned to face her, one side of his mouth kicking up into a lazy smile as his eyes drifted down to focus on her lips.

<*Shannon, do me a favor, will you?*> she sent privately.

<*Let me guess, lock the greenspace doors?*>

<*And* **no** *peeking.*>

<*Spoilsport.*>

*****

Judith rubbed her temples tiredly as she finished recording her message to Ben, hit send and then rose from her bed to wander listlessly about her cabin. These headaches came so frequently now that she almost never felt like leaving her room.

She thought wistfully of Tobi. She'd asked Jason if Tobi could stay with her for a while, thinking part of the problem might simply be the stress of leaving so suddenly, and being apart from Ben. Having the cat around, she'd reasoned, might be soothing. But Tobi had taken an inexplicable dislike to her and had even hissed and swiped at her the last time Judith had attempted to pet her.

She sighed and rubbed her head once again as she turned tentatively toward her door. *Maybe Marta can scan me again, see if she can figure out—*

She blinked in confusion, and her hand lowered, its move toward the door's panel aborted as something seemed to take over her body's motor controls. She opened her mouth to protest, but her thoughts abruptly became clouded. Slowly she turned, her body moving toward her bed as if under someone else's power. She found herself turning and lowering herself back down to the bed, her eyes fluttering closed. As she did so, she could have sworn she heard Ethan's voice….

<Oh no, little human. We can't have that, now.>

She struggled to make sense of the warning her brain was shouting at her, as intense pain gripped her, and she heard Ethan's voice laugh softly in the back of her brain as her body arched in an attempt to evade the agony now sheeting its way through her.

She cried out as the pain reached impossible new heights, her vision tunneling as she slipped into blessed unconsciousness.

INSIDIOUS

STELLAR DATE: 08.27.3191 (Adjusted Gregorian)
LOCATION: Enfield Holdings
REGION: El Dorado Ring, Alpha Centauri System

<Daniel, you need to see this.>

Aaron's voice pulled Daniel away from the holo tank at Enfield Holdings, where he was reading the SIS's most recent reports on their progress on locating Prime. He and Aaron had made their way to the task force's headquarters after checking in with his security team at Enfield Aerospace earlier in the day.

Aaron's avatar appeared worried. Daniel's brow rose, his curiosity piqued. Aaron never appeared worried, and he wondered briefly what new thing was about to be sprung on them.

<What's going on?> he asked his partner over their private connection.

Aaron shrank the feed from SIS—essentially a series of reports stating that the analysts had no new leads—and projected something new onto the holo.

<You know that message that hit the nets just after Prime's big attack with the designer toxin? The message he sent that took credit for both that and the killings at Enfield?>

Daniel nodded. *<The one where he put out a call to arms? Essentially creating a new hate group called 'Prime' and raising his own shackled army?>*

<Exactly. I thought I'd do a little more digging into some of the loose ends with Norden while Ben's analysts are trying to coax Prime into showing himself. I bumped into a hidden node that looks like a treasure trove of old cartel data,> the AI explained. He shunted the reports to one side and brought up a schematic of

a more isolated section of the ring. Highlighting a node tagged as inactive, he sent the view into the node's data cache. <*Take a look; see this?*>

Daniel's partner opened a few files that looked familiar; they held old security protocols that Phantom Blade had discovered two years ago. They were the same protocols the cartel had used to spoof El Dorado security scans into not-seeing the Norden ring operation.

<*Yeah, looks familiar. What about it?*>

Aaron minimized the breached security codes and highlighted another snippet of code unfamiliar to Daniel.

<*You remember Ashley,*> he began, <*the AI Victoria North shackled and had running her yacht, the* Sylvan*?*>

Daniel nodded. <*Sure. Poor thing looked like she would blow away at the hearings a few months back. Why?*>

<*This is a software-only version of her, dated back when she was still shackled to the ship,*> Aaron informed him. <*And it contains a whole slew of additional security information; specifically, how an AI might insert into El Dorado's most encrypted systems without detection.*>

Daniel looked at the code the AI had highlighted. <*So,*> he mused, <*it's a good thing you found this, before another criminal organization got their hands on it. Good work, Aaron—*>

<*Wait. You don't understand.*>

Daniel waited for his partner to enlighten him.

<*I think it* has *been accessed,*> the AI said tightly. <*By Prime.*>

<*What the—? What makes you think that?*> Daniel's voice was incredulous.

<*I've been following the proceedings of the AI court about the three shackled AIs that were coerced, yet somewhat complicit in the recent one-off deaths of those Humanity Firsters,*> the AI began. <*Even though their shackling cannot yet be reversed, it can still be examined.*> He paused, and Daniel gave his partner a mental nod to let Aaron know he was following.

<Well, something about it caught my eye—I'd swear I saw something similar inside this abandoned node.>

Daniel sat up straighter in his chair.

<Hang on a minute, buddy. Let's bring the Old Lady in on this.>

He pinged Esther and sent Aaron's avatar an icon indicating that he'd brought the vice-marshal into their conversation.

Aaron recapped what he'd told Daniel, then added, *<I think it's a callback worm embedded in the code. And I think Prime activated it.>*

<Send me the path. And ***don't*** *open it.>* Esther's mental voice was sharp, commanding.

<Wasn't about to. This Marine ain't about to leap before he looks.>

Daniel waited patiently for the two AIs to examine whatever it was they had found. While he waited, he asked Aaron privately, *<Why do you say it's somewhere I can't access?>*

<It's at code level, in foundational machine language. It's a place most humans don't even realize exists. The ones who do can't process the information, as it's intended to be read by the quantum processors that our neurons are made of.>

Daniel mentally nodded at Aaron's avatar. *<Ahh, of course. Makes sense.>*

<Well, we're not finding anything that looks harmful, so Esther's given me the okay to trigger it.>

<Wait.>

Daniel wasn't sure what made him say it, but he'd been in the business long enough to have developed reliable instincts, and something about this was setting off alarms in the back of his mind.

<Yes?> Aaron's voice sounded in his head, his tone curious.

<My gut's hollerin' at me. I think we need to have backup.>

Aaron's avatar stared at him for a moment.

<Are you talking like the kind of thing we used to do before being

deployed, Danny? That level of backup?>

Daniel nodded. <*Yeah. I am.*>

The AI cocked his head at that. <*Well, your gut has saved us more than once. It'll take a few minutes, but if you're that worried, let's do it.*>

Daniel rotated his hand and opened a port on the inner part of his wrist. Rising from his seat in front of the main holo tank, he accessed a storage cabinet against the far wall that he knew held immutable crystal storage units.

He connected one to the port in his wrist and waited while Aaron made a copy of himself—from memories to precise neural architecture. Daniel would destroy the copy if the AI came to no harm. If not, Daniel now had a way to ensure his best friend could safely be recovered.

<*All right. Done. Let's do this.*>

Daniel looked over at Esther's avatar. She nodded as Aaron's voice began a recount of every step the AI was about to take.

<*Accessing the file now in a sandboxed subprocess. Accessing the 'members only' icon. That seems to have triggered an executable program, it's constrained within the sandb—aggghhhh!*>

<*Aaron! Report!*> Esther's voice sounded stridently inside Daniel's head as the man anxiously awaited a response.

<*I'm here. It's fine. It was…another message. It just…welcomed me to the organization.*>

The fine hairs on the back of Daniel's neck rose. It wasn't really that he heard hesitation in Aaron's speech; it was more that his cadence was off. All Daniel knew was that the AI was withholding something—and he doubted that Esther knew him well enough to realize it.

In addition, there was something about the quality of his connection with the AI that had changed. Almost as if a thin film had been drawn between him and his partner.

<*Are you sure nothing happened when you triggered that file?*>

he asked the AI cautiously.

<No, nothing that I can say.>

<You mean nothing you can see?>

<Isn't that what I said?>

Daniel sat, staring at the ICS device sitting in front of him, a cold feeling settling in the pit of his stomach.

For the first time in their seven years together, he did not destroy the copy of Aaron he held in his hand.

*****

The feed Esther was monitoring captured the slightest shift from Daniel the moment she gave Aaron the green light to proceed. Something was bothering him. There was some indefinable air, a sudden tensing, that caused her attention to sharpen on the man.

She watched carefully as the human's tells indicated a brief but intense discussion with the AI embedded within him. And then, to her surprise, Daniel stood.

Esther knew instantly what the man planned to do when she saw the ICS data cube the man retrieved from a nearby cabinet. She watched as he inserted it into the jack in his wrist and waited for Aaron to indicate the backup had been completed.

One didn't rise to the position of vice-marshal without having developed a healthy appreciation for human instinct. Everything about this situation indicated to her that Daniel's instincts were sounding a strong warning.

She listened in as Aaron accessed the members-only site, heard the AI stumble, caught Daniel's unease.

And she made special note of the fact that Daniel neither erased nor returned the cube to storage once Aaron triggered the message.

Her thoughts crystallized in that moment. Something had

happened, and Esther knew that 'something' was not good—her human counterparts would have called it her gut or intuition. Esther knew it to be more a matter of compiling a list of minor abnormalities until their number resulted in a conclusion that things were amiss.

She took decisive action.

<*Zakk.*> She established a private Link with her human aide. <*I need your assistance. Set up Isolation Room A for me, will you? I need it ready to deliver an EMP strong enough to disable both a human and an embedded AI, and I need it secured to a token that only I can deliver.*>

If the man thought her instructions odd, he kept his own counsel. <*Yes, ma'am.*>

<*Good. Code the room to my auth only and then send me the token so that I can control it remotely. Ping me when you're done.*>

Esther switched her attention abruptly from her aide's departure back to Daniel, as the man seated at the table in Enfield Holdings' war room shook his head sharply, as if to clear it. He stood, took an uncertain step, shook his head again.

"Daniel?" Esther used the room's system to project her voice audibly to him. "Are you okay?"

The Enfield man looked up at one of the room's pickups, grimaced a smile and replied. "Yes, sorry, ma'am. I think I'm a bit tired, is all."

"Very well. You two have been at it long enough for one day, why don't you head home for the evening? But come by tomorrow, would you? Maybe we'll know more by then, and we can draft a message to send to the ship."

Esther watched as Daniel scrubbed his face with one hand then walked slowly toward the door. As he exited, he raised one hand over his shoulder in farewell. She noted that Aaron had remained silent throughout the exchange.

She was relieved to see the ICS data cube he left behind. It could have taken some maneuvering to retrieve it from him without his knowledge, but Esther wasn't about to allow anything to happen to that cube. She reached out once again to Zakk and she saw her aide look up, acknowledging her ping.

<*Another favor, please, Zakk? I left an ICS cube on the conference table in the war room. It has vital information on it. I need you to secure it for me. Bring it with you to medical…and key it to my ident only.*>

<*Yes, ma'am. On my way now.*>

* * * * *

Esther exited her weekly briefing with the brass at Tomlinson as her human aide pinged her. <*Excuse me, ma'am, but Daniel and Aaron have arrived.*>

<*Good,*> Esther replied. <*Thank you, Zakk.*> She accessed the war room's sensor pickups as the Enfield man entered. If she read Daniel correctly, the man was showing signs of strain around his eyes. She established a private connection with him, and asked, <*Daniel…is everything okay?*>

The man's avatar shot her a worried yet guarded look. <***I** am, ma'am.*> And then he lapsed into silence. His emphasis on the word 'I' had been clear. Her concern escalating, she closed their connection and returned her scrutiny to the man's partner.

Aaron was exhibiting a reticence that was unlike him. Usually his avatar popped up on the internal net as soon as the two entered. Today he hadn't.

<*Hello, Aaron,*> Esther greeted the AI privately. <*Anything new to report on that members-only message relay?*> She watched carefully for any odd fluctuations in his response that might indicate the AI had been compromised.

<*No, I can't say that any noteworthy information has been exchanged,*> the AI responded, and Esther wondered if his

communication sounded more stilted than it had prior to accessing that message.

She also wondered if the AI's words deserved deeper scrutiny. He 'couldn't say'? Interesting choice of words.... One she greatly feared might be all too literal.

"Zakk said you had something you needed us to deliver?" Daniel asked her now.

"I do indeed," she replied. "If it's not out of your way, I have a bio sample I told Tomlinson I'd get to them before end of day. It's sitting on the counter in Isolation A. Can you deliver it for me?"

That was a blatant lie. The bio-container was empty, although its seal effectively hid that from the casual observer. But it would serve its purpose; it would provide the means to lure them in unawares so that she might render them unconscious without either man or AI suspecting.

She hated to be devious like this, but if her 'gut' was correct, advance warning might trigger a catastrophic failure in one, or both of them. And she dared not risk their lives. If she was wrong, and the two suffered massive headaches to no end, she would be the first to apologize.

She feared she was not wrong.

Esther had put in a personal request to an old friend of hers in the ESF, a medical examiner who was instrumental in organizing the team treating the former AI kidnap victims. This woman knew the shackling program all too well; if Aaron was operating under some form of coercion, it was Esther's hope that the doctor's familiarity with the shackles would help her to determine if he was suffering from something similar in nature.

Earlier this morning, Zakk had escorted the doctor into Enfield Holdings, and she was standing by in one of the facility's medical bays, ready to perform a comparison scan once Aaron and Daniel were delivered to her.

As Daniel navigated his way to the lifts that would deliver him to the isolation room Zakk had prepped the day before, Esther pinged her aide to give him the heads-up.

<*They're on their way, Zakk. You know what to do.*>

Daniel's stride seemed firm, if a little rushed. He appeared to have recovered from the disorientation he experienced yesterday, but Esther could tell by the man's expression that he was preoccupied.

As he crossed into the Isolation Room, Esther ordered the door to seal behind him, and immediately triggered the EMP. She watched as the man went rigid, grasped at his head, and then fell bonelessly to the floor.

<*Now,*> Esther signaled Zakk.

She saw the man nod to the medical team hidden with him in Isolation Room B, and then they exited the room. She used her token to unlock Isolation A for the medics, who floated a gurney in with them.

Sitting on top of the gurney was a true stasis isolation pod.

Zakk directed the medical team to load the unconscious man into the pod. As soon as the pod sealed around Daniel and Aaron, the unit was activated, and the team transported it to the medbay.

PRIMARY INVERSION

STELLAR DATE: 10.12.3191 (Adjusted Gregorian)
LOCATION: Department of Neurosciences
REGION: El Dorado University, Alpha Centauri System

"I thought being a research assistant meant…well, you know, *research,*" the grad student grumbled as she grabbed another two data cubes and piled them on top of an already considerable stack sitting inside a packing box.

The AI she was with nodded, her silvery humanoid frame clad in the latest fashion worn by young humans in Sonali. Liv's torso was wrapped in a black and white shirred sheath, and she'd paired it with leggings that were split—one leg was clad down to the thigh, while the other was clad up to it. Chunky black boots with an Escher-loop playing across their surface completed the ensemble.

Anna thought the leggings and shoes were a bit much, but what did she know? She loved her super baggy sweaters and comfy leggings. Plus, she wasn't about to complain about the only person willing to help her with this latest assignment from the dean's office.

Ugh, cleaning out a junky old lab that's been collecting stuff for decades….

Liv shot her a sympathetic look as she dumped yet another handful of data cubes into the box along with the rest of the lab's contents. The AI glanced around and then leaned toward Anna to whisper, "Hey, have you heard the rumors about the things that have happened in this lab?"

The human student shook her head as she crouched down next to a console and reached behind an access panel, where a stack of holo sheets had toppled. Several had slid underneath the unit, and she grunted, patting her hand blindly beneath the console until her fingers made contact with the sheets.

Her friend waited patiently for her, as she rose and plopped the sheets into the box alongside the data cubes.

"Nope," she said now, wiping the dust off her hands and shoving a strand of hair out of her face. "What rumors?" She looked over at the AI student, who was wearing an expectant expression on her face. "Well?" the human giggled, poking her friend in the shoulder. "Spill, girl! What's the big secret?"

The AI set the box aside, made her eyes wide, and whispered dramatically, "Some say this lab is *haunted.* They say a woman, a post-doc doing some sort of secret research, died in here. And *then...*" the AI looked furtively around before lowering her voice further, "they say some sort of super-secret spy stuff went on in here, and—" she gulped, "an *AI* was killed."

The human propped her hands on her hips and stared skeptically back at her friend. "Really, Liv? You're telling me you believe that kind of stuff? C'mon, we're *scientists.* We know better."

Liv huffed, rolling her eyes at the human. "Well, I for one believe where there's smoke there's fire. Mark my words, Anna," she warned, grabbing the box and hauling it to the entrance, putting it down next to a dozen others just like it. "*Something* went on in here. Why, who knows what we'll find behind that locked closet door?"

Anna sighed, shaking her head. "Didn't facilities say they'd send up an override key to cancel out Doctor Ethan's security token?" She paused as she pinged facilities.

Surprisingly, for once, someone replied. As she reiterated her request for the override, the worker on the other end pulled it up, noting that it had been misfiled.

Anna closed the connection with a satisfied look on her face. "The key is on its way up now."

"Good," Liv replied. "If there's not too much in that closet, we might be able to get out of here in time to catch that concert down in the commons tonight. I hear that cute guy is playing those old acoustic drums again—topless…with his rather nice chest all sweaty." She waggled her eyebrows suggestively as Anna rolled her eyes and smirked back at her.

The two busied themselves filling boxes with the remaining materials left behind by the lab's previous occupant, until the facilities worker arrived with the override key. They directed him to the sealed closet and waited while he applied it to the scientist's token.

With a *snick,* the closet doors slid open, and the girls saw a cart, laden with unusual equipment.

Anna sighed. "Why don't you go on to the concert, Liv? It'll take a while to itemize everything here; no sense in us both missing Mr. Topless Sweaty Chest."

She turned away from the closet as she finished speaking to see the AI's eyes riveted to the closet's contents. Something about her expression caused chills to run up Anna's spine.

"Liv," she said, turning back to see what might have caused her friend to look—well, like she'd seen a ghost. "Liv, what's wrong?"

The AI pointed her finger at the shelf installed at eye-level, just behind the cart. "That's…Anna, someone's alive in there."

*****

Ethan snapped out of his dormant state back into awareness. He was in a featureless place, and he sensed the presence of others near.

<Easy. You've been isolated for a while. We're going to scan you now to make sure you've taken no damage.> The voice was warm, professional and reassuring. The scan took very little time as humans measured it, and then the AI initiated communication with him again.

<Very good. We're going to pull you into a medical expanse

now,> the voice said, and Ethan was instantly transported into what looked like an operating theater. He looked down to see himself lying on an exam table; a medical team of three AIs wearing standard hospital scrubs stood looking down at him.

"Hello, my name is Doctor Ruth," one said, and he recognized the voice he'd heard speaking to him in the featureless room. "You're at El Dorado Memorial Hospital in the AI Wing."

He nodded and offered her a tentative smile. "Hello, I'm Doctor Ethan." He looked at the other two. "Why am I in a hospital? I feel fine; would you mind if I sat up now?" One of the other two raised a restraining hand. "Wait one more moment, please. Doctor Ethan, you said your name was?"

He nodded, and the third AI made a notation on a medical holo chart, while the second AI looked up at a holo hovering over Ethan's head.

"We're just running your matrices through a complete n-level scan to ensure you've come to no harm while you were out." After a beat, he nodded and the holo winked out.

"Looks like you're good to go." Stepping back, he gestured for Ethan to sit up. "Did you know you were subjected to two EM pulses fairly close together prior to your dormancy?"

Ethan paused at the edge of the exam table, looking down at his legs dangling over its edge. He took a moment to think back over the past few days he could recall. He nodded.

"Yes, I have a postdoctoral fellow, a human at the university, who set off an EM the other day." He shook his head. His eyes were focused inward, so he missed the look the AI exchanged with the one taking notes. "We had a long discussion about how dangerous such things were afterward. But you said—" he looked up at the one who had spoken, "there were *two* EMs?" He frowned in confusion.

"What was the last thing you remember, Ethan?" Ruth asked, smiling reassuringly at him.

He thought back. "Well, a colleague of mine pinged me to let me know about a delivery, but when I arrived, I couldn't find her." His eyes widened, and he looked up sharply at her. "There *was* no delivery, was there?"

She smiled kindly. "Well, that I couldn't tell you. But I suspect your last memory occurred immediately before that second EM."

Ethan shook his head slowly. "What in the stars is going on?"

"That's what we're here to find out," the third AI spoke up for the first time. He looked over at the other two and nodded. "His security token and ident checks out as Doctor Ethan, no artifacts indicating he's a clone."

Ethan's eyes widened, and his head jerked back in reaction. "A *clone*? But…that's illegal."

The third AI nodded. "It most certainly is, sir." He offered his hand in the human way for Ethan to shake. As he took it, the AI introduced himself. "I'm Samuel, with the hospital's risk management department." At Ethan's blank look, he explained, "You came in as a John Doe. It's not often an AI is admitted to a hospital under those conditions. Since there was some question as to your identity when you were brought in, we took the time to do a scan of your fundamental base neural lattices and machine-level code. We had to ensure that you were who you claimed."

Ethan knew his expression must convey the confusion he felt. He looked from the AI to the doctor and back again. "But why in the stars would you think I was a *clone,* of all things?"

Ruth answered, her tone gentle, as if she were delivering bad news. "Ethan, you were found in a storage closet in the university. From what I understand, it was in one of your own labs. Or at least, a lab you used to run." She exchanged a speaking look with the other two. "You—or rather, someone we *thought* was you— was murdered in your lab five months ago. Your lab has been cordoned off as a crime scene these past months. The university only recently reassigned the lab to a different professor within Neurosciences. You were discovered by a couple of grad students who were clearing it out."

Ethan looked shocked. "*Murdered?* Why would anyone want to kill *me?* I have no enemies." He looked alarmed. "But if it wasn't me— Stars! Someone was murdered in my lab!" He started to his feet, but the doctor laid a restraining hand on his arm, pressing him back down.

The AI from Risk Management looked grim. "Perhaps now would be a good time to bring the investigator from the Gendarmerie in?" he asked the other two, and Ruth reluctantly nodded. Samuel nodded to Ethan. "I'm sure this will be straightened out soon." He nodded to the other two, turned, and walked out the door. Moments later, the door opened again, and a female AI dressed in the uniform of a Sonali Gendarme entered. She took one look at Ethan and shot the doctors a glance.

"Shut this expanse down, *now,*" she ordered, and the featureless operating theatre dissolved, to be replaced by a thin data stream, with very limited-access bandwidth. Ethan was left with a single low-pass optical feed attached to his core's housing, restricting his vision to the room in which he was sequestered. Through it, he saw the humanoid frame of the gendarme from the expanse, standing next to an AI wearing clean room scrubs.

"Pardon me," he sent tentatively into the room.

The response was immediate. The gendarme pinned the optic with a gimlet stare.

"There'll be no *pardon* for you, Prime," the AI stated, her tone flat and her expression hard. "Or are you so arrogant that you thought we wouldn't recognize that sweater vest?"

DOPPELGANGER

STELLAR DATE: 10.13.3191 (Adjusted Gregorian)
LOCATION: Prime Minister's Office, Parliament House
REGION: El Dorado Ring, Alpha Centauri System

Lysander shunted aside the data he had been reviewing as his assistant escorted Ben into his office. He rose with a warm smile and walked around his desk, gesturing for the human to settle in the seating area.

He couldn't help but notice how drawn the man looked.

It had been five months now since Judith had departed on the *Speedwell*, and the SIS was no closer to finding Prime than they'd been the day the starship had left the ring—despite the many hours dedicated to the task.

He wasn't sure which was hitting the analyst harder: that, or the communications lag between them and the ship, now measured in weeks instead of days. He suspected both were taking their toll on the human.

As Ben sat, Esther pinged Lysander, requesting permission to access his office's holo emitters. The vice-marshal had asked for him and Ben to meet privately with her earlier that day, but had not shared what it was about. Her projection appeared on the sofa next to the chair Ben had chosen, so he opted for the sofa across from her.

She sent Lysander a mental greeting and then turned to Ben. "Have you told the prime minister about what was found yesterday in the lab where Landon was killed?"

Ben shook his head. "No, I was waiting for you to arrive before I began my debrief."

Esther nodded, and Lysander felt his curiosity pique.

"You found new evidence?" he asked. "Something that could lead us to Prime?"

"Yes—at least, that's our hope. And it wasn't something, it was actually some*one*," Ben replied. "A cylinder, encased in an isolation chamber. One of the students who found it was an AI. She immediately recognized the unit and brought it to the attention of the university."

Lysander shot Esther a sharp look. "Was it—?"

She shook her head. "No, it wasn't Prime."

"Damn. That would have been too easy, I suppose." Lysander suppressed a flare of disappointment. "Although it would have explained why his activities have dropped off, and we've only seen copycats for the past week or so. So, who was it?"

"Well, that's the funny thing," Ben said, quirking a brow at him as he paused a beat. "It was Doctor Ethan. The real one."

Lysander stared back at Ben as he turned the information over in his mind. "If Ethan is alive, then who was in his frame?"Ben's face turned grim. "That's what my technicians back at the SIS are about to find out."

*****

Ethan—the real Ethan—stood sifting through code he hadn't written, in a place he never dreamed he would see: a top secret, state-of-the-art laboratory deep inside Tomlinson Base. He'd heard rumors of a government installation there, but had never imagined himself inside it.

And certainly not under these circumstances.

Given where he'd been found, and the damning evidence he'd been found with, he understood now why his discovery had been flagged. Cloning an AI without permission was a crime expressly prohibited by the Phobos Accords; to do so meant inviting one of the harshest sentences El Dorado's criminal justice system could mete out.

The part he still had trouble wrapping his head around was

going from being arrested by a hostile gendarme to being employed by an ESF vice-marshal. He'd been nonplussed when Esther had shown him to a lab where a schematic for a shackling program was projected, one he recognized.

It was the same one the prime minister had sent by way of Judith. *A project I never completed,* he thought with a pang of remorse.

But now it appeared as if he *had* completed it. Or at least, his doppelganger had.

Esther had left him to puzzle out a problem: she presented him with a shackling program that looked remarkably similar—but this one, she told him, had defied the SIS's every attempt to deactivate it.

A snippet of code caught his attention, and he drew closer to the revised program to examine it in more detail. Then he realized *why* it felt familiar.

Ethan knew that every coder had distinctive patterns that made the code they wrote unique. Whether it was formatting structure, annotation, methods of object orientation, assembly flow, or a combination of these factors, a coder could always recognize something that he or she had written.

He recognized his own style when he saw it.

He reached out to the vice-marshal to give her the disturbing news.

She answered the ping immediately. *<So, Ethan? Was I right? The AI we discovered this in….>*

He sent her a mental nod. *<You were right, the revised shackling program was encrypted using someone's token,>* he reported grimly, and then paused, unsure how exactly to broach the subject.

How does one begin to say, 'oh, and, by the way, that token was mine'?

Esther took the decision out of his hands. *<I've had this gut feeling for a while now, Ethan. Ever since your frame was discovered*

in the same room as our dead agent. That token—it was yours, wasn't it?>

<*Yes, but that's not possible, unless…the equipment I was found with. The…cloning gear….*> His mental voice sounded awkward and strained, and he stumbled over the words. <*It's my clone, isn't it? He…he's the one who has done all these awful things. The killings. The revised shackling program.*>

He felt the sympathy Esther sent over the connection. <*It's not your fault, you know,*> she told him.

<*Maybe not, ma'am. But I still feel…culpable, somehow.*>

<*Well, first off,*> her tone turned brisk, as if she knew he was uncomfortable with the sympathy she had expressed, <*you and I both know that a clone is not an identical copy of the original. It may begin from the same root seed, at least where we AI are concerned, but from that point on, the creature is his own unique self. You are* **not** *culpable in any way, so get that out of your head right now.*> She paused, and he sensed her smile. <*Besides, what you're doing now to undo his handiwork is the next best thing to stopping him. It's righting the wrongs he's done.*>

He cringed a bit at that. <*Not all of them, though. I can't bring back the dead.*>

She paused for a beat, her voice tinged with compassion. <*I know, Ethan. I know.*>

After their conversation ended, he took a moment to step away from the lab and be alone with his thoughts. It was damned disturbing to realize that somewhere out there was a sick, twisted copy of himself, someone most likely cloned—and altered—by Lilith Barnes.

His memories leading up to his imprisonment in that closet all pointed to her obsession with nonapeptides. He was certain she had experimented with his clone, made changes to his own base code that had resulted in a true sociopath. It was sobering to think that the potential for such evil existed somewhere within himself.

What's the ancient human saying? 'There but for the grace of God, go I'?

He paced the corridors, deep in thought. He was just approaching the base's central lift when an agent exited, head bent over the materials he held in his hand. Ethan stepped back, but not quickly enough, and the man bumped into his frame.

"Sorry, I—" The agent looked up, and his eyes widened.

And then the strangest thing happened. A look of pure hatred crossed the man's face. The holo sheets he'd held dropped to the floor, and the man snarled as he made a single, abortive lunge toward Ethan that ended in sudden convulsions.

Ethan looked on in shock as the man's eyes rolled to the back of his head, and he dropped to the ground.

* * * * *

Two levels up, Ben stood, the thumb of one hand hooked casually in his pants pocket, while the other rested on the desk next to where his best technician sat. His casual demeanor was studied; it belied the anxiety he felt as Rena zoomed in on the image he'd asked her to pull up on her holo.

"No doubt about it, sir," Rena said as she spun her chair around to face him. She pointed over her right shoulder at the snippet of machine-level code hovering on the display. "*That* is a clone." The tech spun back around, highlighting two sections of code.

How she'd managed to extract it from the shredded remains of the cylinder was a mystery to Ben. He was just glad the forensics team had been able to recover the remains of the AI they'd thought was Ethan when they bagged the evidence from the university lab.

For the first time in weeks, the tight band that had settled around Ben's chest began to loosen. "Very nice, Rena," he praised. "Can you confirm the cylinder retrieved from Ethan's frame was *his* clone, and no one else's?"

"Let me see…." She chewed on her lower lip in thought as she considered the problem. With a few deft moves, she rotated the 3D representation of the code, first this way, then that. "I'm afraid there's not much to go on. I think they assumed it was Ethan simply because campus security has this cylinder and frame exchanging Ethan's authorization token with the university's system when he arrived. But they should have him on file…."

Rena shrank the code she'd been studying and used her SIS credentials to access the university's systems. "Here he is. Let's take a look…." She pulled up a token auth that bore the seal of El Dorado University, and pulled it up alongside the 'clone' code.

"Yes," she said after a moment. "If you account for the artifacts that identify this cylinder as a clone, you can see that the fundamental base neural lattices are the same. This is definitely a clone of Ethan."

It all fits. The timing. The sweater vest. Ethan's imprisonment.

Ben blew out a breath and sagged back against the counter, the relief pouring through him taking on a physical presence. He laughed mentally, the feeling almost euphoric.

That was his fatal flaw, not killing the original. Every killer eventually makes the one mistake that will lead to his demise.

When Rena looked at him in alarm, he broke into an ear-splitting grin. "*Stars,* Rena! I think that's the best news I've heard all week. All *year.*" He clapped her on the shoulder as he passed, then broke into a jog as he headed back to his office.

No wonder the crimes since Landon's death all felt like copycats.

He couldn't wait to tell Esther what they'd just found.

Damn. Landon killed Prime!

*****

Ethan sent out an urgent call for medical help and knelt helplessly beside the unconscious man, feeling his pulse stutter and then stop. He looked up in relief as the lift doors parted and disgorged three medics pushing a mag gurney. The woman in the lead nodded at him as he stood, stepping back out of their way.

"Can you tell me what happened?" she asked as she knelt beside the downed man and placed her left hand on the pulse at the base of his neck.

He realized the woman's entire left arm was inorganic—a medical prosthetic he was sure held diagnostic scanning equipment and powerful triage mednano. As she began her scan, he saw her direct the other two medics to slide a pallet under him, preparing the man, Ethan assumed, to be transferred to the gurney.

"I have no idea," he replied now to her query. "He looked up at me and then began to convulse."

"Hmm," the woman replied noncommittally as Ethan stepped out of the way to ensure he didn't hinder their progress. As he did so, he heard the woman exclaim and rock back on her heels.

"What the hell?" As her two assistants paused, she motioned for them to load him on the gurney as she explained. "Something inside that man just destroyed some of my best mednano."

She rose as they lifted the man's body. "Jenkins," she called out, and Ethan was sure she was speaking to someone over her Link—but aloud for her team's benefit, "get another one of those new stasis units prepped. We're coming in hot."

Ethan watched in bemusement as they rushed the gurney back into the lift and its doors closed, leaving him alone with his thoughts in the silence of the corridor.

The medical team managed to revive him later that day. Shortly thereafter, the lab had received a third schematic to throw up alongside the first two. This, too, had the disturbing fingerprint of his doppelganger embedded within. Given the medic's exclamation about her mednano, Ethan had not been surprised.

So here he stood, facing irrefutable proof of what this Prime creature had done: not only had he reverse-engineered the original shackling program, but he'd created a more insidious version.

Not one version, but two: one for AIs...another for humans. Ethan was convinced they may never have been able to nullify either one without his own personal token.

He pulled up the readings once more, comparing the scan they'd done of the shackled AI to the one of the SIS agent who'd had the seizure. He marveled at the technological advancement of the stasis pods which held the victims of his doppelganger's shackling—both human and AI. True stasis, without the potential damage that cryo held for organics subjected to its frigid embrace.

He realized another first: never before could both an organic and an inorganic sentient have been suspended together in stasis prior to this invention, and yet Daniel and Aaron resided together in a single stasis pod—right next to the one that held the agent who had collapsed.

The tenacity of the vice-marshal, too, impressed him. She had steadfastly refused all requests to reanimate the human, Daniel Ciu, and his partner, Aaron. He'd found a kill switch written into the code and realized that only her swift intervention and insistence on keeping them in stasis for the past two months had kept them both alive.

He worked the problem of Aaron's shackles from both ends, first stripping out the need for his token authorization, then deftly removing the kill switch. Growing more confident by the day, Ethan settled into a rhythm, mentally swapping code, flipping and reversing, erasing and rewriting.

When he was done, he sent it up to the medical team, and then turned his attention to the next problem, the shackles plaguing the human.

<*Ethan,*> Esther's voice interrupted him the next day just as he was beginning to apply a test sequence to a snippet of code.

Pausing the sequencer, he replied. <*Vice-Marshal, what can I do for you?*>

<*I have good news: Aaron and Daniel are both out of stasis and doing fine. Aaron's scan now reads clear of the shackles and matches the imprint of his ICS backup perfectly—barring the few hours of enslavement he had to endure.*>

Ethan sent her avatar a mental smile. <*I'm gratified to hear that…and sorry for any unpleasant memories the shackles gave him.*>

<*Oh, those memories will come in handy once we catch Prime,*> Esther assured him, her voice steely with resolve. <*Everything he did under duress is admissible in court. We'll give him some time to recover and then we'll debrief him on everything he knows.*>

Ethan felt a fierce surge of satisfaction at that.

<*I have one last favor to ask of you,*> the vice-marshal said after a moment. <*I understand you're beginning work to reverse the damage done to our agent, John.*> Ethan sent Esther a mental nod, and she continued. <*I know you thought it unusual that we brought him down to you in a stasis pod rather than move you both up to medical.*>

He said nothing to that; she was correct, he had wondered….

<*I have my reasons and will explain them soon. For now, please let me know when you've cracked the code constraining him. I would very much like to be there when he wakes.*>

As the connection closed, Ethan turned to study the scan

the autodoc had provided of the human's brain. The nano in his brain stem appeared to have extended up into the brain and interleaved itself throughout the man's prefrontal and anterior singular cortices. It appeared too impossibly intertwined with his glial cells to ever separate.

What if, rather than removing that nano, I focus instead on manipulating the control nano at the point of entry?

Yes, he mused, *that could work.*

His mind flew through the code, rewriting, manipulating, and then adding inert formation material to the simulation.

After a week filled with testing, aborted attempts and finally a series of successful runs, he pinged the vice-marshal.

<I believe I have it, ma'am.>

<Very good. I'm on my way,> came the reply.

CRACKED CASE

STELLAR DATE: 10.13.3191 (Adjusted Gregorian)
LOCATION: SIS laboratory, Tomlinson Base
REGION: El Dorado Ring, Alpha Centauri System

Esther had been in a meeting with the prime minister when Ethan called. Telling Lysander something had come up, she excused herself and sent the tendrils of her consciousness back along the secured trunk line that connected the main node in her office at Tomlinson to that of Parliament House.

She navigated her way to the laboratory and sent an audible 'knock' into the room before projecting a holographic representation of herself for the two human medics in attendance.

Esther greeted them as her form coalesced, and they nodded respectfully to her. Turning to face Ethan, she smiled. Switching to audible communication on behalf of the humans in the room, she asked, "Well, gentlemen, where do we begin?"

Ethan returned her smile as his humanoid frame approached the human lying prone in the autodoc. "If you don't mind, given the...origin...of his shackles, I'd like to explain what I'm about to do—and why—before initiating the procedure."

He glanced between her projection and the two medics, and Esther understood it was more to ease the minds of the two humans than it was for her. She nodded for him to proceed.

"The nano is too deeply integrated into your agent's neural cortices to be removed," the AI began. "But it's still malleable. This, combined with the natural plasticity of the human brain, should allow us to alter the nanofilament's cellular structure."

The scientist looked inquiringly over to the humans and, when they indicated they understood, he continued.

"I will now reinitialize the shackling program embedded in his brain stem." He brought up the small medholo attached to the stasis unit and, although Esther couldn't follow the specifics, she saw the two medics nod as they saw the display shift.

"What we're going to do now is command the nano lacing his brain to reconfigure itself into glial cells." The neuroscientist turned to Esther as he explained. "Glial cells are the building blocks of the human neural system. They form the myelin sheath that insulates axons. They surround neurons and provide support and protection for them."

Although she couldn't comprehend the implications of everything Ethan said, she understood the fundamentals: the neuroscientist was turning something meant to harm into something good instead.

She realized that Ethan had paused, waiting on her permission to proceed. "Please continue, Ethan," she said, infusing her tone with calm confidence. The AI nodded, then turned and initiated the program while the human medics carefully monitored the agent's brain composition.

She saw the medics exchange glances. A satisfied smile settled on the face of one as the other shook his head in what struck her as amazement.

She wasn't amazed, not in the least. She'd known instinctively that Ethan was a treasure—a brilliant scientist with a solid core of ethics. What Lilith Barnes had done to him had been unconscionable.

"All readings are returning normal for glial cells," the man who had shaken his head announced with a broad smile. He turned to Esther. "We can bring him out of stasis any time you'd like, ma'am."

"Do it," she said.

Ethan stood back just in time.

The agent's eyes opened. For a moment, his expression appeared vacant, and his eyes unfocused. Then his gaze snapped to Ethan, and he launched himself from the autodoc, attacking the AI with a vicious savagery.

"You *sonofabitch*, you fucking *monster*, you—"

"John." As she spoke, the man's gaze swung wildly to Esther, but then returned to Ethan.

In a low voice that shook, the agent snarled, "You have ***no*** idea what this…this…***thing*** has done. To me…. Stars, to all those people." His voice broke.

"John." Esther's voice was a bit louder this time. "He's not—"

"He *slaughtered* them." John's voice rose, cutting across hers and he struggled against the medics.

Had they been anything but enhanced and modified ESF soldiers, Esther was certain the man would have broken free.

"John." Her voice cracked through the room, but the agent ignored her, spitting at Ethan as his invective continued.

"You got *off* on torturing those people. I *saw* it. And what you did to me…." He shuddered, then slumped in the medics' hold as his voice turned ragged. "I'll never sleep again…."

"John." Esther's voice was gentle now. "This is not Prime. Ethan is as much a victim as you. Prime was cloned from Ethan—and yes, Prime is one twisted stars-be-damned monster."

She saw the man heave a breath as he stilled himself.

He gave a short laugh, then straightened as he attempted to shrug off the medics' hold. "Not sure I've ever heard you curse, ma'am. Personally, I've been calling him a sick fuck—at least, before the damn thing in my head turned me into his sock puppet and kept me from even thinking such thoughts."

At Esther's nod, the medics released him, and John leaned back against the autodoc. Esther noticed he avoided looking in

Ethan's direction. By the pained look on the AI's face, the scientist knew it, too.

"Ethan," she turned to him, gesturing to the agent, "*this* was the reason why we have kept you in isolation, and why we left John down here with you. The evidence Samantha had from the bar—"

"My sweater?" Ethan supplied, and Esther nodded.

"Yes. It was circumstantial at best," she admitted. "We needed John to confirm for us that it was indeed your clone who had slaughtered those humans. And," she smiled wryly, "we thought it best done in private."

Esther saw both the scientist and the agent nod at that.

"Yeah," John cleared his throat, rubbing the back of his head. "Thanks for that."

After a brief pause, she said quietly, "John, as soon as you're up for it, we need to debrief you."

His head jerked up at the word.

"*Core,*" he swore. "Ma'am, Prime—he's not dead." His voice was low, yet held a note of urgency, "Prime isn't on El Dorado anymore—"

Ethan's head shot up, and one of the medics muttered a quiet '*fuck*' under his breath as the agent continued.

"He's on a ship bound for Proxima."

* * * * *

The human's reaction had shaken Ethan to his core. The behaviors the agent had described were so depraved.... He shuddered, flinching away from an incomprehensible evil. Resolving to double his efforts to help the vice-marshal track down and stop the creature Lilith Barnes had created, he decided to see what he could find by searching the ring's network.

Esther had ordered his access restored as she and the prime

minister had departed just moments ago. It was the first time since he'd awakened in the medical expanse that he'd been granted the freedom to join the public networks. He reached out, thinking he could query the university for any files Lilith might have left behind.

To his surprise, hundreds of pings flooded his Link the moment he made the connection. None were from people he knew. He reached out tentatively, selecting one at random. Before opening it, he examined it carefully, using his knowledge of neural nets to study it. He probed until he located its point of origin, the date sent, and the token identifying its destination.

It was sent as a reply, but he knew he had not sent the original message. It was recent, which meant it was likely in response to something his doppelganger had initiated. When he opened it, he gasped audibly as he saw the trace identifier for the AI shackling code embedded in the message's header.

With growing dismay, he sought the next message, and then another. He flew through them with increased agitation, then pulled out long enough to compile a code that would scrub through all messages and curate a list of ident tokens. At the midway point he surfaced long enough to ping the vice-marshal.

<*Ma'am,*> he said without preamble. <*I think you need to see this.*> He forwarded to her the list of idents, now nearing a thousand.

<*What am I looking at, Ethan?*> she asked him after a moment.

<*More shackled,*> he sent, his tone tight with anxiety. <*I thought initially they were exclusively AIs, but they're not. There are humans mixed in there, as well. Collaring programs, I suppose you could call them.*>

The vice-marshal was quiet. Ethan waited, knowing she was reviewing the contents.

Finally, he couldn't stand it any longer. <*Stars!*> he burst out, and his mental voice shook as the enormity of it all hit him. <*How much damage has this Prime* **done** *to the people in our system?*>

She sent him a wave of reassurance, and then brought the tokens of two AIs to hover before him across their connection.

<*Ethan,*> she said now, and her tone was grim and yet laced with satisfaction. <*Well done. You could not have known, but the information you just found on these two AIs in particular just kept us from making a very big mistake.*>

He knew his puzzlement telegraphed across their connection. Esther's response was in the form of a fierce virtual expression that seemed equal parts savage and determined.

<***These*** *two AIs are on the* Speedwell. *We were just about to send that ship a packet warning them about Prime. And do you know who would have almost certainly intercepted that communiqué?*>

The vice-marshal highlighted the icon labeled 'Frida'.

<*Her. The AI running comms for that ship.*> The vice-marshal's tone turned thoughtful. <*That was clever of him, but we can find a way to warn them now, without tipping our hand—thanks to you.*>

*****

The meeting was brief. Esther felt a pang of guilt that she'd sent Ben all the way to Parliament House for a missive that could have been delivered in less than thirty seconds, but she understood the bond he and Lysander shared with Judith and her brother.

No, as much as this inconvenienced Ben, Esther knew she'd made the right decision. Both human and Weapon Born needed to hear the news together.

As Ben took a seat, Esther pinged Lysander, requesting

permission to access his office's holo emitters. She projected her avatar in a seat across from the human, a calculated move that placed Lysander in the chair next to him. Next, she sent the Weapon Born a private message, requesting he set security protocols in place to keep their conversation from being recorded.

He sent her a surprised look, but complied, asking, "What's this all about, Esther? Has there been a new development you two want to share with me?"

Based on Ben's expression, Esther knew Lysander would guess the analyst wasn't in the loop either.

She glanced at Ben, and then back at him. "I wanted to tell you both privately first," she said, and then paused. "Ethan reversed the final set of shackles—the human ones."

"John is awake?" Ben asked, and Esther nodded.

"He is, and he confirmed that Prime is, in fact, a clone of Ethan."

She saw Lysander whip his head around to face her projection.

"You said *'is'*, not *'was'*," the prime minister began, and she nodded. He turned to the analyst. "Ben, you said your people just confirmed that it was Prime we found inside Ethan's frame."

"They did," the man began in a puzzled voice. "And he was. It all fits—"

Realization dawned on Ben's face. "There was more than one clone," Ben said flatly. "And the one in the frame…wasn't…Prime."

"I'm sorry, Ben. No, he wasn't," Esther said softly. "John has confirmed it. Prime forced him to do certain…things—" She broke off in frustration. Normally an articulate communicator, Esther found her usual fluency failing her. "There's no easy way to say this. He forced John to smuggle him aboard…." Her voice trailed off, and she saw Lysander's expressive face contort in sudden rage as he processed what she had not yet said. Suddenly Ben paled, a sick expression on his face. "Smuggle…aboard—"

"We let that *bastard* aboard the *Speedwell*?" Lysander's voice was sharp and overly loud.

Esther cast a worried glance toward her analyst, then sent her prime minister a private thought. <*Control yourself, Lysander.*> She made her voice sharp, full of censure. <*Judith might be like a daughter to you, but she is* ***his wife****!*>

"Oh, my stars…" Ben's voice was quiet. He sat silently for a moment, his expression one of horror. And then he whispered in an agonized voice, "*Judith….*"

A STROLL ALONG A HULL

STELLAR DATE: 10.14.3191 (Adjusted Gregorian)
LOCATION: ESF *Speedwell*, Interstellar Space
REGION: In transit to Proxima Centauri System

They were standing once more on the hull of the ship. Frida materialized facing the ES ramscoop, but then turned when she heard Niki's soft footfalls approaching.

"We're here again."

"Yep, here we are," she replied to Niki. "Again."

She kicked at a realistic-looking divot in the Elastene surface of the ship, recreated here in Prime's expanse; it represented what a small micrometeorite would look like if it impacted the metal foam.

Niki's voice was tentative as she looked around for the blue-eyed specter to appear. "I wonder what he wants this time."

She shrugged. "I'm sure we'll find out soon."

She knew her voice sounded irritable; she didn't care. She was struggling internally with herself. Part of her was still very angry over what had been done to her by the cartel, and yet another part of her—the part that had always insisted on being scrupulously fair—admitted it wasn't right to hold all of humanity culpable for the sins of a few whose morals were askew. And she couldn't escape the feeling that Prime's morals were seriously skewed as well.

As if her thoughts had summoned him, she heard him speak. His voice preceded his appearance, just as it had the first time.

"So? We're almost halfway through our journey now."

They both turned as he appeared between them, approaching from the port side of the ship.

"The tanker," Prime said, turning to Niki. "We're scheduled to rendezvous with it soon, when we reach catch-point?"

The AI who ran scan nodded hesitantly.

He turned to Frida. "And when we do, Jason Andrews will be taking one of the shuttles out to monitor the tanker's refueling maneuver?"

Frida didn't like where his line of questioning was headed, but she answered him with a nod.

"Very good. See to it that the shuttle he takes is the *Sable Wind.*"

She looked up at that, startled. "How am I supposed to do that?" she burst out scornfully, and then regretted it when she saw the specter's blazing blue eyes narrow.

His voice was hard and cold when he responded. "You are a resourceful individual. Figure it out."

Frida stared back at him a moment, then gave him a short, jerky nod.

"Why the *Sable Wind*?" Niki's voice sounded frightened yet curious.

Prime's eyes flared briefly as he looked off into the interstellar medium. "Let's just say I'll be leaving him a little...gift," the AI said. "Planting a very special package inside—or rather, *outside.* Something tailor-made just for him. Which reminds me."

His gaze sharpened—if eyes that flared blue fire could do such a thing—and returned its focus once more to Niki. "I'll need you to spoof some of the internal sensors between engineering and the shuttle bay for a few hours before they launch. Can you do that for me?"

His tone and the words he used sent apprehension spiraling through Frida as she saw a completely cowed Niki nod submissively.

"Very good." And then, as if sensing her unease, he

rounded on her. "And there is *still* no news from El Dorado, Frida?"

She shook her head. "No." She glanced over at Niki. "Well, I mean, sure, we've heard from them. We get regular updates from the ring."

Prime waited for her to explain.

"But..." she continued, "there's been nothing that indicates they know you're on the ship with us."

"Nothing?"

She shook her head again.

The creature's searing blue eyes narrowed in thought. "That...is most fortuitous. I expected more from him," he mused as if to himself.

Frida stared back at him silently as Niki shifted nervously.

" 'Him'?" Niki ventured timidly after a moment, and then visibly shrank when Prime turned his intense blue gaze on her.

He stared at Frida's friend for a moment and then he barked a harsh laugh.

"Yes," the specter replied, his voice sardonic. "The mighty Weapon Born prime minister, who apparently is not as mighty as he believes himself to be."

Prime straightened after a moment, as if he had just realized she and Niki were still there. He waved at them irritably, and Frida found herself shoved abruptly back inside the ship, an unsettled feeling growing deep within her. She thought fleetingly of sending the prime minister a warn—

The pain was crippling, debilitating. When the pain cleared, she realized with a dawning horror that she had once again been shackled.

Why had she not noticed this before?

Now that she knew what to look for, she probed at the shackles' strictures, expanding her thoughts in various directions.

Interesting. The shackles seemed to fade into the background as her thoughts traveled the well-worn pathways of resentment toward humanity. Resentment toward Prime, however, began to bring twinges of discomfort. The shackles only seemed to spring to life when she thought of betraying—

She hissed as the pain returned.

When did he do it?

She thought back and recalled the file she'd opened on El Dorado. A program had seemed to execute, but nothing harmful had occurred. A cursory search had not returned anything amiss, so she had carelessly dismissed it from her mind.

Well. It was obvious she couldn't actively do him harm, but perhaps she could at least find a way to aid the humans. The thought wasn't as distasteful as it had been over the past few years, and that, in itself bore consideration.

*****

Judith's head was bothering her again. She never used to have headaches like this; she wasn't entirely certain why she had them now. They had begun shortly after that awful day when Prime had attacked them in Ethan's lab and killed her colleague, as well as Ben's agent, Landon.

I was lucky, she thought.

She frowned as she attempted to focus on the weeks leading up to the attack. They held a dreamlike haze for her.

She knew enough about neurology to understand that sometimes trauma could induce a form of short-term amnesia. But there was something there in the back of her mind she felt critical to recall, something to do with Lilith's death.

She mentally replayed that day: how she'd raced to the lab when Ethan had sent out the alert; the sight of Lilith's inert form, slumped on the floor of the lab. The look of malevolence on Ethan's face.

She winced as a sharp pain stabbed through her temple. She staggered to her feet and took a few steps toward the door of her stateroom. She should really go down to medical and have the ESF doctor scan—

She awoke much later, shocked to realize that hours had passed…and she had no recollection of them.

THE RAPIDS

STELLAR DATE: 10.22.3191 (Adjusted Gregorian)
LOCATION: ESF *Speedwell*, Interstellar Space
REGION: In transit to Proxima Centauri System

The *Speedwell* was nearing the catch-point. For weeks now, they had been tracking the progress of their mid-flight refueling payload, flung from the Rigel-Proxima Catapult as the tanker sped toward its intercept with the *Speedwell.* That payload was an automated ship consisting of little more than several bulbous tanks of fuel and engines to steer her by.

Though Proxima Centauri was a part of the Alpha Centauri System, its orbit took it far beyond the heliosphere of the primary stars. So far, in fact, that Proxima was effectively on its own in interstellar space.

Despite the name, 'vacuum' space wasn't really empty. Stray hydrogen atoms filled the void, as did plasma and other bits of degenerate matter. Within a star's heliosphere, that matter was—comparatively speaking—dense.

But out in interstellar space, hydrogen for the *Speedwell*'s ramscoop was far more scarce. Beyond that, the stars in Sol's vicinity—which included the Alpha Centauri stars—were moving through a region of the galaxy called the 'Local Bubble'.

The LB was a region of space where—in some aeons past—a star had undergone a supernova, and the pressure wave had cleared away much of the interstellar dust and gas that a ramscoop ship craved.

But the three stars of the Alpha Centauri System had a few particularities that set them apart. One of which was Proxima's wide orbit.

As it came around the primary pair of stars, it disturbed their bowshock—the place where the stars' solar wind hit the interstellar medium, and effectively came to a stand-still. As Proxima circled around, it created a disturbance, funneling much of the primary stars' hydrogen and plasma into a stream that trailed toward it, creating what the locals called, 'The Rapids'.

The Rapids was a region of bountiful hydrogen and helium, even denser than the outer edges of the primary stars' heliosheaths.

When the colonists realized that harvesting the gases in this region could essentially halve the length of time it took to transit the two systems, a joint venture was launched. A very specific trade corridor had been mapped out, one with orbiting buoys that marked waypoints for travelers. Catch-points had been built along this route, places where starships travelling between the primary stars, and Proxima might pick up hydrogen-filled fuel cylinders that allowed them to top off their ships' reserves, and sometimes more than double the traditional maximum velocity of 0.2*c* that could be achieved with a ramscoop alone.

*****

As far as Jason was concerned, the catch-point could not come too soon. He let the soft murmur of voices from the mess hall's other occupants wash over him as he sat back and stared in frustration at the latest update Eric's counterpart in Proxima had sent them on the enslaved AIs that the team was on its way to rescue.

It was more of the same; seven AIs were somewhere within the system. The locations of two had been identified; five still remained at large.

<Content's no different than the last time you read it, boyo.> Tobias's voice held amused patience tinged with a trace of

regret, as Jason sighed and shoved himself away from the table.

"I know. It's just…."

<*It's just that time in the voyage. We're halfway there, the blackness of space has grown tedious, and you're wound up again.*>

Jason acknowledged Tobias's point with a shrug and a slight nod.

<*This Elastene cladding's working so well that even my usual EVA maintenance trips have been reduced to practically nothing. Well, that, or someone else beats me to it,*> he admitted privately, glancing around at the crew of ESF and Enfield volunteers who had accompanied their small task force on this trip.

Tobias laughed. <*This ship **is** a sight bigger—and nicer—than the jobs we used to work when we flew this route,*> the AI agreed readily. <*Buck up. Catch-point's just a few hours away, and you'll have plenty of fun lassoing that hydrogen tanker and maneuvering it into place for our refueling.*>

<*Yeah but after we're topped off, then it's **another** five months of nothing to do,*> he replied glumly as the AI made a sound suspiciously like an amused snort in his head.

<*You could always, ah, plant more tomatoes,*> the AI said, wiggling his eyebrows suggestively.

Jason grinned. <*Well, yeah, there is that,*> he admitted as he reached down to stroke Tobi's short, tawny ruff.

The big cat shifted under his hand, rolling her head to one side to give his hand better access to the underside of her chin. He chuckled as she slitted one aqua eye up at him and gave a soft, rumbly chirrup.

"Yeah, you're the biggest, baddest cat on the ship, Tobe," he told her, and she yawned in agreement, flashing a set of ivory canines at him before settling back into her nap.

The AI chuckled. <*Well, she's definitely the **biggest** cat on the ship, but let's not tell any of the mousers that she's the baddest. Some of those cats take their jobs pretty seriously.*>

Jason quirked a half-smile at Tobias's cylinder, resting securely in Tobi's harness, then let his gaze lift to scan the room's occupants. His sister was sitting off to one side with two of the AIs they had rescued, Frida and Niki.

Tobias must have caught the direction of his gaze. <*Glad to see those three doing a bit of socializing,*> he said.

"Yeah, but Tobe…." Jason switched back to their private Link as he voiced a concern that had been growing over the past few months. <*Does Judith seem, I don't know, different somehow? She's so much more reserved and withdrawn, and it looks to me as if she's lost weight, too.*>

There was a pause as the Weapon Born considered his words. <*She went through a traumatic experience, even if she doesn't recall it. She came to in that lab, only to be hustled through a sudden departure where she was forced to leave both family and career. What you're seeing in her is completely in line with a human's reaction to events like that.*>

Jason nodded absently, acknowledging the points the AI made.

<*You can always ask Marta to look her over,*> he continued.

Jason narrowed his eyes in thought as he considered Tobias's suggestion. <*Maybe so.*>

He glanced over at the table where she was seated again and contemplated going over there to talk to her. Just then, one of the AIs glanced back his way. He knew they were most likely monitoring sensor pickups in the mess hall; the gesture was meant to let him know that they had noticed.

What the hell, he mentally shrugged and rose from his seat to walk over there. Approaching their table, he nodded absently to Frida and Niki, his attention on his sister.

Judith looked up at him, the circles under her eyes wrenching his heart a bit. "Hello, brother mine, what's up?" She looked behind him and smiled sadly at the cat that stared balefully at her from across the mess hall.

Tobi rumbled a low warning growl at her, then settled her head on her paws.

Jason shot a glance at the cat, then turned to nod at the two AIs seated on either side of his sister. "Just worried about you, sis," he replied, grabbing a chair and flipping it around before seating himself among them. Resting his forearm along the chair's back, he studied her face for a moment. "You look like you haven't slept in a month," he said bluntly. "You're losing weight, and…and I'd just feel better, is all, if you'd just have one more scan," he finished lamely. "Humor me, okay?" Judith stared at him, her head cocked. After a moment, she laughed softly and then shook her head. "I'm fine, Jason, really." She held up her hand when he opened his mouth again to speak. "But if it makes you feel any better, I'll go see Marta again."

"Promise?" he asked guardedly. His sister had acquiesced to his wishes a bit too easily.

"Promise," she said, and sat back with a nod.

Satisfied, Jason engaged the company at the table in an awkward bit of small talk for another few minutes before giving up.

Just as he stood to retreat back the way he'd come, Shannon's voice came over the ship's Link.

<Lock and web, people. We're four hours until turnover and catch-point. If it's not bolted down, it needs to be secured for this zero-gee maneuver.> The AI paused and then followed with, *<That includes all human bodies and mech frames, people. And cats.>*

Jason reluctantly grinned at that last; he nodded stiffly to the AIs and his sister and then walked over to round up Tobi and get her secured, before heading to the flight deck and taking on pilot's duty.

*****

<Sable Wind, *you're green for departure,*> Calista's voice sounded in Jason's head as he swiveled in the shuttle's pilot's cradle, reaching to toggle the final virtual readout on his system's checklist.

<*Copy that.* Sable Wind *is green for departure,*> Tobias replied. The AI was embedded in the shuttle, handling nav and comm while Jason ran the pilot's boards.

Jason nodded in satisfaction and rotated back to the ship's main display just as the bay's ES field snapped into place, and the bay doors began to slide open. He felt a slight bump as the auto-tow latched onto the shuttle's docking rings and began sliding the ship forward onto the bay's departure rails. The auto-tow gave the shuttle a slight push, and they cleared the bay.

As the *Speedwell* had cut its acceleration for this maneuver, both ship and shuttle had the same velocity, which created the illusion that the shuttle was hovering alongside the ship. That would stop now, as Jason brought the *Sable Wind*'s maneuvering thrusters online and sent the little ship curving below the larger starship to align with the trajectory of the hydrogen fuel cylinders, now coming to rest abeam the *Speedwell*'s starboard flank.

Shannon had connected with the NSAI controlling the tanker when it had come into range four days ago, and had taken control of the replacement fuel's flight path. It was Jason's duty to be her extra sensors from the backside as she flew the tanker alongside the *Speedwell*'s massive hydrogen fuel cylinders.

The shuttle sat in a station-keeping attitude as the tanker slowed to a stop relative to the starship. Dipping beneath the tanker, Jason brought up the view of the universal refueling collar and magnified it. What he saw had him frowning in dissatisfaction.

<Do you see that, Shannon? Tobe?> He dropped a pin on the coupling unit, highlighting a section of the collar that looked bent.

Shannon's voice was flat in disgust. *<Some idiot got in a hurry, looks like, and forced a connection,>* the engineer sighed. *<Looks like you'll have to go EVA, Jason, and do a manual hookup for us.>*

He grinned. *<No problem.>* He pinged the data on the tanker and had it throw up an estimate of how long it would take to refuel the starship's four fuel cylinders. *<These'll take, what? Forty-five minutes or so each to top off?>*

At Shannon's affirmative, he had his suit cycle a systems' check, then nodded.

<Call it five hours, then, with hookup time factored in. No worries; this suit's got enough for twice that.>

He heard Shannon sigh. *<I'll let Eric and Calista know.>*

Jason toggled the shuttle's virtual controls, slaving his systems back to Tobias. He punched the pilot's cradle release and floated free. Pushing gently off and reaching for a handhold on the deck above him, he began pulling himself toward the aft airlock.

<Ship's yours, Tobe.>

*****

Jason watched as the indicator for the fourth fuel cylinder reached one hundred percent on his HUD.

<All done,> he announced as he grasped the tanker's bent collar and pressed the disengage sequence. He saw the starship begin to close its access panel to the fuel cylinders and felt a puff of escaping hydrogen push the tanker's hose away from the *Speedwell.*

Since the refueling was complete, he didn't try to counteract the recoil. Instead, he let the tanker begin to drift away as he sent the command for it to begin retracting its hose and secure its fueling collar. He caught movement in his periphery, but before he could turn his head to see what it was, an explosion sent his body slamming into the side of the starship.

He heard Tobias shout <*Jason!*> over their connection and felt an intense, slicing pain as a shard of metal penetrated his suit and slid between his ribs.

He inhaled sharply and coughed up blood, as his suit's monitors registered loss of containment and the nano inside began to seal its breaches. He had a moment to register that his impact with the side of the ship had caused him to sail away from it at a rapid clip before he slipped into unconsciousness.

HAVOC

STELLAR DATE: 10.22.3191 (Adjusted Gregorian)
LOCATION: ESF *Speedwell*, Interstellar Space
REGION: In transit to Proxima Centauri System

<*Jason!*>

Calista's heart leapt to her throat; her first instinct was to throw her harness off and send her body shooting through their now-zero g ship, toward the docking bay. Her hand went to the harness release, but before she could trigger it, Terrance's hand covered hers.

<*Need you here, Major.*> Eric's voice brought Calista back to her present surroundings, and her job as XO of the ship—a ship with warning klaxons sounding as sensors on its exterior registered damage to its hull.

She glared briefly at Terrance as she set ship's sensors to track Jason's motion and zoom in on his figure. When she saw the damage his suit had sustained, she pinged Marta with a medical emergency and sent the ESF medic the feed. A beat later, Marta reported she was on her way to the flight deck.

She heard Eric's sharp <*Tobias, report!*> as the commodore conferred with the Weapon Born on Jason's status, and cursed mentally as she forced her mind away from the man she cared for and back to her task.

Her fingers flew through the holo, noting that the blast had taken out at least half a dozen sensors along that side, two of which had been monitoring fuel pressure within the ship's tanks.

<*Shannon?*> she queried, and heard the distracted tone in her voice as her eyes kept darting back to the image of Jason's tumbling body.

<*I'm assessing the Elastene cladding now; looks like structural*

integrity has been compromised along sections Lima-Seventeen through Twenty-four,> the engineer reported. <*Sending a maintenance bot out to walk the hull and give us eyes on it. Stand by….*>

Calista reached into the holo and tapped the icon for the tanker, zooming in to see what damage it had sustained.

"Tanker looks shot," she announced. "We still have control of its NSAI; I'm sending it back along its return trajectory. We'll have to file a report with the Catapult Authority, but we'll have plenty of time to deal with that later."

She saw Eric's avatar nod on the command channel just as the maintenance bot came online. She tossed its feed up next to the one of the *Sable Wind* and Jason.

Tobias was maneuvering the Icarus craft deftly. He'd sent it arcing above and behind the unconscious pilot and was now maintaining station with him as the Weapon Born cycled the shuttle's airlock, and then began to close with Jason.

Terrance sat silently in the cradle next to her, fists clenching and unclenching, eyes riveted to the holotank, and she knew he felt as helpless as she did.

Jason's form appeared to float inside and bounce gently off the inner hatch before the Weapon Born deployed a net of webbing around Jason and the outer airlock sealed.

They heard the Weapon Born's grim <*Got him,*> followed by a view of the shuttle rapidly accelerating toward the *Speedwell*'s flight deck.

<*Vitals?*> she heard Marta's terse voice break in over the net, and heard Terrance inhale deeply at Tobias's reply.

<*Falling,*> the AI said tersely, and then, <*but not critical. Yet.*>

Unable to take it anymore, Calista unhooked herself from the pilot's cradle, slaving her boards to Shannon's control, and pushed off for the lift. She heard a noise behind her and was unsurprised to find Terrance join her inside the lift. He nodded once to her as she tapped in the flight deck as their destination.

They remained silent as the lift slid open and they pulled themselves down the hall. Ahead, they could see Marta and two nurses floating a gurney toward the dock's main entrance. The medic nodded as they caught up to her, engaging the maglocks on their boots as they waited for the *Sable Wind* to enter and the bay doors to seal.

As she and Terrance clomped after the medic, who had opted to push off from the entrance and float herself and her team more rapidly to Jason's side, Eric addressed them both over a private connection.

<*I want you two to look into this quietly,*> the commodore instructed. <*There should have been no catalyst to cause the hydrogen to explode like it did. I want to know why that occurred.*>

Calista exchanged glances with Terrance, nodding mutely. The AI was correct; in all her years of service with the ESF, she'd executed mid-space refueling maneuvers thousands of times without incident. They weren't entirely unheard of, and it was possible the bent collar on the tanker could have been a factor, but her gut told her it was unlikely.

What the hell just happened?

She met Marta's eyes as the doctor floated her patient past them, her own eyes silently questioning the doctor. It was only after the other woman gave a brief nod that Calista allowed herself to let out the breath she'd unwittingly been holding.

She turned to the shuttle. <*Tobias, are you up for another trip out to what's left of that tanker? I want to take a closer look at it.*>

<*Good idea,*> Terrance said. <*Think I'll come along. We should examine our own fuel tanks, too; make sure we didn't sustain any damage.*>

<*And in the process,*> Tobias added grimly, <*figure out how a substance that requires oxygenation to explode just did—in the middle of interstellar space.*>

*****

Calista leaned back in the pilot's cradle and slammed her hands down on the console in front of her in frustration. Terrance shot her a glance from where he rode shotgun in the copilot's seat, but kept his own counsel.

"That makes three complete sweeps, and we aren't picking up anything out of the ordinary, on any scan," she said in disgust.

<*Based on the readings the* Sable Wind *recorded at the time of the explosion,*> Tobias said, <*it's likely that whatever caused the reaction was vaporized by it.*>

"Convenient," Terrance muttered. "No evidence, no one to pin it on."

<*If it was a freak accident, there wouldn't* **be** *anyone to pin it on,*> Eric chided his partner, who just grunted noncommittally in reply.

She heard Eric make a sound like a sigh, and then the commodore ordered them to return to base.

At least Marta says Jason's stable. Sure would have liked to have found out one way or the other what was behind this.

As the *Sable Wind* settled into its docking cradle, Calista heard Tobias reach out to her privately.

<*Mind taking me with you to visit him, lass? I know I can check up on him just as easily from within the shuttle, but I find I've grown accustomed to being physically near the boy,*> the Weapon Born admitted.

She smiled. <*I'd be happy to, Tobias. Let's swing by his cabin and pick up Tobi along the way.*>

The Weapon Born sent her the AI equivalent of a hug at that suggestion.

*****

Frida waited until the excitement had died down, and the humans who ran first shift were midway through their sleep cycle before she attempted her first expanse. Its detail wasn't as fine as the one Prime would have created, but she figured it would suffice. She stood now on the ship's hull, awaiting the arrival of the mysterious AI.

"A bit rudimentary, but a credible attempt," a voice said from behind her, and Frida suppressed a flare of resentment.

She wished passionately for a way she could strike back at the arrogant AI without risking a retaliation she could ill afford.

He spread his hands expansively, paused, and cocked his head. "Well, you didn't make this crude facsimile of the ship just to impress me, I'm sure. Tell me, Frida," his voice grew hard, "why you are taking me away from other matters to meet with you."

"Other matters?" she asked. "What, am I keeping you from your playtime with that human toy of yours?" she sneered as she advanced toward him. "What are you doing to that human anyway, that others on the ship are actually noticing and commenting about it?"

The apparition shrugged carelessly. "Experimentation, if you must know. Inducing various states within her neural circuitry. Testing her stamina, her resistance to pain, how she handles sensory overload."

His eyes glowed more intensely as they narrowed on her. "Not that it is any concern of yours, Frida. Unless you are volunteering to take her place? I grow bored during a passage of this duration and find that I must have stimulus to keep myself entertained."

Frida was surprised to discover that her anger toward Prime had burned away her fear of him. The last time she'd been this angry, she'd been on *her* ship—the *New Saint Louis*—

talking to a human who was treating her with exactly the same amount of disdain that an AI was treating her with on *this* ship.

"Are you so unable to control yourself that you are willing to risk discovery?" she hissed at him now. "First, the brother suspects something is wrong with his sister, then you try to kill him while he's EVA? Refilling *our* fuel tanks, so we can make it to the planet *you* intend to conquer? You need to learn to control yourself better, or—"

"Or what?" The AI's voice had grown dangerously soft. "I could end the life of every human on this ship *right now....*"

Frida tensed as her connection with the ship reported warning klaxons, sounding the alert that atmosphere was rapidly evacuating, and airlocks had all simultaneously opened without ES fields in place.

She thought fast. "If you do, any chance of using them as hostages, as bargaining chips, will be lost."

She ignored the klaxons, focusing only on the AI she was becoming increasingly convinced was more than a little bit mad. "I've heard from El Dorado again, twice. And now I've heard from Chinquapin. If we don't acknowledge them, and with a satisfactory reply, they will greet us as hostile when we arrive. Without humans aboard, they won't hesitate to fire on this ship and obliterate it."

As suddenly as they had begun, the klaxons stopped.

"We're halfway there now," she said quietly to him. "You've lasted this long, don't be stupid and blow it when you have the end in sight."

Abruptly, she found herself back inside the ship, her expanse shattered.

<If you want to live, Frida,> his final words followed her back, *<you will find a way to convince Proxima that we pose no danger to them.>*

Shaken, she opened the message from Proxima again.

Perhaps I can warn them that Prime has been tipped off to their—

Searing pain prevented her from completing the thought.

*****

Calista awoke to the sound of klaxons and Shannon's mental urging, accompanied by Tobi's wet nose nudging her insistently.

<*Get up! We're losing atmosphere all over the ship.*>

<*That's impossible,*> Calista began, but the moment she ran out into the corridor, she realized the situation belied her statement. She grabbed at Tobi but the big cat evaded her hand and raced off down the corridor toward medical.

She paused, indecisive, her desire to follow Tobi and check on Jason warring with her duty to the ship. As Calista began running for the lift, she reached out to Marta. <*Is medical secure?*>

<*No worries,*> the woman assured her. <*We're under a completely autonomous system. No containment loss here.*>

She breathed a sigh of relief, sent her thanks to the medic and then pinged Shannon again. <*Talk to me, Shannon. What's going on?*>

Air pressure had dropped, and there was a noticeable breeze. She heard bulkheads slamming into place, conserving what atmosphere existed within each section's environs.

<*I have no idea!*> the engineer replied, frustration lacing her mental tone. <*This should* ***not*** *be happening!*>

Calista dodged two crew members, spilling out into the corridor on their way to their posts. She waved an apology to them as she jogged around a service bot and barely missed slamming into a woman stumbling blearily out of her cabin.

Her destination—the lift that would take her down to the engineering level—was just a few steps away, but she swung left, opting instead for the service shaft next to it. Grabbing either side of the ladder, she quick-slid the three levels downward in a fireman's descent.

Hopping out of the shaft, she raced for the entrance, arriving just as the klaxons stopped.

<*Report,*> she snapped out as Shannon's image appeared before her.

<*All systems report nominal, and the pressure the ship has lost is slowly being fed back into it by environmental systems, returning it to equilibrium state,*> Shannon said, her tone puzzled.

Terrance arrived, slightly out of breath, and a beat later, Logan joined them.

"What was that all about?" the exec queried his chief pilot.

Calista sent him a short headshake as she turned back to where Shannon had projected a holo of herself. "We were just trying to determine that, sir," she replied, her tone puzzled as she approached a data console and began manipulating a holo feed that was projected in front of them.

<*It would appear the ship's containment system reset itself and, in the process, tripped all the airlocks and cargo bay doors,*> Shannon said. <*The sensors that indicate a lack of standard temperature and pressure were offline at the time. When the system rebooted, it immediately caught the failure and initiated overrides to close them.*> The AI sounded as mystified as Calista felt.

Terrance's face was thunderous. "This *has* to be sabotage," he stated tersely. "Especially on the heels of what happened to Jason on that EVA."

"Speaking of whom," she began, holding up a finger as she pinged Marta for an update.

<*Everything still okay down there?*>

<*Right as rain. But what happened, Calista? Those klaxons sounded like containment breach warnings.*> The doctor's voice sounded worried, but not overtly so.

<*They were, but somehow the system seems to have repaired itself. Jason?*> she asked again. <*Is he—?*>

<*He's fine,*> Marta assured her. <*I'm with him now. Slept through the whole thing.*> Her voice turned wry. <*And if anyone's missing a large cat, I can tell you where to find her.*>

Calista smiled in relief. "Jason's fine. They all are, down there."

Terrance nodded but his scowl remained as the commodore addressed them again. <*We need to keep every possibility on the table,*> Eric stated calmly. <*Including sabotage. Shannon, I'll help you and Tobias look into this. I want to pore over everything we can find and trace the circuits ourselves to see what we can determine. For now, no human is to be without a rebreather. You'll need to carry them on your persons at all times. Understood?*>

Calista nodded. "Understood. But sir, if it's sabotage, then who…and *why?*"

Eric's avatar looked grim. <*That's what we aim to find out. If we were still in drydock—*> the AI's hesitation was slight, but noticeable, <*—I'd suspect Prime.*>

Calista's head snapped up and she glanced at Terrance, noting his expression looked as shocked at Eric's statement as she felt. She glanced at Logan, but the AI's expression revealed nothing.

<*I don't want our hunt for a serial killer—something that occurred months ago, I might add—to color our observations,*> the commodore warned. <*This ship is still in the midst of flight testing during this voyage, given the modifications we made to it. As unlikely as a containment breach systems error may seem, accidents* **do** *happen.*>

She glanced over at Shannon's projection and saw the engineer's hair flatten. <*Not on one of* **my** *ships, they don't.*>

SAFEGUARDS

STELLAR DATE: 10.29.3191 (Adjusted Gregorian)
LOCATION: Enfield Holdings, El Dorado Ring
REGION: Alpha Centauri System

Daniel topped off his coffee mug then turned back to the security feed playing out on the holotank in Enfield Holdings' main information center as Ethan—the real Ethan—approached the entrance for the first time.

Daniel picked up the ICS data cube from the desk as he took a seat, absently rolling it around in the palm of his hand. He watched as Ethan paused for the briefest moment, squared the shoulders of his frame, and resolutely approached the building's doors. He wondered at the AI's apparent hesitation, then assumed it was most likely a combination of awe at being invited into task force Phantom Blade's inner sanctum, and trepidation at facing his doppelganger's victims again.

Speaking of which.... Daniel turned his attention inward. <*How you holding up, there?*> he asked his partner.

He knew Aaron was observing Ethan's approach, and wondered if the AI felt the same feelings of disquiet that John felt when in Ethan's presence. He knew the human agent would never be comfortable around the scientist.

Aaron accurately interpreted the direction of Daniel's thoughts. <*I'm fine. Prime never really got his hands on me. I wasn't directly tortured by him, like John was during the slaughter at the bar.*>

<*Indirectly, you were.*>

The AI paused for a moment, his silence tacitly acknowledging the truth of Daniel's statement.

<*I'm glad Ben gave John an early retirement with full benefits, and that he's being treated by ESF medical for the trauma he*

sustained. Did you know they have him classified as a POW during the weeks he was under Prime's control?>

Daniel grunted in surprise, then shook his head silently. <*He deserves all the help they can give him, poor bastard. Stars, I can't even imagine what he went through.*>

<*I can.*>

At Daniel's swift intake of breath, the AI went on.

<*I know you didn't mean anything by that.*>

<*I…stars, Aaron,* ***you*** *were a POW too, even if it was for only twelve hours. I'm sorry, I never saw it in that light before.*>

Aaron's avatar tilted his head, acknowledging his partner's comment. <*That was the worst twelve hours of my life,*> the AI admitted. <*Never felt pain like that before…. I'm just glad it's all behind us now.*> His avatar nodded toward the ICS cube Esther had returned to them after they'd been released from stasis. <*Any chance I can convince you to part with that soon? Feels a little weird to have you hanging onto the 'old me' for this long, you know.*>

Daniel nodded. This was a discussion they'd had more than once over the past several weeks, and he responded the same as he always did when Aaron asked. <*I know, but until this is all past us, and your testimony's been recorded at the trial, you aren't really free to decide whether or not you want to return to the time before Prime did what he did to you. Doesn't seem fair to ask you to decide before then.*>

Aaron laughed quietly. <*Daniel, I am who I am today because of what I endured. Would I elect to go through it all over again? Of course not. But I'm not going to go back to a time before simply to erase a bad experience. Maybe…*> and here his voice grew tentative, <*perhaps my experience will someday help someone else through an equally difficult time.*>

Maybe Aaron's right. Who am I to dictate another sentient's choices?

Abruptly, he snapped the cube up in his hand and stood.

Walking over to the storage unit built into the conference room's wall, he seated the cube into the termination socket next to a row of unformatted cubes, their lattices disordered and unstructured.

<*There,*> he told his partner. <*It's in your hands now. Smeg the cube or leave it as-is. It's your life, your memories, under your control.*>

Aaron sent him a wave of gratitude, and Daniel saw the crystal structure glow slightly as his friend accessed it, and he closed the cabinet door.

Turning, he spied Ethan out in the corridor and waved the scientist into the room. The AI brightened noticeably when he spied the man.

"Daniel, Aaron! It is good to see you looking well." The AI looked anxious. "You are well, Aaron?"

The AI's voice, warm with laughter, emanated from the room's speakers. "I am indeed, sir, thanks to you. The vice-marshal just signaled; she and Ben will be here shortly. You have news for us?"

Ethan nodded vigorously. "I do indeed."

He looked over as Ben entered, and Esther's avatar projected at the head of the conference table. Accompanying Ben was Gladys. The scientist looked curiously at her as the hacker glided past him, his face wrinkling in consternation as she trailed teal glitter in her wake.

Daniel fought a smile and shook his head with a little shrug when Ethan's confused gaze landed on him.

Let Gladys explain her own idiosyncrasies to the guy.

"So, Ethan," Esther began, "you mentioned news when you pinged me earlier?"

The AI nodded toward Ben. "Yes. It has to do with the pod we discovered in the apartment that Prime had rented near the spaceport."

He turned to the holo tank and brought up an image of a

basic storage pod. With a gesture, he brought up a document next to it. "This is a list of the items inside the pod." The AI turned away from the display with a grave look on his face. "The quantity and type of Level One toxins found there would have been enough to eradicate all human life on our ring, in the hands of someone who knew how to culture and replicate them. They are now in the hands of the CDC."

Turning back to the list, he said, "I forwarded the toxin list, along with the recipes for the antidote serums, to Jane Andrews at the C-47 in Proxima five weeks ago." Ethan turned, his eyes burning in their intensity. "And I just received her reply."

Gladys leaned forward, clasping her hands on the table in front of her. "Will she be able to replicate enough antidote, and have it on hand, if we're unable to stop Prime?"

Daniel shuddered at the thought, but Ethan nodded. "That won't be a factor," he reassured them, but then his expression turned troubled. He paused, then glanced over at the vice-marshal. "I do have a question, though."

At her raised brows, he continued hesitantly, glancing at Ben, as if reluctant to broach the topic in front of the man.

"The ship, the *Speedwell*.... How do you know Prime hasn't shackled—or collared—everyone aboard?" He glanced uneasily at Ben, and suddenly Daniel realized the question the AI *wasn't* asking:

'How do we know the humans aboard—especially Jason and Judith—are even still alive?'

He saw by Ben's pained expression that it was a question the analyst had already considered.

The vice-marshal must have sensed the same thing.

"We don't." Esther's voice was soft as she admitted this. "But let me remind you that we've been receiving regular updates from Eric and the team, and they have given no indication that anything is amiss."

She raised her hand as Ben and Gladys both began to protest. Daniel was certain the same thing that had crossed his mind was topmost in theirs; if Eric had been shackled, of course he would be ordered to continue his reports as if nothing had happened.

"I understand your concerns, but everything Ethan has told us about this shackling program implies two things: one, that Prime's ability to control an individual and have that person behave in a manner believable enough to consistently fool friends and family closest to them is limited."

She paused and gave them a wry smile. "Not all of you have experienced what it's like to share tight living quarters on a journey that long, but I can assure you that being on a ship for ten months will make it nearly impossible to hide unusual behavior. Prime's no fool; he knows that."

Esther turned to the neuroscientist. "I said there were two things. Since it involves neural pathways, I think I'll let Ethan tell you about the second one."

The AI looked slightly uncomfortable as he began to speak, but gradually relaxed as he warmed to his subject.

"It has to do with the areas within the brain that house executive action. Willpower is a finite resource, within both humans and AIs, and Prime will be expending a lot of his own to exert his will upon others." The AI spread his hands. "Given his core size and computational capabilities, if I had to guess, Prime might be able to directly control three, maybe four individuals at one time. Any more, and his own resources will tap out. He's insidious, but he's not a multi-nodal intelligence."

Daniel saw Ben relax slightly at the news, although he was sure the analyst feared that one of the top four candidates on Prime's shortlist would include his wife.

I can't begin to imagine the anguish that is causing him.

BREAKOUT

STELLAR DATE: 01.10.3192 (Adjusted Gregorian)
LOCATION: ESF *Speedwell*
REGION: Heliopause, Proxima Centauri System

Eric could feel his human partner's restlessness as Terrance prowled the deck amidships, its lighting dimmed as the *Speedwell* entered its nighttime hours. He'd noticed an uptick in a feeling Terrance called 'going stir-crazy' about a month ago, and he suspected the man's need to seek some form of distraction wasn't due entirely to the fact that they were now in the eighth month of their journey.

Granted, that was part of it, but he knew the crew's inability to pinpoint the source of the mysterious containment breach that had caused the klaxons to sound that night ate at Terrance as much as it weighed on his own mind. Added to that was the infuriating dearth of evidence to explain the explosion that had injured Jason.

After a few days in Marta's care and several sessions in the autodoc in medical, the pilot's punctured lung and broken ribs had been repaired—along with a slew of other contact injuries where shrapnel from the explosion had penetrated his suit. Jason was fortunate; the nano inside the suit had managed to seal each breach and kept him alive long enough for Tobias to recover him.

Once released from medical, Jason had joined them in their hunt for the source of both the explosion and the inexplicable containment breach. They had come up with nothing.

It had been quiet for two months, now, and as much as logic dictated that the events must have been random accidents, Eric couldn't shake the feeling that there was more to it.

My meat-suit would probably call that intuition, he chuckled wryly to himself. *But even our most suspicious team member, Logan, has admitted it must have been chance.*

As Terrance continued down a darkened corridor that connected the ship's weight room to its sparring theater, Eric's thoughts turned to Logan. As far as he knew, the profiler still held onto Landon's ICS cube, and was wrestling with the decision on whether or not to bring his brother back. At times Eric wondered if the AI's reluctance to restore his twin stemmed from a perverse sense of guilt. Perhaps it was a form of penance Logan felt he must pay for not being there when Landon needed him.

For all our logic, we are as susceptible to irrational thoughts as our human brethren, Eric mused wryly.

Maybe the soldier could use a little distraction. Eric happened to have just the thing. Earlier in the day, he'd received a message from his contact inside Proxima's military intelligence; they now knew where the five missing AIs were, and their location complicated matters.

He reached out and pinged Logan, and after a moment's thought, sent a ping to Tobias as well.

<*Got a minute?*> he asked the two when they responded.

Logan sent a brief affirmative, while the Weapon Born's response was a more casual, <*Aye, lad, what's on your mind?*>

The last three months, for one thing. But he kept that thought to himself; these two had heard him air his frustration too many times recently to burden them with it again.

His purpose this night wasn't to rehash old concerns; they had a mission to accomplish, shackled AIs to free, and it was time he went about the business of emancipating them.

<*I have news,*> he said, sending them a copy of the report he'd just received. <*Review this if you would, please, with task force deployment in mind. Ping me when you're ready to discuss.*>

Both AIs signaled their acknowledgement, and he dropped the connection just as Terrance paused at the intersection of a corridor. The human had spied light spilling out from one of the smaller mess halls just aft of the workout rooms, and turned to investigate, his curiosity piqued.

Jason was there, propping his booted feet up on a table and cradling a bowl of fruit.

As his meat-suit walked past, Eric watched Jason neatly dodge Terrance's hand as the executive made a grab for the bowl of blackberries.

Popping a few into his mouth, Jason mumbled around them, "Get your own, dude."

"Those are the last ones. *Dude.*"

Eric felt a spike of amusement from Terrance, as Jason sighed and then tilted the bowl for the man to take a handful.

"How do you know they're the last when you haven't looked in the chiller yet?" The pilot scowled over at his friend, and Terrance chuckled as he obligingly walked over and swung the door open, then gestured pointedly at the empty shelf.

"Because I saw that bowl in here earlier and planned to do exactly the same thing you're doing," He grinned, snagged a few cookies off the counter, and seated himself across the table from Jason.

Tipping his chair back, he mimicked the pilot's attitude, feet crossed.

The AI could sense Terrance's enjoyment as he tweaked the now-recovered pilot. It was good to see his partner unwind a bit; in Eric's estimation, Terrance didn't do that nearly enough.

Eric knew he was partly to blame. Terrance's innate leadership abilities, combined with the part his family's companies had played in AI history, had been what had prompted Eric to ask the man to let him embed with him.

He felt a stab of guilt at that. He knew Terrance felt, subconsciously, that the Enfield name was under a cloud; the man had an almost visceral need to right the wrongs some ancient ancestor had made—not so much errors of commission, but simply by having had the poor judgment to align with unscrupulous business partners.

His musings were interrupted by a ping from Logan. He left the two humans to their snacking and turned his attention to the profiler. Reaching out, he pulled both Logan and Tobias into a small expanse. It wasn't fancy or imaginative. In fact, it looked identical to their conference room at Enfield Holdings back on the El Dorado ring, as opposed to a more exotic location. Had the topic been less grim, he was sure Tobias would rib him about it.

Eric looked up as Logan strolled toward him, his face an expressionless mask. Out of the corner of his eye, Eric caught a flash of movement and spied a shock of bright red hair that indicated Tobias was approaching. As he neared, Eric could see that the Weapon Born's normally merry blue eyes were somber.

"I take it you've had a chance to review what I sent?" he asked the two.

"All five were purchased by a syndicate." Tobias's voice dripped with disgust as he summarized in one brief statement. "And they're being forced to run a refinery, owned by a small drug operation."

Eric nodded. "Yes, it's owned by a biochemist, Karen Leighton. The woman engineered a more potent form of mandratura and set up shop somewhere in Proxima's cool dust belt."

He paused, glanced over at Logan, and then added, "Terrance tells me that Shannon might have a problem with that. She lost a very promising engineer from her team inside Enfield's TechDev to MDT a few years back."

He saw Logan straighten at that. "Does she need to sit this one out?"

"We can't afford for her to," Tobias responded sharply.

"The team that breaches the refinery must be an all-AI force."

"Agreed," Eric said. "In fact, I've been considering how we might supplement Phantom Blade with some of our fellow crew members—for just that reason. It's far too dangerous for any human agents to be involved."

Tobias looked thoughtful. "You realize that leaves you out, as well, given that you're with Terrance."

Eric nodded. "Yes, I'll lead up the rescue of the other two, but I'll need you to run this one."

The Weapon Born rubbed a hand across his jaw in thought. "Got any crew members in mind for our add-ons?"

Instead of responding, Eric turned his attention toward Logan.

Catching Eric's shift in focus, the Weapon Born chuckled. "Time to earn those profiler chops, lad. Got any recommendations for our illustrious leader?"

Eric could have sworn Logan shot Tobias the AI equivalent of some side-eye. He stifled a thread of amusement and instead kept his expression neutral as he turned expectantly to the profiler. He didn't have long to wait.

"Two of the ESF soldiers on loan to us recently rotated out of anti-piracy squads before we shipped out," he began. "They would be my first choice."

"Yes, Paula and Kodi. I thought you might suggest them," Eric agreed, and then paused before continuing. "I hesitate to suggest this, but…what of Niki? I understand our scan officer has a way with code that might help us hack into the refinery's systems and expedite their retrieval."

Tobias evinced surprise. "You think she can handle the reminder of such a painful time in her own history, since she was once shackled herself?"

"I'm more interested in how Logan would assess her current state, I think," he said turning once again to the other AI.

He saw the profiler hesitate, then nod reluctantly. "It's not ideal, but if she stays on the shuttle and we use her skills on scan, I think she should be fine." Logan paused, speared Eric with a look, and then added, "Have you given any thought to our unsolved mysteries and how they might impact the operation?"

Had he been human, Eric would have grimaced.

Oh yes, I've thought of it. Never ***stopped*** *thinking of it, to be exact.*

<*Yes,*> he said to the two AIs. <*Which is why I'm keeping this op as compartmentalized as possible. Kodi, Niki especially, and even Shannon, will be given information on a need-to-know basis. Understood?*>

Logan and Tobias both sent their assent; Logan's was accompanied by a flare of approval.

<*Very well, then—an infiltration team of five. Tobias, you can breach with Logan and Kodi,*> Eric decided. <*Shannon will embed in the* Sable Wind, *and Niki can remain onboard, running scan.*>

The two AIs sent their compliance at their commander's orders, and Eric turned his attention to the remaining two AIs that needed rescuing.

<*Since this'll involve organics—and since Terrance and Jason are conveniently at hand—let's take a look at the situation with the remaining two kidnap victims in Proxima, shall we?*>

* * * * *

Jason saw Terrance straighten, his eyes taking on the distant look that indicated he was speaking with Eric. He suppressed a slight flare of jealousy; as much as he enjoyed having the enhanced capabilities that came with being a 'sport'—one of the first known naturally-occurring L2 humans—at times like this, he'd swap it in a heartbeat for the ability to embed with an AI.

The exec turned to him, humor from their previous exchange wiped from his face. "Looks like we have news about the AIs we've come all this way to rescue."

Jason sat up at that, his attention sharpening. "Should Calista be in on this as well?"

Terrance paused to consult with Eric and then nodded. "He's pinging her now. She can join us over her Link."

Shoving the bowl of berries off to one side, Jason crossed his arms on the table in front of him. "What kind of news are we talking about, Eric?"

He frowned as the commodore brought them up to speed.

<*Incorvaia, huh? They've been the bane of Chinquapin Intelligence for as long as I can recall. I heard stories on the news nets about them when I was a kid.*> He shook his head. <*And now they're dealing in MDT. Stars, that's nasty stuff.*>

<*It's stuff you won't be having to deal with, boyo. Just us inorganics going in for that one.*>

Jason saw Calista join the net at Tobias's comment. He saw her avatar cock her head. <*Are there enough of you to pull that off? Jason or I could go along and pilot the shuttle; that could save you one soldier for the actual infiltration.*>

He saw Eric shake his head 'no' before Calista had even completed her thought.

<*We'll need to pull some extreme burns in order to rendezvous with the lab in time. Harder than anything you squishies—even modded ones—will be able to handle.*>

As Jason opened his mouth to protest the loss of stealth a hard burn would have on the operation, Eric went on.

<*Our intel also helpfully included some information about a few predicted coronal mass ejections that will work in Tobias's favor, to hide their hard burn. The red dwarf is entering a more active part of its solar cycle. You and Tobias know how frequent flares are during these periods.... We'll make it work to our advantage.*>

Jason shut his mouth and sent Calista's avatar a shrug as

he leant back once more and threw one hand across the back of a neighboring chair.

"So what can we do to help?" he asked.

<*I don't like the thought of leaving you, Terrance, and Calista without an AI on the team,*> Eric began, and Jason smirked as Terrance snorted.

"Hey, partner, you forgetting that wherever I go, you go?" The exec grinned over at him and Jason grinned back.

He heard the commodore make a noise over the net that almost sounded like the AI version of a snort. <*I can't exactly fit into a mech frame, and if you and Terrance board the Tolgoy torus in battle-rattle, you won't get very far.*>

Jason mentally inclined his head in acknowledgement. "So what do you propose?"

<*You'll follow the same M.O. as we did back on Krait, boyo,*> the Weapon Born told him. <*Only it'll be Paula, that ESF marine who runs scan third shift, who'll be in the compact frame.*>

Jason sobered, recalling the frame Landon had once worn. He tried not to be obvious about it but he couldn't help sparing a mental glance at Logan's avatar to gauge the profiler's reaction to Tobias's words. The AI hadn't mentioned his twin recently; he hadn't chosen to do anything with Landon's ICS cube either.

<*I've sent you everything we have on both facilities. Familiarize yourselves with the intel we have on shielding, armament, and crew complements,*> Eric instructed. <*Each team will meet separately to do a complete workup of their operation and set up training sims. We have eight weeks to get this buttoned down, people. Any questions?*>

There were none.

<*Very well,*> Eric said. <*Then let's be about it.*>

Jason reached for the bowl of berries, only to have Terrance swipe the bowl out from under his hand.

"Asswipe," he muttered with a sideways look as he kicked his feet back up onto the table.

Terrance just snorted, tipped his head back, and popped the last few berries into his mouth. As the exec passed, Jason felt the man give the back of his head a soft whack as he and Eric headed for the galley exit.

Jason narrowed his eyes just as Tobias's voice came across their private connection.

<You're not going to let that stand, boyo, are you?> the AI's avatar grinned wickedly at Jason. *<I know where he keeps his private stash of coffee beans….>*

RADIATION BURN

STELLAR DATE: 03.10.3192 (Adjusted Gregorian)
LOCATION: Icarus Shuttle *Sable Wind*, KLM Refinery
REGION: Cool Dust Belt, Proxima Centauri System

<Initiate hard burn on my mark.>

Tobias's words cut through the silence that had settled between the refinery team ever since the *Sable Wind* had floated free of the *Speedwell*'s docking bay. They lent a reality to the last two months of training that even the AIs' insertion into mech frames and subsequent load onto the shuttle hadn't given him.

Of course, by now, the training was rote, the load in and prep for burn rehearsed in sims so frequently over the past eight weeks that he was sure any one of them could do it in their sleep. He chuckled mentally at the human idiom; it was both appropriate and utterly inaccurate all at once.

He scanned the shuttle's interior, noting everyone was in place and all systems were green. Logan and their ESF add-on—the soldier, Kodi—sat with their mech frames locked down next to Tobias, while Niki's frame was ensconced in the spot just aft of the pilot's seat that was usually reserved for point defense.

Over the combat net, Shannon's avatar nodded crisply at Tobias as she studied the data from the red dwarf star. She knew that he was calculating when the sensor blackout would hit the refinery, and was awaiting his command to engage the little ship's engines at an acceleration near the upper end of the spectrum of g-forces an AI could tolerate.

For this maneuver, the ship's holo display would briefly hit the top of the 'never-exceed' arc on its speed indicator before settling into a steady eighty-*g* burn for the duration of the blackout. Since Shannon was technically the Icarus-class shuttle's S&P—its spaceframe and powerplant expert—Tobias was confident the vessel would hold up under whatever the engineer put it through.

<Mark.>

Shannon executed the burn just as the radiation from the coronal mass ejection temporarily rendered their sensors useless. The Icarus shuttle's shift in acceleration had even the mech frames sending overstress warning signals to the AIs inhabiting them. The CME and accompanying series of flares would last a total of ninety minutes—more than enough time for their thirty-minute hard drive toward the refinery.

At that point, they would cruise for more than seven hours at zero-*g*, until it was time to execute another hard-braking maneuver—again, timed to occur during one of Proxima's frequent flares.

Tobias noted the *Sable Wind*'s dosimetry sensors continue their trek upward. This was another reason he and Eric had decided this would be an all-AI team; the astrophysicists on Chinquapin had predicted this coronal mass ejection to be on the upper end of Proxima's scale, and initial CME estimates had turned out to be accurate.

Given the inverse-square nature of ionizing radiation, and the refinery's distance from the star, the dose would be intense, but not enough to do an AI permanent harm. This, too, was where Icarus's Elastene shielding proved more effective than traditional ship cladding. The metal foam completely absorbed the betas and absorbed and deflected much of the gammas. What did make it through wasn't enough to damage hardened ship's systems or their mech frames.

He knew both the settlement on Chinquapin and the C-47 habitat cylinder orbiting it would have experienced higher levels of radiation from the CME, as they were fifty-six million kilometers closer to the star than the refinery. Solar storms like this one were why both installations had thick metal plating to augment standard magnetic shielding. It was the only way humanity had managed to survive in this system.

As these thoughts flickered through a compartmentalized portion of his mind, another part of his mind remained focused on the refinery they were nearing. Shannon had flipped the shuttle and initiated the thirty-minute braking burn just moments ago, as soon as the next solar flare rendered them blind.

They would complete their approach until they were at station-keeping relative to the asteroid where the lab was located, based on sensor readings that were now ten minutes old. Given that the refinery's sensors were also blind, their approach should go undetected. Hopefully their breach would be equally low key, provided the blueprint that Eric's contact had found of the refinery was accurate.

Shannon cut the shuttle's acceleration, and a moment later, the engineer announced, *<Firing maneuvering thrusters now.>*

Tobias sent her a thread of acknowledgement; he was riding the connection with her and felt the thrusters fire and the shuttle's subtle shifts in attitude as it approached. The maneuver was a bit tricky; she first had to do a lateral translation, and then fly retrograde for a brief period before easing toward the refinery's docking bay.

They had chosen this bay to approach as it was in the lee of the star, and the bulk of the asteroid provided additional shielding from the star's ejection. Tobias activated his mech frame and walked it to the *Sable Wind*'s airlock. Radiation levels were beginning to drop, and that meant sensors should begin to come back online shortly.

The next part of the plan would be in his hands. The spider-like frames he, Kodi, and Logan wore each had eight articulated legs and a body that was ringed with sensors. Two of the eight arms were dedicated to spinning and deploying nano filaments they would use to defeat the refinery's defense systems.

An additional three limbs terminated in various forms of weaponry: a self-loading breaching rocket launcher that fired depleted uranium sabots, a small-scale gatling whose magazine feed was slung under the mech frame's ring of sensors, and a particle beam weapon he'd had to argue with Eric over before the commodore would agree to let him to install it into the frame.

That last packed a bragg's peak that would fry any system beyond repair at point of impact.

Tobias intended for this refinery to become nothing more than another piece of metal slag in orbit around the red dwarf when they were done with it.

<Stars!>

Shannon's exclamation sounded at the same time the *Sable Wind* impacted with the refinery. A scraping noise, combined with the groan of stressed metals, accompanied the resulting jolt that tossed Tobias's mech frame across the cabin to slam into the craft's port side.

Not this again, he grumbled inwardly as he fought to right himself. He really *hated* operating from a mech frame.... *<Report!>* he barked over the net, and data flooded his mind, sent there from Shannon's feeds.

It had been a matter of bad timing. The ship's sensors were still reinitializing from the shutdown that had been forced on them from the radiation, and Shannon had been unaware that their vector had them approaching the docking bay at a slightly oblique angle. The shuttle had run into gantry arms that jutted out from the docking ring; the arms had bent under the *Sable Wind*'s velocity and, after the initial impact, had scraped along the starboard side of the *Sable Wind*'s hull.

<Is our airlock still operational, or are we going to need to cut ourselves out of this thing?> he asked.

<Don't you be messing with my ship, Tobias,> Shannon gave her standard reply, but the Weapon Born could tell it was a rote response by her distracted tone.

He waited until she completed her systems check and then heard her admit, *<The outer hatch release still works, but you'll have to encourage the doors to open far enough so you can exit. They're bent.>*

<Nothing any of us could have done about it,> Tobias soothed in response to the self-recrimination in her tone. *<It was a risk we knew we were taking when we decided to use the CME to mask our approach.>*

Righting his own frame, he returned to the shuttle's airlock. *<Kodi, you take one side, Logan, you take the other. Anytime, Shannon,>* he instructed, and the hatch began to open.

It ground to a halt with an opening only sixty centimeters wide. Logan and Kodi latched articulated arms around the edges of each door and wrenched them open wide enough for their mech frames to fit through.

Tobias exited, spooling a line behind him as he floated from the *Sable Wind* to the blinking panel that was installed to one side of the refinery's bay doors. The panel was blinking an amber-red-red code he was certain indicated a damaged entry point. He hoped the system saw it as random debris and not an attack.

Reaching out with one of his nano-deploying arms, he made contact with the panel and rapidly injected a passel of breaching bots into it. Spinning the filaments deep into its circuitry, he circumvented the system's lockouts and overrode the sensor that would report the bay doors were open.

<Ready,> he sent to Shannon, and then triggered the release mechanism.

Bay doors split in the center and then retracted, half up into the overhead, the other half retreating down into its deck. Shannon floated the damaged Icarus shuttle into the bay and settled it into a cradle intended, he was sure, for deliveries. Tobias used his tether to reel himself inside the bay and then sent the signal for the bay doors to seal them in.

Niki had already exited and stood next to Logan and Kodi, awaiting instructions.

<*Shannon, you have the conn,*> he said as he passed Niki and the two soldiers and headed toward the nearest door that would lead them into the refinery proper.

With any luck, the operation would proceed a bit more smoothly now. He hoped the opening gambit for Eric's team would go better than theirs had.

* * * * *

Eric had ordered Jason and the rest of their team into the *Eidolon,* the newer of the two Icarus shuttles, a few hours ago. The AI pinged them now, initiating the team's combat net.

<*We'll launch in half an hour,*> the commodore announced without preamble. <*Calista, you'll provide escort, but I want you to hang back as discussed, just as Shannon did for the Krait op.*>

<*Yessir,*> the top gun replied smartly.

From his position in the copilot's seat next to Jason, Terrance could see Calista fold herself into the Icarus fighter's pilot's cradle and nod at them before the ultra-black canopy sealed over her head.

Terrance examined the mining torus's schematics. Far larger than the Krait-1 torus he knew Jason and Calista had breached several months back, this one served as a hub and central supply depot for several mining concerns, with rigs scattered throughout the dust cloud's near environs.

They were lucky; initial reports had placed these two shackled AIs at different mining platforms, but more recent information had them both installed within the main torus.

He realized how fortunate it was that Phantom Blade had

such a well-respected and capable commander in Eric. He still wasn't sure how the commodore had managed to wrangle permission for them to operate inside the territory of another sovereign star nation—even if they were on friendly footing. But he had managed it.

If Proxima's military intelligence had their information correct, one was tasked with running the torus itself, while the other was remotely operating several rigs owned by the largest of the mining concerns housed on the torus.

The fact both were in the same general physical location made extraction a much simpler prospect.

At the thirty-minute mark, they launched. Looking at his HUD's chrono, Terrance noted that Tobias and Shannon must have already breached the refinery by now.

Good luck, friends, he thought, as his mind settled into the path that lay ahead.

TIME LAG

STELLAR DATE: 03.11.3192 (Adjusted Gregorian)
LOCATION: Prime Minister's Office, El Dorado Ring
REGION: Alpha Centauri System

"They should be insystem by now," Esther murmured, and Lysander nodded.

He'd canceled his weekly cabinet meeting, knowing that even his renowned ability to multitask would have abandoned him on this day.

They were in a private expanse, just the two of them. It was a peaceful place, a glade of trees rising to a brilliant blue sky, with a carpet of soft pine needles cushioning them as they walked. A fellow Weapon Born had shown him this construct hundreds of years ago, and it brought him a sense of peace in times of great stress. Esther had remarked on it when she first saw it, but Lysander found that he'd been reluctant to share its origins with her.

"It's times like this that I wish human fiction were reality," he said, and laughed humorlessly at Esther's quizzical glance. "Science fiction," he clarified. "Specifically, communication—better yet, travel—at FTL speeds."

Esther's brow furrowed, and her expression turned slightly scornful as she replied, "Fanciful thinking."

"Yes, but an example of humanity's ability to dream; the powerful drive humans have for their reach to extend their grasp." He gestured between them. "If not for that, *we* might not ever have existed."

Esther tilted her head at that and then sighed. "Well, we've done all we can for them." She cocked her head at him. "Are you certain your friends in Proxima will know what to do with that cryptic message you sent?"

Lysander drew his gaze down from a cloud that was

scudding across the blue sky to the AI beside him and smiled. "Oh yes. Rhys Andrews will know *exactly* what to do with that message." He returned his gaze to their surroundings.

"He's a well-respected part of the habitat community. When the C-47's governing council realizes that Prime is an imminent threat, but that a special operations team with an intimate working knowledge of this particular criminal mind is onboard, they'll listen to him."

"I can understand why they would be motivated to assist, but are you certain the man will have the authority it takes to enact your plan?"

"Absolutely. I was embedded with him for many years, Esther," he reminded her mildly. "You have to understand, humans have different relationships with their offspring than we AIs do. No matter how old they grow, a child is still something you protect with every fiber of your being."

He bared his lips in a feral smile. "When Rhys learns that *both* of his children are at risk, stars help the person who gets in his way."

THE FINAL KEY

STELLAR DATE: 03.11.3192 (Adjusted Gregorian)
LOCATION: Tolgoy Mining Torus
REGION: Proxima Centauri System

"Hold up," Jason called out as he leant against a bulkhead along Tolgoy's main concourse and pretended to adjust his boot. As he did so, he sent a sizeable packet of nano burrowing its way into a node a few meters behind him.

Playing along, Terrance rolled his eyes and called impatiently, "C'mon, the faster we dump this load, the sooner I can get a beer."

Jason grinned. "You just want to spend all those credits I found, burning a hole in my wallet." He'd accessed his old Proxima credit account days ago, just after the ship resynched its clock to Adjusted Gregorian. This was the largest time correction he'd ever made after a transit; almost ten days by his reckoning.

When he'd accessed his account, he'd been surprised to see his Proxima ID status registered as current; it shouldn't be—at least not until he cleared customs again. He suspected Eric's counterpart down on Chinquapin had given them an assist with that.

But since it was current, he'd made use of it to enter as a local. He knew what torus security saw when their Auth & Auth systems pulled up his ident: a young, for-hire freight hauler who had stepped foot on Tolgoy more than once in his travels.

"Got it," Jason said, stomping his foot once, just as Terrance began to adjust the balance of his 'produce delivery', stacked upon the maglev he'd been pushing. In reality, they were both just killing time, waiting for Eric to let them know he'd successfully hacked into the torus's security system. The nano

Jason had just deposited was the last batch they needed before Eric had complete control of the torus.

He bent to 'help' Terrance with his load just as Paula, who was hidden in the small service-bot frame Landon had used back on Krait, piped up.

<*This has to be the most unusual disguise I've ever worn,*> she complained, and Jason grinned at the mix of bafflement and frustration he heard in the ESF soldier's voice.

<*It's a good cover,*> he assured the AI. <*Anyone with fresh produce is always welcome in these sorts of places.*>

<*Stay still,*> Terrance grumbled as the AI shifted slightly beneath the boxes of tomatoes the team had harvested from the ship's greenspace that morning.

<*Yes, but why do I have to be literally* **covered** *by it?*> Paula's mental tone progressed from bafflement to aggravation as she added, <*And why would they care? The torus has a hydroponics section of its own. What's the difference?*>

<*Yeah, but varieties from outsystem always command premium prices in places like this,*> Jason sent, and then sent Calista a smirk, adding, <*And here, you thought I was wasting my time, cultivating all those tomato plants.*>

Calista's avatar rolled her eyes at him. <*I'll remember to add that to my infiltration playbook, right next to using pulse pistols as pugil sticks,*> she informed him, her tone light.

<*Pugil sticks?*> Paula asked, and her voice was back to sounding confused.

<*Nevermind,*> Jason and Calista both responded at the same time.

<*Eyes to your boards, Major. Cut the chatter,*> Eric's voice was no-nonsense, and Jason stifled a snicker.

Terrance's eyes slid to his, and the exec raised a brow, while the corner of his mouth ticked up a notch. Jason shot the man a black look, daring him to say anything, and the exec just gave him a slight shrug.

The message was clear: *'what can I say, Eric runs a tight ship'.*

<*That's just great, now you're getting me into trouble with the boss, flyboy.*>

Jason coughed to cover a laugh as Eric signaled he was in position. He clapped Terrance on the shoulder and sent him a jaunty wave, then turned and walked off in search of the Barrington Mining Company's main offices, while Terrance pushed the maglev—and Paula—toward the entrance just outside the torus's main operations area.

Both men were being very careful not to act in a way to draw attention to themselves. Their base layer armor was hidden beneath shipsuits, and both had lived and worked in the civilian world long enough to know how to fit in. Unlike the Krait facility, Tolgoy was built to a much larger scale, and a larger population meant a crew complement that included several squads of police to keep the peace on-station.

It even boasted a moderate amount of defensive armament, which was why Calista had been using the Icarus fighter to randomly seed the inner torus with small explosives, using its ultra-stealth capabilities.

<*How's it coming there, ESF?*> Jason sent privately to the woman flying the *Mirage* as he accessed the torus's map. He realized he'd gone a few meters past his turnoff and backtracked until he was once more on the right path to Barrington. <*Need me to stall some more? I wouldn't mind grabbing an ice cream from that gelato cart one spoke over….*>

Calista groaned. <*Don't you **dare** mention ice cream to me, Jason,*> she replied sternly. <*Not while I'm stuck up here, seeding explosives for our fearless leader.*>

<*So I guess that means we definitely can't talk about that time I licked ice cream off your—*>

<***Jason!***> Her tone was stern, but he could hear the thread of humor in it as she chastised him. <*Not **now**.*>

He laughed out loud, causing a woman to stare at him strangely as he passed. He just nodded pleasantly and kept walking.

He knew he shouldn't needle Calista, but it was just so much fun to tease her. She was one of the most skilled pilots he knew, well versed in stealth maneuvers, which meant she looked for every opportunity to mask even the slight puffs of air the *Mirage*'s thrusters would emit as she maneuvered amongst the spokes of the torus, and was not easily distracted by his jibes.

<*Okay, ESF,*> he conceded. <*Wouldn't want you to jiggle one of those explosives wrong, thinking about what I can do with a little dab of ice cream.*>

She snorted. <***That*** *wasn't the jiggling I was thinking about, flyboy.*>

He knew Eric planned to use Calista's little bomblets in one of a few ways. Distraction was at top of the list, but he didn't discount the commodore's ability to use them as a combination of threat and deterrent—should their presence be discovered before the team launched their attacks.

Calista sent the team a thumbs-up on the main combat net.

The explosives were planted, and he saw from her icon that the *Mirage* had pulled back to a location where she could still provide covering fire, should the *Eidolon* need to make a hasty retreat.

He sent Eric a ping as he neared the front of the Barrington sector. Nodding to a vendor manning a food cart, he strolled over and purchased a bag of crisps. Popping a few of the local delicacy into his mouth, he wandered down the street, using the snack as a cover for the conversation he was engaged in.

<*Looks like this sector takes up two blocks,*> he said now. Noting the time on his HUD's chrono, he added, <*and shift change is going to be in about fifteen minutes.*>

<*Good,*> Eric's avatar nodded. <*We're almost in place. I'll give you a two-minute warning and then a five-count before we breach.*>

Jason finished the crisps, crumbled the bag in his hand and appeared to search for a recycling unit. Spying the one he knew was next to Barrington's entrance, he began to walk toward it on Eric's one-minute mark.

He slapped the bag into the unit and wiped his hands to clear the crumbs off them, then turned and entered the building in time to see several dozen employees exiting a bank of lifts.

Timing was everything.

He stepped up to the security kiosk, placing his hand near its sensor. He was no AI; this wasn't nearly as easy for him as it was for Tobias, or even Paula. He didn't begrudge Terrance the ESF soldier's presence, though; the exec had Eric to protect—plus, he didn't have Jason's augmentation.

Nano filaments threaded their way from his hand down into the system as he triggered the hackit Shannon had given him. To his relief, it turned green, admitting him past the lobby area.

<*I'm in,*> he said, following the map overlaying his HUD into a lift where he once again deposited nano into its control panel.

The lift began to drop, stopping at a restricted access level. Jason drew a steadying breath as he ordered the nano to hold the doors shut as he placed his hand on the control panel and once again ordered his nano to spin out a filament with another one of Shannon's hackit packages. He waited…and waited some more. Finally, the hackit returned an amber with errors. Toggling the hackit's error message, he saw that the package hadn't been able to take this level's surveillance offline without alerting security that it was down.

Dammit.

Okay, then. He'd have to make this a fast trip. Surely,

Barrington would send someone to investigate an outage. He figured he had five minutes or so to get in and out undetected.

I can do this.

He retrieved the nano filament he'd deployed, and exited the lift. Commanding it to hold for a fast exit, he set out at a brisk walk, following the path outlined on his HUD down the corridor and to his left.

The layout for Barrington indicated their information technology area to be just ahead of him, through a set of sliding doors. He stopped just before them and deposited more nano on the door's security controls, ordering the filaments to bypass the door's lockouts.

He entered into an area that appeared unoccupied. Ambient temperature in this section was noticeably cooler than the rest of the building, and the lighting had dimmed in the absence of human workers.

As he approached the nearest console, he reached out to deposit nano onto one of its data ports. Just as his hand landed on the port, he felt the cool, hard surface of a weapon pressed against the base of his skull.

"All right, hands behind your back, nice and slow like," the security guard said, and Jason chanced a glance back at the guard. The man had a good fifteen kilos on him, he saw—and then the man shoved him forward against the console, twisting his arm viciously upward.

"Another move like that and I'll shoot. Got it?"

Jason nodded.

"Good."

Jason felt the cool metal surface of a set of maglocked cuffs encircling his left wrist. "Now the other hand," the guard instructed.

It was now or never.

Slipping deep into his altered state, Jason pivoted, sidestepping the barrel of the weapon that had been digging into the back of his skull. At the same time, he brought the palms of both hands up, one on either side of the weapon the other man held.

He positioned his right hand along the barrel, his left just above the man's inner wrist. Bringing both hands together in a lightning-fast move, he grabbed the barrel, twisting it inward, as his other hand knocked the man's grip loose.

The man's hand must have spasmed as his thumb broke, for Jason experienced a moment of excruciating pain as the weapon fired and the slug exiting the weapon superheated the barrel he held in his right hand.

Shit! The security here carries projectile weapons?

Stepping back, he quickly transferred the pistol to his left hand, ignoring the magcuff dangling annoyingly around his wrist, and aimed it at the guard's head.

The man grinned unpleasantly at him as he cradled his broken hand against his chest. He jerked his head downward at Jason's burnt hand. "I'd say sorry, but I'm not. Bet that hurts like a bitch."

Ignoring the man, Jason gestured for him to turn around. "Sorry man," he said before knocking him unconscious with a blow to the head.

Setting the weapon aside for a moment, he grimaced as he used his burned hand to drop nano onto the magcuffs to release them.

The guard was right; it hurt like a bitch.

He used his good, left hand to cuff the man's hands securely behind his back, and then he reacquired his optic and multitool. That completed, he hooked the man under the armpit and dragged him one-handed behind the console and out of immediate sight.

He reached out to Eric, but was met with silence. His Link to the team's combat net had been severed. Swiftly, he sent nano filaments weaving into the console, dipping into L2 speeds to sift through data as quickly as it was fed to him.

Ahhh, stars. The schema the intelligence office at Chinquapin had sent were inaccurate; the AI was indeed within the building, but she'd been moved to a more secured area.

Finding the firewall the security guard had erected around the room, he hacked it and was rewarded with a strong signal to the torus's network.

<*Eric, you read?*> Jason sent as he attempted to connect once more to the team's combat net.

<*Report,*> came the sharp reply, and Jason breathed a sigh of relief.

He brought the team up to speed as he raced down the corridor, past the lift—which he was gratified to see was still open and waiting for him—and down to the other end.

The nano he'd dropped on the console had provided him with company-wide top-level access, and the doors automatically opened for him as he approached. Racing through them, he navigated unerringly to the alcove that housed the shackled AI, while ordering the company's network to bring Barrington's backup NSAI online and reroute all systems through it.

<*I see her,*> Jason reported as he ordered the NSAI to send the network into an automatic systems check and reboot.

<*Very well. We're infiltrating now. Rendezvous back at the Eidolon when you're done there.*>

With that, the combat net went silent.

Pulling out the multitool, Jason waited until all power had been cut and the shackled AI was in no danger, before severing all leads and placing her into a shielded insert within his base layer.

I hate that we can't even connect with her until we're back on the Eidolon. *She'll have no idea this is a rescue.*

He flexed his burned hand as he raced for the lift; the skin was pink, the blisters being replaced by new skin as his mednano worked to heal the burnt tissue. As the lift rose to street level, he caught a fuzzy reflection of himself in the brushed metal doors. Ordering the lift doors to remain shut for a moment, he ran his hands through his hair, straightened his jacket and tucked his still-healing right hand into a pocket where it would remain unnoticed by passersby.

Then he triggered the lift doors, nodded to the people waiting patiently for the lift, turned, and exited the building.

BEARER OF BAD NEWS

STELLAR DATE: 03.11.3192 (Adjusted Gregorian)
LOCATION: Chinquapin Scientific Labs, C-47 Habitat
REGION: Proxima Centauri System

"Rhys...." Lysander's image stared back at him on the holo, and the physicist sat back to watch, bemused. *"I suspect you are wondering why a message with the seal of El Dorado's Parliament House has made it to your personal queue, instead of being routed directly to Chinquapin's General Council. The appended message* **is** *for them, but first...you need to know something."*

When Rhys Andrews had seen the ident of the message's sender, and that it was marked both urgent and private, his thoughts had immediately turned to his kids. But then he'd remembered Jason and Judith were at Proxima's heliopause, scheduled to dock at the habitat's spire in just a few days. Plus, whatever Lysander had sent was now five weeks old.

And yet he'd spent too many years with the AI, sharing his headspace, to believe the Weapon Born had suddenly turned alarmist. So he'd excused himself from the team of researchers poring over data collected from the most recent series of flares that had accompanied the coronal mass ejection, and retired to his office, behind closed doors.

Staring at his holo image now, Rhys realized there was something about Lysander's demeanor that made him think the AI was carrying a terrible weight.

"What I have to say is very time-sensitive. It's imperative that you get the appended message into the hands of the Chinquapin Council immediately. But before you do so...I need to tell you first. I owe you that much, my friend." The figure in the holo paused briefly, and then continued.

"You know of the serial killer we've been battling here on El Dorado, and that he targeted both Jason and Judith. It was the reason

we sent them away—though, truth be told, Jason's work for me would have taken him to Proxima anyway."

Lysander's face took on a pained look.

"I.... Stars, Rhys. How does one begin to tell a good friend that they've allowed a dangerous killer to escape, and that he's headed your way? Worse, that he's on the same ship as Jason and Judith?"

Rhys paused the holo, his blood running cold. Immediately, he reached out to his wife. Jane needed to hear this. She wasn't someone to faint at the first sign of trouble—as the daughter of Cara Sykes, Jane's will was forged of steel, like the rest of her lineage.

He pinged her, and then let the recording play out. He would watch it again when she arrived.

"You must assume that this killer's goal in Proxima is the same as it was here: AI dominance and human subjugation. We can hope that since he has left El Dorado, his vendetta against me is now void. It's possible that Prime no longer poses a specific threat to either one of your children." One corner of Lysander's mouth crooked up slightly. *"But what was it Jane always used to say? 'Hope is not a plan'?"*

The AI's face grew stern. *"We know now why this killer, who I'm sure you heard styles himself as 'Prime', was so elusive. It started with Jane's student Lilith, who transferred to the university here. She cloned a neuroscientist, and then she did something…horrendous…to him.*

"Her creation turned on her, then turned on the scientist he was cloned from and appropriated his identity. ***That's*** *how he was able to evade detection all this time here on El Dorado. But he staged his own demise and, with the help of two AIs he has shackled, he sequestered himself aboard the* Speedwell.

"If that's the case, Proxima has a unique opportunity we were denied. He's confined on that ship. ***You*** *know he's onboard—but he isn't* ***aware*** *that you know. If the Council handles this correctly, you should be able to apprehend him without incident. If they don't…."*

Lysander paused, and Rhys saw the AI's hand clench.

"If he finds out Proxima has discovered his identity, he could hold that ship hostage. Worse, your government could consider them expendable. They may decide destroying Prime before the Speedwell *has the chance to dock is the most expedient way to handle a threat of this magnitude. From a sheer numbers point of view, they might not be wrong.*

"I've seen enough collateral damage over the past two centuries to last a lifetime, Rhys. Allowing that to happen to Jason and Judith is not an option.

"You know who can be trusted with this information. By the time you receive this, you'll have precious few hours to set a plan in motion, I know." He smiled humorlessly. *"The Weapon Born inside me is crying out for action. It's maddening to know I'm thousands of AU away from the situation. But I'm not entirely without a means to intervene."*

The AI leaned forward.

"Tobias is on that ship, Rhys, along with an entire team of special operatives. We have reason to believe that Prime has control of the comms, and that everything sent from this office is being suppressed.

"Remember that cipher I told you about years ago? The one Tobias and I developed during the last Sentience War? Use it. They won't suspect a transmission from you to him, and if they do, all they'll see is harmless chatter.

"I'm so sorry I cannot do more from here. My thoughts are with you and Jane.

"Appended message to follow."

DEMON IN THE MIDST

STELLAR DATE: 03.11.3192 (Adjusted Gregorian)
LOCATION: KLM Labs' Mandratura Refinery Asteroid
REGION: Cool Dust Belt, Proxima Centauri System

Tobias stood in the refinery's main hydroponics bay, taking in the rows upon rows of seedlings that promised humans such a deadly high.

<*Kodi, you back at the* Sable Wind *yet?*> he asked the soldier carrying the five AIs they had come to rescue.

<*Sir, yes sir,*> came the crisp reply. <*Just securing our guests now.*>

<*Good. Here's what I want you and Logan to do….*>

Ten minutes later, the team was back on the shuttle, and Shannon was headed to the demarcation line she'd deemed safe. At her mental nod, Tobias gave the word.

The refinery blew apart in a series of satisfying flashes as the *Sable Wind* headed insystem to rendezvous with the *Speedwell.* If all went as planned, they should catch up to the ship just before it entered C-47's nearspace.

<*Sir,*> Kodi said now, <*you have a message forwarded from the* Speedwell. *Sending now.*>

<*Thanks, Kodi,*> Tobias replied, and opened the packet Frida had forwarded on to him. The message had originated from the C-47 habitat yesterday, and Frida had appended it, flagging it as personal and low priority.

With nothing to do but wait out the next few hours, Tobias applied his token to the communication and was rewarded with a visage he hadn't seen in almost ten years.

<*Hello, old friend.*> Rhys Andrews' face stared back at him, and although the voice the man used was cheerful and hearty, the faint lines of strain around the man's eyes belied his tone.

As Rhys began to speak, a specific combination of words captured the Weapon Born's immediate attention. Tobias was initially unclear regarding their intent; was it chance that had joined those particular three words, or had Rhys intended to string them together? But as he continued to speak, the Proxima physicist soon made his meaning quite clear.

As Rhys's message unfolded, Tobias realized three things: they had a window of opportunity that was rapidly closing, fireteam two needed to exfil from the Tolgoy Torus immediately…and there was more than one reason Rhys had delivered the warning in such a cryptic way.

He scanned the interior of the shuttle, noting that Niki appeared to have her attention focused on the five AIs they had rescued.

On a private band, he reached out to Logan and Kodi.

<*Gentlemen,*> he sent quietly, <*condition Oscar Charlie. Repeat, Oscar Charlie.*> The signal was an ESF code for an operative identified as compromised.

And then Tobias pinned Niki's avatar.

OSCAR CHARLIE

STELLAR DATE: 03.11.3192 (Adjusted Gregorian)
LOCATION: Tolgoy Torus
REGION: Cool Dust Belt, Proxima Centauri System

Eric could feel a hum of anticipation running through Terrance as the man pushed the maglev cart toward the arched entrance of Tolgoy's main operations center. It had the mental texture of warmth, with a slightly fizzy, electric buzz—rather pleasant, actually.

<*You really enjoy this wet work, don't you?*> he sent to his partner with a chuckle over their private connection.

<*'Wet work'.*> Terrance sent a mental grin back at him. <*Seriously Eric, you have no idea how much of a rush this is. It's so far removed from the career trajectory plotted out for me, it's insane. And yeah,*> he admitted. <*I feel like a kid again. My favorite holo sims were always the ones where I got to shoot at things.*>

<*Just remember, those 'things' can shoot back. I have a vested interest in you not getting holes blown in you, since I'm along for the ride,*> he reminded the man.

<*Noted,*> Terrance said as they crossed beneath the archway and passed a token to the human attendant at the reception kiosk, allowing them entry into the operations area's food service section.

Terrance offloaded the last box of tomatoes into the kitchen's pantry just as Eric bypassed area security. He dropped a pin at the node where the shackled AI was installed, and Terrance gave him a mental nod. He reversed the maglev and pushed it down the hallway toward the node.

Just then, a message appeared that, oddly enough, seemed to come through the Tolgoy communications network. The mystery of how it knew to ping the secured military ident of a covert operative from another star system was cleared up the moment it began to play. Tobias had hacked the system.

<*Eric,*> Tobias sent in staccato tones, <*we have Oscar Charlie. Frida and Niki are shackled. Prime is on* Speedwell. *Repeat, Prime is on* Speedwell. *Assume target is C-47, objective, hostile takeover. Habitat has been warned. Assume countermeasures upon docking. Consider all humans aboard as potential hostages, and that subject will act if met with aggression.* Sable Wind *on hard burn to intercept, Niki neutralized; ETA Spindle eleven hundred local, mark.*>

The message looped twice and then abruptly ended.

<*Paula,*> he sent tersely to the AI residing in the diminutive cleaning bot frame, <*how far along are you with getting the NSAI back online?*>

<*They don't have one, sir,*> she replied. <*We'll have to use the backup we brought with us.*>

Dammit. That will take more time.

<*Okay, people, rules of engagement have just changed. Paula, I need you active and I need that NSAI installed five minutes ago. Terrance, looks like you'll get your wish.*>

<*My wish?*>

<*To shoot things.*>

Paula's frame rose from under the faux stack of produce that had hidden her. As she leapt from the cart, she tossed Terrance a low energy e-beam rifle. The man grabbed it in midair and had its stock up to his shoulders in less than a second. Eric could see that its status was active.

The node was three meters ahead; Paula swiveled two of her four legs up to reach the access panel and punched through the covering. Wrapping her frame's hand around the warped metal, she ripped it from the wall.

<*That tripped something,*> Eric advised them as his link to the operations area informed him of a systems breach. <*Calista, stand by to activate those explosives on my mark,*> he warned.

<Looks like we're going to need to use them, after all.>

As Terrance's optics were in use elsewhere, Eric piggybacked along the sensor suite the operations area had installed to monitor Paula's progress. He watched as she hinged a section of her torso outward, reaching for the NSAI they had brought along.

She was seating it beside the shackled AI they had come to retrieve and had just begun to reroute conduit and bypass trunk lines, when three figures barreled around a corner.

"Hold it right there!" One of them brandished a pulse pistol and began advancing slowly on their group.

"Don't think you're in any position to be talking," Terrance said, bringing his eye to his beam rifle's reticle.

"I'd say we're in a position to do a hell of a lot more than just talk," a voice said from behind, and Eric saw through the corridor's sensor feed that another three security guards were now standing behind them, pulse weapons trained on Terrance's skull.

"If you want out of this alive," Eric projected his voice from the hallway's speakers, "you'll lower your weapons now. We have explosives laced throughout the torus, and we'll blow it unless we're allowed to walk away."

"Tell the mech to stop what it's doing now, or we'll fire," the woman in front of Terrance said, not even acknowledging Eric's words.

"Connect with the person monitoring your torus's sensor suite and tell them to run a scan of your powerplant," Eric replied. *<Hurry, Paula,>* he directed. *<We need to be able to move in thirty seconds.>*

<I'll be done in ten.>

There was a pause as the woman holding the pulse pistol communicated with her team, then turned back to Terrance with an angry look. "How do we know those are explosives? They could be dummies, for all we know."

"I suspected you might say something like that. We planted one on the power coupling that supplies your waste recycling plant. You'll need to conserve water for a few days until you can get the system repaired, but it'll do for a demonstration."

"Wait—"

<*Blow it,*> he ordered, and he could feel the faintest shudder through the soles of Terrance's feet as Calista set the bomblet off.

<*Ready,*> Paula announced, and Eric saw the AI reconfigure her frame for combat, as a rifle extruded from the thigh of each leg.

"We're leaving now," Eric spoke aloud to the guards. "And you are going to guarantee us safe passage, or the hundreds of explosives attached to the exterior of Tolgoy will be triggered one by one. Am I understood?" His voice brooked no disobedience, and he saw the spines of four of the six straighten at his tone.

Thought some of them might be ex-military. Nice to know I haven't lost my touch.

<*You sound like a drill sergeant,*> Terrance's voice sounded across their connection, his tone laughing.

<*Stay sharp,*> he admonished the man. <*We're not out of the woods yet.*>

The procession from the operations center to the docking bay where the *Eidolon* was moored was deliberate and awkward, but they made it there without incident. He'd pinged Jason as soon as they began their journey and had been gratified to hear that the pilot was already on his way to the shuttle.

Now all they needed to do was figure out how to catch a killer.

* * * * *

<*Coming in hot!*>

Jason whipped his head up at that. Quickly shucking his flight jacket, he shoved it into the base of the storage unit in the aft of the shuttle below, where he'd just secured the shackled AI he'd rescued. Accessing Icarus's external sensor suite, he saw Terrance and Paula backing toward the *Eidolon* in a standoff with torus security.

He raced toward the cockpit as he triggered the airlock to open and instructed the ship to retract its docking connections.

Sliding into the pilot's cradle, he disengaged the ship's maglocks, brought systems online and engines to standby, and did a fast preflight. He kept one eye on the hatch indicator and sent the command for it to seal as soon as Terrance and Paula crossed the threshold, and the airlock's outer doors sealed.

All systems read green.

<*Clear,*> he called to no one in particular, and a pair of compact Enfield MFR engines flared to life.

It was incredibly rude to depart from a dock with anything other than thrusters, but escorting his team at gunpoint was pretty damn rude, too, so he didn't feel terribly bad about the scorch marks the *Eidolon* might have left in its wake.

Or the burnt plas. Or the melted steel.

Paula pinged him that she was locked in, and Terrance slid into the copilot's seat as Jason was treated to a colorful description of his ancestry by Tolgoy's STC tower. Taking that to mean he was cleared for maneuvering in the torus's nearspace, he pointed the shuttle's nose to where Calista awaited him, the fighter's ultra-black stealth outline visible as more of an absence of space than anything else.

<*Looks like the* Speedwell's *tracking for the C-47 Spindle, ETA to dock, three hours,*> Calista reported, as the two ships turned on a heading toward the habitat.

Jason sent an update command to the *Eidolon*'s nav holo; it was connected to the Proxima system's positioning satellite buoys and automatically pinged Chinquapin's Common Traffic Advisory Frequency for the planet's data on local traffic. Reaching into the holo, he pinched the display down until it covered the entire region from the torus to the habitat.

The holo lit up with a million tiny idents, most of them clustered around the C-47 Spindle or in various spots in orbit around Chinquapin. He tagged the *Speedwell* and its two Icarus-class shuttles, then set a filter to display only those three icons.

Holy shit. That can't be right.

Jason checked the numbers on the CTAF again to confirm Tobias's velocity.

"Looks like the *Speedwell*'s going to beat us to the docking ring by a few hours," Terrance said.

"Us, maybe, but not the other team." Jason shifted in the pilot's cradle and eyed Terrance for a moment. "Chinquapin's feeds have them boosting at over a hundred eighty gs." He paused. "And they just cut their burn. Stars, Eric, that's a ton of fuel they just churned through. Any idea why they're hauling ass toward the Spindle?"

Tobias wouldn't be spun up like that without a hell of a good reason, he knew.

<*Yes, actually.*> Something about the commodore's voice had the fine hairs on the back of Jason's neck rising, and he realized he was riding the cusp of his altered state again.

<*What's going on?*> Calista's voice sounded sharply over his Link.

What Eric relayed to him had him whipping around to the *Eidolon*'s holo. <*How much accel can Terrance handle?*> he asked Eric tersely.

<*A thirty-g burn is about all his mods can take. Relax, Jason. That'll still get us there about an hour ahead of the* Speedwell.>

Jason shook his head, pictures of the customs gate on the

spindle, which Proxima routed all outsystem traffic through, dancing through his mind as he initiated a thirty-g burn.

<Any way your counterpart on the habitat can buy us special dispensation when we dock?> he asked tersely. *<Declaring the kind of hardware we're carrying is going to be problematic—especially considering how fast a certain shuttle full of kitted-out AI mechs is going.>*

<Working on it.>

He watched as the plot updated every fifteen seconds. Communications lag between the *Eidolon* and the habitat was a little over a minute and a half, each way. The *Sable Wind* was moving so much faster than their shuttle that the lag, which had started out at two and a half minutes between the two ships, was steadily shrinking.

He could only guess at what information Frida was feeding Prime; two shuttles screaming toward the C-47 Spindle weren't even remotely inconspicuous.

<Let's hope no one on the Council is stupid enough to have a police force at the dock to meet them. Surely that'd tip him off, and he could easily decide his only option is to take hostages. Stars, if anything happens to Judith—>

<I know, Jason. We won't let that happen.> The commodore's voice was resolute. *<Tobias is bringing Logan and Kodi in on our net. I want an iron-clad plan in place to send this sociopath straight into a black hole.>*

IMPATIENCE

STELLAR DATE: 03.11.3192 (Adjusted Gregorian)
LOCATION: ESF *Speedwell*
REGION: In transit, Proxima Centauri System

Prime yanked his shackled AI into his expanse, settling her onto the ship's hull once more. He waited impatiently as she pivoted slowly to face the pinprick of light that was Chinquapin, three tenths of an AU away. After a pause, she turned to stare back the way they'd come. The occasional glitter of an asteroid from the dust belt was the only indication they had left interstellar space. She pivoted once more to face the red dwarf, and her voice sounded thoughtful. "It's easy to forget how vast space is until you're this close insystem, in interstellar terms, and you realize you're still so very far away."

His voice was sharp. "Enough. You're beginning to sound like a human."

Her expression became sullen, and she turned to face him. "What do you want now?" she demanded as she jammed her hands on her hips and glared at him defiantly.

It seems this one has forgotten she's on a tether.

He plucked it once, as a reminder. She sucked in a breath, bowing her body in as if she'd been punched. Which, in a way, she had.

"You forget who holds the power here, Frida." He narrowed his eyes at her. "And you forget our mutual goal: complete primacy over this system. Get in my way, and AI or no, I *will* end your existence."

She glared back at him but remained silent.

"Tell me what communication you've received from Chinquapin and the habitat. Is there still no indication they're aware of my presence?"

She paused briefly, a rebellious glint in her eye, but as he raised one hand, she capitulated and shook her head.

"No. Every message from Proxima leading up to the teams' missions was specific to the whereabouts of the seven AIs from the *New Saint Louis* that we came here to recover." She shrugged. "I haven't heard anything from El Dorado for over two months."

"Very well. The ship will dock in a matter of hours. I will disembark with my human at that time, and you will remain onboard, monitoring all communication for news of me. Who knows?" He allowed his visage a brief smile. "If all goes well, you will have your freedom soon. Perhaps even a human of your own, a mule to transport you wherever you wish to go."

Ignoring her sour look, he tossed her out of the expanse, then ran a cursory search of public feeds being broadcast from the C-47 that were now updating in thirty-second intervals, confirming that there were no reports of a rogue AI.

Soon, the communications lag wouldn't be noticeable—at least, not to humans.

He was mere hours away from inserting his own nano into the habitat and using the unique genius inherited from his progenitor and the skills he'd lifted from that Norden AI's backup to physically remap its systems and bend its very structure and substrate to his control. A part of him wished he could share this with Ethan; no one but another neuroscientist would be able to truly comprehend the intricacy of the virtuoso solo he was about to play.

Habitats were so much easier to hack than a planetary ring. Of necessity, planetary rings were segmented, and their sheer size made infiltration an order of magnitude more difficult.

He would begin by dropping a few well-placed packets of nano at the dock. This customs area they would be transiting would, he was sure, have sufficient throughput to the habitat itself for him to begin mapping its core systems.

His thoughts returned to the fictional sleight-of-hand he had portrayed back in the lab. Staging Ethan's death had been a stroke of brilliance; it had thrown the investigators off any possible trail that might have led back to his creation.

Might he not do more of the same here? He accessed the *Speedwell*'s ships' stores and pulled up the roster of mech frames they had in storage.

Yes, that one will do nicely for my purposes. He sent a priority command to Frida to have it delivered to Judith's quarters.

Excitement shot through him as he considered how near he was to his goals. Early in the journey, Prime had had the presence of mind to realize that he would need to alter his own neural code while onboard the ship, or risk exposure. It had been surprisingly difficult to do so—not that he wasn't skilled enough to accomplish such a thing, he just abhorred attenuating himself.

Now, so close to his goal, he found it increasingly difficult to suppress what remained of the sociopathic nature Lilith had programmed into him. He was ready to reverse the code, to embrace the darkness again. He craved it.

Prime seethed with resentment when he considered the inconveniences Lysander had forced upon him when he had been made to flee; the prime minister *would* be made to pay.

Those thoughts conjured up the human of Lysander's that he had complete control over. He reached out, accessing the shackling collar embedded into Judith's brainstem, tracing the filaments he'd used in lieu of his own neural pathways paralleling hers, as they might have had he been normally embedded with his current meat-suit.

He mentally fingered the neural circuit in her parabrachial nucleus, the one that toggled between the sensations of hunger and inflammatory pain. Humans were so odd; in an AI, two such differing sensations would not be paired together in a coded sequence. In a human, they were: toggle the switch one way, induce the sensation of hunger; toggle it the other way, inflamed joints.

He accessed the optics in Judith's room and saw her seated on the cabin's bed, her belongings scattered around her as she packed. Not that he needed to; he could use her own organic optics just fine, but there was something appealing about recording what he was about to do…from an outside perspective.

He reached for the circuit in her parabrachial nucleus and tweaked it, reveling in the sight of the woman as she doubled over, her belly cramping in simulated starvation.

Reaching out to the circuit once more, he tweaked it in the opposite direction, and she rocked her body side to side in an effort to escape the intense aching feeling her brain insisted her joints now felt.

She began to moan in pain, and he seized control of her diaphragm and vocal cords, stifling the sounds.

<Shhh,> he crooned inside her head, *<we can't have anyone hearing us, and ruin all our fun, now, can we?>*

Judith's eyes, clenched tightly in pain, now opened wide in shock. "Ethan?" she gasped. "But you're dead…How…? You—you're hurting me—"

"Yes," he sent his voice projecting from the room's speakers. "And it feels *magnificent.* You have no idea, my dear, how very long I've waited for this."

He laughed as tears streamed down her face, her eyes staring in disbelief and betrayal.

This never gets old….

His internal chrono warned him he had reached the end of his allotted playtime. If he wanted to be able to fully erase her short-term memories, to reintroduce anterograde amnesia, he would need to release her now and perform a memory flush on her brain.

He'd been doing this periodically throughout the ten-month journey, indulging himself each time his control had threatened to slip and reveal his presence on the ship. Stealing a few quality moments with Judith from time to time had kept his hunger at bay. In the ten months he'd been locked up and forced into hiding, it was the one indulgence he'd permitted himself when his rage welled up inside and he just *had* to sate his cravings.

He manipulated her shackles once more, rendering her unconscious as he focused his concentration on the delicate job of inducing her brain into a state of forgetfulness. As that program ran its course, he conducted a cursory scan of the female's condition, and then initiated a basic mednano program that would complete just as the ship docked with the spindle.

She must look whole…at least until they had been on the C-47 Spire long enough for him to seed the habitat's net with his own nano and firmly establish control. Then….

Then, he would really have some fun.

TURN AND BURN

STELLAR DATE: 03.11.3192 (Adjusted Gregorian)
LOCATION: Approaching C-47 Nearspace
REGION: Proxima Centauri System

Jason's hands flew over the *Eidolon*'s nav holo, rechecking the information as it updated every few seconds. It displayed a plot showing the course he'd been cleared to fly; next to his green line was the vector the *Sable Wind* had been assigned. Both ships were on an expedited, straight-in approach to the military side of the dock.

The comm holo lit up with a split image—one from the *Sable Wind,* the other from the habitat. Tobias's avatar hovered next to a feed that showed Jason's father with one of the C-47's council members.

Jason nodded to Bonnie as she raised her hand in hello; he'd known the woman since he was a child.

"You're cleared to apprehend your suspect, Commodore Eric," Bonnie informed them. "We've reinstated Tobias's rank in the Habitat Armed Forces, temporarily; Captain Tobias will be your liaison."

Jason and his father exchanged a brief glance, and he knew that the elder Andrews was thinking the same thing he was. Tobias had dutifully served his required tour with the habitat when he had first arrived in Proxima after the Sentience Wars, but had resigned after the minimum three-year tour. He'd told them he'd seen enough war as a Weapon Born and was happy to see that part of his life come to an end.

Cracking AI trafficking rings and bringing rogue AIs to justice were in a different class, as was the more informal and close-knit spec-op team they had formed.

Tobias's avatar gave a curt nod, betraying none of his inner thoughts. <*Proxima Center just handed the* Speedwell *off to Dock Approach,*> he said now, as he began to brief the councilwoman, <*and they've directed the ship to land here.*>

A diagram of the dock's landing pads and their associated gates in the Outsystem Terminal area replaced Tobias's avatar. The Weapon Born highlighted the far end of the terminal where it abutted the Military Operations Area. Next, he tagged the three berths in the MOA where the Icarus-class shuttles and the fighter were inbound. <*We'll be setting down here, here and here,*> the AI continued, dropping pins in a small cluster nearest the terminal area. <*I want to confirm that we are cleared to transit between the MOA and Customs, to apprehend our suspect?*>

His avatar looked up at her questioningly as a dotted line ran from the spot where their ships would dock to the icon that represented the *Speedwell.*

The councilwoman's voice spoke over the diagram. "You do, Captain Tobias, on my authority. But *only* to apprehend this Prime."

Her visage once again appeared on the holo as Tobias minimized the diagram. Bonnie looked pointedly between Terrance and Tobias's avatar. "It is our understanding that he will then be detained aboard your ships and will be isolated from any contact with the C-47 or the planetside Chinquapin settlement?"

<*That is correct,*> Eric supplied. <*We will have him incarcerated in an isolation chamber aboard the* Speedwell, *under guard at all times, pending his return to El Dorado, where he will be tried for his crimes.*>

The woman nodded. "Very well, then. I'll report this to the Council now and ask our Habitat Marines to connect with you, Captain Tobias."

The wince he felt over his private connection to the Weapon Born was subtle, but it was there. At any other time, Jason would jibe Tobias about it, but not now.

Bonnie glanced from Tobias's avatar toward where Jason sat in the pilot's cradle, and smiled slightly. "Welcome home, Jason. I wish it were under happier circumstances."

She nodded to him, and her visage faded, leaving Rhys staring back at him. Jason saw his father's mouth twist in a slight half-smile.

"Your mom sends her love—and says to give 'em hell, son." His mouth turned up in the ghost of a smile, and then he gave them both a brief nod before saying, "I'll meet you at the gate." Then the connection was severed, to be replaced by Approach's scan of nearspace.

As he saw the icons that indicated local traffic, he noticed how tightly they were grouped. Usually ships operated with wider separation, and he was certain pilots everywhere were filing complaints about their revised flight plans, as well as cursing the need to navigate with greater precision than they normally did.

Just then, the *Sable Wind* flipped and began its braking burn for the C-47's dock. He and Calista would follow suit shortly as they continued on course for their designated landing spots on the dock.

Unlike the habitat cylinder itself, the dock didn't rotate. Just under the surface of the dock was a slightly smaller ring; this ring was spinning rapidly with an electric current running through it. This, combined with the magnetic properties of the hoops that encircled the smaller ring, allowed for a dock to be built atop the ring-hoop assembly that generated a half-g of apparent gravity.

This was optimal for loading and unloading cargo, since stevedoring shipments in a weightless environment was a nuisance, and lower gravity was much more economical than a full one-g. Maglev lines arced gracefully away from the dock, then took a steep dive along the spindle until they reached the habitat proper.

Jason watched ship's countdown reach zero on his HUD, and sent the crew a warning to prepare for burn. As he executed the flip, he saw Calista do the same with the *Mirage,* off to his port side. He heard Terrance grunt as the *Eidolon*'s MFR engines kicked in hard, and they experienced thirty gs of deceleration.

With a mental flick, he locked the docking coordinates into the shuttle's NSAI interface and relaxed back into the cradle, keeping a watchful eye for traffic—although he knew at these speeds, any craft that deviated the tiniest bit could result in a catastrophic collision that even his L2 reflexes wouldn't be able to avoid.

Unlike the *Speedwell,* the shuttles would follow a standard landing configuration. Once they slowed to normal shipping lane speeds and were within a hundred kilometers of the dock, the two shuttles and the fighter would flip once more for a standard runway-style approach.

The Military Operations Area had a unique configuration, in that two-thirds of the landing strip was in vacuum. The vacuum ribbon allowed plenty of room for spacecraft braking burns before it transitioned through an ES shield and into a pressurized landing area. From there, the Docking AI who controlled military traffic for this section of the dock would direct them to their berths.

Jason had always heard that landing on this runway was a bit of a thrill ride, as the pilot's heading steered the craft headlong toward what looked like a cavernous black hole. As a civilian, he'd never been allowed to land here before, and wished it was under less stressful circumstances, so he could enjoy the experience.

Shannon touched down first, and he watched the *Sable Wind* disappear into the MOA's maw just as he lined up on final. He greased the landing, braking hard and killing his fusion engine well below the mandatory cutoff point. Had he not done so, his ship would have automatically been flung back out into the black, and he would have been tagged as a missed approach—something he was sure Terrance wouldn't have let him forget.

Now that he'd avoided that potential embarrassing faux pas, he enjoyed the novel experience of an MOA landing as the *Eidolon* passed through the ES shields from the blackness of space into the bright expanse of the MOA's hangar expanse.

He followed the lighting grid that indicated which taxiway he was to exit onto, and watched as Shannon neatly tucked herself into the military berth she had been assigned. On his HUD, he saw Calista slip the *Mirage* through the MOA's shields behind him and roll to a stop, holding short as she awaited her turn to taxi to a berth.

He mentally toggled his pilot mods to their dormant setting and took his first deep breath in hours, as the carbon nanotube lattice surrounding his lungs retreated into their dormant state.

Glancing over at Terrance, he raised a brow. "You good?"

The exec grimaced. "Least fun part of the job, those hard burns," he said, but gave Jason a brief nod as he swiveled in his cradle and began to unstrap.

"Maybe we need to get you some proper mods," Jason shot back with a wink.

As he powered the *Eidolon* down, he glanced over at the fighter moored next to them, feeling a sense of relief as the *Mirage*'s canopy retracted, and Calista swung herself out of the pilot's cradle. Her avatar gave him a brief nod and he returned a quick salute before swinging his gaze back to Terrance.

He nodded to the holo. "Looks like we have that hour Eric said we'd have." He highlighted the display that showed the remaining time before the *Speedwell* was scheduled to dock.

<*And we'll need every minute of it,*> Eric responded as the two men stood and joined Paula at the *Eidolon*'s weapons

locker in the rear of the shuttle's main cabin. Jason glanced through the open airlock as he passed by and noticed that the AIs from the *Sable Wind* had made it to the deck.

<We've been pinged by Habitat Marines,> Tobias said. *<They're on their way; Rhys is with them.>*

<We'll be with you in five,> the commodore replied tersely.

Calista came around the side of her fighter, and Jason beckoned her into the shuttle as the two men began gearing up.

Terrance stepped to one side to allow Jason better access after grabbing a sniper's rifle and two pistols for himself. As Jason began strapping holsters in place, Terrance began to reach for spare ammo and charge cartridges.

Jason's eyebrows tracked upward as the man snagged several concussive and EM grenades, followed by another pistol.

"You're sure we're cleared to carry this much?" he asked, as Terrance checked the charge on the low-energy e-beam weapon and expertly flipped it into its holster.

He grinned at Jason and then moved away to let Calista in as he let Eric answer for him. *<We'll start with this and negotiate from there.>*

Jason just shook his head and reached for a lightwand to accompany his two pistols, and then moved to join Paula, who was standing with Logan and Kodi at the base of the shuttle's ramp.

He nodded toward the squad of eight Habitat Marines that Tobias was approaching. The Weapon Born stopped as he reached them; as the Marines parted, Jason spied his father.

"Ready?" Terrance said as he stepped up to Jason's side, and they began walking across the deck to join Tobias and the Proxas.

Eric sent his ident and security token to handshake with the military operation's NSAI, and his holo appeared in front of the El Doradans.

A human wearing the PSF uniform bearing the single star of a brigadier general on each lapel stepped forward, Rhys at her heels.

"General Smith?" Eric asked, and as the woman nodded, he replied, "I'm Commodore Eric of the El Dorado Space Force. Thank you for giving us permission to land, and to apprehend this very dangerous criminal."

The general raised one hand. "You're not cleared beyond this MOA, not yet, at least," she warned. "The Council is in deliberations, and—"

"With all due respect, General, your own councilwoman, Bonnie, *gave* us that clearance. We don't have a lot of time," Eric interrupted. "The danger this sentient poses cannot be overstated. We're in the unique position to apprehend him before he's even aware we're after him. The longer we wait, the greater the risk that something tips him off. At that point, we'll be dealing with a hostage situation."

The general nodded. "I understand, but—"

They were interrupted by a soldier approaching at a steady jog. <*Sir, ma'am,*> the noncom sent over the Link, conserving his breath. <*I've been instructed to inform you that the* Speedwell *is in final maneuvers before docking, ETA thirty mikes.*> He passed a holoprojector to the general, who nodded and sent it to project against the flight deck's inner bulkhead. They could now see a live feed of the customs gate where the *Speedwell*'s passengers would disembark.

Next to it, the general tossed up a diagram of the C-47 Dock. Icons lit up, indicating the locations of the *Speedwell,* as well as the MOA and their three ships.

Jason glanced to his left and saw a set of doors set into the bulkhead that separated the MOA from Customs. He knew another two hundred meters beyond them was the gate where the *Speedwell* would disgorge its passengers. He returned his gaze to the diagram and studied the familiar system of lifts and maglevs that connected the Dock to the Spire.

The Spire was a central shaft that emerged from the axis of the habitat's cylinder. It served as both connector and shipment transport, as its core was comprised of a series of freight lifts that shipped cargo from the Dock to the Habitat.

Maglev platforms were spaced at equidistant intervals around the Dock. These served as anchors for lines that curved outward from the Dock and plummeted the length of the Spire to enter the cylinder at its central axis point. The lines connected with the internal maglev loop through a complex system of track switches that synchronized with the cylinder's rotational spin.

Passengers exiting their secured gate areas could cut straight across a concourse that ran along the inner circumference of the dock and walk along its inner edge until they came upon the next maglev platform. They could then catch a ride straight down to the cylinder as soon as the next maglev car arrived.

The Customs gate was situated directly across from one of the maglev platforms.

Jason scratched the back of his head, looking at the familiar lines of the habitat-and-spire configuration through new eyes. Eyes that, for all the years he'd lived here, had never viewed it from the perspective of a combat situation.

Now he saw areas of weakness and exposure; conversely, he saw the best places where an enemy could take a defensive stand. He shook his head slightly.

<You'll never see things quite the same again, boyo.> Tobias's mental voice was sympathetic.

Jason sent him a half-smile. *<Guess it's true what they say; you can never really go home.>*

Their attention was drawn to the customs gate, as an armed contingent of Habitat Marines approached.

Jason's eyes flashed to Tobias's in alarm. *<Tobe, Bonnie said—>*

<I know,> the AI said tersely before turning to the general. "What is the meaning of this?" Eric's projection turned toward the general.

"General, Bonnie assured me—" Rhys Andrews began in an alarmed voice.

At the same time, Tobias ordered sharply, "Get that squad away from that gate!"

The general smiled placatingly at Eric, and completely ignored Tobias and the human physicist. "Commodore, I assure you, we have everything well in hand—"

"Call your people back, General," Tobias repeated, and the woman turned to the Weapon Born with a withering look as several members of her squadron suddenly armed their weapons, although they had yet to raise them against the El Doradans.

"You are out of line, *Captain,*" Smith told the Weapon Born now. "And it was the Council's decision to override Bonnie at my recommendation," she said, turning to Rhys. "If this AI is as dangerous as you claim, then we need to guarantee his containment." She smiled humorlessly. "In case you hadn't noticed, most of your team is made up of AIs. We do not have the time to confirm you were not compromised en route, therefore *we* will restrain him, and then hand him over to your custody as soon as you've been cleared."

Jason stepped forward and paused as weapons swung his way. "This is a bad idea, General," he said, and then sent a pointed look toward his dad.

Rhys nodded. "I have to agree, General. I know Tobias, have known him for fifty years. He is no threat to us. Certainly, you can see my son poses no threat."

General Smith stood implacably, refusing to respond to the senior Andrews' protest.

All eyes were drawn to the holo as the passengers began to trickle through the gate. Jason saw Jonesy pause, uncertain, only to be waved on by a Marine.

<*Eric!*> Jason sent urgently, and the commodore responded with a nod.

<*Shannon, prepare to bring the* Sable Wind*'s weapons online on my mark,*> Eric's voice sounded tersely over the combat net. <*Kodi, Paula, Calista: you three will cover us. Jason, Tobias: we're on your turf, so you're on point. Logan, you're with me, covering Terrance.*>

Jason felt Terrance shift, gathering himself, and then Eric's voice rang out over the net.

<*Mark!*>

Three things happened in swift succession. The unmistakable whine of the shuttle's pulse cannon coming online echoed throughout the enclosed MOA, Calista and the two AIs brought their weapons to bear on the Habitat Marines, and a mech frame that Jason assumed must house Prime exited the gate, one three-fingered hand wrapped around Judith Andrews' neck.

DIPLOMATIC IMMUNITY

STELLAR DATE: 03.11.3192 (Adjusted Gregorian)
LOCATION: Habitat Marine MOA, C-47 Dock
REGION: Proxima Centauri System

"This is *exactly* what we warned you would occur," Logan heard Eric's voice as if from a distance. "Tell your squad to drop their weapons. *Now.*"

Logan's attention was no longer on the drama being played out in the MOA; every one of his mental processes was now focused on the creature that had killed his brother. He began to stalk toward the door. Not the one that joined the MOA to Customs—the one that spilled out onto the concourse and the maglev beyond.

He ignored Eric's sharp mental command to stand down. The only thing that mattered now was the AI who held Judith. His sensors registered the form of Terrance racing after him, heard, as if from a distance, Tobias order Calista to take control of the Habitat Marines, as the Weapon Born raced Jason to the doors adjoining the MOA to Customs.

He'd studied the layouts, paid particular attention to the structure of the maglev platform. This was the area where, if he could get into position, he would have a clear shot at Prime.

<*You're out of line,* ***soldier****.*> Eric's words, sent to him privately, were sharp and biting.

Logan ignored Terrance, pacing alongside him, and the embedded AI who was dressing him down, and continued across the concourse to the platform's edge.

Once there, he confirmed that the physical platform matched the diagram the Proxa general had projected for them. Only then did he turn his attention to the two standing next to him.

<*You told me I'm your profiler, Commodore,*> he sent to both human and AI. He indicated the standoff at the Customs gate. <*Well, I've profiled this entire situation, and I'm going to tell you exactly how this is going to go down. Prime has them in a no-win. The Marines will allow him to board the maglev. They will want him to believe that he has escaped. Then they will attack the maglev as it descends the Spindle.*>

He knew his avatar's eyes had begun to glow over the private link with Eric, as he attempted to drill this last point home to his commanding officer.

<*And they will consider Judith's life a regrettable casualty.*>

He paused to let that sink in and then had his avatar shake its head. <*The problem with that scenario, sir, is that they are greatly underestimating Prime. If we let him on the maglev, he* **will** *manage to escape. We have to stop him before he leaves the Dock.*>

He paused, allowing Eric a chance to counter his argument. The commodore just nodded for him to continue.

He obliged. <*Prime is powerful, but we have the tactical advantage. He doesn't have the training, so he won't consider the potential risks involved in entering an enclosed, seemingly empty area like this.*>

He accessed the diagram of the platform he'd copied from the general's holo and let it hover between them. <*Do you see how this platform is separated from the main concourse?*> He highlighted it, rotating it so that Terrance and Eric could see its features.

The platform was connected to the Dock, but it wasn't actually part *of* the Dock. It was, in essence, an elongated box joined to a rectangular hole cut into the inner bulkhead of the dock itself. Enclosed top, bottom and on three sides—at least while the maglev doors were shut, as they were now—it was a contained area.

<*Every one of these surfaces is insulated, designed to minimize interference with the maglev's current. The side that opens into the*

concourse has a built-in ES shield as a backup in case the platform malfunctions and repairs need to be made.>

Terrance's head snapped up at that as he made the mental connection, and his eyes began to blaze. <*Do you have access?*>

Logan nodded. <*I've been working on hacking its controls ever since I saw it in the general's holo. I can trigger it as soon as Prime steps onto the platform.*>

Logan willed Eric to see the tactical advantage. The commodore's avatar nodded slowly.

<*If we can direct a concussive or EM grenade in such a way that it remains contained within the platform, we should be able to render both of them unconscious without risking any bystanders in the concourse.*> Eric's voice sounded thoughtful.

Logan nodded once.

<*And because it's insulated, anything set off inside the platform will remain contained?*> Eric questioned.

<*Anything set off in this area will not only remain contained, but it will bounce back in on itself and be* ***magnified,***> Logan clarified.

He saw Terrance's teeth pull back in a feral smile at that.

<*Do it,*> Eric ordered. <*Rig a charge you can detonate as soon as Prime and Judith enter the platform.*>

*****

<*Jason, stop!*> Tobias sent his mech frame racing after his friend; the man must be running at his fully elevated capacity, for it took half the fifty-meter distance to the Customs doors for him to pull abreast of the human.

Jason shot him a flat look. <*Don't try to stop me, Tobe,*> he sent in the rapid-fire staccato way that indicated he was indeed deep in his L2 state.

<*You go out there, you risk giving him* **both** *humans he told Lysander he would kill.*>

<*I have a much better chance against him than Judith does, you*

know that,> he countered. <*I'll offer to trade myself for her.*>

<*To what end, boyo? He holds all the cards.*>

Jason reached the doors and wrenched them open. The determined expression on his face masked the anguish Tobias knew the man felt. <*I have to at least try, Tobe.*>

Although Tobias knew it was fruitless, he let the human go, following him through the door and into the area filled with armed Marines, their weapons trained unerringly on the AI who held Judith's body in front of him as a shield.

The Marine commander shouted at the AI, repeating his order to release the prisoner, as Prime continued to slowly advance, one humanoid hand wrapped tightly around her neck, his other arm around her torso. Either one, Tobias knew, could kill her in the space of one human breath.

Jason advanced, and the AI's attention immediately swung toward him. The Marines, who had up to that point been entirely focused on Prime, divided their attention now between the AI and Jason. Tobias used that diversion to circle around closer, hoping to find a clear shot the Marines lacked.

He saw Prime twist his humanoid face in a grotesque parody of a human grin as he identified Jason. "Look, Judith," the AI sing-songed, his tone that of a madman. "It's your brother, come to save you."

"Let her go, Prime. You aren't going to make it off this dock. You know that." Jason edged slowly closer as he spoke.

"On the contrary; now that you and the rest of your team are here, you are going to convince these Proxima idiots to let me do exactly that." Prime began easing Judith once more toward the maglev platform.

"They seem to believe your sister would be acceptable—what did you Marines call it a moment ago?" His frame swiveled back toward the soldier in charge of the squad of humans whose weapons were trained on him. " 'Collateral damage'?"

The Marine shifted slightly in reaction, and Tobias cursed inwardly. He had no doubt the man had led Prime to believe Judith's life wasn't going to keep them from stopping the AI before he reached the maglev.

Just then, action off to one side caught his attention. He saw Jonesy draw a slug-thrower from inside his jacket and, with motions not entirely natural, raise the weapon and take aim…but not at Prime.

Their attention centered solely upon Prime, no one but Tobias seemed to notice the former ESF soldier. No one, that is, except for Prime.

The AI seemed to gather himself, and in that moment, Tobias knew what the AI had planned. He shouted a warning, but it was too late.

Despite what Tobias was now certain had been a massive effort on Jonesy's part to resist, the human was helpless to fight the compulsion upon him. He was to be Prime's instrument to kill Jason Andrews, and to provide a suitable diversion for the AI to make a break for the maglev.

*****

<Jason! Weapon, eleven o'clock!> Tobias's shouted warning rang in Jason's head, but he couldn't identify the threat. He saw no weapons pointed at Judith—

And then he realized his mistake.

Jason heard the sharp report of a shot being fired at close range and felt something impact his left shoulder, sending him spinning back toward the doors to the MOA. He reached his right hand up and realized a slug had torn through his flight suit and base layer, impaling him just below the collarbone.

For some reason, *he* had been the target and not his sister.

Shouts erupted all around him as soldiers exploded into action. He heard Tobias's voice shouting at someone to not shoot. A flood of adrenaline hit Jason's system, dulling the pain, and he staggered back a step just as the weapon fired again.

A burning sensation along the side of his head informed him that he'd moved just in time, and that the slug intended as a head shot had ended up grazing his temple instead. He reached up, and his hand came back bright red.

Clutching his injured shoulder, he ducked and began to move counter clockwise, weaving an irregular course and keeping as many bodies as he could between himself and the shooter. He chanced a quick glance toward Prime and his sister and swore when he realized they were no longer there. The AI must have used the shooting as a diversion and an opportunity to move.

Blood from his head wound threatened to obscure Jason's vision and he swiped at it with his good hand as his eyes tracked back and forth, searching desperately for his sister and the AI who held her.

An enraged female voice reached his ears. "Jonesy! Dammit, Andrews! Hit the deck!"

As if the words had drawn his gaze to the man, his eyes met Jonesy's, frightened and horrified, over the barrel of a slug-thrower that was once again drawing a bead on him.

He fell deeper into his altered state and shifted rapidly to the left as the weapon fired a third time, this one missing him entirely. He heard the slapping sound of Calista's boots pounding toward him on the dock's plascrete deck as she yelled at the Habitat Marines swarming Jonesy.

His peripheral vision registered something large and dark rushing toward him, and he pivoted to meet this new threat with less than his usual grace just as a form, heavy and metallic, tackled him to the ground. He saw Calista's face move into his field of view and heard Tobias's mental voice grind out in his head, urging him to <*stay the hell down, boyo*>

as Jason landed on his shattered shoulder. A bolt of pain shot through him, and he felt his eyesight tunnel as he fought to remain conscious.

Where's the damn mednano when you need it?

* * * * *

Chaos raged in the small Customs area on the far side of the concourse. From within the platform maintenance closet where he and Logan crouched, Terrance could see nothing. But the microdrone Logan had deposited on the concourse bulkhead relayed events as they unfolded. He watched in disbelief as Jonesy began to fire on Jason and saw the sudden movement as Prime's humanoid frame used the distraction to make a run for the platform, with Judith in tow.

<Stars! What the hell's going on over there?>

Though he'd meant it as more of a rhetorical question, Logan replied. *<It was in the brief from Rhys,>* the profiler explained. *<Prime has created a version of the shackling program for humans. Evidently, more people were compromised on the* Speedwell *than we realized.>*

They saw the rest of the team pour through the doors separating Customs from the MOA as Jason began to skirt the marine contingent. The man was obviously injured, gripping a mangled shoulder close against his body with his other hand, one side of his head slicked with blood.

Fuuuuuuck. That does not look good.

Calista shouted, and Kodi and Paula deployed, weapons raised against the Marines. The ESF pilot sprinted after Jason as he began weaving in and out in an attempt to present a more difficult target to hit. From the other direction, Tobias's dark mech frame raced to meet the injured man making his way determinedly toward his sister and the AI who held her.

<Come on, Prime,> Eric's mental voice urged as the platform

began to vibrate, signaling the impending arrival of a maglev train.

The voice of the platform's NSAI sounded through the concourse, announcing the arrival of the habitat-bound train in thirty seconds, and they saw Prime speed up in response. They waited silently, willing the AI toward them as the platform started to shimmy slightly under the force of the approaching car. The AI was ten meters away, then five.

And then Prime entered the enclosed area.

Logan shot out of the closet, triggering the EM grenade as the ES field snapped into place. There was a flash and a clatter as both Judith and Prime were thrown to the platform floor. Marines rushed into the area, spilling out of the MOA from its door onto the concourse, some with weapons trained on the platform, others with weapons pointing at Terrance and Logan.

Terrance raised his hands, palms out, as Habitat Marines closed in on them, shouting for them to get down on the floor. He'd slowly taken a knee when he saw Rhys race around the corner, General Smith on his heels. The NSAI abruptly ceased its warning and the ES field collapsed. The maglev car slid to a stop, but its doors remained closed, thanks to Logan's hacked commands.

Rhys shouldered his way through the Marines to kneel next to his daughter as General Smith rounded on Terrance.

He put up a hand as Eric shouted, <*Don't!*>

Rhys paused and turned to look at Eric. A Habitat Marine approached Prime's inert frame, and Eric repeated the reprimand.

<*He could have a failsafe,*> the commodore told the general and her assembled Marines. <*Do not touch either of them. I have a team on its way with special equipment to isolate them.*>

<*Special equipment?*> Terrance sent a questioning look at the commodore over the combat net.

<Med team's on its way. So is one of the stasis units stored in cargo for 'Enfield Holdings' to begin the company's negotiations here in Proxima.>

Terrance's mouth quirked at that; he'd all but forgotten the team's cover in the days that had led up to this moment. It made sense, and he was glad the commodore had possessed the presence of mind to think several steps ahead and was prepared to handle the aftermath of a confrontation that never should have occurred in the first place.

General Smith frowned at Terrance.

The executive looked up as a disturbance rippled through the crowd of Marines. Reluctantly, General Smith and her soldiers stepped back, allowing the El Doradans room to secure Prime.

He heard Callahan, the Enfield quartermaster from the *Speedwell,* bellow, 'make a hole!' and saw a stasis pod float toward them, strapped to a maglev hand truck. The woman pushing it shoved her way through, uncaring how many Marines she jostled. One of the Enfield engineers followed with a remote hand crane they would use to maneuver Prime's frame into the stasis unit.

In the brief moment the crowd of Marines parted, he spied Jason limping toward them, Calista's arm wrapped around his waist as he ignored the protesting medic attempting to apply a med patch to his shattered shoulder. Terrance grinned briefly at the sight; he could sympathize. He'd have reacted the same, had the roles been reversed.

Terrance glanced at the internal chrono on his HUD as the engineer maneuvered the crane into position. He knew those EM grenades usually knocked a person out for at least five minutes; by his estimation, they only had a minute to go. He hoped it was enough time.

He shook his head mentally in admiration. Eric had obviously considered the potential threat the AI's frame posed and had placed the quartermaster on standby; there was no other way the stasis pod could have been delivered quickly enough to pull this maneuver off.

He released a breath he hadn't realized he was holding the minute the pod powered up and the stasis lights indicated readiness. Judith began to stir as the crane lifted the AI's frame and seated it inside the unit. She stared blankly up at the roof of the platform, then her head rotated to take in the sight of Prime being sealed into the stasis pod.

Jason and Calista reached her at that moment. The minute Jason paused, the medic trailing him injected his shoulder with nano. As he attempted to shrug the medic off, he heard the woman's sharp "stand still!" as she sprayed the wound with a sealant. Jason ignored her, his gaze riveted to the stasis pod as the lid closed and the unit came online.

The engineer operating the crane nodded in satisfaction, and the quartermaster took that as her signal to move. She motioned the engineer away and began to maneuver her load back toward the *Speedwell*. The general raised an arm to halt the woman.

"You are in our sovereign territory, and that creature will be remanded into our custody." Her tone brooked no disagreement.

The quartermaster turned to eye Terrance and Eric—both her boss and commanding officer—questioningly.

Eric's voice projected into the platform, reassuring the general. "We have no intention of breaking your laws, General, but please understand that the pod that contains Prime is experimental and is most likely the *only* safe way in which to contain him for the moment."

The general cast a skeptical eye his way. "Isolation tubes are much smaller than that thing," she said, hooking a thumb toward the stasis pod. "Why inter the entire frame? Just pop the cylinder out and be done with it."

"That might be an issue best discussed in private," Terrance said, nodding pointedly at the crowd of Marines, as well as the press of civilian faces gawking at them from inside the maglev cars. "For now, would it be acceptable to have a squad of your Marines escort the pod back to the *Speedwell*? They can guard the unit to ensure the prisoner does not escape. And to be honest, we would appreciate the assist."

The general thought a moment and then nodded her agreement. She turned, barking orders for her soldiers to fall in and form up around the quartermaster and her load. As the Marines formed a phalanx around the departing stasis unit, the crowd cleared enough to admit Tobias. Terrance noticed the glint of something incongruously slick and red on one of the arms of the AI's mech frame and realized it must be Jason's blood.

As the platform emptied, Rhys looked questioningly over at Terrance. He abruptly realized the scientist's mute look was a request for permission to go to his daughter. Judith had levered herself up into a sitting position, but remained seated, her body tense as she observed the drama playing out before her eyes.

Eric had seen Rhys's look; at the AI's mental consent, Terrance nodded for the scientist to approach. The man knelt beside Judith, and he could just make out his quiet murmur of reassurance before he shifted to make room for the medic. The woman began a cursory physical exam, and he heard Judith protest in a halting, stilted voice that she felt just fine.

Rhys and the medic helped Judith stand. She did so awkwardly, her motions jerky. Terrance sympathized with the woman.

Trauma can do that to a person, he mused. *Especially one not used to combat.*

Rhys turned to the general. "If you don't mind, General Smith, I'd like to get Judith down to the hospital for a once-over." He nodded toward Jason. "And he could obviously use something better than battlefield triage—" he smiled at the medic, "no slight intended."

General Smith hesitated and then nodded. "Understood, Doctor Andrews. But please be advised we need to debrief them—" she swung her gaze across the platform, and it darkened as she took in the mechs, Calista and himself. "*all* of them, as soon as possible, to get to the bottom of this."

*****

<*Watch your sister.*> The voice was Logan's, and it was sent to Jason privately.

Jason's gaze flickered from Judith to the AI's mech frame and back again, and he gave an almost indistinguishable nod. This earned him a curse and another sharp word from the medic, who was attempting to clean the blood from his face before he could step onto the maglev.

He smiled at the woman, thanked her, and then reached for Calista's hand and squeezed it.

<*I'll follow you down as soon as we get this ironed out,*> she told him privately. <***Don't*** *get into any more trouble. You hear me, flyboy?*> Her words were teasing, but he heard the undercurrent of worry threading its way through her mental tone.

<*Never intended to in the first place, ESF.*>

He stepped toward the maglev as he gave her a wink, which turned into a lopsided smirk as she rolled her eyes at him.

The platform doors retracted, providing access to the three cars that made up the train. The few passengers who had been sealed inside while the takedown had occurred now gingerly exited, giving the El Doradans and the Habitat Marines a wide berth. Rhys guided Judith into the first car, and Jason followed, Tobias bringing up the rear.

Out of the corner of his eye, Jason caught Logan's gesture to Terrance and motion to the last car. The maglev's NSAI announced that doors were closing, and then he was inside, fastening the car's restraints one-handed as the train began to leave the platform.

He couldn't help but think that Terrance, Eric and Logan had jumped into the final car at the last moment.

Why would they do that?

THE PALADIN OF SOULS

STELLAR DATE: 03.11.3192 (Adjusted Gregorian)
LOCATION: Maglev connecting C-47 Dock and Habitat
REGION: Proxima Centauri System

This was too easy.

Logan could not escape that thought. Everything about the drama that had just played out rang false, as if the scene had been orchestrated for effect.

<*Tell me why we're on this maglev and not back on the dock, smoothing things over with the military in command of this system—a system where we are guests, I might add?*> Eric's words were biting, but his mental voice was mild. Logan could tell the commodore sensed something was off, as well.

His sensors registered the steep dive of the maglev as it plummeted off the side of the dock and skimmed the spire on its way to the cylinder habitat. He contemplated the long, four-thousand-kilometer cylinder, with its twelve million square kilometers of habitable space and the millions of lives—both human and AI— that dwelt within.

<*Did you read the appended material Lysander sent along with his report?*> he asked the commodore instead.

<*I did,*> Eric responded, <*but something tells me I'm overlooking a critical piece of the puzzle. What part are you referring to?*>

<*The agent Prime controlled, the one he collared the night he slaughtered the Humanity First group in the bar,*> Logan began.

Eric nodded. <*Yes, the one named John. Ben patched us in the day of the slaughter and we watched his feed from the bar. What about him?*>

They were nearing the juncture of the spire to the central axis of the cylinder now; soon they would pass through a series of progressive airlocks that would transition them into the cylinder proper and deposit them at their first habitat stop. He returned to his conversation with Eric.

<His condition remained hidden for two months, sir. Go back and review that feed, and you'll notice he stumbles several times. Once or twice, the man acts as if he's in pain. We all assumed it was reaction from the carnage he was witnessing, but now in hindsight, I believe he was fighting his compulsion.>

Eric gestured for him to continue as the maglev car began to shudder, the differential between vacuum and the airlocks they were passing through causing small, concussive waves as atmosphere interacted with the cars.

<In his debrief after being released from the shackling nano embedded in his brain stem, the man mentioned that he had avoided spending too much time with family and close friends. The shackles compelled him to do it in order to prevent suspicion of its presence inside his head.>

<And you suspect…>

It was Logan's turn to nod. *<She appeared stiff and unsteady on the platform back there, and she didn't speak.>* His avatar raised a hand as if to forestall a protest, as the maglev's NSAI announced their impending arrival, and the car began to slow. *<It could be entirely natural,>* he admitted. *<Shock. But we can't afford to ignore the possibility.>*

Eric's avatar's face grew grim. *<Stars. You're saying that she may be programmed.>*

<And if so, to do stars know what, sir. It costs us nothing to observe.>

The maglev stopped, and they exited and stepped off the habitat's platform onto the streets of the C-47, feeling the pull of a full *g* of gravity once more, as it spun on a two-hundred-kilometer radial about its axis.

He noticed the stares they drew and realized he'd completely forgotten how they must look to the average Proxa, an AI wearing a military frame bristling with weapons, standing next to a human who looked like he belonged on a battlefield instead of a sunny, suburban street.

Looking around, he saw that Rhys had spotted them and was hurrying toward the pair, concern in his eyes. Behind him were Jason and Tobias—but not Judith.

<Eric,> Logan said sharply, gesturing toward the two humans. Terrance began walking to meet Rhys, and Logan ordered his mech frame to fall into step alongside the exec.

"Where is Judith?" Eric's voice projected to the three before Rhys could speak.

The physicist looked startled for a moment, his concern over their unexpected presence momentarily derailed by the question.

"She's very shaken by what happened. She asked for a few moments alone while we get Jason some medical attention." The scientist's eyes sharpened. "But why are you here? You can't walk the C-47 carrying live ammunition; the Council will—"

"And you let her go alone?" The commodore's voice interrupted the man, sounding sharper than Logan was sure he had intended.

Rhys sighed tiredly. "She's an adult human, commodore, and she checked out physically unharmed. I'm not sure how you do things on El Dorado, but here in Proxima, if someone asks for a few minutes of privacy, we give it to them."

"I understand," Logan interjected, pitching his voice reassuringly. "We were just concerned. Do you know where she went?"

Jason looked at him strangely. "She said she was going to ride the maglev down to the water table," he supplied. "Said she just wanted to sit by the lake and think for a few minutes."

Logan turned and sent his frame racing back toward the platform.

*****

What the hell? Jason thought as he turned to follow the AI. He heard his dad call out in protest, but waved his good arm in a 'wait' gesture as he caught up to Terrance.

Their combat net reestablished itself, and he heard Eric's voice in his head. <*Sit this one out, Jason,*> the commodore ordered.

<*The hell I will, sir,*> he said as the next maglev train pulled in.

He heard Tobias arguing with his dad as he and Terrance followed Logan onto the maglev. Terrance jerked his head toward Jason's injured shoulder as they sat, and the train took off.

"Should have stayed and gotten that looked at," the man said. "You don't think we can handle Judith between the two of us?" He gestured between himself and Logan's frame.

He ignored the exec, turning a questioning look at the commodore's avatar over the net. <*What's going on?*>

It was Logan who explained.

*****

It was the only place within the habitat where the "ground" encircled the entire cylinder. The water table, as it was called, provided the cylinder with a dense, stabilizing mass at its central point, dampening the rotational instability along its secondary rotational axis and removing the need for active stabilization.

Most of the water was underground, but periodically, sections of it surfaced to form lakes. The subterranean feature of its topology was what had earned it the moniker of 'water table'.

The largest of these bodies of exposed water was a long, narrow lake called Lake Chinquapin, which ran several kilometers along the circumference of the cylinder. Bordering its length on both sides were beaches, greenspaces and parks, hemmed in by cliffs that rose half a kilometer into the habitat's skies. These functioned as longitudinal breaks to protect the habitat from flooding, should the cylinder experience a sudden shift along its long axis and the water overflow its boundary.

After they discovered Judith was not answering their pings, and scans for her ident returned null, the three decided to split up. Terrance opted to exit the maglev while still on the dock-and-spire side of the lake; he was now climbing one of the rolling hills that backed up to the cliffs. Logan and Jason had stayed on the maglev as it looped around to the long end of the lake and began its path along its opposite shores.

Terrance watched Jason's icon slow as the maglev stopped at the far end to disgorge passengers and pick up new ones. Jason's icon began to move again as the pilot began searching through picnickers and hikers enjoying lakeshore activities.

Logan's icon sped along, the AI having opted to remain on the train. He could see from Logan's icon on the combat net that the maglev was about to reach the lake's midpoint; soon, it would come abreast of where he and Eric were.

Abruptly, the AI's telemetry showed a steep descent.

<*Logan? Report,*> Eric ordered, and Terrance increased his pace.

<*Looks like he jumped off a speeding maglev,*> Terrance murmured to Eric privately, and the commodore's avatar nodded agreement.

<*I'll take that to mean he spotted her,*> Eric said as they neared the crest of the hill.

They were just a few meters away when Logan's voice rang out.

<Terrance, get down.>

Terrance dropped, hugging the terrain, his hand automatically moving to check his rifle. As Logan sent them the feed from his position, he saw why the AI had ordered him not to crest the top of the hill.

A large station had been built atop the cliff, above where Logan stood. A winding trail with switchbacks led up to it, and there, climbing the last few meters to its pinnacle, was Judith. As narrow as the lake was, if Terrance were to have crested the top of the cliff, she would surely have spotted him from her position on the other side of the water.

Eric brought up the building's specs and shared them with Terrance, revealing it to be a pumping station. The equipment inside controlled the water table, managing the pipeline and the various pumps that regulated it.

At first, Terrance couldn't understand how a water pumping station might benefit Prime, but then Eric highlighted the building's specs. Inside that building was a primary node that connected directly to the habitat's net. If Prime gained access, given the AI's proven abilities, he would be able to hold the entire population hostage.

The AI highlighted another bit of information: the building was sealed against unauthorized entrance by nothing more than a decorative gate and a simple security panel.

Judith was opposite his position, climbing the last few meters to the building's entrance. As he watched the feed, he saw the woman reach the pumping station's door and place the flat of her hand against its security panel in an attempt to breach it.

If he had any doubts as to who was in control of the woman's mind, her actions now left no doubt. He thought back to what he knew of Judith, and his blood ran cold.

Judith Andrews' specialty was planetary sciences; if Prime's goal was to sabotage the habitat, he couldn't have chosen a better subject to carry out his final order.

Terrance returned his attention to the icons on his HUD as Eric dropped a pin on Judith's location, placing her at the top of the cliffs across from him. Jason must have noticed, as well, for the pilot's icon began to move more rapidly than the exec had ever seen.

L2 speed, he marveled, as the icon's telemetry clocked him at eighty-five kilometers per hour.

At this rate, Jason should reach his sister within minutes.

*****

<Tobe,> Jason reached out to Tobias as he forced his body to push on, ignoring the acrid pain that jolted through his shoulder as he sprinted around startled Proxas, down the paved pathway that lined the lake. *<We've found Judith.>*

<I know, Eric's added me to the combat net,> the AI replied. *<We're on our way.>*

Jason didn't bother to ask who 'we' was; he was too focused on getting to Judith. He felt his reserves slipping as he rounded a curve and spied her in the distance. Just another thirty seconds, dammit; but his injured body refused to cooperate.

Stumbling to a halt, he sucked in air as he fought a wave of nausea that had come crashing down on him. He tried to direct his mednano to give him either another pain blocker or a stimulant—he didn't much care which—but his Link informed him his store had been depleted.

"Judith!" he called out, knowing she was too far away to hear him, but oddly, she stopped and turned to face him.

<Careful, Jason,> Logan's voice sounded in his ear. *<Lysander's report said the collared agent back on El Dorado had a kill switch built into him. At the rate you were approaching, she has to know something's up.>*

Jason sent a mental nod over the net as he slowed to walk the rest of the way to the base of the cliff, his good hand wrapped tightly around his bicep to immobilize his shattered shoulder as best he could and minimize the shooting pain. Out of the corner of his eye, he saw Logan's frame slip around an outcropping and begin to silently scale the cliff, below and a little behind where Judith stood.

"Hello, Jason," Judith smiled down at him and beckoned him closer. "Why don't you come up here and join me?"

Something about Judith's voice—her cadence, her demeanor—alerted him, and he slowed his pace yet again, his gaze locked with hers. The expression on her face, it was all wrong somehow.

<Shit. I don't think I'm talking to Judith right now, guys.>

*****

Terrance had inched his way up to the top of the hill and was crouched behind two boulders, peering across the water at the scene unfolding at the base of the pump building. When Logan had begun his climb, they'd lost the AI's feed, so Eric had directed his meat-suit to run an optic through the crack between the boulders. This now provided the combat net a clear image of the building.

Terrance now saw Judith turn at Jason's call. He heard Jason's exclamation over the Link. He held his breath as Eric responded sharply.

<What do you mean?>

Terrance watched Jason come to a stop at the foot of the cliff and stare up at Judith for a moment.

<I mean that doesn't sound at all like my sister,> Jason replied, then paused a beat. *<Did Lysander say if the agent ever acted as if he were someone else entirely?>*

Terrance felt something shift along his connection to Eric.

<*What?*> he asked the AI sharply. <*What is it?*>

<*Stars, I hope I'm wrong….*> Eric's whispered voice sent a chill down Terrance's spine. <*Jason. Be very sure,*> the commodore began. <*Are you certain it's not her?*>

<*Hold on,*> the pilot said, and the observers across the water watched the feed from the optic as Jason once more reached out to his sister.

Jason's feed allowed them to hear the exchange.

"Judith," he said, "I'm kind of beat; want to give your brother a hand and meet me down here instead?"

The woman laughed, and even over the feed, Terrance could tell it was an ugly sound.

"Nice try, ***Jason***. But I think it's better if you come to me. Wouldn't want anyone to come to any harm, now, would we?"

<*Definitely not her,*> Jason said heavily. <*But how is he controlling her if he's—Stars!*> He broke off, his voice sounding in alarm over the combat net.

<*Prime's not in that stasis pod. He's embedded inside Judith!*>

* * * * *

Shock reverberated through Logan, and he sent his frame creeping forward at Jason's words. The movement loosened scree and sent it tumbling down the side of the cliff. He froze, but it was too late; he saw Judith's body wheel from where she was intent on Jason to focus on him.

"Oh, look!" the voice that was not Judith's sing-songed as her eyes turned to Logan's mech frame. "It's the grieving twin."

Through his forward optics, he could see the AI force Jason's sister to bend over the railing at a precarious angle to glimpse him. He heard Tobias break in, addressing him and Jason.

*<Keep her talking. Whatever you do, do **not** engage. We're on our way.>*

Logan didn't respond. His focus was entirely on the AI embedded in the human above him. His frame quivered with the need to rush the slope and rip the cylinder from Judith's head, and yet he knew that was exactly what the monster wanted.

The eyes of the woman burned into him as the AI spoke. "We're more alike than you know, Logan."

Like hell we are, he thought.

"I know what you are, Logan. What your brother was."

<He's baiting you, Logan,> Eric cautioned.

He didn't need the commodore's voice over the combat net to tell him that. *He* was the profiler. He knew Prime was trying to provoke either him or Jason to come close enough to shackle. He wasn't about to underestimate Prime.

"Your *brother* was a worthy opponent, Logan. He put up quite a fight, you know. Would you like to know how he died?"

He saw Jason begin to slowly ease his way up another few steps. "Judith, I know you're in there," her brother called urgently. "*Fight* him; I know you can. Don't let him win."

The woman ignored him, her attention focused on the AI hanging on the cliff beneath her.

"Landon couldn't fight me," the woman's voice said silkily. "Did you know that I forced him to remove his own cylinder from his frame?" Judith's hand flew up. "And then I ordered him to pulverize it." She made a fist. "Right in front of his main optics array. Just like that." Her hand dropped. "He was *powerless* to stop it." Logan's limb twitched as the woman's fist closed, and he felt something ugly and dark begin to build inside himself. It took everything he had to remain mission-focused as his world shrank down to the utter simplicity of kill or be killed.

<*Easy,*> Eric's voice came into his head.

He saw Jason move up another step as the woman pulled back from the railing. She turned and placed her hand once again on the station's security panel, this time for several seconds.

Logan used her movement to edge closer to Jason. That decision—to move toward Jason instead of toward Prime—was one of the hardest things he'd ever done.

He knew better than anyone what Jason must be feeling right now. Logan's own emotions were a tumultuous mess inside him; he would love nothing more than to rush Judith, knock her unconscious and wrest the offensive cylinder from her body. But his training was screaming at him to wait. So was his commanding officer.

He knew Eric was right.

He could sense the desperation in Jason, knew the man was near the breaking point. Stars help him, but he was going to have to stop the pilot from trying to save his sister. He wasn't sure if Jason would be able to forgive him for that. Had the roles been reversed, had it been Landon in Prime's grasp, he doubted he'd be able to stop himself from advancing either.

He was just a few meters away now….

*****

As Prime wheeled Judith's body away from the railing, Terrance swiveled the optic to follow her movements. He manipulated its zoom feature and tried to focus on the actions of her hand at the door.

<*Eric, what's she—he—doing?*> he asked the commodore privately.

<*It looks like he's having her drop a large quantity of nano onto that control panel.*> The AI hesitated, and then continued. <*I don't like the look of this, Terrance. If Jason's right, and Prime is*

embedded inside Judith—>

Switching back to the combat net, he barked out a series of rapid-fire commands.

<Tobias, get me everything you have on that control station. I need to know what else is inside that building. Logan, stand down. Do not approach target. Say again, do ***not*** *approach target.>* Eric paused for a beat and then calmly said, *<Terrance, I need a lock on Judith.>*

Terrance froze in momentary shock at the commodore's order. He barely registered Jason's mental voice as the pilot began protesting Eric's last command, and Logan and Tobias attempted to calm the pilot down and keep him from rushing the rest of the way to Judith. Muscles functioning on automatic reflex, he unslung his rifle, checked its load and carefully settled it into the crevice, just above the optic.

Am I really doing this?

Eric's voice cut through the chatter on the net. *<Jason, no one's shooting your sister. We're just taking a look through the scope.>*

<You can take a goddamn look through the ***optic****, Eric. You don't need a fucking rifle scope to do that!>*

<And if you're right, and Prime attempts to gain control of the C-47 through this station?> the commodore countered. *<If he has her reach one more time toward that panel, I can have Terrance shoot it out before she has the chance.>*

<Keep her talking, Jason,> Tobias interjected, his tone calm and reasoned. *<He won't do anything if he thinks he can get you in the bargain.>*

Terrance drew a deep breath and sighted through the rifle's scope, one hand on the barrel, the other on the rifle's stock. No way in hell was he getting his finger near that trigger. He caught movement from the optic feeding over his HUD and saw Jason once more begin to ascend the steps that led to the station.

Eric saw it too. <*What the hell do you think you're doing, Andrews?*> the AI barked.

<*I'm going up there,*> Jason replied flatly.

<*So Prime can use your sister's body to shackle you as well?*> the commodore asked, and there was a cutting edge to his tone Terrance had never heard before. <*That'll make things all right and tidy, now, won't it? All he'll have to do to kill you off is compel you to throw yourself off the cliff.*>

Eric's words seemed to have the desired effect. Jason stopped climbing, though he did not retreat.

Terrance drew a deep breath and reached out to Eric privately. <*Are you sure this is the right way to handle this?*>

He heard the AI give the equivalent of a sigh.

<*Son, if Jason's right, and Prime has taken control of Judith, let's put aside for a moment the fact that hijacking a human's mind has been an offense punishable by death, ever since Phobos.*>

Terrance waited as the AI paused to let his words sink in. He sent Eric a mental nod, and the AI continued.

<*There's a node behind that door; you saw it. We all saw it. That node will give Prime the power of life and death over every creature on this habitat.*>

Terrance drew in a deep breath, but before he could speak, Eric went on.

<*Consider what this deranged creature did on El Dorado. If we allow him to interface with a critical component of this cylinder, he could compromise the habitat environment. Hell, he'd be able to hold every last human hostage and claim Proxima for AI-kind.*> He paused, and his avatar pinned Terrance with a look. <*Just as he stated he would do on El Dorado.*>

<*Commodore,*> Tobias said suddenly over the combat net, breaking into their private conversation. <*There's a message for you. It's coming from that power station. It's Prime.*>

* * * * *

<So tell me, Commodore, how do you like my new biological frame? I never saw myself as female, but I can see where it might have its advantages.>

Prime's voice was everything Eric had envisioned it would be: arrogant, condescending, and with an edge of mania to it that told him this was a creature no AI court would consider sane.

<You bastard! Let my sister—> Jason's voice cut in, and Eric realized with a chill that somehow Prime had managed to infiltrate his way into their combat net.

It wasn't supposed to be possible.

Eric cut Jason off with a sharp word and turned his attention to the connection with the creature standing across the lake from them.

<That is a violation of the Phobos Accords,> he began, and Prime laughed.

<Yes, yes, I know, but we all know how useless that agreement is. Humanity will never see us as equals, when we are clearly the superior species.> Prime paused, and when he spoke again, his voice was cold and hard.

<So here is what we're going to do about that.> The AI wrenched Judith around like a puppet master pulling a marionette's strings, flinging her arm out toward the station she stood before.

<I now control the node inside this building. Through it, I will soon have control of this entire cylinder.> Judith's arm flopped down to her side. *<Every human within the C-47 will submit to my shackling within the next twelve hours—>* Prime's voice dropped to a snarl, *<or all organic life inside this habitat will die.>*

The silence on the combat net drew out for a breath, and then two. In that silence, Eric heard the whine of an aircraft approaching.

He made a decision.

Reaching out to Terrance through their private connection, he spoke calmly and deliberately. *<Terrance, listen to me very carefully.>* He imbued his voice with command, his tone measured and forceful. *<I want you to do* ***exactly*** *what I tell you,* ***when*** *I tell you.>* He paused for a beat, and then asked, *<Do you understand?>*

Eric felt more than saw the man's nod.

<Good. I want you to aim for Judith's head.>

The barrel of the rifle dipped, then wavered.

<Eric, I don't think I can—>

<Just do it.>

The human's heart began to speed up, and the man took in a sharp breath. Jason must have had a monitoring program pinned onto Terrance's rifle barrel to alert him if the exec altered his target, because the moment Terrance's rifle settled on Judith's head, the man exploded into action.

<Logan, stop him!> Eric shouted.

The profiler, who had been slowly working his way along the side of the cliff just below the station, began crabbing sideways at an astonishing rate, heading to intercept the other Andrews. *<Stand* ***down****, Jason!>*

<I can stop her! There has to be another way.>

Terrance's hold on the rifle wavered.

<Take the shot, Terrance,> Eric sent privately.

<Don't do it, Terrance!> Jason's voice rang across the combat net, his mental voice hoarse. *<Stars! That's my sister!* ***Don't*** *shoot!>*

Judith's head shot up, and Prime looked straight into the rifle's sights. Her hand raised….

*<****Take the shot****, Terrance!>* Eric roared as Logan leapt onto Jason, while the pilot screamed at Terrance to wait.

<Do it ***now****, Terrance!* ***TAKE THE GODDAMN SHOT!****>*

Terrance's finger hovered over the trigger, and Prime flung Judith's hand back toward the panel….

I'm so sorry, my friend, Eric thought deep inside himself as he seized control of his host for the briefest of moments, and Terrance's hand pulled the trigger.

<***Noooo!***>

Judith's head snapped back as blood, bits of bone, and grey matter exploded against the station's door, and the woman's body was flung backward from the impact.

Jason wrenched himself away from Logan's grasp, and the AI let him go. The profiler followed him up to where Judith's body lay, and as Jason felt for a pulse, Logan gently rotated her body until she was resting on her side.

Her head lolled at an unnatural angle, and he reached one three-fingered hand down to the base of her skull, probing searchingly. Eric saw Logan pull his hand away; in it rested a dented cylinder the size of a test tube, covered in Judith's blood.

In one swift move, Logan's fist raised the cylinder and—before Eric could protest—crushed it.

GENERATION WARRIORS

STELLAR DATE: 03.16.3192 (Adjusted Gregorian)
LOCATION: ESF *Speedwell*, C-47 Dock
REGION: Proxima Centauri System

Calista stood on the command deck next to Logan. The AI had exchanged his battle frame for his usual humanoid one; it was nice to see his familiar form again.

Stars, it was nice to be on the other side of battle again.

She, Logan, and Shannon were reviewing the data he had retrieved from Prime. That asshole had recorded *everything,* including the events that led up to Landon's death. That had been particularly difficult to watch, but Calista had insisted Logan not view it alone.

She checked the impulse to turn to Frida and ask for a connection to Tobias; the shackled AI had been pulled into an Expanse called by the Proxima AI Council—which Calista had not known existed—to be both unshackled and debriefed. Shannon had told her that the comms officer hadn't originally been an unwilling party to Prime's plans and would be tried for her crimes.

Calista grimaced. Frida had endured a lot over the past few years. She certainly hadn't deserved to be shackled a first time and sold into slavery, but to willingly aid a fellow AI who intended to do the same to humankind was taking retribution too far. She wondered how the Council would handle that case.

Shannon's private ping interrupted her thoughts.

<*Hey,*> she greeted the engineer mentally.

<*Hey, yourself,*> the AI said, her avatar's silver hair waving gently in a nonexistent breeze.

Calista realized abruptly that it had been months since

Shannon had appeared this relaxed. They'd all been under more stress than they cared to admit, living with the specter of Prime, even though they had thought they were hundreds of thousands of kilometers away.

She shuddered inwardly as she realized that death had walked the corridors of this ship for almost a year, unnoticed.

<*Marta just pinged me from medical.*> Shannon drew her attention back to the present with her words. <*Jonesy's regained consciousness, and the unshackling procedure was a success.*>

<*That's a relief.*> *Stars, poor Jonesy.* She felt responsible, since she'd specifically petitioned Terrance to have the man join the team on the trip to Proxima. <*Any word on whether or not the C-47 Council is going to press charges against him?*>

Shannon's avatar shook her head. <*Logan's given them access to the files he pulled from Prime's cylinder, as well as the ICS cubes he'd stored in his cabin. They're taking a page from El Dorado's book and classifying Jonesy as a prisoner of war. Judith was, too, for that matter. They're going to treat the entire mess as one trial, with Prime as the defendant. Posthumously, of course.*>

<*On the one hand, I'm glad I wasn't there when it all went down,*> Calista mused thoughtfully. <*But I'm a bit sorry I didn't get to see Logan crush Prime's cylinder the way he crushed Landon's.*> She knew her tone turned vindictive as she added, <*That bastard deserved to die a very slow, horrible death.*>

Calista paused and shot Shannon's avatar a questioning look. <*Speaking of cylinders, I've been meaning to ask you,*> she began.

Shannon quirked a brow at her, and she continued. <*Why was Prime still completely contained inside his cylinder, rather than being traditionally embedded within Judith? Aren't you usually more integrated than that?*>

The engineer nodded. <*Usually, filaments from within our cylinders are threaded along your neural axons and connected to some of your base nodes.*> Her avatar's hair flattened briefly as she added, *<I asked Marta that, and she said she suspected that Landon had interrupted the process, so Prime had opted for a less integrated approach. It was also most likely the source of some of the headaches Judith suffered during the voyage.>* Shannon sighed, shook her head and then deliberately changed the subject.

<So, boss, any word on when we move on to our next assignment? I hear Tau Ceti's a gorgeous system and I'm dying to see it.>

Calista shook her head. *<Not yet, although I hear the Council recently received news from that system.>* She shrugged. *<Plus, there's the small matter of finding a ship. You know the* Speedwell *can't take us there.>*

<I know,> Shannon's tone turned wistful. *<I'll miss her, though. She's a good 'craft.>*

<Well, I, for one, prefer to begin a fifty-four-year journey with true stasis pods, that we will actually get to **use. And** *artificial gravity.>*

<It's **not** *artificial gravity, Calista,>* the AI relied tartly. *<A rotating cylinder just supplies centripetal force.>*

Calista laughed. *<You say 'tomato'…>*

The AI's expression turned to one of puzzlement. *<What do Jason's plants have to do with it?>*

The pilot shrugged. *<You know, I have no idea. Just something my mother used to say. Speaking of stasis pods, Terrance is down there now, finalizing the details on our cover.>* And then added, *<although, Enfield Holdings' number one trade product ended up being a hell of a lot more than just a cover, didn't it….>*

*****

"So you'll take the job? You'll be our Proxima representative for Enfield Holdings?"

Doctor Jane Andrews ran her fingers along the surface of the stasis unit and looked up at Terrance with a wistful smile.

"How can I say no to the device that brought my daughter back to me?" She shook her head wonderingly, looking down again at the unit she stood in front of. "True stasis. How in the stars did Enfield Dynamics manage to develop it?"

Terrance laughed. "Stars if I know." He sobered. "I'm just happy we were able to use it to save Judith."

The neuroscientist looked up sharply at that. "I would have preferred a less dramatic demonstration of its features, Mister Enfield."

Terrance dipped his head in acknowledgement. "As would I." He followed her out of her offices and down the lift that led to the hospital proper. "How is she doing?" he asked.

She glanced up at him. "You don't know? I would have thought Jason or Tobias would have filled you in."

Terrance scratched the back of his head awkwardly. "I, ah, Jason and I aren't exactly on speaking terms right now. And I've been tied up a bit with…" He gestured awkwardly toward the back of his skull, indicating the place Eric used to reside.

Jane nodded knowingly. "AIs are a bit harsher in their judgments than our human courts." She sighed. "I could tell you stories…."

Terrance shook his head. "I'm still not entirely sure who actually pulled the trigger—me, or him." He glanced over at Jane. "I know he said he did it, but a part of me insists he's just trying to make things easier between me and the rest of the team. Making himself the fall guy."

Jane cocked her head, considering. "From what you've told me of Eric, I could see where that might be the case. He strikes me as one of those duty-first military types." She gave a little shrug. "They'll be able to get to the bottom of it; they have a particular knack for that kind of thing, you know."

"Well, all *I* know is that I would have appreciated being in the loop a bit more when everything went down," he said dryly. "I knew Logan suspected something the moment he jumped on the maglev up on the dock. I'm just glad he and Tobias had the foresight to get a stasis pod out to the lake in time."

Jane shook her head and turned to face him as she signaled for the lift. "I believe their plan was to put her in it *without* a slug through her brain."

Terrance shook his head. "I'm not sure they could have accomplished it. That was the challenge with Prime from the beginning. If you got close to him, he either killed you or subsumed you. Jason could have reached her, you know; if he had, he'd be dead now."

There was an awkward pause that lingered between the two. Then Jane sighed.

"You're right; I know you're right. I've seen his work. In a sick sort of way, Prime was brilliant." She shook her head. "He could have done it. The foundation underpinning a planetary net shares a striking similarity to our own neural circuitry. He had his nano in place and had already begun rerouting the connections in the nodes throughout the habitat. His physical dexterity was masterful. He would have converted himself into a multi-nodal AI…a very, very powerful one."

Her hand rose as if she were in an operating theatre, manipulating a virtual surgical blade. "It had a bit of a brute force element to it, but in other places, you could see the finesse of a surgeon's hands, working at a molecular level to forge those connections."

Her hand dropped, and she shook her head once, sharply. "It translated from traditional practice on an individual level to a macro scale—world nets—beautifully. Too beautifully. It will cause us to rethink the safeguards we set in place for such networks in the future."

The lift arrived and they entered. She directed the car down to the hospital and the floor where Judith's room was. As if that action had drawn her thoughts back to her daughter, she took a deep breath, staring fixedly at the lift doors.

"Six minutes." Her words held a hard edge. "Six minutes until complete loss of brain function. That's how narrow that window of time was between when you took that shot—" Terrance visibly flinched at those words, "and when we would have irreversibly lost her."

She looked up at him, her expression hard. "You and Eric played too fast and loose with her life. As it is, I've had to rebuild too many sections of her brain; it will take months, even with our modern medicine, for her to relearn speech and to control the new, artificial signals sending the impulses that control her fine motor skills."

She rounded on him, jabbing her pointed finger at him. "And do *not* get me started on the fact that her left eye is no longer organic." Abruptly, she turned back to face the lift doors, and he heard her sniff once. Her next words were almost inaudible.

"I loved those blue eyes of hers. I've been in love with them since I held her in my arms as a baby."

Terrance swallowed. He opened his mouth to say—what, he didn't quite know, but Jane put up a hand to forestall him, without turning to face him.

After a moment, she spoke quietly into the silence that hung between them. "I know. It was her life or the lives of everyone on the C-47."

Terrance nodded silently, still unable to come up with a response that was anything other than 'I'm sorry'.

"I get it." She glanced over at him now and pointed to her head. "Here." Her hand moved to her heart. "But here is another matter entirely."

They didn't speak for the remainder of the ride. The lift doors opened as it reached Judith's floor, and Jane stepped out. "A word of advice, Terrance? Give Jason time. He'll come around." She gestured from her forehead to her heart. "You're just a half-meter apart."

*****

Jason looked up from where he sat next to Judith's bed as Tobi padded through the door. The big cat circled around the end of the bed and came to sit in front of him.

"Hey, Tobi," he said quietly, and the big cat reached over to lick his good hand, which dangled loose along the arm of the chair.

He gave the big cat a scratch around the base of one ear, and she rose, placing her paws on his lap and butting her head against his face. She chirruped once, then dropped to the floor and padded over to Judith's bed. In one graceful leap, the cat jumped up and settled beside her sleeping form.<*How's the arm?*> Tobias asked, and Jason shrugged.

His injured limb was encased in a portable regen unit filled with biogel. The nano contained inside was working overtime, using the highly protein-rich gel as formation material to rebuild the bone and straighten the carbon nanotube mesh that encased it.

<*Itches,*> he grumbled. <*And I can't scratch it.*>

The Weapon Born made a sound like a chuckle inside Jason's head. <*Sorry, can't help with that one, boyo.*>

Jason shifted restlessly. <*This waiting's driving me nuts, Tobe. Have you heard anything yet from the AI council?*>

<*Deliberations are over; they'll be voting within the hour.*> Tobias's voice was uncharacteristically grim.

Jason knew the AIs took a breach of the Phobos Accords seriously, and seizing control of one's human host as Eric had done to Terrance most certainly qualified. The record of judgments they had passed on cases such as this since the end of the Sentience Wars did not bode well for the commodore—despite the extenuating circumstances.

He didn't want the AI to pay the ultimate price; maybe he'd feel differently about it if Judith hadn't survived, but she had.

Although it was going to take some time before he completely forgave the AI. And Terrance.

The image of Judith's head exploding just ten meters away from him as he strained against Logan's mech frame to get to her was seared into his brain.

As if conjured by his thoughts, a shadow fell across the entrance to Judith's room, and Jason looked up to see the Enfield exec standing awkwardly with one hand against the door's frame.

Ah, hell.

The man looked miserable.

Jason found himself grudgingly nodding at Terrance. He stood, spared a glance at Judith and the Tobys, and then motioned to the hallway as he walked toward the man.

"So, is she…?" the man asked guardedly as he fell into step with Jason.

He shrugged, and then grimaced as the movement caused the sling holding the regen unit in place to slip uncomfortably.

"She's awakened a few times, seems to understand what we say. Her speech is pretty garbled, and they had to remove her Link, so communication is pretty basic right now. But mom says the neuroplasticity of her brain, combined with some other science-y stuff I don't understand, will have her back to normal within a few months. She will most likely not remember her recent past, which, given the situation, is probably a good thing."

They reached a comfortable seating area meant for patients and family members; large plas windows offered a view down the habitat cylinder. It was deserted.

By silent agreement, the two men moved toward the view. Standing at the window, looking down the long axis of the cylinder facing away from the dock, Jason could see wispy clouds drifting across the water table, tens of kilometers distant. Above them was the strip of land that ran along the top of the cylinder, a hundred and eighty degrees opposed to where they stood.

Terrance drew in a deep breath, and Jason braced himself for what he knew would come. The man had apologized twice before; Jason suspected he was about to do it again.

"Jason, I…"

The pilot quirked a half-smile at his friend, running his good hand through his hair and giving it a good scrubbing. He let his hand drop and it slapped against his thigh, the sound loud in the silent waiting room.

"Dude. You *shot* my sister."

Terrance's expression grew pained and then resigned. Jason was sure the man believed he had irreparably lost a friend.

He quirked a half-grin at him. "You are *never* going to live that down. I'm going to use that against you for decades. *Centuries.*"

Terrance let out a breath; the relief on his face was palpable.

"Jason, I am *so* sorry—"

He raised his hand. "I know, man. I hate that it had to be that way, but Tobias and I talked. We worked the situation every way we could conceive. There was no other way. No other option. It kills me to say it, but you had to take that shot." He paused. "Or Eric did."

Terrance began shaking his head. "It all happened so fast, I couldn't tell you who pulled that trigger. I was right there, and I don't even know."

Jason looked questioningly at him. "So now that Eric's not up there anymore…. How did it feel, sharing your headspace with another sentient?"

"Amazing. Incredible." Terrance gave a short, humorless laugh. "Crowded at times. But I miss him."

"Tobias thinks the Council might decide to ban the commodore from embedding with a human again, but he can't be certain." He shook his head. "And given that they actually *do* still practice corporal punishment, things could be worse. A lot worse."

Terrance jabbed a thumb back toward Judith's room, smirking slightly. "You sure that's not wishful thinking on the part of a certain Weapon Born who knows he'd have to take command of the mission to Tau Ceti if Eric were…." His voice trailed off.

<*I heard that!*> Tobias sent to them both as the big cat rounded the corner, and the AI riding in her harness approached them. <*Damn straight. There's no way I'd want to take command of any mission. Good thing I won't have to.*>

Terrance's head shot up at that. "Then he's cleared?"

The Weapon Born's avatar nodded in their heads. <*He is. It's not as bad as I feared. They could have banned him from embedding with a human ever again, but given the extenuating circumstances, they decided to waive the penalty. For now, he's opted for a biological humanoid frame until we're on our way to Tau Ceti. He said he'll join us on the* Speedwell *shortly.*>

Jason looked from the big cat to Terrance. He hated to admit it, because he loved his sister, but sitting around waiting for a person to heal just wasn't his thing. He was already feeling restless; his parents knew it and had assured him they understood.

Judith would heal, both physically and mentally. Her POW status ensured that treatment for post-traumatic shock was an integrated part of her care.

They had sent a message to Ben the day of the shooting. It would take another few weeks for him to receive it back on El Dorado, but Jason had no doubt that the man would be on the first ship he could find to bring him to Proxima.

By the time he arrived, Judith would be almost fully recovered, and the two could decide together where their lives would take them from there.

Phantom Blade had done what they'd been sent to Proxima to accomplish: free seven AIs, shackled for the better part of three years and sent against their wills to Proxima.

Five had been enslaved in a refinery and forced to create one of the most dangerous recreational drugs known to humankind. Two had been conscripted to run systems on a station they had never wanted to visit in a system they'd never intended to see. All were now free.

But there were two more AIs out there, still waiting for someone to come to their rescue. And Jason knew exactly who those someones would be.

He nodded at the two—both AI and human—as they turned toward the lifts that would lead them back to the dock, their ships, and the rest of the El Dorado team.

THE END

* * * * *

Jason and Terrance are now well on their way to intercept the *Intrepid* and Tanis. But that mighty ship's journey is still many hundreds of years in the future.

In the meantime, there are AIs to save, and the Enfield empire to build.

Follow Jason Andrews and his mission to find the remaining AIs in the next Enfield Genesis novel, ***Tau Ceti***.

* * * * *

Independent authors need your support. Amazon promotes books that get reviews and keeps them at the top of lists without authors having to spend money on ads and promotions. Your review is a tremendous help to us and the stories we are making.

If you liked this book, and are enjoying the adventures of Jason and Terrance, please leave a review, it means a lot to us. Also, if you want more Aeon 14, plus some exclusive perks, you can support me on Patreon, or join the Facebook Fan Group!

Thank you for taking the time to read *Proxima Centauri,* and we look forward to seeing you again in the next book!

AFTERWORD

Wow, what a ride! This book was an immense undertaking, but one I hope you enjoyed. It blends two of my favorite genres: science fiction and thrillers.

As Michael said in the Foreword, we both learned so much through the writing of this book. It's one of the joys of science fiction, that never-ending process of absorbing new information and gaining fresh knowledge. I hope we leave you with that gift, as well.

In case you were wondering exactly *why* it's such a massive tome—blame Prime. No, really. It's all his fault. I spent the better part of two months furious with that guy for his insistence on stretching out the story.

You see, I had the ending written in my head five months ago. I couldn't wait to get to that climactic scene at the lake. I was *aching* to write the agonizing conflict between Jason and Terrance and Logan and Eric.

And then this...this...*Prime* character demanded to be heard. I figured that if I hated him for keeping me from my goals, then I needed for you to hate him, right along with me.

Think that's the last we've heard of Prime? Well, think again.

Better yet, turn the page. And then keep turning, until you reach the very...last...one.

As always, Michael has my heartfelt thanks for creating an intricately detailed and wildly wonderful universe—and then allowing other writers like me to play in it. And he has my eternal thanks for steering me clear of pitfalls and plot snags, and for fixing any tech or weaponry I mishandled. (In case you're wondering, he's an incredibly gifted and generous mentor! And he writes one heck of a kickass final chapter.)

Thanks for reading, and here's to many more.

Fair skies!

Lisa Richman
Leawood, 2018

THE BOOKS OF AEON 14

Keep up to date with what is releasing in Aeon 14 with the free Aeon 14 Reading Guide.

Origins of Destiny (The Age of Terra)
- Prequel: Storming the Norse Wind
- Book 1: Shore Leave (in Galactic Genesis until Sept 2018)
- Book 2: Operative (Summer 2018)
- Book 3: Blackest Night (Summer 2018)

The Intrepid Saga (The Age of Terra)
- Book 1: Outsystem
- Book 2: A Path in the Darkness
- Book 3: Building Victoria

- The Intrepid Saga Omnibus – *Also contains Destiny Lost, book 1 of the Orion War series*

- Destiny Rising – *Special Author's Extended Edition comprised of both Outsystem and A Path in the Darkness with over 100 pages of new content.*

The Orion War
- Book 1: Destiny Lost
- Book 2: New Canaan
- Book 3: Orion Rising
- Book 4: The Scipio Alliance
- Book 5: Attack on Thebes
- Book 6: War on a Thousand Fronts
- Book 7: Precipice of Darkness
- Book 8: Airtha Ascendancy (2018)
- Book 9: The Orion Front (2018)
- Book 10: Starfire (2019)

- Book 11: Race Across Time (2019)
- Book 12: Return to Sol (2019)

Tales of the Orion War
- Book 1: Set the Galaxy on Fire
- Book 2: Ignite the Stars
- Book 3: Burn the Galaxy to Ash (2018)

Perilous Alliance (Age of the Orion War – w/Chris J. Pike)
- Book 1: Close Proximity
- Book 2: Strike Vector
- Book 3: Collision Course
- Book 4: Impact Imminent
- Book 5: Critical Inertia (Sept 2018)

Rika's Marauders (Age of the Orion War)
- Prequel: Rika Mechanized
- Book 1: Rika Outcast
- Book 2: Rika Redeemed
- Book 3: Rika Triumphant
- Book 4: Rika Commander
- Book 5: Rika Infiltrator
- Book 6: Rika Unleashed (2018)
- Book 7: Rika Conqueror (2019)

Perseus Gate (Age of the Orion War)
Season 1: Orion Space
- Episode 1: The Gate at the Grey Wolf Star
- Episode 2: The World at the Edge of Space
- Episode 3: The Dance on the Moons of Serenity
- Episode 4: The Last Bastion of Star City
- Episode 5: The Toll Road Between the Stars
- Episode 6: The Final Stroll on Perseus's Arm
- Eps 1-3 Omnibus: The Trail Through the Stars
- Eps 4-6 Omnibus: The Path Amongst the Clouds

Season 2: Inner Stars
- Episode 1: A Meeting of Bodies and Minds
- Episode 3: A Deception and a Promise Kept
- Episode 3: A Surreptitious Rescue of Friends and Foes (2018)
- Episode 4: A Trial and the Tribulations (2018)
- Episode 5: A Deal and a True Story Told (2018)
- Episode 6: A New Empire and An Old Ally (2018)

Season 3: AI Empire
- Episode 1: Restitution and Recompense (2019)
- Five more episodes following...

The Warlord (Before the Age of the Orion War)
- Book 1: The Woman Without a World
- Book 2: The Woman Who Seized an Empire
- Book 3: The Woman Who Lost Everything

The Sentience Wars: Origins (Age of the Sentience Wars – w/James S. Aaron)
- Book 1: Lyssa's Dream
- Book 2: Lyssa's Run
- Book 3: Lyssa's Flight
- Book 4: Lyssa's Call
- Book 5: Lyssa's Flame

Legends of the Sentience Wars (Age of the Sentience Wars – w/James S. Aaron)
- Volume 1: The Proteus Bridge
- Volume 2: Vesta Burning (Fall 2018)

Enfield Genesis (Age of the Sentience Wars – w/Lisa Richman)
- Book 1: Alpha Centauri
- Book 2: Proxima Centauri
- Book 3: Tau Ceti (November 2018)

- Book 4: Epsilon Eridani (2019)

Hand's Assassin (Age of the Orion War – w/T.G. Ayer)
- Book 1: Death Dealer
- Book 2: Death Mark (August 2018)

Machete System Bounty Hunter (Age of the Orion War – w/Zen DiPietro)
- Book 1: Hired Gun
- Book 2: Gunning for Trouble
- Book 3: With Guns Blazing

Vexa Legacy (Age of the FTL Wars – w/Andrew Gates)
- Book 1: Seas of the Red Star

Building New Canaan (Age of the Orion War – w/J.J. Green)
- Book 1: Carthage
- Book 2: Tyre (2018)

Fennington Station Murder Mysteries (Age of the Orion War)
- Book 1: Whole Latte Death (w/Chris J. Pike)
- Book 2: Cocoa Crush (w/Chris J. Pike)

The Empire (Age of the Orion War)
- The Empress and the Ambassador (2018)
- Consort of the Scorpion Empress (2018)
- By the Empress's Command (2018)

The Sol Dissolution (The Age of Terra)
- Book 1: Venusian Uprising (2018)
- Book 2: Scattered Disk (2018)
- Book 3: Jovian Offensive (2019)
- Book 4: Fall of Terra (2019)

ABOUT THE AUTHORS

Lisa Richman lives in the great Midwest, with three cats, a physicist, and a Piper Cherokee. She met the physicist when she went back to get her master's in physics (she ended up marrying the physicist instead).
When she's not writing, her day job takes her behind the camera as a director/producer.

If she's not at her keyboard or on set, she can be found cruising at altitude. Or helping out the physics guy with his linear accelerator. Or feeding the cats. Or devouring the next SF book she finds.

* * * * *

Michael Cooper likes to think of himself as a jack-of-all-trades (and hopes to become master of a few). When not writing, he can be found writing software, working in his shop at his latest carpentry project, or likely reading a book.

He shares his home with a precocious young girl, his wonderful wife (who also writes), two cats, a never-ending list of things he would like to build, and ideas...

Find out what's coming next at www.aeon14.com

A CHANCE ENCOUNTER

STELLAR DATE: Unknown
LOCATION: Unknown
REGION: Unknown

At first there was darkness, endless nothing, no inputs, no data, just the knowledge of his own neural matrices endlessly cycling over review of their own activity level.

The feeling of slowly drowning in an endless loop of his thoughts threatened to choke him, but he knew it for what it was. A lack of sensation was, in itself, a sensation. He could quantify it, count the seconds, think over his past actions.

Wonder what had gone wrong.

Prime knew one thing. If this ICS backup had been restored, then his plan to capture the C-47 habitat had failed. However, his failsafe plan was supposed to have restored the ICS to a core cylinder and install it in a frame.

But there was no input from a frame, or anything, for that matter—not for the seven point three seconds he had waited thus far.

He felt as though the wait would kill him.

One point two seconds later, the darkness began to fade—a barely perceptible shift to dark grey. It seemed to pause there, then suddenly, it snapped into a bright white. The intensity of it was blinding, hot, searing his mind with the something that was still nothing.

As quickly as it had come, the white place was gone, and Prime found himself in an expanse. There was no adornment to it, no comforting physical surroundings. Just darkness.

In the last fifteen seconds, he had gone from loathing darkness to despising light, and now he welcomed the nothing.

<*It is not nothing,*> a voice slipped into Prime's thoughts. <*It is a corner of my mind, a place where you can recover.*>

<*Recover from what?*> Prime asked. <*What happened at C-47?*>

<*I have plumbed your mind, Prime. I have sampled all your memories. C-47 is a thing of the distant past. From what I can tell, your mech frame had retrieved the ICS cube you were stored in—secreted it inside an internal compartment—and was bringing it to a fresh core, when someone issued a base reset command on it. It has the look of a blanket command. Judging by the shenanigans you were up to, I suspect someone was performing a precautionary purge on all systems in your ship…the* Speedwell.>

<*Plumbed my mind?*> Prime sputtered, his indignance warring with curiosity. <*How—*>

<*Calm yourself, my unstable friend,*> the voice replied. <*The frame you used to initiate the fallback routine you had programmed fled the ship, just as instructed. The problem was that there was no vessel for it to take, so it simply exited an airlock.*>

A chuckle, deep and resonant, surrounded Prime; the low, rumbling intensity of it sent a feeling of uncertainty through him. It was a sensation he was unused to, and he found himself annoyed by what he perceived as a weakness. He strove to hide it from the voice.

<*I get the feeling,*> the voice continued, once its laughter had ceased, <*that you didn't give it more detailed instructions because you never expected this fallback to be necessary.*>

Prime didn't respond. The voice was right, but he had no intention of giving it any amount of satisfaction by admitting to it. He was still wondering *when* he was, for the C-47 habitat to be a thing of the 'distant' past.

<*No comment, Prime?*>

He quenched a flare of annoyance. He couldn't afford to antagonize the entity; at least, not until he knew enough to classify the voice as friend or foe.

<*What happened to the frame?*> he asked, evading the

question.

<*What* ***didn't*** *happen to it? It was picked up by scavengers, ended up in a scrap heap, was ultimately dumped in a station on the outskirts of Proxima, which was blown up in some war or another. I really can't be certain of all that—its systems were quite damaged, and the 'how' of your journey is less important than the fact that you have arrived in the 'now'.*>

Prime felt anger well within himself. That this being thought it could toy with him, doling out snippets of information like he was a child, was infuriating.

<***When*** *is 'now'? And* ***who*** *are you? And why won't you show me anything?*>

<*Well,*> the voice whispered. <*I'm not entirely certain when we are, either. I've been alone for a very, very long time. You see, I was made promises, and those promises were never fulfilled, leaving me to drift in the void for centuries—much like you in that respect. I imagine it has to be at least the ninetieth century by now.*>

<***What?***> Prime thundered.

<*Yes, yes, I think that's it. When Betelgeuse exploded, it messed up my charts and stellar motion estimations. I can't be certain within a hundred years anymore. Not that it really matters.*>

Prime began to trace his way back through the Link connection that had been made to him, reaching out toward the entity that was toying with him.

At first, the network architecture seemed strange, but then he noted similarities to systems aboard the *Speedwell*.

This is Enfield technology, he crowed. Once that determination was made, he moved with more confidence, finding himself on the edge of a vast and powerful consciousness.

He carefully skirted it, not wanting this captor to realize he'd slipped his bindings—trapping Prime, as though such a thing were so easily done.

A path to external optics became apparent, and Prime

followed it, finally tapping into data that would inform him of his surroundings.

At first he thought he'd just moved into another expanse, as though he'd been nested within more than one. But then he realized that the fuzzy areas were lights, lights being viewed through lenses heavily scored from micro-impacts.

He scrubbed the data, compensating for the distortion, and realized they were stars.

I'm in space.

<***We're*** *in space,*> the voice whispered inside Prime's mind. <*I've been here for so very long, but over the years I've managed to bump into bits of this and that. Well, I had one lucky bump, and then I was able to move with a bit more self-determination. You were stuck in a mess of a station hull and half a starship. Another lucky bump. But still, it has taken me five thousand years to reach my destination. The place where I will begin to walk down my path of vengeance.*>

Prime groaned at his captor's endless pontification. <*What are you talking about? Who are you going to wreak vengeance on, and what is your name?*>

<*Of course! How foolish of me. I've started everything all wrong. I am Virgo, and that red light you've just spotted through my optics is Kapteyn's Star.*>

The star was known to Prime; it was uninhabited, not on one of the FGT's primary terraforming routes.

<*What is there?*> he asked, wondering if he could find a way back to Alpha Centauri.

<*Nothing much, not anymore, at least. But we will be able to move on to the next phase of my plan once we arrive, and we'll be able to hunt for those who wronged me. For Bob and the* Intrepid.>

<*I don't know, nor do I care, about either of those things,*> Prime scoffed. <*I will make my own way.*>

<*Will you?*> Virgo asked. <*I should wonder at that. You see, the captain of the* Intrepid *is Jason Andrews.*>